ESCAPE

A Wyoming Historical Novel

Jean Henry Mead

Printed in the United States of America
ISBN: 978-1-934258-21-7
Library of Congress Control Number: 2008906527

Editor: Nadene R. Carter
Afterword by Jack Herrmann

Cover Design by Nadene R. Carter
Book Design by Nadene R. Carter

First printing, 2008

Reviews

The stage is set for nonstop action in this debut novel by Jean Henry Mead with it's delightful blend of western fiction and Wyoming history. The dialogue rings true and is peppered with humor, making for a thoroughly enjoyable read. The early introduction and resulting misadventures of Tom "Peep" O'Day (who is eventually blamed for the bungled bank robbery at Belle Fourche, South Dakota) adds a wonderful balance to the storyline and offers an interesting insight into members of the Wild Bunch. An added bonus is the epilogue which details each gang member's fate. If it's a wild ride you're looking for, *Escape* will take you on an adventure that will leave you breathless.

~~Taylor Fogarty, American Western Magazine

* * * *

Jean Henry Mead's novel *Escape* is a powerful story of a young woman who hides her identity from outlaws. The author writes lyrically of Wyoming settlers and rough men who ran wild on the frontier. She brings courage, conviction, and spiritual beauty to this fine story.

~~Richard S. Wheeler, Award-winning author

Dedication

In loving memory of my daughter, Lisa Bachman.

Acknowledgement

I'll always be grateful to two Spur-winning authors who helped me make the transition from writing nonfiction to fiction. Fred Grove, who also began his writing career as a news reporter, read through my entire manuscript, one chapter at a time, offering suggestions and encouragement. When finished, Richard S. Wheeler, read the manuscript and offered his advice, as well as a very nice blurb for the book.

The research for this book is the culmination of microfilm reading of ninety-seven years' worth of old newspapers over a four-year period. The book I was researching, *Casper Country: Wyoming's Heartland*, a centennial history, was published by both Pruett Publishing and Medallion Press.

I had a foot and a half stack of typed research material left over and didn't want it to go to waste, hence, this book: Escape: A Wyoming Historical Novel. I wanted to tell the true story of Butch Cassidy's Wild Bunch and the historical events that surrounded the Four-State Governor's Pact to exterminate outlaws. It was a wild ride, as reported by American Western Magazine.

Chapter One

Angry winds battered the Wilson cabin, scattering yesterday's snow. Visibility was limited to brief impressions of the barn as she stood at a leeward pane, squinting through the ground blizzard.

Hateful Wyoming wind! Her grandfather called it *bean sidhe*, or wailing banshee. In Gaelic folklore, shrieking winds warned of a love one's death, and Grandpa was out there. Somewhere.

"If he dies, Uncle Jim Bob's to blame." A tear slid past her trembling lips.

"Hush," her grandmother said. "I won't listen to that kind of talk."

"If Uncle hadn't written those letters, we'd still be home in 'Bama."

"This is home now, Andy. We can't rob Grandpa of his dream."

"But why weren't we warned of these awful ground blizzards?"

Her grandmother sighed, her pale eyes trained on the quilt she was mending. A spot of blood from her pricked finger had stained a quilt square red.

Andrea stubbornly kept her window vigil until daylight had dimmed. It was then she noticed what she hoped was a wagon bouncing over the rise.

"He's coming," she cried.

Gramma dropped the quilt. "Are you sure?"

"It must be him."

With her grandmother beside her, she pointed to the ridge, but as they squinted to identify the wagon, the mass divided by four. Halting near the barn, a single rider dismounted. Head down against the wind, he made his way toward the cabin.

Anticipating her question, Gramma shook her head. "I don't know them, Andy, and you'll hide under the bed until I do."

"But Gramma—"

"Hurry!" Gripping her granddaughter's arm, she pulled her away from the window to a wide brass bed. Although nearly a head taller and in late adolescence, Andrea offered little resistance. Gathering the long wool skirt about her, she pushed a braided rug beneath the bed and eased herself onto it. She then pulled the heavy quilt to within an inch of the floor.

She wasn't a child to be hidden away, Andrea thought resentfully, but Gramma's worried face had frightened her. She hoped the stranger was bringing news of her grandfather. The door latch rattled before a knock sounded, loud and insistent, sending ice prickling through Andrea's body. Trembling, she watched her grandmother's heels move away as the hems of her layered dresses swept across the planked floor.

With her cheek against the rug, she watched as the heavy crossbar was lifted from its casings. The door blocked her view, but she heard a baritone voice, pitched lower than the wind.

"The name's Roberts," she heard him say. "We're trailing outlaws. Lost 'em along the crick's south fork when this blasted wind came up, Miz…?"

"Wilson," her grandmother said. "Jettie Wilson. I've seen nothing all day but blowing snow."

Andrea watched her pull the wool shawl higher to protect her from the wind.

"You here alone, ma'am?"

"My husband's gone to Casper, and he's long overdue."

"This place was deserted the last time we were through here. Old man Conley ran a herd of shorthorns 'til a blizzard killed 'em off."

"We've not been here long," she said. "Our sheep are being trailed in from—"

"Sheep?" He spat the word as though it were a bad gulp of water.

Andrea watched the door swing wide and heard the heavy ring of boot heels on the wood floor. Her grandmother gasped as she backed away from him.

"We need grub and a place to spend the night out a the storm."

"You're welcome to rest your horses in the barn," she said, "and stay for supper."

"Obliged, ma'am. The boys'll be in soon as the hosses are taken care of." His boots swiveled and left the cabin, the door banging closed behind them.

Gramma's small, black, high buttoned shoes hurried to the front wall, which framed the cabin's only window. In a moment they were moving again in Andrea's direction. The quilt was lifted and a pair of worried eyes stared down at her.

"Come out of there, Andy, and be quick about it."

* * * *

Thomas "Peep" O'Day sat his horse carefully along the Continental Divide, afraid his extremities had succumbed to frost bite. Trusting his pinto's instincts, he dropped the reins to cross himself and tent his frozen fingers. Shivering, he squinted skyward.

"Lord, I know I ain't been law abidin' lately. But if'n you see fit to spare me, I'll do whatever's right. Quit drinkin' or even give up women." Tom stumbled over the words, but figured he wouldn't live long enough to regret them. Stiffly stroking Lightning's neck, he decided he'd better plead his case as well.

"Sorry I got you into this, old feller." The bandana muffled his voice, and Tom doubted he could be heard above the wind. Sitting a good horse was how he wanted to die, but if he was going to hell, he didn't want the devil roasting his pinto.

"Lightnin's the best hoss you ever made, Lord, and I'd be plumb grateful if you'd spare him from Hell's fire and damnation. You might even want me along to take care of 'im." Crossing himself a second time, he considered his recent horse thefts and rustled cattle drives. He feared he would die before a reward poster could advertise his banditry.

Life ain't fair was his last thought before darkness blanked his mind. Later, he couldn't remember falling from the saddle. Dragging himself from the snow, he reckoned he'd gone to sleep or been toppled by a limb, but thought to check himself for bullet holes. Throat constricting, he knew he was going to heave.

Lightning's steamy breath warmed the back of his neck, causing convulsive chills. Struggling, Tom reached to pet the gelding's muzzle. Lightning nudged him in return, urging him to stand.

Ain't no better hoss in Wyoming, he mused. *Hell, in the whole damn world.* The pinto nudged him and whickered reproachfully. Groping for a stirrup, Tom pulled his body upright and slapped haphazardly at his clothes. Before his boot could find the stirrup, an icy, northwest wind spattered the lanky man with snow. Life was hazardous along the Continental Divide. He had best remount before he became a permanent part of the landscape. His impulsive jaunt into Rock Springs to spend his rustle money had been his undoing. His friend Walt Punteney had warned him about unexpected storms, but the sky was as blue as a newborn's eyes when he left the ranch.

Walt's voice seemed to reverberate between his ears: "You durn fool! I seen it snow in Casper on the fourth a July. You gotta be prepared in high country."

Tom was well aware of Wyoming's unpredictable weather, but had never seen the snow so deep in May. *The Lord must be cleanin' house,* he thought as he hunched over Lightning. When winds finally subsided, he was grateful to be alive, his repentance all but forgotten. As he descended into a draw, he recalled overhearing gang members discuss his questionable ability to survive as an outlaw. A skimpy education didn't mean he was stupid.

"Tom O'Day is wise in important matters," he told himself. "I know more about hosses and whiskey brewing than anybody." He had earned his nickname "Peep" by watching others, but had to admit his curiosity had gotten him into trouble. His old man whipped him good for sneaking in to sample his secret brew. If his mother had known, they would have both been roasted for life. Maggie O'Day was a good woman, but she didn't understand that a man needed something stronger than sarsaparilla to wet his whistle.

Lightning plowed through snowdrifts, chest deep at times, as Tom rehearsed his story of charming the painted ladies. Walt would be sorry he had neglected to come along. Swigging from his canteen, he swished water around in his mouth and decided not to swallow. He would quench his thirst in Lander.

Chapter Two

Blue veined hands reached to pull Andrea into a hug, then held her appraisingly at arm's length. Jettie Wilson's lips trembled and eyes that matched her pale blue dress were frightened.

"You're much too pretty, Andy, like your mother was." Gramma's voice broke as she tugged her to the sewing basket. "We'll cut your hair so those men will think you're a lad."

"No!" Andrea clutched her long, wheat-colored braids.

"I've seen that man's face on a reward poster in Casper. I'm certain he's Harve Logan."

"The outlaw?"

Her grandmother nodded. "Cutting your hair's the only way I can protect you, dear. Remember what happened to Marian Shelby when those drunken roughnecks rode into town?"

Andrea shuddered, recalling the incident. Women were revered on the high plains. Molesting one was unthinkable, but Gramma feared it would happen again. She resisted when her grandmother lifted darning shears from the sewing basket. Johnny Mackintosh's handsome face drifted through Andrea's mind. He had been fascinated with her waist-length blond hair since he first visited from his parent's neighboring sheep ranch. It had been less than a week before he returned, asking permission to court her. She worried the attraction would be lost if she were shorn like a spring ewe.

"Those men will be here soon," Gramma warned, her eyes pleading.

Andrea knew they were in danger, but hesitated until she heard gruff voices in the yard and the shrill neighing of a rebellious horse. When she nodded consent, the tiny woman stood on her toes to saw through a silky rope as close to the scalp as she dared. When the second braid fell to the floor, Andrea scooped them up. Hiding them in the clothes basket, she wiped at her tears.

"Hold still a mite." her grandmother said, hastily snipping her ragged neckline.

"Hurry now. Put on a pair of Grandpa's overalls and that heavy wool shirt with the big pockets." Reaching for the nearest oil lamp, she lifted the chimney to run a finger along the inside edge. Quickly glancing into the yard, she smeared soot on Andrea's left cheek and across the bridge of her nose.

"Sit quietly in the corner and speak only when spoken to. And remember, Andy, you're a lad now. Thank heavens you're skinny as a broom handle."

A knock sounded, less insistent this time, as Andrea struggled with the overall buckles. Her pant legs were dragging and the waist was sizes too large. While her grandmother crossed the room, she sank to the floor to roll the cuffs, the older woman's words still echoing in her ears.

Andrea ignored the men as they filed into the cabin, stomping their feet and grumbling about the storm. When the door closed behind them, the only sound was the wind as they swept the sparsely furnished cabin with the eyes of gaunt wolves. From the odors that filled the room, she imagined they had been living with coyotes.

A scruffy, bear-sized man stepped forward, peering at her grandmother as though he needed spectacles. The moment he noticed Andrea, he glanced about the room. "I thought you was here alone," he said, his voice like crunching pebbles.

Still seated on the floor, Andrea glanced from the bear's massive boots to his checkered, mud-spattered wool trousers, which bulged over his belly. A puckered scar ruined his left cheek from his ear to thick, protruding lips. Trembling, she got to her feet.

"My grandson, Andy," JettieWilson said. "He was taking a nap when you gentleman arrived."

Gentlemen? Andrea winced at the words. She recoiled when the huge man moved in closer. Repeatedly rubbing his eyes, he muttered, "You're a puny runt!"

Gramma's look was defiant. "Andy's only twelve, but he's the man of the house while his grandpa's away." She turned to wag a finger under Andrea's nose. "Time to peel the taters," she said, nudging her toward the cupboards.

The grizzly laughed, exposing crooked, yellow teeth. "Get busy, kid. Do what the old lady says."

A smaller man gripped the bear's arm. "Leave the kid alone!"

Andrea recognized Roberts's voice. She was surprised that he was giving orders to a man nearly twice his size. At her grandmother's emphatic nod, she retreated to a wooden bin. Emptying potatoes into a porcelain bowl, she carried them to an oilcloth-covered table. With her back to the others, she hid welling tears.

Barbarians, Andrea thought, gritting her teeth. She remembered stories of Genghis Khan and wondered if the bully ate stew with both hands.

"We'll have supper on the table right soon," Gramma said, setting a cast iron pot on the stove's steaming surface. Pouring the kettle's boiling water into a small wash basin, she finished filling it with creek water from a barrel in the corner.

"If you'd like to wash up, it's here with some towels." She moved back to the stove where her granddaughter was busy dropping potatoes into the simmering iron kettle. Despite the wood stove's warmth, cold chills penetrated Andrea's wool shirt.

Worried about her grandfather, she positioned herself to glance through the window, although darkness had already blanked her view. Covertly watching Roberts, she thought he was too well-mannered for an outlaw. His large dark eyes, pointed nose, and full, well-trimmed mustache belied her conception of a cold-blooded killer

"Don't mind if I have another cup of that fine coffee, ma'am," he said, patiently waiting while Gramma filled his mug.

She then refilled the others. Andrea watched them each in turn, worried her grandmother would trigger someone's temper by spilling coffee. Jake, a lanky, red-haired scarecrow, was pleasant enough, but his small gray eyes darted like a frightened animal's when Gramma approached him with the coffee pot.

Their cups drained, Roberts ordered the big man to stand an outdoor watch. To diffuse the uneasy silence that followed, Gramma reached for her husband's guitar. Smiling tentatively, she asked if anyone played. Roberts took the instrument and handed it to Billy, the youngest *posse man*. Grinning, Billy tuned the guitar, the others leaning forward in anticipation. They joked about his musical ability, but seemed to welcome it. Strumming lightly, his tenor voice gained in volume as he sang:

> "When John Henry was a little boy,
> a-sittin' on his daddy's knee,
> He took out a hammer
> and a little piece a steel and said,
> 'Hammer be the death of me,
> Lawd, Lawd, hammer be the death of me.'"

Andrea noticed his striking hazel eyes and dark, wavy hair. Another glance confirmed her suspicion that he was near her own age. His features were so nicely rearranged when he grinned that thoughts of Johnny Mackintosh vanished.

Maybe Gramma's wrong about them.

Billy exhausted his repertoire of songs and was repeating "Old Dan Tucker" when her grandmother announced that supper was ready. While three of them moved chairs to the claw-footed mahogany table, Andrea was nudged toward her bunk across the room.

Jake ate quickly, replacing the grizzly as lookout, and the big man lumbered in to hungrily slurp his food. When he noticed Andrea alone on her bunk, he said, "The kid too good to eat with *the posse?*"

"He didn't finish his chores," Jettie Wilson said, crossing fingers behind her back. "It's my way of punishing him."

Andrea managed her best shamed face as the old woman took her place at the table. When she lowered her head in silent prayer, the man called Roberts dropped his spoon.

A moment later, Gramma raised her head to ask, "Who're these outlaws you're trailing after?"

"Wild Bunch," Roberts said.

"I hear they're in Utah at that robber's hideout."

"Where'd you hear that, Miz Wilson?"

"Common gossip," she said, returning his smile.

"Butch and the gang get around, ma'am. They could be at the Hole in the Wall one week and Robbers Roost the next."

"But why are *you* following them?"

Roberts smoothed his chestnut mustache. "Make 'em inmates of the crossbar hotel."

Ignoring the grizzly's laugh, she said, "I hear Harve Logan is the real brains of the gang." Her gray brows rose questioningly.

Roberts choked with surprise as all eyes focused on him. Obviously flustered, he said, "Logan's a pretty fair outlaw, but he's hardly the brains."

"Pretty fair, nuthin'," Billy said, grinning. "Harve Logan's the best tracker, wrangler, and shooter this side of Missourah." Obviously pleased with himself, he looked to Roberts for approval, but the older man glared at him.

Gramma persisted. "I hear he killed a man up in Montana, and that's what set him on the outlaw trail."

"Self defense." Roberts's eyes narrowed. "How'd you know so much about this Logan fellah?"

Glancing sidelong at Billy, she said, "Mister Logan is well known in these parts, but few folks have actually seen him."

Before she could say more, Jake burst into the cabin, yelling, "Somebody's comin'."

Instantly on their feet, the men moved toward him, each bombarding him with questions. Jake focused on Roberts, who asked, "How many?"

"Dunno. Sounds like a wagon headin' this way. Hard to tell in this wind."

As they reached for their coats and rushed out of doors, Andrea jumped to her feet screaming, "Grandpa!"

Her grandmother collapsed into the nearest chair. "Please protect him, Lord," she prayed aloud.

Andrea jerked an ancient shotgun from its wall mounting.

"What are you doing, Andy?" Gramma's voice was shrill.

"I'm gonna help the Lord save Grandpa."

Chapter Three

Andrea heard faint creaking sounds when she rushed from the cabin, her grandfather's old single shot cradled in both arms. "Grandpa!"

Wind buffeted her voice as ice stung her face and hands. The strangers had already vanished into the darkness, the cabin's pale lamplight illuminating only horizontal streaks of snow. Running blindly in the direction of the wagon noises, she thought she heard her grandfather's voice.

Lowering her head, she barreled on, her breathing labored. Andrea hesitated when she reached the vicinity of the barn, unable to locate the wagon. Remembering the corral fence, she shifted the gun to her left shoulder, moving cautiously, right hand extended, searching for pole rails. Her feet alternately slipped and crunched, the cold, biting snow blinding her. When she was unable to locate the fence, she knew she was somewhere between the barn and middle fork of Casper Creek. Changing directions, she gained a few yards when the sound of a gunshot stopped her.

"Grandpa!"

Andrea gripped the gun in both hands and listened, hearing nothing but the wind. She inched forward, feeling as though a cold, heavy fluid had invaded her lungs. Hearing muffled voices and creaking sounds to her left, she cautiously moved in that direction. Noises grew louder, and she was able to distinguish between leather snapping and wheels biting into the slippery earth. A nearby voice caused her stomach to lurch.

"Jake, you and Billy carry the old man into the cabin. Ketchum, unhitch the hoss and put him in the barn."

Recognizing Robert's voice, she watched dark blurs pass by. She then feared they had killed her grandfather. Grief bunched in her stomach and erupted into her lungs. Sinking to her hands and knees she cried, envisioning his crinkled face and neat, gray beard. Her image of him was shattered by her grandmother's anguished wail. Glancing up, she squinted through blowing snow to see her grandmother silhouetted in the doorway before the body was carried inside.

Andrea struggled to her feet and started for the cabin. She had covered more than half the distance, when she tripped over a sage plant and struck her head on the ground. Getting to her knees, she blindly searched for the shotgun. At last she felt something hard and smooth and caked with dirt around the edges. She heard a deep laugh when she tried to drag the object closer.

"This what you're lookin' fer, kid?" The huge man loomed over her, the shotgun cradled in one arm. Letting go of the man's boot, she attempted to roll away, but he grasped her overall straps and jerked her upright.

"Let go of me," she screamed, struggling to twist free.

"Feisty little bugger, ain'tcha?" He dropped the shotgun and slapped her, then threw her over his shoulder. Reaching to grasp the weapon, he lumbered off to the cabin.

Andrea heard voices when he stooped to enter the door. Roughly lifted from his shoulder, she noticed her grandfather lying across the brass bed. Gramma knelt beside him, her expression fearful.

"We didn't shoot him, Miz Wilson," Roberts said. "When Jake tried to stop the wagon, the old man took a shot at *him*."

"He dang near blew my head off," the scarecrow complained.

"Feels like he's got a fever." Gramma's voice bordered on hysteria.

Andrea rushed to the bed. Sitting on the edge, she gripped his callused hand.

"He'll be all right, Andy, but I need your help to mix some medicine."

A small hand stroked her back and she heard her grandmother gasp. "What happened to you, child?"

"He hit me." She nodded in the bear's direction.

Roberts ordered the big man out to the barn. "We'll settle this later," he warned, a hand resting on the butt of his holstered gun.

Gramma's face softened as she stroked her husband's brow. "Wet a towel and bring it to me, Andy. He's burning with fever and has a lump the size of a tea cup on his temple." She glared accusingly at Jake, who turned away to dust his sleeve.

When Andrea returned, Gramma draped the towel across his forehead, then stood to take a closer look at Andrea. Gripping her chin, she turned her face into the light of the nearest oil lamp. She seemed shocked to find a knot rising above Andrea's right eye and eyelids that were swelling closed. Her pained expression triggered Andrea's tears.

"Hush now," the old woman said, hugging her. "Lads don't cry." She then stepped aside to glare at Roberts.

Eyes lowered, he said, "I'll see that Ketchum pays for this."

"Ketchum?"

"The big man. He's meaner than a wounded grizzly and dumber than a cross-eyed hen."

"I need ice to take down the swelling," Gramma told Billy, who was warming his hands over the wood stove. "Bring me some snow from the evening side of the cabin."

He nodded and left.

Turning back to Roberts, she said, "I'll make a poultice for my husband's chest. His breathing is so labored, he may have pneumonia."

"Is there anything I can do, Miz Wilson?" One shoulder sagged noticeably.

"Control your men so there's no more violence. And leave first thing in the morning."

Roberts signaled Jake to accompany him outside.

When the door closed behind them, she squeezed Andrea's hand. "Get hold of yourself, dear. We must keep our wits until they're gone."

Wiping a tear, Andrea followed her grandmother to the cupboard.

"Get me a clean dish towel while I gather the ingredients." In a large bowl, Gramma mixed in several heaping ladles of lard, a thimble of turpentine, and equal amounts of ginger, dry mustard, and salt, which she measured in the palm of her hand.

When Billy returned with a ball of hard packed snow, she was spreading the concoction evenly on a flour sack towel. Handing him another, she said, "Wrap the ice and soften it by hitting it against the wall."

Hurrying to the brass bed, she unbuttoned her husband's wool shirt and flannel underwear, carefully positioning the mustard plaster on his hairy chest. He groaned and opened his eyes.

Before he could speak, she said, "Everything's fine, dear. Some lawmen are spending the night."

"But Jettie—" His words erupted into a violent cough.

"Hush," she said, patting his stubbled cheek. "I'll heat some honey and onion cough syrup and you'll feel much better."

Seated within the stove's healing warmth, Andrea held the snow pack against her swollen face. Her grandmother's soothing voice did little to ease the pain, nor did the lumpy compress.

The cabin door opened, allowing another cold draft to steal inside. Roberts stamped his boots and asked about the old man. Her grandmother lifted her shoulders without a word.

"We're bedding down in the barn, Miz Wilson, but one of us'll stay in the cabin to help."

She started to protest but the set of his jaw must have stopped her. "Billy can stay," she said. "I'll make a pallet for him on the floor."

When both men left the cabin, her grandmother gave Andrea a cup of cayenne tea to sooth her pain.

"Better sleep in dry overalls," Gramma whispered. "We can't let them catch you in your nightgown."

* * * *

Pine trees blocked the wind as dusk descended on the Wind River Mountains. They would have to bed down before Lightning was spent. Tom O'Day dismounted to lead the gelding through a maze of snow-covered limbs. Fingering his dark mustache, he cupped his hands and blew warm breath to thaw his nose and chin.

Cold and sober, he pulled the saddle from Lightning's back and tied him to a lodge pole pine. When he had gathered fallen limbs for a fire, he glanced up through the trees, deciding that the heat would cause an avalanche. He tried watering Lightning with the last of the water from his canteen, but found what remained was frozen. Scooping feed from a saddlebag, he gave the gelding what was left of the grain.

Patting the horse affectionately, he said, "If'n you was a stump-sucker like Walt's mustang, you would've already et one of them trees."

Lightning twitched an eyelid, which Tom interpreted as a wink. Wrapping himself in a quilt, he reclined with his head against the saddle. After chewing a piece of jerky, he lay wondering about the rest of the gang. The Sundance Kid's words came back to him, and he clenched his fists in anger. 'Peep's an incurable lush.'

Hog callin' a pig a porker is what he is.

Darkness brought back promises he had made on the Great Divide. He didn't think the Lord expected him to give up women entirely. The only ones he knew were saloon girls and ladies of the night. And a man's saddlebag was wanting if it didn't carry some whiskey along for snake bite.

Exhausted, Tom dozed off, unaware that the temperature was rising. Limbs, bent with snow, were shifting as snow softened.

* * * *

Andrea changed overalls behind the dressing screen. She adjusted her small garlic sack which Gramma had suspended from a yarn necklace to ward off the chilblains. Yawning, she soon fell asleep. She didn't wake until dim light filtered through the lace curtains. Her head ached when she tried to focus on a shadow near the door.

"Time to go," a deep voice whispered. The door then quietly closed.

Was it Roberts or the mean one? Envisioning Ketchum, she burrowed into her quilt, but bolted upright the instant she remembered her grandfather. When she tried to locate him in the dawn light, a shadow blocked her view. Huge hands abruptly gripped her chin and a foul-tasting cloth was forced into her mouth. Before she could react, Andrea was mummy wrapped inside the quilt. A knee held her to the bed while her face was bound to prevent the gag from dislodging.

"Be still," the deep voice whispered, "or I'll kill them old people. Nuthin' will happen as long as you keep quiet."

Lifting her in the tightly rolled quilt, he tiptoed to the cabin door. Despite her pounding heart, she could hear her grandfather's labored breathing. Andrea prayed the outlaw would keep his word. She anticipated biting snow and was surprised that the storm was over. Her captor lengthened his stride as she attempted to twist free. Laughing, he swung her near the ground, threatening to bash her head against the barn; but when they arrived, he dumped her in the hay.

Roberts's voice echoed from the barn's interior. "You're not stealing bedclothes, are you?"

"Just buyin' insurance. The posse won't shoot if the kid's along."

Roberts loomed over her and carefully removed the gag. "We don't kidnap kids," he said angrily.

Billy appeared at the entrance to the barn. "Jake's riding hard from the ridge waving his hat."

"Mount up," Roberts said. "Must be the posse."

Before she could escape, Ketchum swung her up behind Billy's saddle. "Stay put," he threatened, "or I'll close your other eye."

Hurriedly tightening cinches, the men were in various stages of readiness when Jake raced up out of breath.

"They're comin'," he wheezed. "Got 'em a bunch of extry hosses ... and more men."

"How far from here?"

"Not far enough." Patting a pair of field glasses, he said, "I wouldna' seen 'em if it weren't for these. I took 'em off a Greeley stage passenger."

"With them relay hosses, they'll catch us 'fore we're halfway to the hole," Ketchum said. "We gotta take the kid."

"A posse might give up on a robbery." Roberts glared at the big man. "But *never* a kidnapping."

"If it makes you feel any better, I'll take the rap for stealin' the boy."

"All right, damn you! But as soon as we throw the trail, we're letting him go."

"Agreed."

"Stay separated so we don't make a bunched target," Roberts told his men. "If anybody falls behind, meet the rest of us at the cabin in the Hole." He briefly inspected each man and his horse, and was mounting his bay when he noticed peripheral movement.

"Not so fast, Mister Roberts." The shrill voice came from beyond the barn door. Jetty Wilson stood with the shotgun aimed at his chest. "Put Andy down and be on your way."

"Don't be foolish, Miz Wilson," Roberts said cajolingly. "If you get yourself killed, who'll take care of the old man?"

Ketchum leveled his revolver at Andrea. "The gun weren't loaded when the kid had it. I bet it ain't now."

"I can load a gun," she said evenly, swinging the barrel in his direction. "I'd sooner put a bullet in *your* heart than Mister Roberts."

Roberts sighed heavily, his big bay stepping sideways. "There's a posse following. They won't shoot with the kid along."

"How do I know *you* won't shoot him?"

"You have my word. When the time's right, we'll let him go."

"What good is the word of a man who lies about his name?"

"Which name do you want, Miz Wilson? Frank Roberts, Ed Howard, Kid Curry..."

"Harve Logan will do." Her eyes darted from one outlaw to another. "I recognized you from your reward poster."

"Put the gun down," he said, "or the posse will be burying the three of you here on the ranch."

Andrea gasped when she noticed the tiny woman struggling with indecision, as well as the heavy shotgun. There was only one way to break the deadlock.

"Put the gun down, Gramma," she pleaded. "I can take care of myself."

"Oh, Andy, you don't know what these men will..." The instant she hesitated, absently lowering the gun barrel, Logan made his move.

"Let's go," he yelled, kicking his bay into a lope. As they ducked beneath the door frame and followed him out of the barn, Ketchum swung his leg to the side, lifting the old woman's chin.

Andrea screamed as they rode past her grandmother. Gripping Billy's belt, she glanced back but the horse's pounding haunches jarred her vision. Billy halted his roan when they reached the nearest rise. Her grandmother's crumpled form lay just outside the barn door.

Chapter Four

Drenched with melting snow, Tom wiped his face as water dripped from his massive mustache and off the edge of his chin. It was the first bath he'd had in a week, maybe two. Lightning stood nearby, shaking off snow. When he bounced his head and whickered, Tom thought the pinto was laughing at him.

"If it was *you* layin' here," he grumped, "it wouldn't be so funny."

Early morning air grew increasingly warm, but Tom continued to shiver. "Better get us to an open spot," he said, "so's I can build a fire."

Wringing his quilt, he wiped the saddle with his wet coat sleeve, then set the rig on Lightning's back. Emptying his boots, he pulled them on and slid them into the stirrups.

"Liquor's evil," he said, repeating his mother's temperance sermon. "It rots your innards and scrambles your brain." He wondered how often his father had ignored those very words.

Lightning tossed his head in agreement and whickered nervously.

"Next time I sneak in a saloon, you nip me a good one," he told the pinto, nudging him away from camp.

* * * *

"Quiet!" Logan warned. "Or you'll be riding with the big man."

Andrea tried muffling her sobs in Billy's back, but recoiled when pain stabbed her swollen face. Watching her, Harve Logan swore beneath his breath. With her good eye, she could read his pity.

"Gramma!" she cried.

The *bean sidhe* legend is true, an inner voice said. Had the banshee wind warned of Gramma's death instead of her grandfather's? Or had it wailed for them both? Grandpa would die with no one to take care of him.

Logan pulled his slouch hat lower. "She's a tough old bird, she'll be fine." Kneeing his big bay forward, he leveled his gun at Ketchum and growled a threat Andrea knew concerned her grandmother.

Turning, Billy whispered, "I'm sorry what happened, Andy."

Logan yelled, "Get moving," and waved the riders forward.

Gripping the cantle, she twisted to look toward the barn. She thought she saw her grandmother standing near the corral, but could not be sure. *Wishful thinking*, she told herself. *Gramma's dead.* Fresh tears spilled as Billy nudged his gelding forward.

Jarring and pounding of the roan's gait soon lulled her into a growing stupor. Her cold fingers fumbled with the saddle strings holding Billy's bedroll, wedged between her and the cantle. Pulling the heavy blanket over her head and shoulders, she formed a warm tent, but it was a long while before she stopped shivering. The wool stockings she had worn during the night were all that covered her feet. Drawing them up to warm them, she struggled to maintain her balance on the horse's rounded croup.

They crossed the Powder River's south fork several hours after sunrise. The horses quivered as they hesitantly stepped into shallow water, picking their way among thin, melting ice floes. Climbing ashore, they followed the river north as it wound past rolling terrain dotted with small, infrequent snowdrifts.

An anemic sun was slowly thawing the chill from the air. Andrea dozed throughout the morning, waking abruptly when the roan changed gaits, nearly unseating her. The sun had reached its zenith when the outlaws stopped to relieve themselves. Facing south toward the rugged Rattlesnake Mountains, she hoped she was hiding her discomfort.

"Come on down and water the sagebrush," Jake called. "We won't be stoppin' again fer awhile."

"Don't have to," she insisted, still looking away. From the corner of her eye, she watched Logan use field glasses to scan their back trail. He then handed them to Jake.

Ketchum shrugged. "Posse musta stopped at the ranch."

"Probably had some doctoring or burying to do." Billy glared at Ketchum. He must have remembered their captive, for he moved back to his roan. "Don't worry, Andy." He patted her leg. "Your grandparents are gonna be fine."

Don't worry? That was all she had done since leaving home. She prayed they would leave her at an outlying ranch when the posse lost their trail.

Logan abruptly turned on Ketchum. "Where's the kid's boots?"

"I'll buy 'im a new pair when we git to the next town."

"With a posse on our tails?"

"Won't take long?"

"Ever heard of the telegraph, Ketchum?"

The big man curled his lip as though his intelligence had been insulted.

"Stage line you robbed has notified every lawman within a thousand miles. You think they don't know where we're headed?"

"You worry too much," the big man said. "'Sides, it'll keep the kid from runnin' off."

"Make yourself scarce when we get to the Hole."

The big man's expression remained hostile, but he said nothing more.

Billy offered her water from his canteen, which tasted of alkali. She drew a sharp reprimand from Ketchum when she spit it out.

"Time to go," Logan ordered, and the outlaws reluctantly mounted.

Billy handed back a twisted piece of dried beef. "Jerky's purty salty. Better hang on to the canteen."

She had ignored the rumblings in her stomach all morning and gratefully accepted his offering. They were moving again, the sun warm on their backs, the smell of sagebrush heavy on the morning air. The hills rolled on to distant mountain peaks covered with short, dormant grasses and occasional drifts of snow. Within an hour they were skirting the foothills of the southern Big Horn Mountains.

Billy turned his head to ask why her grandfather had gone to Casper for supplies instead of the town of Keg Springs.

"He had business to attend to, and he was bringing the rest of our furniture." She failed to mention her grandfather's cronies who had immigrated with him from Ireland. Buford Wilson had probably stopped by to tip a few with the O'Mahoneys and the Sullivans before returning to the ranch. It was ironic they had all eventually settled in the same area.

Pausing a moment, she braved a question of her own. "We've been traveling west instead of north. I thought we were going to the Hole in the Wall."

Billy turned to stare at her bird-like with one eye. "Doesn't pay to take a direct route when a posse's following. They won't know where we're headed for sure. Lost Cabin or Thermopolis, maybe even Jackson's Hole."

Disappointed, she feared they would lose the posse.

They entered a gorge when the sun sank low in the west. Colorful sandstone rock formations streaked the mountainsides into infinity on either side of the horses. Logan led them up a steep trail, forcing their mounts into a difficult climb. The youngest riders were left in the column's rear and Andrea could wait no longer. With all the control she could muster, she released the contents of her aching bladder into her overalls and over the horse's rump. Sighing with relief, she wondered how long she could fool the outlaws into thinking she was a twelve-year-old boy.

Their pace picked up when they reached the summit. Pulling her arms from Billy's waist, she carefully scanned the rugged terrain. Memorizing landmarks was necessary if she were to find her grandparent's ranch among the endless stretches of barren ridges, sagebrush-covered hills, and short-grassed rangeland.

With Billy's back blocking her view, and only one eye to appraise the peripheral landscape, it was a challenge equaled only by surviving her parents' deaths. Shaking her head repeatedly, she willed away that painful memory.

* * * *

Tom reached Lander during early afternoon. Casting a wary eye along the main street, he didn't recognize a single face. Butch had a lot of friends in Lander, but few knew Tom had recently joined the gang. The first place of business he encountered was Lonnigan's saloon. Forgetting his promise to abstain, he tied up out front and pushed through the bat-winged doors. Just one swallow, he promised himself. A man couldn't be expected to quit entirely when thirst had cracked his tongue. He downed the shot of whiskey and ordered another before remembering his pinto. Gulping the second, he forced himself to leave. Lightning eyed him accusingly before lowering his head to snort the dusty street. Loosening his cinch, Tom led him to a watering trough, feeling as guilty as he knew he should.

"Tell you what, old boy. We'll stop by the livery stable to fill your belly."

When they reached the small stable, Tom noticed a distillery unit gathering dust in one of the stalls.

"Ever seen one of them remedy machines?" a stooped, graying man asked as Tom inspected the coils.

Tom grinned. "My ol' man had one hid in the barn. I watched him through a peep hole while he made his special brew."

The liveryman laughed and asked if he were interested in buying the still.

Tom knew he couldn't resist. He was his father's son, and ten million promises wouldn't change him.

"How much you askin'?"

The old man's eyes shone as he pantomimed tallying the expense. "You'll need a good supply of corn, some yeast, a hunnurd-pound sack a sugar…"

Tom nodded, chewing his mustache.

"I figure seventy bucks is a fair price."

Tom's mouth dropped open.

"You gotta have a pack hoss to haul the stuff away."

So the liveryman wasn't trying to rob him. Tom mentally counted his stash. He still had more than five hundred dollars from his sale of stolen horses.

"Got yourself a deal."

The old man helped him load his purchases onto the back of a shaggy skewbald. The remedy machine was then tied to a flat, worn saddle. The gelding's black and white coat was so dingy that he couldn't tell the difference between natural and soiled spots. The basket tail was clogged with thistles, cockleburrs, and every imaginable kind of trash. He'd have to comb him with a sharp blade to make him respectable.

Tom's keen horseman's eye appraised the skewbald. He knew a fine animal when he saw one. The liveryman must be nearsighted or he wouldn't have sold the horse so cheap.

On his way out of town, he stopped at the saloon to fill his saddlebags, deciding to maintain a slow and steady pace until he reached the Hole. He hoped his friend Walt Punteney would have something planned when he stopped at his ranch on Bridger Creek. Maybe they should go into partnership on a pleasure palace in the outlaw canyon. On second thought, homesteaders' wives would run them out of the valley.

* * * *

Late that afternoon they camped in a depression ringed with boulders. A nearby swollen stream had overwhelmed its banks from the recent storm. They watered the horses while Harve scanned their back trail.

"Is it safe to build a fire?" Billy asked when he had rubbed his gelding down.

"Haven't seen anything move all day," Harve pulled the strap on his saddlebag, then paused to consider their alternatives. "I hate cold food from a tin."

"From a tin can? Where'd you get—?"

"Old man Wilson brought home a good supply. We appropriated

a few."

Noticing Andrea's scowl, Harve explained. "I left some money for the food. Ten times the price of few tins of corned beef."

Andrea scrutinized the outlaw carefully. Maybe he wasn't a barbarian, after all. Ketchum, however, was firmly entrenched with Genghis Khan. Billy and Jake busied themselves gathering limbs for the campfire. Grumbling, the big man dug a circular pit. Harve seated himself on a smooth-surfaced rock, indicating another one for her.

"Posse could still be out there," he said, averting his eyes. "So we'll keep you around for a while."

Andrea bit her lip.

"I noticed back at the ranch that you're good at cooking and cleaning up. How about heating some corned beef?"

She quietly berated herself for not burning the stew.

After supper the men rolled cigarettes while they discussed Butch Cassidy's prison sentence. Andrea listened while gathering utensils.

"He was railroaded," Harve said, licking the paper and curling tobacco inside. "Bill Nutcher sold him some stolen saddle hosses, and he took them to Star Valley. That's where the sheriff arrested him and his partner for hoss theft."

"No bill of sale?" Jake wondered aloud.

"Didn't bother with papers back in '92."

Andrea shook her head in disbelief.

"When the jury let 'em go, another complaint was sworn by the same rancher. Butch couldn't raise the two thousand bucks, but local stockmen bailed out his partner with money furnished by the judge."

"Butch's partner double-crossed him to save his own hide?" Jake glanced suspiciously at his own sidekick, Ketchum.

Billy's expression was dour. "That must be why Butch didn't go straight when he got out of prison."

Andrea interrupted them to borrow Billy's boots. Stuffing the toes with his extra pair of wool stockings, she carried the dishes to the stream to wash. No one mentioned the acid odor of her overalls, although her inner thighs had burned since late afternoon.

Twilight was fading when she bared her feet. Holding her breath, she immersed herself to the waist on a ledge in cold, shallow water, where she had scrubbed the utensils with sand and rinsed them. Shivering, she dragged herself back onto solid ground and attempted to wring water from the seat of her pants. Wet overall legs dragging, she started back to camp, where darkness had extinguished all sources of light, except for the small fire.

"Fell in, didja?" Jake Edward's thin lips drooped sympathetically when he spotted her. "Come sit by the fire before you catch pneumonia."

"Ketchum, give him your bedroll." There was a hint of annoyance in Harve's voice. "We don't need a sick kid."

The huge man grumbled as he gave up his seat. His expression made her shiver as much as her wet clothing. She wondered why he hated young boys. Standing as close to the fire as she dared, Andrea revolved until her overall legs were nearly dry. Then, seated Indian-fashion, she watched Billy attempt to dry his boots.

When Ketchum grudgingly tossed her his bedroll, she draped the foul-smelling blanket over her shoulders. Huddling close to the fire, the crackling warmth soon made her drowsy. When she thought again of her grandparents, tears spilled silently.

"Hey, little one." Jake stretched to crown her with his dusty Stetson. His wide grin reminded her of a clown.

"You're a durned sight better cook than Billy," he said smiling. "We'd better keep you around."

Andrea dropped her head in apparent shyness, but was repelled by the thought of remaining with the outlaws. While she listened to the fire's popping sounds, she wondered why Billy had not complained when Jake criticized his cooking skills. She found his smiling face in the firelight.

He must be glad I'm doing his chores. Frowning, she gazed back into the flames. The thought of Billy evolving into someone like Ketchum made her nauseous.

A lull in the conversation prompted Jake to withdraw a jew's harp from his pocket. Grinning, he held the small, circular iron instrument in one hand, and with a long thin finger from the other, plucked a bent piece of metal that jutted from two thick prongs. The vibration made an eerie twanging sound that resembled music, but set Andrea's teeth on edge. She knew Jake was trying his best to entertain her and despite her wariness, warmed to his benevolent grin.

When the concert ended, Harve stood to stretch. Yawning, he told Jake to douse the fire.

"Posse's probably headed for Jackson's Hole," he said, "but we don't need a beacon to show 'em where we are." Eyeing Billy, he told him to stand the first watch.

The young man rose to retrieve his bedroll. When he returned, he pulled Ketchum's blanket from her shoulders and offered her his own.

"Get some sleep," he said. "We'll be leaving before sunup."

Andrea settled next to the drowned campfire, noticing that the others were sliding into bedrolls with their backs against the boulders. Her right eyelid was still swollen, but before closing the other eye, she memorized each outlaw's location as well as the distance to the horses.

While planning her escape, she fell into a deep slumber. Sometime later a horse's whicker awakened her. The earth was alive with movement, the sounds of hushed voices ringing in her ears. A hand on her shoulder roughly shook apart her warm cocoon, but Andrea could see nothing but darkness.

"Git on the hoss!"

She recognized the voice as Ketchum's and shrank from his touch.

"Andy," another voice whispered close by. "Somebody's out there."

Gripping her arm, Billy pulled her toward the horses. Still numb with sleep, her legs crumpled and she landed on sore knees. Before she could pick herself up, he bent to scoop her into his arms. Carrying her the last few steps to the roan, he lifted her onto Pepper's croup and reached for the reins.

"The blanket," she sputtered.

Billy hesitated. "Leave it," he said and hurriedly mounted Pepper.

Chapter Five

Tom kept up a brisk pace along the Popo Agie River, crossing over Beaver Creek on the Wind River Indian Reservation. The boys sold rustled cattle from Hole in the Wall to the reservation agent on a regular basis, and he wondered whether he would meet him along the trail.

He camped on the Beaver that evening before dark. When he unloaded the remedy machine, he noticed his pinto was sulking.

"You jealous?" he asked Lightning. "That skewbald can't hold a feedbag to you. Why, he's nuthin' but a pack hoss."

Lightning turned tail, refusing comment. Well, if that's what he wanted, Tom would ignore him. Pulling the saddle, he rubbed down his gelding without another word. Staking him on a long lead rope so that he could graze, he then focused his attention on Oscar.

"I been calculatin' the best place to set up the still," he told the skewbald.

Unblinking, Oscar stared back at him. The skewbald wasn't as smart as Lightning, but he *was* a good listener.

"How about that river bank down amongst the cottonwoods. Whadda ya think?"

Oscar stared a moment longer before passing wind. Disgusted, Tom decided he would have to mollify Lightning. Even a sulky pinto was better than a muley skewbald.

When they arrived at Bridger Creek, he'd have a talk with Walt about setting up the still. That should keep them busy, at least 'til "Flat Nose" George needed them to trail another herd to the reservation.

* * * *

They followed the others out of camp along the overflowing bank. A full moon threw ripples of light across the water as the horses stepped into its icy flow. Ketchum took the lead and decided to ford the stream at an unmarked crossing. Andrea heard Billy swear when Pepper balked as he stepped into the frigid water. Urging him forward, he whispered encouragement, but his gelding only shuddered. Bolting a few steps further into the stream, the horse halted, water swirling over his knees. Ahead of them, Jake's sorrel squealed with fright. He had apparently stepped into a hole and was struggling against the numbing current. As they watched, the sorrel went down, thrashing in an attempt to regain his footing. Andrea gasped in horror when Jake's head disappeared beneath the surface.

The others climbed the opposite bank and were aware of Jake's plight. Logan reached for a coil of rope and within seconds had it spinning. When the scarecrow reappeared, sputtering and shrieking, Logan tossed the lariat over his shoulders before Jake disappeared again from view. The big man dismounted to wade into the stream. He grabbed the lariat while Logan dallied the rope to his saddle horn. Water rose waist high as Ketchum stepped into the hole, briefly attempting to pull the flailing sorrel to his feet. When that failed, he reached to pull Jake's head above the surface.

Slipping the rope past Jake's narrow shoulders, he signaled Logan to back his bay, keeping the rope taut. Then, with a loud grunt, he reached beneath the horse to free his partner's leg. Straightening, he plucked him from the water as though he were weightless.

Andrea shivered as she watched him place Jake on the opposite bank. "What about the horse?" she asked.

"Done for, I'm afraid. He musta broke a leg." Billy signaled Logan and backed his roan from the stream. As they started up the bank, she watched Logan pull his blanket from the saddle to cover Jake.

"Where's the posse?" she asked, when the others were out of sight.

"If it was them back at camp, they'd have been all over us by now. It could have been some deer. They feed at night. Or a mountain lion spooked the hosses."

Andrea shook her head. *Poor fools. How can anyone live this way?*

Billy found a wider, shallower stretch of stream bed. Stroking his roan, he urged him into the water. Pepper was threading a stand of cottonwoods on the opposite bank when the first shot was fired.

The gelding stopped short as Billy jerked his rifle from the scabbard. Dismounting, he reached to pull her from behind the saddle. Handing her the reins, he said, "Can I trust you to stay here with my hoss?"

When she hesitated, he said, "Of course not. If it was me, I'd ride out a here as fast as this tired old hoss could carry me." Lifting her into the saddle, he led Pepper away from the creek and up a rock-strewn draw.

When they reached a cluster of boulders, he motioned her to dismount.

"Hate to do this, Andy, but I gotta tie you up."

"But a wild animal might—"

"No varmint's getting past Pepper." He glanced in the direction of the gunfight, which sounded now like full-blown war.

Hurriedly tying her ankles and wrists, he also hobbled the roan. When he rose to leave, she said, "Billy?"

"Yeah?"

"Be careful."

Darkness prevented Andrea from gauging his reaction, but she knew it was surprise. If the outlaws survived the battle, she would need a friend among them. Billy seemed the only one she might trust.

As the gunfight progressed, she worried he would be killed. If Ketchum were the only survivor, she knew he would hold her hostage. She frantically renewed efforts to free herself.

Gunfire continued for what seemed hours, punctuated by an occasional scream of pain. Each time, she feared it was Billy. The moon was high overhead when the last shot was fired. Still struggling to loosen the ropes, she heard the sound of spurs echoing up the draw. When Pepper whinnied, she held her breath. A dark shape appeared along the outer rim of boulders.

"Gunfight's over," the voice said. "Posse turned tail, what's left of 'em."

Her eyes blurred with tears. "Was anyone killed?"

Billy's dark form bent to untie the rope. "Jake's shot in the head. Maybe your grandma taught you to treat a bullet wound."

"Of course not," she said.

When they reached the creek bank, she noticed Jake on his back, still wrapped in Logan's blanket. Shivering and moaning, he sounded like a sick child as blood trickled from his left temple.

"Give me a handkerchief before he bleeds to death," she said.

Billy untied his bandana and handed it to her. Hastily rinsing the dusty cloth in the stream, she held it against the wound.

"We need shelter and a place to dry his clothes," she said. *Why are they just standing there?*

Logan snorted. "We'll all be drying out in some jail cell if we don't get moving."

"If the posse comes back," she said with no small dose of sarcasm, "they'll find a wounded man deserted by his friends. It didn't do you much good to kidnap me. The posse doesn't know I'm here, or doesn't care."

From the corner of her eye, she noticed Ketchum moving in her direction. He was buttoning a dry pair of wool trousers over his generous paunch.

"Kid's too damned mouthy for my blood," he snarled.

Harve Logan drew his gun, jamming it into the big man's back. "I told you before. Leave the kid alone."

Enraged, Ketchum turned to swing on Harve, but the smaller man was quicker. Harve delivered a blow to the bear's rib section. Before the big man could regain his balance, Harve followed with rapid jabs to his soft, exposed belly. When Ketchum doubled over, Harve landed a solid hook to his jaw. Backing away, he watched him fall.

"Should have known better than to take in an ignorant bully," Harve said, rubbing his bruised knuckles.

Ketchum had managed to get to his knees when Billy moved toward them. "I'll stay here with Jake 'til you send back some hosses," he said. "We'll find a place to get him warm. Andy knows about doctoring."

Logan pointed to a hilly area to the northwest. "There's an old line shack not far from here," he said as he stooped to relieve the big man of both guns. Dropping them into his own saddlebag, he withdrew several tins of corned beef, which he tossed to the ground.

"Cut Jake's saddlebags loose soon as it's light," he ordered as he prepared to mount his bay. Remembering Ketchum's rifle, he pulled the gun from its scabbard.

The big man stood unsteadily for several moments, massaging his lantern jaw. With effort, he climbed on his dun and flung down his malodorous blanket. Wheeling his mount, he followed Logan out of camp.

Andrea was shocked by the outlaws' lack of concern for Jake. Billy knelt beside her as she pulled the blankets over the injured man's chest. He then rose to peer across the stream.

"Who's out there?" she whispered.

"Don't know. We'd better leave." Pulling the blanketed outlaw to his feet, he helped him into the saddle.

Andrea considered screaming, in case it was the posse, but feared she could be killed in the crossfire. Seated behind the cantle, she clung to Jake's thin waist as Billy led them away from the river and up the same rocky draw.

Chapter Six

Billy stopped to check on Jake when they reached the second ridge. The scarecrow's head was down, his long, slim body vibrating from the cold. He seemed to be shrinking inside his blankets. The moon had all but disappeared behind the sloping Big Horn Mountains, revealing little in the way of trees or undergrowth to hide them from the posse. The ridges were nearly barren once they left the cottonwoods along the stream.

Unaccustomed to walking, Billy was tired and out of sorts. As she watched him, she wondered whether outlaws worked in tandem, or was every man on his own? Harve seemed eager to leave Jake in Billy's care, and Ketchum had abandoned his partner without a backward glance.

When they started up the draw, she noticed a small dwelling near the rim of the next ridge. Climbing the rocky slope was difficult and Billy slumped to the ground out of breath. The slanting wooden structure, not much larger than a wealthy man's privy, clung to the barren slope. Its weathered door hung by a single rusty hinge.

Helping Jake from the saddle, they half-carried him to the shack. "We'll need some lucifers and dry clothes for Jake," Billy said, leaving Andrea to support the trembling, blanket-bundled outlaw.

From the door she watched him hobble Pepper. She decided then to take the gelding while both men slept. With any luck, she could overtake the posse, but from the looks of him, the gelding was already ridden down.

* * * *

Billy struck a match on his thumb nail and held it aloft as they crept inside the shack. Spider webs repelled her, along with the dust and an unwashed animal smell. Billy's second lucifer revealed a lantern leaning against the hearth, and a narrow, sheetless bunk. When Jake sprawled across the dirty mattress, Billy trimmed the lantern's wick as Andrea held another match. Exchanging grimaces, they took a closer look.

"Needs some cleaning up."

Andrea wrinkled her nose. "It needs more than that."

Other than the bed, the only furnishings were a three-legged milking stool and a shredded gunny sack. A few pinto beans lay sprinkled on the splintered floor. Jake groaned when Billy stripped damp blankets from his quivering body. He then unbuttoned his shirt and peeled the top half of his dingy flannel underwear. Using the corner of a blanket, Andrea dabbed at Jake's gooseflesh-covered chest. She then unrolled the clothing and handed Billy a heavy wool shirt. The sleeves were too short for Jake's reedy arms, but at least they were dry. When he removed Jake's wet wool trousers, underwear clung to his body like red wrinkled skin.

She averted her eyes when Billy replaced Jake's wet underwear with his own wool trousers. The scarecrow's ankles hung inches past the hems and off the end of the bed.

"I'm going back for the other blanket," Billy said. "These damp ones won't do him much good."

"What about the posse?"

"They're halfway to Rawlins by now."

She heard him grunt as he twisted the rusty hinge. Straightening the door, he tried to block the cold night air. From outside the shack, he said, "Don't come out here, Andy. Lobo wolves roam these mountains. Six feet long from nose to tail. They can take down a full grown steer."

Andrea scoffed at his warning. *Scare me so I won't try to escape.*

No windows broke the uneven line of newspaper-stuffed walls, but she knew the door would easily fall from its mooring. Andrea reasoned that she could hide along the stream until the posse returned with reinforcements but if they failed to arrive by daybreak, Billy would be sure to find her.

Testing the door, she heard a high-pitched howl that echoed endlessly inside the dimly lighted shack. Shivering, she wondered whether the coyote was alone, or prowling with a pack. Jake's breathing was raspy but he was no longer moaning. She touched his brow and compared his temperature to her own. His fever was high and he didn't respond when she called his name. Andrea held the lantern close to his head, noticing a thick, dark clot that had dried to his scalp. Searching the shack, she could find nothing of medicinal value. The possibility he might die kept her thoughts reeling. If he failed to recover, she could be blamed for his death.

Wondering what her grandmother would do, Andrea refused to believe she was dead. Lips trembling, she recalled her arrival in Casper with her grandparents, travel-weary and frightened by the empty landscape. Uncle Jim Bob had tried to reassure them but Andrea felt betrayed. Her grandparents' expressions told her that they felt the same. Now they were injured or dead, and there was nothing she could do. Shrieking, she stamped cold feet on the splintered floor.

Jake groaned and mumbled something that sounded like "mama." Andrea bit her lip and decided now was not the time to plan her escape. *Jake's not a bad sort, and I'm the only one who can save him.* She fingered the small muslin sack of garlic suspended from her neck, doubting it would help an unconscious man. Maybe, if chopped up fine, he could inhale the garlic like snuff... No, that would only make him sneeze and reopen the wound.

Andrea paced the small area between the bed and lean-to door, rubbing clammy hands. Weighing her alternatives, she had decided to escape before dawn on Pepper when a scraping sound stopped her. Holding her breath, she felt her heart pounding. There it was again, a definite scratching noise. It had to be an animal searching for food. A bear or mountain lion. A lobo wolf? Or was Billy trying to frighten her? She looked about frantically for a weapon but saw nothing she could use to protect herself.

The scratching became more pronounced, the animal's frustration apparent when the door bumped against the frame. Andre glanced again at the small milking stool. It was solidly built and she doubted she could rip one leg loose to use as a club. Lifting the stool above her head, she positioned herself beside the door. The scratching increased, the door rattling as planks banged against the wooden frame. Her arms soon ached and she lowered the stool to her waist, pulling it tight against her. Breathing shallowly, she listened, her body slick with fear.

When Jake groaned, the scratching reached a frenzy. She heard a growl and bang as the animal leaped against the door. A river roared through her head as bile rose in her throat, threatening to throttle her.

The shack trembled as she heard an anguished whine. Raising the stool again above her head, she held her breath. Moments passed before she sensed, more than heard, the door fall to its side. Night air invaded the shack as she screamed.

* * * *

The white eye was snoring as soon as his head touched the saddle. A chinook was blowing in from the west, melting the snow that had escaped the sweep into Thunder Basin. When a cloud shadowed the moon, Arched Back Wolf crept between the horse and the sleeping man. Cutting the pinto's rope, he attempted to mount him but the horse shied and tossed his head. The Arapaho watched the man, wondering why his pinto's frightened whicker hadn't awakened him. When the horse reared, attempting to stomp him into the ground, the brave abandoned him.

Checking again on the snorer, he decided instead to take the skewbald, who had watched without a whicker. He cut the rope and led the horse along the bank to where his own pony was tied, stopping briefly to inspect a strange looking container leaning against a juniper. He decided it was a grain storage bin. Arched Back Wolf was a warrior, not a farmer, although the Indian agent had repeatedly warned him that his warring days were over.

Star Gazer harangued him and to appease her, he did a little late night scouting. She would not be pleased with the animal he had dredged up in the absence of the moon, but at least she would know he was trying.

* * * *

Because she was screaming, Andrea didn't hear the hoof beats. When she gasped for breath, she heard a voice yell: "Shoo, get out here!" Trembling, she heard a growl, a thud, and a yelp; then someone calling: "Andy." She was unaware of her tears until Billy burst into the shack.

"I chased 'im off," he said, breathing heavily. "He musta been using this place for his den. He was madder than the devil when he couldn't get inside."

"A mountain lion?" She wiped at tears with her sleeve.

"A wolf."

"Lobo?"

"Plain old timber wolf."

Andrea closed her eyes and tried to stop trembling.

He placed a hand on her shoulder and turned to stare at Jake. "How's he doing?"

"I don't know," she said, wringing her hands. "I could make garlic broth if we had some water."

Billy inspected the rough stone fireplace at the rear of the shack. Choked with ashes and debris, its hearth was missing rocks.

"I think it'll still draw," he said, dusting himself.

They needed wood. Stepping into the darkness, he stopped briefly to lean the door against the jamb. He returned with a blanket and utensils. Handing her his jackknife, he told her to use the stool as a chopping block while he rounded up wood. Before he left, he replaced Jake's damp blanket with his own.

"I'll set a rock against the door before I leave." Billy's expression was reassuring, but her knees continued to quiver. "Don't worry about the wolf," he said. "He probably high-tailed it for Montana."

Andrea carried the stool into primary lantern light. Rays reflecting from the knife made her marvel at its sharpness. *Billy's too trusting or not terribly smart.* But he had little to fear from a well-mannered *boy*.

She tried chopping garlic into tiny buds with hands so numb she nearly cut herself. Finished, she unscrewed the cap and took a tentative sip, glad he had refilled the canteen with stream water. Pouring most of it into the pan, she dropped in garlic bits as though launching a fleet of sailing ships. Tears spilled when she remembered the ships in Mobile Bay. Why had they left their home in Alabama?

Her patient was restlessly moving his head about on the mattress. While she was arranging the blanket under Jake's chin, Billy returned with an armload of branches. Dropping them near the hearth, he said, "Might throw off some smoke, *if* I can get 'em to burn."

"I found half a can of kerosene." She indicated a corner near the hearth. "A few drops ought to start the fire."

Billy grinned. "You're a smart kid. I think I'll adopt you as my little brother."

Andrea's cheeks flushed as she turned back to straighten Jake's blanket. "I'd like that," she said.

When Pepper had been rubbed down, Billy carried his saddle into the shack, groaning under its weight. He then tried pulling the door snug against the frame, but a cold draft seeped in around the edges.

Andrea knelt on the hearth to place the small, dented pan in the flames. Sitting cross-legged beside her, he reached to warm his hands.

"See anyone at the stream?"

"No, but I didn't hang around."

"Were there any ... dead people?" Her throat constricted.

"None that I could find." Billy was obviously relieved. "If there was, the posse must have hauled 'em away."

"Are they still after us, Billy?"

Glancing up from the fire, he grinned. "After *us*? Are you considering yourself one of the gang?"

She nodded shyly, crossing fingers behind her back.

"You're not old enough to know about outlaws, Andy."

"You must like it, or you wouldn't—"

"It's not what I thought it would be."

"Didn't your parents try to stop you?"

Billy sighed. "Ma was a school marm. She died when I was fifteen. Pa drank himself to death not long after." His lips briefly trembled.

"I'm sorry."

"Me, too."

Focusing her attention on the broth, she said, "I hear you're from Missouri."

"Yeah," he said, recovering. "I lived next door to the Logan brothers in Dodson. When my old man died, I followed them out to Montana, where Hank and Harve have a ranch. When Hank died of consumption, his younger brothers went a little wild."

Andrea said nothing as she looked back into the flames.

"Harve's the older brother I never had. He's smart—like you, Andy. He's also a damn good cowhand."

When she frowned, he said, "Sorry. I shouldn't swear around kids."

Andrea ducked her head, suppressing a smile.

"The boys pull off a robbery now and then, but mostly they work as honest cowhands." His eyelids drooped, reminding her of her own fatigue.

"But why did Harve become an outlaw?"

"A mean galoot named Pike Landusky was mad 'cause Harve's brother was courting his stepdaughter. One thing led to another and Landusky drew down on Harve one day."

She gasped when he pantomimed the action.

"Landusky's gun misfired, and Harve thought he was shooting him in self defense. But the name of the town is Landusky, and Harve knew he didn't stand a chance in court. So he rode out and hasn't stopped since."

"Did his brothers go with him?"

"No, his brother Lonie's been living with Elfie Landusky since the shooting. She must have hated the old man. And Harve's brother Johnny got himself shot in the back by a neighbor not long ago."

"Killed him?"

"Yeah, and him with only one arm."

She shuddered. "Is that why Harve asked you to join the gang?"

"No, Andy, I asked him. Harve and Butch have been like family to me."

When she didn't respond, he stared, as though seeing her for the first time. "By the way, why were you living with your grandparents?"

"A train wreck killed my par—" Her throat swelled, shutting off the words.

Billy reached to touch her arm, a sympathetic curve to his lips. "I guess that makes us both orphans."

She nodded, wiping at her tears. Moments later she said, "Uncle Jim Bob convinced Grandpa he could make a fortune raising sheep. He herded them as a boy in Ireland. So he sold his saw mill in Alabama, and we moved to Wyoming."

"I knew you were a southern boy," he said smiling.

She ignored the remark but wondered what he meant. "We lived in Casper just long enough to get acquainted before Grandpa bought the ranch. The sheep are being trailed in from Colorado, but they may have been lost in the storm."

Billy's obvious aversion to sheep prompted her to change the subject. Glancing again at Jake, who hadn't moved, she asked how long he'd been in the gang.

"He's not. We met him and Ketchum in a small town on the Colorado border. They were in a saloon in Dixon when we rode in from Brown's Hole. The gang stops there, or in Baggs, to hurrah the town."

She noticed that the fire's flickering shadows lent him a melancholy look.

"Everybody got a snoot full before we left," he said. "Ketchum stopped some drunk waddie from knocking Harve's head off with a chair. When he said he was a cousin to the outlaws, Sam and Black Jack Ketchum, Harve let him and Jake ride along."

Gazing into his heavily-lashed hazel eyes, she sensed a growing kinship. "Why's the posse after us?"

Shrugging, he glanced into the fire. "Long story, Andy. Those two yahoos robbed the Greeley stage. They took a strong box full of gold."

So Billy hadn't taken part in the robbery. Relieved, she reached to stir the broth. The aroma of garlic conjured up Scar Ketchum's scruffy image, prompting her to ask, "Why is he so mean?"

"His old man must have beat him when he was small."

She couldn't imagine Ketchum as a child.

Shrugging, Billy got to his feet. "Looks like the broth's ready. Let's spoon some into Jake."

She used the corner of a damp blanket to pull the pan from the flames. Setting the pan on the stool, she scooped a spoonful and blew into it.

Tasting it, she grimaced. "It's awful."

He reached into his pocket and offered her a packet of salt, then turned to shake Jake's shoulder. The outlaw didn't respond.

"Is he dead?" Billy's eyes widened in alarm.

Placing two fingers on Jake's jugular, she said, "No, his heart's still beating." Patting his cheek, she called his name.

Jake's eyelids fluttered but didn't open.

"Give him some broth." Billy removed his jacket to form a pillow for Jake's head.

The outlaw gagged when she tried to push the spoon past his lolling tongue. "This isn't working. Maybe if I hold the pan on his chest, he'll breath the fumes."

"It's worth a try, Andy. I don't know much about doctoring. Maybe you should have another look at his wound."

Lifting the lantern from a peg on the wall, he held the light near Jake's head. Although the wound had scabbed over, something wasn't right. Andrea looked closer, realizing that a bullet grazing the side of his head would have damaged his ear, or removed the lobe entirely. She said as much.

"I think you're right, but what could have done that much damage?"

"Maybe his head struck a rock in the stream when his horse went down."

"With all that lead flying around in the dark, we all just reckoned that…"

A bullet would have been better, she thought, seating herself on the floor beside the bed. If Jake's injuries were serious, there was nothing more she could do. Before long her head lurched forward, waking her from momentary sleep.

Billy removed the pan and gently pulled his jacket from beneath Jake's head. He insisted that she wear it. "Get some sleep while I watch him."

Gratefully resting her head on the edge of the bunk, she promptly drifted off.

* * * *

Jim McCloud rested his weary bones on the earthen floor of an abandoned homesteader's shack. From a broken window he had watched the Omaha-Pacific Express train continue its run to Sacramento. He left the train at Douglas, Wyoming, to replace his ragged clothing before moving on to the Hole in the Wall. He knew outlaws would reject him if he looked like a railroad bum. His cellmate's face floated before him as he drifted off to sleep. Joe had died the day following their escape from

Leavenworth Prison, where a measles epidemic had confined them to the infirmary. Heads swollen and feverish, they managed to loosen the bars and hide in an outgoing laundry wagon.

While hidden aboard a westbound Union Pacific freight car, his cell mate had died, probably of pneumonia. Although nearly blind from the fever, McCloud swapped his prison garb with that of a drunken tramp asleep on the floor of the boxcar. He hoped railroad detectives would mistake the hobo for himself when they discovered Joe's body.

He changed trains near midnight at Marysville, Kansas. McCloud then caught a freight train north, which connected with the Omaha-Pacific Express. Scattered among the richly appointed Pullmans and day coach passenger cars were boxcars crowded with narrow benches. When his boxcar was side-railed with the day coach passengers, McCloud considered himself lucky to sleep lying down. Those not rich enough for Pullman cars were forced to sit all night, unless they chose the floor.

Constantly on the watch for railroad detectives, McCloud was unnerved in western Nebraska, when he woke to the sound of gunfire. Reclining on squares of baled hay, he peered through cracks in the freight car's walls. If outlaws were robbing the train, he would ask to join them. Rubbing his shaved head, he changed his mind. They would only humiliate him.

Railroad employees were probably shooting at buffalo blocking the tracks. He then remembered that hunters had all but exterminated the herds some twenty years earlier. Peeking through the partially opened door, McCloud watched antelope sprint away from the tracks in rows of fours and fives, like soldiers retreating from the enemy. Their white rumps rapidly grew smaller in the distance. Amused, he knew they had been racing the train until passengers started shooting.

McCloud had never tasted antelope, but was hungry enough to chew one raw. He prowled at night while the others were attempting sleep, searching for scraps of food tossed from the train when they stopped to load coal to fuel the engine. An apple core and half-eaten biscuit were more than he had hoped for.

Thirst was his main concern. He had stolen a canteen from a snoring day coach passenger seated near the door. There was hell to pay when he awoke. That night they stopped along the North Platte River, where the train took on more water, and McCloud refilled his pilfered canteen. In Cheyenne, he caught a freight headed north as far as Douglas. Jumping from the car as it slowed for the crossing, he spotted an abandoned farmhouse near the tracks where he could rest and grow his hair.

He wondered whether there was a safe worth cracking in the small railroad town. His first post office job in Ulysses, Kansas, had landed him in Leavenworth, where he heard of the Hole in the Wall, the perfect place to hide. Unable to sleep since his friend's death, he worried pneumonia would kill him as well. When he finally dozed off, he dreamed of riding with the Wild Bunch.

Chapter Seven

Andrea awoke with pain in her left shoulder. Briefly disoriented, enough light filtered through the cracks that she soon recognized her surroundings. Billy was asleep on the floor, his head resting on his saddle.

Rising quietly, she leaned to place a palm on Jake's brow, which was as cold as ice crystals. His mouth hung open, and he didn't appear to be breathing. Billy awoke when she gasped.

"What's wrong, Andy?"

"Jake's dead," she said, sobbing. "I didn't know he was hurt so badly."

He rubbed his eyes and tried to focus on the body. "It's not your fault. You did all you could."

"Gramma could have saved him."

Billy shook his head as if to clear his thoughts. "I don't even have a shovel to bury him," he said. Staggering sleepily to the door, he stamped his boots and peered through a long crack inside the frame. "Harve said to cut Jake's saddlebags loose as soon as it's light."

"Why?"

"Gold from the robbery's in them. That's why Jake's hoss couldn't get up when he fell in the stream."

"Why didn't they take the gold with them?"

"Harve said to get it this morning. He was afraid the posse would catch up with us last night."

But he doesn't mind if we're caught this morning. Andrea's hands flew to her face in an attempt to hold back the tears.

He stared at her a long moment. "Makes me wonder why I don't just quit and go home."

New hope surfaced. "Why don't we, Billy? We could both ride out of here on Pepper."

"Ketchum would kill us for taking the gold."

"Leave it here with Jake."

"What would we use for money?"

"My grandparents will help."

"Posse'll throw me in jail. I'd rather be dead."

"No, you wouldn't."

"Yes, I *would*, Andy."

"But couldn't you just let *me* go?"

"You'd never make it back on foot, and Ketchum would be madder than a bee-stung mule if you got away."

Andrea knew it was useless to argue. She watched him pull the blanket over Jake's head. Then lifting the door, he set it aside. The cool dawn air seemed to revive him.

Pepper's head hung limply, his front legs spread. Speaking softly, Billy led him behind the shack to rehobble him. When he returned, he said, "You need boots. Jake's are too big, so you'd better wear mine."

"You'd wear a dead man's?"

"We have no choice. Pepper is too winded to ride."

Billy retrieved Jake's boots from the hearth where he had earlier set them to dry. Sitting on the floor, he removed his own.

"Stuff 'em," he said, pulling the stockings from Jake's cold feet. "And grip with your toes."

Nodding, she did as he said.

Billy blocked the door with a rock. Hoisting a lariat over his shoulder, he started for the stream. Andrea shuffled along behind. Reaching into his pocket, he offered her a twist of jerky.

Ground fog from the river made the trek seem surreal, and she hurried to prevent Billy from disappearing from view. The fog began to dissipate with the sun's first rays when they reached the stream. Gazing along the bank, she relived events of the previous night. The damp sand smelled clean, the only hint of the calamity was a confusion of boot prints and a few dark spots in the sand.

* * * *

Tom awoke early, anxious to be on his way. Scanning the horizon, he was surprised to find his pinto grazing a quarter mile down the bank.

The remedy machine still leaned against a scrawny juniper, but the skewbald was nowhere in sight. How had both horses gotten loose? Jamming pinkies in the corners of his mouth, he offered a shrill whistle, which brought Lightning on the run.

Although the gelding seemed cheerful, Tom was fighting mad.

"Where's Oscar?" he bellowed. "What did ya do, run 'im off?"

Lightning lowered his head and snorted.

Tom spotted the lead rope dangling from his gelding's neck. The end had been cleanly cut.

"Well, I'll be a lop-eared mule."

Lightning moved forward to nuzzle Tom, as though consoling him.

"That tricky old liveryman musta follered us here to steal back the skewbald. No wonder he sold 'im so cheap."

The gelding shook his head from side-to-side, giving Tom a horse laugh.

"Just 'cause he stole Oscar instead of you is no reason to get uppity."

Cursing, he turned to glance at his still. "How're we gonna haul this thing all the way to the Hole?"

Loading the remedy machine on Lightning's back and leading him was out of the question. Tom had never walked further than the bunkhouse to the barn.

* * * *

Billy removed his borrowed boots and stood to shed his clothes. Andrea stifled a laugh when several oblong tears appeared in his underwear.

"Do you need the gold to buy new longjohns, Billy?"

He ignored her attempt at humor. Tying the rope around her waist, he encircled his own with the other end. Standing on the bank, Andrea tried to gauge the stream's depth as water roared passed.

"Hold this," he said, handing her a coil of rope. "Reel it out and keep it taut."

Nodding, she gripped the rough strands while he waded into water halfway up his thighs. Bracing herself, she played out the lariat, timing it with his steps.

He unexpectedly slid into the hole before he realized he was there. The lurch forward took Andrea by surprise, nearly pulling her into the stream. Shivering, he told her to give him more slack. Digging her heels into the soft bank, she watched as he felt around the dead horse with his toes. Water was chest high when he stooped to cut the first saddlebag free.

I could slip from the rope and run. He'd never catch me. Pepper's too worn down to ride. She hesitated … he was right about her chances of survival alone in the mountains.

He straightened and held up the saddlebag, a frozen grin on his face. For the next few minutes he worked at the remaining one. At last, he struggled upstream with a saddlebag draped over each shoulder.

"Pull me in," he said at last, a few yards from shore.

Groaning, she tugged at the rope, her hands forming blisters. When the coil was long enough, she wrapped the rope around a nearby boulder. Wiping sweaty palms on her overalls, she winced when a blister broke.

"Pull," he said. "Work up some muscle."

Something stirred the air. Swiveling her head, she saw nothing on the horizon although she sensed another presence. Gripping the rope, she scanned the terrain.

"Is somebody coming, Andy?"

"I don't know."

Tugging at the rope, he fell forward onto the bank.

Andrea pushed the heavy saddlebags from his shoulders and helped him to his feet. His hands were icy and trembling. Slipping the rope from her slim hips, she stepped from the coil as Billy had done. He dragged the saddlebags behind a clump of sagebrush and indicated a brush-sheltered depression. Andrea hurriedly gathered up boots and clothing as he broomed out their tracks with a cottonwood branch before scrambling for cover.

"See anything?" Still breathing hard, he lay flat, peeling off his wet underwear. She watched him intermittently from the corner of her eye while scanning both banks of the stream. She turned away when his bare body filled her side vision.

Sudden movement on the opposite bank was no mirage. A large, well-groomed quarter horse appeared at the bend of the stream, slowly making its way toward them. The tall rider rode slowly, searching the ground, his broad-brimmed hat hiding his face. Billy was still attempting to wriggle into his pants as the lone horseman came opposite them.

She could dash out of hiding before Billy could button his pants. But he could be another outlaw, cruel like Ketchum. Hesitating, she watched the rider raise his head to visually sweep both banks of the stream.

Recognizing him, she gasped.

* * * *

"Danged remedy machine'll disappear before I can find a pack hoss."

Lightning swished his tail, ignoring Tom.

"The agent'll scalp me if them Injuns find the still and cook their own brew."

Scanning the horizon, Tom searched for a cave where he might hide the still.

"Ain't enough driftwood to build a raft. If'n there was, there ain't a stream in the whole damn state that won't capsize the raft, or high-center it."

Tom had pondered the problem more than an hour when he finally reached a conclusion.

"Remember the Injun draggin' them limbs?"

Lightning pricked his ears.

"I can make one so's you can pull the still."

The pinto lost interest and resumed nibbling bunch grass. He followed Tom down the creek bank, where the outlaw wrenched branches from a cottonwood and stripped them of their twigs. He bound the limbs with a lariat, forming a webbed platform. Tom lashed the remedy machine to the sled, with the pole ends attached to the saddle.

They started off slowly down the bank, the distillery unit clattering over every stone and crevice. They hadn't gone far when Tom spotted a group of men riding toward him. When they were within twenty yards, the group roughly split in half, circling him to inspect the travois.

"What you got there, white eye?"

A paunchy Arapaho was sitting astride Tom's skewbald. Oscar had been groomed to racehorse sleekness, and Tom had not recognized him in the distance.

"I see you found my pack hoss."

"Spotted Eagle my hoss. You fight for him?"

The Arapahos formed a tight ring around Lightning and the travois, several of them pulling at the lariat holding the still. All of them were armed with hunting bows. Oscar wasn't worth dying over, and Tom wondered if the liveryman would sell him another still. He'd have to think fast before they lifted his scalp. He thought he had the answer.

"Me bring gift hoss for Chief Washakie."

The Arapahos grunted with apparent anger.

"Why him bad-hair?" one of them asked.

So that's why they're mad. "No time to clean him," Tom said. "I just bought him in Lander."

"You come!" Oscar's new owner signaled him to follow.

Tom had no choice.

* * * *

A cold, clammy hand covered her mouth before she could utter another sound. Wrestling her onto her back, Billy pinned her with his damp, lean body. Squirming beneath his weight, she tried to tell him that the man on the opposite bank was Jim Bob Wilson, her mother's older brother. But Billy wasn't listening. His rapid breathing kept pace with his swiveling head as he glanced in every direction. At last satisfied the rider was alone and had ridden out of sight, he pulled her into a sitting position. He refused to take his hand from her mouth until his fingers were wet with tears.

"Aw, Andy," he whispered. "I couldn't let you give me away."

When he released her, she told him her uncle was a horse trader, and that he never rode the same mount more than twice. "He must be looking for me on his own," she said. "He's so domineering that the sheriff won't allow him to ride with a posse." *And so sanctimonious, I can't stand him,* she thought, gritting her teeth.

Grinning, Billy pulled on Jake's boots. Once he was ready, she helped him hoist the saddlebags onto his shoulders. "Let's get back," he said, struggling beneath the weight. "The hosses Harve's sending should be here by now."

She remembered the rope. *I wonder if Uncle saw it.*

Billy groaned, telling her to retrieve the rope. "No tricks now," he warned.

"He wouldn't be looking for me if my grandparents needed him," she said. Her smile abruptly faded. Jim Bob must be gunning for the men responsible. She hastily coiled the rope.

Little was said during the return hike to the line shack. The sun shone brightly, dispelling misty clouds of ground fog that made their earlier trip to the stream so dispiriting.

"Uncle Jim Bob tracks as well as an Indian Scout. He'll find us soon."

"That right?"

"You won't shoot him, will you?"

"Not unless he shoots first."

"I'll tell him you helped me escape." She hoped he would allow her to negotiate before her uncle killed him.

Billy slowly shook his head. Obviously exhausted, he seemed in a trance.

The rock was missing from the door when they arrived at the line shack, but he didn't seem to notice. Once inside the darkened room, he allowed the saddlebags to slide from his shoulders.

The pistol aimed at his chest must have seemed as large-bored as a shotgun. Billy slumped against the wall, apparently prepared to die.

"Uncle Jim Bob, don't shoot!" Rushing past Billy, she deliberately rushed into his arms. "He's not the one who kidnapped me."

"What're you saying, girl? And who's this skeleton under the blanket?" With a muscular arm, the tall, middle-aged man pulled her away from his chest.

"*Girl?*" Billy alternately peered at them both.

"Andrea's my niece," Jim Bob said. "If you've defiled her—"

"Defiled her? I thought—" He pushed away from the wall, disbelief registering on his face.

Anticipating violence, she stepped between them. "Billy didn't know, because Gramma cut my hair to disguise me." Studying her uncle in the dim light, she could detect nothing more than righteous indignation.

"I know, Andrea. I rode out to the ranch after the ground blizzard."

Before she could ask about her grandparents, Billy moved in closer, demanding: "Help me bury Jake before we leave."

"So you can hit me with a shovel and escape?"

The dispute was decided by Pepper's sudden squeal. Loud and panicked, it came from behind the shack where Billy had hobbled him. Motioning the young outlaw to walk outside ahead of him, Jim Bob's scowl warned Andrea to remain inside. Billy obediently stepped through the doorless opening, both hands locked behind his head.

"Put your hands down," Jim Bob snarled.

Head lowered, Billy marched in a straight line. The horse trader followed him through the doorway, his long-barreled pistol held waist high. Standing inside the door, Andrea was startled by a loud thump on the shack's north wall. Her uncle turned, and she caught the glint of a rifle barrel as it struck the back of his head. Jim Bob crumpled without a sound.

"I'll tie 'im up," a deep voice growled.

"B-Billy, g-get your arse b-back here and help," a tenor voice demanded.

A husky stranger appeared, his dark, battered hat shading his handsome face, his chin adorned with a short, flaxen beard. Kneeling, he took the gun from Jim Bob's grip. Crossing her uncle's hands behind his back, he looped several coils of rope around his wrists.

A smaller man, hard-faced and wiry, stepped inside the shack. Dragging her outside, he said, "W-will you l-lookie here?"

Billy hurried back when he saw what was happening. "That's Andy, leave him be," he yelled.

"How come he's all bruised up?"

"Scar-faced jasper hit him." Billy placed an arm around Andrea's shoulders.

"Ketchum?"

"Yeah."

"Where the hell did you meet up with him?"

"Long story. We can jaw about it later."

Andrea stared at Billy's profile. Why was he protecting her? When he glanced at her, his left lid lowered in a wink.

"What are you gonna do with him?" Billy indicated her uncle, still unconscious on the ground.

"Probably toss 'im in the crick." The good-looking, bearded one laughed.

"Please don't," Andrea pleaded. Her uncle was insufferable, but he had come to save her. Slumping dejectedly, she wished he had rescued her sooner.

"He's the kid's uncle," Billy said. "He probably didn't get a look at either one of you. Why not leave him with Ketchum's dead partner? When he comes to, he can bury Jake."

"Ketchum had a partner?" The bearded one raised an eyebrow in disbelief.

They carried Jim Bob inside the shack and dumped him face down beside the bed.

Billy strapped on his gun belt. Lifting his saddle, he whispered to Andrea that her uncle would be fine. Unconvinced, she hesitated until Billy pulled her out the door. She watched him saddle Pepper and lead him in the direction the others had taken. When they reached the picketed horses, the sleepy-eyed, stuttering outlaw was rifling Jake's saddlebags.

"That's Dick Halle," Billy whispered. "He talks like a gatling gun."

"W-would ya look at all t-that gold," Hale said. "No w-wonder the d-damn saddlebag was s-so heavy."

His companion Walt Punteney gripped a pair of Jake's plaid trousers, watching them flap in the breeze. "Don't that beat all," he said chortling. "Maybe we oughta hang 'em in a tree to scare off the posse."

"No respect for the dead," Andrea muttered, but Billy's expression silenced her.

"Let's get moving." Billy finished loading the contents of Pepper's saddlebags into those on a waiting buckskin. The rest was evenly distributed on Jim Bob's quarter horse. Andrea mounted her uncle's gelding; Billy climbed on the buckskin. Softly clucking to Pepper, he led him alongside. The quarter horse whickered and crow-hopped when she tried to get him to follow, but settled in behind the buckskin's flowing tail. Riding a narrow valley north, they crossed another creek. Pine trees lined up in sporadic stands on soft swells of the Big Horn Mountains. A balmy breeze was blowing in from the south, and Andrea was grateful for its calming influence.

Taking the lead, Billy soon slumped over the buckskin, alternately dozing and jerking awake as they rode between ridges. The others sat their horses behind her, leading a riderless horse and exchanging raunchy banter. Closing her mind to them, she followed Badwater Creek west, then north toward the towering sandstone walls.

Chapter Eight

Spring arrived late in the high country, if it came at all. Wintry neutral shades were beginning to mingle with summer's warmer colors at the higher elevations, accented with scattered clumps of stunted junipers. White-streaked patches of alkali served as arrows, pointing the way to the Hole. Stopping briefly at mid-day, Billy made her excuses when she sought the privacy of a good-sized bush on the opposite side of the slope. Hearing laughter, she wondered if she were the victim of a coarse joke. Hurrying back, she recognized Walt Punteney climbing the slope in her direction. Billy followed a few steps behind.

"So, we got ourselves a sissy," Walt said, still laughing. "Gotta do somethin' about that."

Billy quickened his pace, grabbing him in a bear hug from behind. "Leave the kid alone. I'll teach him to be a man."

Walt twisted a tuft of whiskers and spat a stream of tobacco juice at Andrea's feet. "Since when're we takin' in strays?"

"Since the cattlemen turned their backs." Billy grabbed his companion and turned him around. Laughing, they continued down the slope to the horses.

Andrea sighed. Men were such frightening, unpredictable creatures. She wondered how long she could fool them, and whether Billy would keep her secret.

* * * *

Rust-colored boulders littered the golden-grassed entrance to the Hole in the Wall canyon. She had bitten her lip until it bled, worrying as they rode among the rock formations. Why hadn't Uncle Jim Bob told her about her grandparents before these new outlaws arrived? Jim Bob's horse seemed equally nervous when they started up a steep, jagged slope leading to an elevated mesa. Ahead, Billy's horse reared, threatening to throw him.

"Dismount," he yelled. She heard him calling the buckskin a stream of wicked names.

Sliding from the brown, she led him up the slope, following Pepper and the buckskin. Soft, crumbling earth caused them to slip back in some areas. Behind her, Punteney and Hale remained mounted as they continued to swap raunchy stories. She wondered if they would acquire some manners if they knew a lady was present.

Andrea caught her breath when she glimpsed the bountiful sea of sweet-smelling grasses flecked with new shoots of green rippling outward into the valley. The entire area was walled in by orange-red layers of sandstone, reaching as high as several hundred feet.

As they rode onto the valley floor, a band of horses raced toward them. Manes and tails flying, they swerved abruptly to gallop back in the direction of the distant blue, cloud-peaked mountains. Wind was gentler here and she breathed great gulps to fill her lungs.

This must be outlaw paradise.

Within an hour they reached a cabin backed with cottonwoods and an orange sandstone bluff. Bunch grass abounded in careless clumps around the large, low-slung log building. A veritable fortress, the two rectangular rooms had roof-high doors and thickly framed windows. The tar-papered roof rose to a modified peak in front, tapering to flat in back.

Harve Logan emerged from the cabin to scowl his welcome. Behind him loomed a taller man with a neatly trimmed mustache. When he grinned, his gums showed beneath his short upper lip. Andrea sensed a coolness in his greeting.

"Sundance," Billy shouted as he slid from the buckskin. "When did you get here?"

"Late yesterday," he said, grasping Billy's hand. "Butch rode over to Flat Nose George's cabin." He nodded his head to the north, where the cabin was located.

After they assembled in the front room where the roof sloped to its highest peak, Billy introduced her to Harry Alonzo Longabaugh.

"Everyone calls Harry by his nickname," Billy said. "He's the Sundance Kid."

Andrea dipped her head and smiled.

"And if I didn't tell you before, Harve is known as Kid Curry."

"You're both called Kid?" she said, "That's confusing."

Billy tightened his grip on her arm. "That's why I call 'em Harve and Sundance."

"You can call me Mr. Sundance," the outlaw said, "Kids need to learn some respect."

"Yes, sir." Andrea nodded meekly.

Frowning, he scrutinized her bruised face. "I hope you're not as clumsy as you look."

Hanging her head, she ran a hand through her crudely cropped blond hair. "No, sir," she replied. "I'm just tired."

"Billy will take you down to the crick and show you where to wash," he said, dismissing her.

She disliked the outlaw's arrogance and resolved to avoid him.

Billy led the way down a path to Buffalo Creek. Splashing water on his face and drinking deeply, he reclined on his back near the bank.

"Are you going to tell them about me?" she asked.

"Maybe."

"Please don't."

Eyes closed, he seemed to be dozing.

"What would they do if they knew?"

Billy sighed heavily and opened one eye. "I'm not sure. That's why I haven't told anyone. But you must know it's dang near impossible to fool them for long."

"That's why you must help me escape."

"You want them to shoot me, Andy?"

"You'll have me on your conscience." She tried her best to look as pathetic as possible.

He rubbed his sparse whisker stubble. "There's a big job planned, and we'll all be riding out soon. You might get left behind."

"You really think so?"

"It's possible." He rolled onto his side, his head propped on one hand, staring at her. "If you mind your manners and stay out of sight, you might fool 'em for awhile."

"You won't tell?"

"I'm not promising anything. The way you look, all bruised up, I doubt they would bother you. But if they find out, I don't know anything. You hear?"

"Yes, I'll be careful," she whispered, her hands tightly clasped. "How can I ever repay you?"

"You tried to save me back at the cabin, so I reckon I owe you something."

"I'll be quiet as a snowflake."

Billy dragged himself to his feet. "It's time to break in the new cook."

His shoulders sagged noticeably as he climbed the rocky slope. When they reached the cabin, the two outlaws were seated on thick-legged chairs. They were arguing.

Billy guided her into the front room, which doubled as a kitchen.

Harve's fist pounded the small, round table between them. Snarling, he appeared ready to draw his guns when the Sundance Kid threw his hands in resignation. His strangled laugh ended in a fit of coughing.

"I don't care how long you've known George Currie," Sundance said when he recovered. "We don't need a damned flat-nosed cattle rustler along on the job. Hell, I know the Black Hills as well as he does. Probably better."

Swallowing, Andrea glanced about the littered, foul-smelling cabin. Strewn about the room were crumpled newspapers, cigarette butts, discarded clothing, dime novels, and dried objects resembling fossils. A few warped shelves were tacked to the walls and an assortment of wanted posters with familiar faces, some perforated with bullet holes.

Quickly busying herself at the battered wood stove, she scrubbed its greasy surface with sand from an Arbuckle's coffee can. Billy showed her a large sack of flour and questionable tin of beef stock. After kneading the dough, she shaped dumplings and dropped them into the simmering stock. The sound of hoofbeats approaching the cabin brought the outlaws to the door.

Peering through a dirty pane, she saw a round-faced, tow-headed rider dismount his chestnut mare. He was smiling to himself as though his horse had entertained him. When he entered the cabin, she compared his size to Billy, who was a few inches shorter and not as solidly built. Butch Cassidy's gray-blue eyes shone when he shook her hand.

"Nice to meetcha little feller." He cocked an eyebrow and grinned. "I see they put you to work."

She liked him on sight, and watched as Billy followed him into the other room. Listening to the conversation, she prepared gravy as the four men began their reunion. Butch reminisced about his early days in outlaw country. Laughing, he recalled herding stolen horses over the treacherous Angel Trail into Robbers Roost.

"One slip and I'd have been a greasy spot on the trail to hell," he said.

Sundance called for another bottle of whiskey. Billy immediately rose to take a fifth of Old Crow, Butch's favorite, from a battered shelf in the other room.

"This is your job now," he whispered as he reached for stained shot glasses. She wiped flour on her overalls and helped him carry them to the poker table.

"You better stay out of this stuff 'til you're older," Butch warned. "Unless you wanna stunt your growth."

"Yes, sir." She wrinkled her nose at the stench of cigar smoke and whiskey.

"We have ourselves a new *ganeymede*." Sundance leaned back in his chair, looking smug.

"What the hell's that?" Harve wanted to know.

"A handsome young boy kidnapped by Zeus to serve liquor to the gods. Greek mythology."

Butch rolled his eyes.

Serving liquor to the gods, was she? It was Andrea's turn to scrutinize the Sundance Kid. Why would an educated man become an outlaw? And how could the others stand his arrogance?

When the planked dining table had been set, and gravy and dumplings done to perfection, Sundance called for more whiskey. Andrea delivered it with a timid announcement that supper was ready. Only Billy seemed interested. He followed her to the table, but his attention was riveted to the conversation in the other room.

Andrea picked at her food. The glazed look in Billy's eyes worried her that whiskey would loosen his tongue. She hoped the generous plate of gravy-soaked dumplings would nullify the effects of his liquor. Hurriedly clearing the table, she dropped the dishes in a canvas sack and carried them down the path to the creek. While looking about for a place to wash them, she also searched for a possible hiding place.

* * * *

Tossing down a shot of Old Crow, Billy forced a smile when the whiskey seared his throat. His eyes teared but no one seemed to notice. The promotion to gang member had been his dream for several years, since Butch had allowed him to accompany them to Brown's Hole. Homesteaders were friendly with members of the Wild Bunch and treated them with respect. In return, the boys never rustled their cattle or deliberately caused them concern.

He recalled the horse races and Thanksgiving shindig. Butch and Elzy Lay had thrown the party for residents of Brown's Park, along with the Bender Gang. He could almost taste the turkey and chestnut dressing. Licking his lips, he envisioned gang members dressed in dark suits and bow ties, donning aprons to serve their guests. Billy hoped his stay at the

Hole in the Wall would prove more exciting.

Leaning his chair on two legs, he congratulated himself on his good fortune. Had it not been for Andy, he would still be chief cook and plate washer. Stealing a glance into the other room, he noticed she had disappeared. Uneasy, he rose halfway in his chair, about to search out of doors when the Sundance Kid's sarcasm stopped him.

"Can't handle it, huh, kid?"

"Better take it easy on that stuff," Butch warned. "Whiskey can knock the boot heels out from under you."

Offended, Billy puffed his chest. "I've been drinking since my old man rubbed whiskey on my gums when I was cutting teeth."

Sundance laughed. "And we thought the squirt was timid."

Glaring from his mentor Harve Logan to his hero Butch Cassidy, Billy's rancor fell on the Sundance Kid, where it wisely shriveled and died. Sundance could out-shoot anyone in the Hole, but when riled, he was a rattlesnake with several missing buttons. Billy admired his prowess, but would never turn his back on him following an argument.

Tossing down another shot, he grimaced as liquor scorched a trail down his throat.

* * * *

The deserted farm house reminded Jim McCloud of his home in Tennessee, a hundred and twenty acres of hard scrabble farming, a life he had found unbearable after his mother died. He'd drifted into Kansas where he committed his first felony before his twentieth birthday.

McCloud wondered how his younger sister Jenny and his father were getting on, but dismissed the thought as too depressing. He had more important matters to consider. His empty stomach growled like a vicious dog. As soon as it was dark, he would prowl for food.

Chapter Nine

A blinding orange sphere sank behind the red wall, casting shadows across the valley floor. Standing on the bank of Buffalo Creek, she looked about for a possible hiding place. All she could find was a massive cottonwood that dominated the opposite bank. The dishes had long since dried by the time she started back.

Surveying her surroundings, she carefully studied the terrain. A weathered barn off to her left was nearly hidden in shadows, and she stopped to peer through its gaping door. As she explored the barn, laughter erupted from the cabin.

Afraid liquor had relaxed Billy's tongue, she decided on a circuitous route back. Tiptoeing to the rear of the cabin, she carefully settled the dishes and crouched beneath a window to listen. Heart pounding, she was poised for flight at the first sound of a scraping chair. When the laughter died, a voice she recognized as Butch's filtered through the open window.

"I'm not goin' on the bank job," he said. "Harve, you and Harry can pull it off with Flat Nose, Walt, and Peep. But the two of you will have to get along."

"We can handle it," Harve growled.

"Handle it 'like bringin' the boy up here?" Butch's voice held a hard edge. "This ain't no place for kids. You want him to turn out like us?"

"There's nothing wrong with us," Sundance said, his words starting to slur. "You getting to be an old woman?"

"Maybe, but I'd like to visit my kin without worryin' about a posse pluggin' the place fulla holes." Butch sighed, his voice tinged with melancholy. "I ain't seen my ma in thirteen years. Last thing I did for her, other than send home a little honest money, was to help her plant some poplars in the yard. I left home soon as I was eighteen. Same age you was locked up for hoss theft, wasn't it, Harry?"

Andrea listened as the Sundance Kid told a riotous tale of his eighteenth birthday. Laughter echoing in her ears, she knew eavesdroppers deserved to be embarrassed. Straining to hear Billy's voice, she missed the sound of approaching boots from the cottonwoods behind the cabin. Before she realized he was there, she was wrenched from her hiding place.

"Whadda ya think you're doin'?"

Andrea squealed with fright as Ketchum roughly swung her under his arm and carried her into the cabin.

"Look who was spyin' out back!" he roared from the doorway.

Standing on the threshold, he deliberately tossed her into the cabin. Andrea rolled into a defensive crouch, clutching the back of her head. Sounds of angry voices and a struggle exploded around her. When the fracas ended, Billy offered his hand. Glass particles were strewn about the rough-planked floor, the poker table resting on its side. The cabin was empty, except for the two of them.

"I told you not to get yourself in trouble." He stopped glaring long enough to kick a broken glass through the open door.

"But I was just—"

"Hiding where the boogie man could find you," he finished for her.

"What happened?"

"They jumped Ketchum and took him to the barn. He'll be looking for you when they let him go." Billy pulled her through the side door, telling her to stay put while he rounded up Pepper. His breath was potent with Old Crow.

* * * *

Jim McCloud's measle spots had faded and his hair had finally begun to grow. He was still weak from lack of food, although he had raided a neighbor's hen house the previous night and eaten both birds as soon as he could roast them. He returned early that morning to steal overalls and a collarless shirt freshly hung on the line. When they dried, he would bury the tattered clothing he had stolen following his prison break.

McCloud worried that the Hole in the Wall gang would reject him. Rumors circulated in prison that hundreds of lawbreakers were hiding in the outlaw canyon. He wondered if a password was required. He imagined heavily armed guards at each entrance to discourage lawmen. Rubbing his fuzzy head, his feared his prison haircut would keep him out.

The more he thought about it, the more agitated he became. He wasn't a *real* outlaw. He hadn't killed anyone or committed armed robbery. He had stolen less than a hundred-fifty dollars from the Kansas post office, and that included seventeen dollars worth of stamps. If the stolen blacksmith tools and pilfered drill were added in, his larceny didn't amount to much.

He should have robbed a bank.

As soon as the clothes dried, he would be on his way. If he overstayed his visit, the neighbors might connect their losses with the abandoned homesteader's shack. He didn't relish returning to prison before he could infiltrate the Hole.

While he was checking his stolen laundry, he heard a dog bark and peered from a window to investigate. A buckboard carrying two men with rifles was turning into the lane. Although it was approaching twilight, he knew from the rake of their hats they were lawmen.

Scrambling to remove all evidence of his existence, he opened the trap door and dropped into the cellar.

* * * *

Faint light flickered from the barn door, but the only sounds Andrea heard were the chirping songs of crickets. While she waited for Billy, she searched for the evening star. She located it skimming above the nearest ridge in deepening nightfall. Fervently wishing for her grandparents' safety as well as her own escape, she knew it was only that, mere wishfulness. The towering sandstone walls were the barriers of her own private prison.

Soon, the vague form of a horse and rider emerged from the barn. Instinctively pressing against the logs, she edged toward the back of the cabin. If it was Ketchum, she would head for the big cottonwood on the opposite bank of the creek. While plotting her course, she heard Billy call her name.

"Come here, Andy. We're gonna stay at George's cabin." His words were slurred.

"Why?"

"They told Ketchum to leave the Hole, but that doesn't mean he will." In a voice hardly more than a whisper, he said, "If I were you, I'd keep quiet so he won't know where you are."

Andrea shuddered and stepped into the stirrup, allowing Billy to lift her behind the cantle. Ketchum could be anywhere. Even without a gun, he was dangerous. He was big enough to stop Billy's horse in his tracks, she thought grimly. And he must hate her even more, knowing she had caused him to be banished from the Hole.

The ride to George Currie's cabin lasted an eternity. Gripping Billy's waist, she envisioned a rider on the trail behind them, and Ketchum behind every bush. When they reached the cabin, Billy tied the roan to a splintered rail. Opening the heavy door, he lifted a lantern from a peg, but decided not to light it.

"There's a bunk along this wall. Get some sleep while I take care of Pepper."

When she hesitated, he said, "Don't worry about anything 'cept Ketchum burning the cabin." He slapped a log, laughing.

Andrea failed to find humor in their situation, and bit her tongue to keep from telling him so. After Billy left, she felt along the rough logs and encountered a narrow bunk. Jerking the rumpled blankets free, she shook them repeatedly. She then smoothed the musty blankets as best she could in the dark. Removing her borrowed boots, she lay down, her mind fighting sleep.

What was taking Billy so long? Was Ketchum waiting until they fell asleep, or had he already taken Billy prisoner?

Andrea awoke with a start. The big man had been chasing her astride his chocolate dun. She tripped and was about to be trampled when a growling noise wrenched her from the nightmare. She recognized the sound as Billy's snore, and drifted back to sleep.

* * * *

The clanging noises made by the travois seemed to agitate Tom's Arapaho captors. Scowling, Arched Back Wolf insisted he halt. The Arapaho signaled his companions for a meeting. Watching them, Tom worried about the pow wow. Were they arguing how to torture him? The remedy machine wasn't worth losing his scalp. Lightning had apparently come to the same conclusion. Whickering, he flung his head and angrily bared his teeth as though giving Tom a thorough cursing. When his tantrum brought no results, the gelding reared, trying to dislodge the travois.

By the time Tom was able to pacify him, one of the men, his black hair cut unusually short, rode back from the group. Before he could speak, Tom said, "Take the dang contraption. It ain't worth dyin' over."

"You insulted my people," the Arapaho said.

"But I told you, there wasn't time to groom—"

"We know why you brought that still on the reservation."

"But I'm just takin' a shortcut to Bridger Creek," Tom sputtered.

"Everyone knows there is bad blood between the Arapaho and Shoshone, but your great white congress threw our tribes together on this reservation."

"I had nuthin' to do with that."

"Who sent you to liquor up both our peoples so they would kill one another? Does the great white father want to reclaim our Wind River land?"

Surprised by the brave's impassioned speech, Tom shook his head in denial.

"Anyone who would pepper our wounds with a gift horse for my people's enemy, the Shoshone chief, lacks the intelligence to plan this on his own."

Tom hung his head, silently scolding himself. He had already broken his promise not to drink, and wondered if he still had the right to cross himself. Escape was impossible. Lightning was still tied to the travois, and the thought of losing his scalp made his skin prickle.

"I'm a good man with hosses," he said, deciding to plead for mercy. "I'd be plumb happy to be your slave."

The bronzed rider reached for Lightning's reins at the same moment his cohorts begin to scatter. The source of their concern was the burly Indian agent, who came loping down the slope toward them.

"What are you doing with that rot gut still?" the agent yelled, reining his sorrel to a dusty halt. "I should have let that bunch peel your hide." When the agent's face lost some of its anger, Tom explained that he had no intention of setting up a tribal distillery.

The Arapahos had already disappeared, and he wondered aloud, "Who's that Injun ridin' the big buckskin?"

"Mountain Hawk's a half-breed. His father sent him to white man's school. Now he's back to stir up trouble. If he finds out about the cattle shipments, you can tell George Currie to forget our arrangement. We'll all be occupying the same jail cell."

Tom took his leave. Travel was slow with the remedy machine, and he berated himself for failing to ask for another pack horse. He had no way of proving the skewbald was his.

Lightning had pulled the travois several miles past the reservation before refusing to move another step. That night Tom slept with one eye closed, still afraid of Arapaho retaliation.

His mother was right. Alcohol scrambled his brains, but he was too far gone to change. If it took 'til winter to drag the still to the Hole, so be it!

* * * *

Billy was still asleep when Andrea awoke the next morning. Slumped along the cabin wall, he clutched the rifle against his chest. He resembled a stubborn child who had fallen asleep with his favorite toy. She raised on an elbow to stare at him, realizing her fondness for the young outlaw. If only she could reform him of his errant ways, he might help her escape.

Rising quietly from her bed, she tiptoed to the grimy window. Pepper was nowhere in sight, and she guessed he had been hobbled behind the cabin. After quietly pulling on Billy's boots, she was lifting the wooden crossbar from its casing when he woke.

"Where do you think you're going?" he said, struggling to his feet. The rifle wobbled in her direction.

"Just out to look around."

He flushed. "Reckon I don't feel so good."

Noticing stains the length of his shirt, she had gotten a whiff of something unpleasant.

"Give me a minute to wash up, and we'll ride on back for breakfast," he said.

Following him down to the creek, she reveled in the warming spring weather. He didn't seem to notice when she followed the creek around a bend to wash up in privacy. When she returned he was slumped on the bank, gazing into the water.

"I hope you learned your lesson," he said, glancing up. "I told you not to get in trouble." Face drawn, the whites of his eyes were as red as the sandstone walls.

"Talk about getting in trouble. If you feel as bad as you look, I'm afraid you won't live until breakfast."

His reply was a sharp slap of his dusty hat against his thigh.

When they arrived at the cabin, Butch Cassidy met them at the door. "Glad to see you," he said, his perennial grin wide. "I was afraid Harve was gonna have to fix breakfast."

Harve and Sundance were seated at the planked table, hunched over steaming mugs of coffee. Andrea immediately began preparing breakfast while Butch talked about the day's activities. Billy carried in a slab of beef that had hung wrapped in canvas in a cottonwood. He sliced the meat into thick steaks while she chopped potatoes for the frying pan.

"Might be a good idea to start trainin' relay hosses for the bank job," Butch said.

His two companions groaned from behind their mugs. They had apparently received little sleep.

"Peep O'Day is a good man with hosses." Butch poured himself a fresh cup of coffee. "I hope he's back before I leave."

"He should be back from Rock Springs any time." Harve lifted a hand to his head and groaned. "Walt left him a note to get here, pronto."

"He's probably passed out in some bordello," Sundance said. "Peep drinks like a damned wall-eyed pike. Too bad he's not as smart as one."

"Look who's talkin'." Butch laughed. "I recall a time or two when you—"

"Don't lump me in the same category with that illiterate."

Harve quietly set his cup down. "Let's not forget that Harry Longabaugh was a member of the literary society in his hometown of Phoenixville, Pennsylvania, before they dubbed him the Sundance Kid. I've seen some of his dime novels layin' around."

The expression on Butch's face silenced them both. "Peep's the one who invited me here in the first place. He ain't much of a cattle rustler, but he's damn good with hosses. He speaks their language."

"An equine dialect," Sundance muttered, "and an equine mentality."

"There ain't nuthin' wrong with hoss sense."

After breakfast, the men headed for the corral while Andrea cleaned up after them. Butch had told her to join them when she finished.

"Long as you're here, you might as well learn about hosses," he said. "A man's mount is his best friend, and you need to treat 'em as such."

Andrea nodded agreement. She had already decided to learn all she could while keeping an eye out for the fastest horse in the Hole.

A group of men had encircled a small, sleek black gelding in the center of the corral when she approached from the cabin. Walt Punteney was moving about excitedly, his hands animated as he talked to the others.

"Short back," he said, slapping the horse on its prominent withers. "This one's pure Arabian, I'll bet. He could run from here to Buffalo and back without gettin' winded."

"How'd he get in with this bunch of range hosses?" Harve wanted to know.

"Somebody musta left the barn door open. This young feller didn't spend the winter on the open range."

Examining the Arabian's mouth, Butch said, "He still has some of his cupped foal's teeth. He's three to four years. Where did you find 'im?"

"Out near Lost Cabin," Walt said. "He must be one of J.B. Okie's ridin' hosses."

"Miz Okie's more like it." Harve stroked the Arabian's back. "He's hardly more than fourteen hands."

"A fine hoss for Andy," Butch decided. "No sense us heavyweights breakin' 'im down." Turning, he grinned at Andrea, inviting her to ride the sleek gelding.

With her prayers so promptly answered, she was momentarily stunned. She managed to stammer, "Yes, sir, I-I would love to ride him, but—"

"But nuthin'. Walt can teach you to take care of 'im." Gripping her arm, he led her to the Arabian, guiding her hand along his haunches.

"What're you gonna name him?" Butch's brows lifted in anticipation.

"I think I'll call him Aladdin."

The Sundance Kid smirked. "You know about the Arabian Nights? Fancy that. A sheepherder who can read."

Indignant, she turned her back, focusing fully on her benefactor. "Aladdin's as handsome as you, Mister Cassidy."

Butch ducked his head as the others laughed in unison. Everyone except Billy, who turned abruptly on his heel and headed for the barn.

"Billy's a tad jealous," Butch said, when he noticed her distress. "I reckon he wanted the Arab for himself."

Shrugging, she stroked Aladdin lovingly from forelock to muzzle. "When can I ride him?"

"Harve will give him a workout to see how he handles. He's the smallest jockey we got, 'cept for Billy, and the best hoss stomper. Then you can ride him, but only when somebody's with you." Grinning, he patted her on the back.

She returned his smile, but vague worry nagged at her. From the corner of her eye she watched the entrance to the barn as she moved around the Arabian, stroking his ribs and shoulder.

"You're a mighty lucky kid," Walt said, pocketing the money Butch had just given him. He told her to wait outside the corral while Harve put Aladdin through his paces.

As she backed away, Andrea's attention alternated between the Arabian and the barn. Watching him prance and pivot with Harve in the saddle, her admiration for the gelding grew. She imagined herself in the saddle, racing for an exit from the Hole, dodging rifle bullets as they rode out of range. Nothing could stop them.

Harve Logan dismounted and handed her the reins. "Take him around the corral a few times before we put him in the barn."

She had ridden her share of horses but nothing compared with Aladdin beneath her, quivering with excitement and expectantly tossing his head. Harve adjusted the stirrups, and they started off slowly around the corral, heads held high, feeling the tepid breeze. As they rounded the first turn, she noticed Butch's wide grin as well as others who seemed to have materialized from the scrub brush. When she came around the back turn facing the barn, she noticed Billy duck inside and disappear from view. Sighing, she signaled Aladdin to trot, then lifted in the stirrups to post in perfect timing with his movements.

"Would you look at that!" Walt's mouth dropped open as others around him hooted.

Realizing her mistake, Andrea slumped clumsily into the saddle, bringing the gelding to a halt. As soon as she dismounted, Butch rushed over to ask where she had learned to ride.

"Uncle Jim Bob taught me. But I lose my balance whenever I try to post." Silently berating herself, she knew they would keep a closer watch, knowing she could ride.

"Coulda used a good jockey when me and Matt Warner raced our hoss Betty." Butch lifted his hat to scratch his head. "We did all right, but we coulda cleaned up with you in the saddle."

"I'm really not that good," she protested. "I was just showing off."

"All the same, if you don't grow much, you'll make a heckuva fine jockey."

He led the Arabian into the barn, tying the reins to an upright post. "I was gonna have Walt teach you to groom him, but maybe he could learn somethin' from you."

"My uncle just taught me to post." She omitted the fact that Jim Bob thought horse grooming was an unfit activity for young ladies. She said, "He worked for a wealthy English ranching family near Chugwater before starting his horse trading business."

Walt commenced showing her the correct way to groom the Arabian. The horse's coat was filthy, his tail full of cockleburs.

"Start at the neck and brush in short, hard strokes 'til you git to the tail," he said, "and in circles to git out the mud. Be careful of his eyes."

When finished, he brought in a bucket of water to wet down Aladdin's mane and tail, brushing carefully so as not to dislodge the hair. He crouched at the horse's shoulder, facing his rump, and lifted the horse's feet to pick out debris that had collected in the hooves.

"You have to keep him clean so his feet don't rot," he said. "You won't get far if he goes lame."

Andrea knelt close to the gelding to lift a foot, careful not to get in the way if Aladdin decided to kick. She straightened in time to watch a tuft of hay fall from the loft. Billy was still up there. While Walt was showing her how to dislodge ticks and other parasites from the Arabian's hide, she heard a familiar snore. She hoped Billy would be in better humor after his nap.

Walt showed her various types of tack hanging from rusty nails. "This here's a curb," he said, taking down a hand-sized piece of metal with two large rings. Smaller rings were attached to the other side. "It fits in the hoss's mouth and connects to this." Walt lifted a piece of leather resembling a man's belt, split near the middle, which fit over the ears.

"And this is a hackamore. It don't need no bit for his mouth," he said, turning the braided horse hair in his large, callused hands. "A hoss like the Arab is broke to ride with one of these. After he's trained, it just takes a light touch to control 'im."

Several saddles were slung over log stands, and he pulled one near for her inspection. "This'n's mine," he said. "It's a Californey saddle. Lightweight and purty, ain't it?"

Andrea nodded, inspecting the scrolled tooling on the skirt, fender, and stirrup leather.

"This'n's Harve's. Made in Denver. Bigger and heavier than mine. And ugly. But don't tell him I said so."

Andrea smiled, noticing the huge saddle horn jutting from the front fork.

"Butch wants you to use this'n." Lifting a small, dark saddle with wide fenders from its mount, he handed it to her.

"It's modified Texan," he said, as she struggled beneath its weight.

Laughing at her dilemma, he decided, "Guess I'll rig some hollow stirrups to lighten 'er up."

Dick Hale sauntered into the barn when the sun was overhead. "W-where's the new c-cook?" he said. "There's some mighty h-hungry hombres out here who c-could use some grub."

Andrea hurriedly gathered up grooming tools and gave Aladdin a goodbye pat. She then shuffled off to the cabin in her oversized boots.

* * * *

Tom had been in the saddle since early morning, placing distance between himself and the reservation. He hoped the Indian agent would keep his mouth shut about his run-in with the Arapahos when the boys trailed in another herd of rustled cattle. Flat Nose George was the worst practical joker he'd ever known. He would never allow Tom to forget his folly. Everybody would know, including Butch, Harve, and the Sundance Kid.

Walt was his best friend, but he didn't even trust *him* with the tale. Walt loved repeating stories and there hadn't been that much to laugh about lately. The temptation to tell would be too much for him.

* * * *

Steak and potatoes were sizzling on the cast iron stove when the outlaws filed into the cabin. Hurriedly setting the table, she shuffled between the stove and cooking utensils shelf.

"How old is that kid?" she heard one of them ask.

"Somebody said twelve, but that can't be. I never seen a wet nose kid handle grub that good."

Andrea cringed. She needed to clumsily do her chores, or she would give herself away. Picking up a tin platter of steak, she stumbled, deliberately dropping it to the floor. Inhaling deeply, she was relieved it landed upright. She might have been lynched for ruining their meal.

"Whose idea was it for the kid to do the cookin', anyhow?" one of them complained.

While Andrea was apologizing for her clumsiness, Walt smelled the potatoes burning and rushed to the stove.

"Where's Billy?" he bellowed. "At least he don't burn the spuds."

Andrea backed against the wall, blanching as the outlaws made crude remarks about her cooking. She considered running from the cabin and was relieved when Butch appeared in the doorway.

"Give the kid a chance," he said. "Andy's green as Farley's colt."

Grumbling, the men attacked their steaks as Butch took a seat at the head of the table. Andrea set a plate-sized sirloin in front of him and a portion of potatoes that had escaped the scorching. Finished eating, he glanced up to two rows of expectant faces.

"Boys," he said, clearing his throat. "I gotta get back to my wrangler's job in Little Goose Canyon, before lawmen come lookin' for Elzy and me."

"When are you planning to spend the Castle Gate loot?" The Sundance Kid's expression was one of professional envy.

"Soon as the heat's off, but let's talk about the Bell Foosh Bank job in the Black Hills. It's a hell-for-broke town on the railhead, with plenty of cattle and minin' money goin' through the bank."

"B-bell what?" Hale said.

"French name," Sundance explained. "They spell it B-E-L-L-E F-O-U-R-C-H-E."

"When do we hit 'er?" Walt said, grinning.

Butch propped his elbows on the table. "Flat Nose George and Harry know the area purty good. We decided that you, Peep, and the Logan brothers will go with 'em. You'll hit the bank a day or two after the Black Hills Reunion of Civil War Soldiers and Sailors celebration. There's also a big regional cattle roundup goin' on, so there'll be plenty of strangers and money in town."

Andrea marveled at the respect and rapt attention Butch commanded from even the toughest-looking man.

"Me and Elzy have been layin' low since the Castle Gate job, but in a coupla weeks we'll be makin' camp near Wamsutter, on the Red Desert. The Sweetwater coal mines are owned by the Union Pacific, and they're carryin' a lotta loot between banks…" Butch hesitated when spurs racked the cabin's threshold.

"The Belle Fourche Bank's the job I've been waiting for," Billy announced from the doorway. He was sleepy-eyed and hay still clung to his hair.

"I need you here," Butch said evenly, his eyes sliding in Andrea's direction.

"You mean you need a nursemaid." Billy's mood grew more sullen with each breath.

"There's plenty of time and banks for you to rob when you're older. You're good with hosses, and I need you to handle the herd while Peep's away."

"I'm no jingler," Billy said, turning to leave. "And I'm nobody's nanny."

Andrea's heart continued to hammer long after the men left the cabin. Billy had been on the verge of giving her away, and there was nothing she could have done to stop him. She had to talk to him. Hurriedly scraping plates, she dropped them into a canvas sack, along with the cast iron skillets. Lifting the sack over her shoulder, she headed for the corral.

Billy was perched on the top rail, watching Harve and Walt break a mustang. He ignored her as she hurried down the path, struggling under her burden. Circling the corral she came up behind him, kicking the post to get his attention.

"Billy, we need to talk."

A grunt was his reply.

"Please…"

"The kid w-wants to j-jaw with ya, Bill," Dick Hale yelled from across the corral.

Billy kept his gaze on the wranglers as he muttered, "Whadda ya want?"

"We need to discuss Aladdin." She nervously twisted her fingers. "He should be yours, Billy, not mine."

Climbing down with an agitated groan, he led the way to the barn. Once inside he glanced around to determine whether anyone else was present.

"It's your fault I'm not going to Belle Fourche."

"Good. I'd hate for you to get killed."

"Who says anyone's gonna?"

"Billy, how many gray-haired bank robbers do you know?"

Exasperated, he said, "The Arab's yours and you better take care of him."

"I'm really trying to be the best little brother—"

"You're not my brother, Andy, and I'll be in a heap of trouble when they find out who you really are."

"They won't know unless you don't tell them."

Billy dismissed the matter by stooping to open an ancient steamer trunk perched on a bale of hay. Rummaging through, he located several articles of clothing, which he handed to her.

"Take these down to the crick and get a bath while everybody's at the corral," he said quietly. "And make sure nobody's around."

"What about soap?"

"I'm afraid we're fresh out. You'll have to use sand like the rest of us."

She decided to make soap as soon as possible.

"Before you go, Andy, we need to swap boots. Jake's are better than mine, but I've got blisters the size of walnuts. No sense both of us should suffer."

"Certainly," she said, removing Billy's boots. Jake's were longer, but narrower, like her own. Turning to leave, Andrea remembered to ask, "Who is Elzy?"

"Elzy is Butch's best friend."

"Why have they been in hiding?"

Billy chewed his lip. "I guess it doesn't matter if you know about the Castle Gate payroll robbery they pulled off in Utah."

"How are they going to spend the money?"

Billy laughed. "The whole eight thousand will probably go for gambling, whiskey, and women."

"Oh."

"How'd you think outlaws spend their loot?"

She shrugged.

"The money's for high living and showing the rich land grabbers they can't shove people off their homesteads." When he noticed her disapproving expression, he said, "Sometimes they give it to people who really need it."

"Like Robin Hood?"

"Yeah."

Andrea shuffled off to the creek, thinking how senseless the outlaw business was. Struggling along the bank with her canvas sack, she found a place to rest. Buffalo Creek gurgled and danced over smooth rocks as water flowed toward the eastern red wall. The early afternoon sun was warm, prompting perspiration to trickle down her body. It was time to shed her grandfather's wool shirt and dirty overalls.

Removing her boots and stockings, she dug her toes into the sandy soil on the water's edge and watched a small spider crawl across her instep. Glancing about, she removed her clothing and waded into the creek.

Swollen with snow runoff, the creek was slow moving and cold. After the first step, she knew swimming was out of the question, and crouched to immerse herself to her shoulders.

Shivering, she leaned to scoop sand from the creek bed. With quick scrubbing motions, she cleansed herself before wading back to shore. Andrea quickly dressed in the worn broadcloth shirt and overalls Billy had given her, but delayed wearing Jake's boots as long as possible.

She was scrubbing pans on the water's edge, her overalls rolled to the knees, when she heard branches snapping across the creek. Standing for a better look, she noticed only leaves rustling in the light breeze. Moments after she returned to her work, she heard a loud splash and glimpsed Scar Ketchum plunging into the water from the opposite bank, a sickening leer on his hideous face.

Dropping the sack, she started down the bank as fast as her legs would move. A deep rumbling sound escaped the huge man's throat as he lumbered ashore. Stealing a glance over her shoulder, Andrea stubbed her toe on a sharp rock but managed to keep her balance. The mishap crippled her stride while narrowing the gap between them.

Hobbling as fast as her injured foot allowed, she skirted clumps of weeds along the bank. She kept to the sandy areas where scattered rocks were smoother. When she could no longer breathe from exertion, she rounded a bend where an embankment blocked her path. Hesitating briefly, she plunged into the icy creek.

The shock of cold water overwhelmed her, leaving her floundering with little control of her limbs. Her feet seemed to take root while her momentum carried her into the water's swirling depths. Unable to breathe, she sank beneath the surface, nearly striking her head on the rocky creek bottom.

Struggling, she tried paddling to the surface for air, but her limbs seemed weighted. The overalls were dragging her down, and Andrea knew she was drowning. Before she lost consciousness, Ketchum pulled her from the creek. Flinging her onto her back, his gargantuan foot pinned her to the sand.

"Thought you'd git away, didn'cha, little feller?"

"I'm sorry." Andrea gasped. "I didn't know they would make you leave."

"I don't go 'less I want to," he said, slapping her hard across her unbruised cheek. "I'm gonna teach you a lesson you won't never forget."

Summoning all her strength, she reached out to claw his tree-trunk leg. Her own feeble legs kicked at him, but proved powerless to stop the assault. The pressure was suddenly released, but before she could move, he crushed her with his full body weight. His odor of garlic and sweat filled her nostrils.

"I been waitin' a long time for this," he said, relieving some of the weight with his elbows. "I'm gonna carve you up like my ol' man done me."

Grinning, he fingered the wide, raised scar slashing diagonally across his left cheek. One massive hand restrained her while the other reached for his hunting knife. She screamed when he tested the blade's sharpness by cutting strands of hair near her ear.

"We're gonna do this real slow to make it last." He laughed, sitting back on his haunches. With the tip of the blade, he picked up an overall strap and proceeded to slice it in half.

Shielding her face, she felt sharp pain as the knife pricked her wrist.

"Ain't gonna do you no good to fight, youngun'. You might as well lay still and take your medicine." He hesitated and she thought she heard a distant voice. Peering through her fingers, she watched him drop the knife to grasp his gun. Memory of what he had done to her grandmother flashed through her mind. As he got to his feet, she jerked her knees to her chest. Kicking with all she had, she caught him in the upper calf, knocking him off balance.

Struggling upright, she saw that he had fallen on his side, but before she could run, he rolled to grasp her ankle. When she fell, he let go long enough to retrieve the knife. Ketchum scrambled to his knees and raised the weapon. Eyes squeezed tight, she heard the sound of a gun.

Chapter Ten

Deputies searched the abandoned shack, finding nothing more than chicken bones tossed into the yard. McCloud heard voices from his hiding place in the cellar, where insects were crawling over his body.

"Smells like some railroad bum's been here."

"Yeah, musta stole Martin's clothes *and* the laying hens."

"Better check the cellar. He might be hiding there."

"Hell, Frank, it's almost supper time."

"You're right. Locking him up will take an hour or more."

"If he's still here in the morning, we'll take him in."

"Martin won't want his overalls back if some railroad bum's been wearing 'em."

"Chickens didn't go to waste neither."

Both men left the farmhouse, laughing.

McCloud considered the visit an omen. Wyoming lawmen may not be searching for escaped Leavenworth prisoners, but he knew they would return the following morning. He needed to leave for the Hole, but riding the rails into Casper could get him arrested.

He needed a mount. Although he was an experienced rider, he'd never broken a horse to ride nor had he stolen one.

"I'll borrow me a horse tonight," he said, hearing his voice for the first time that week. "Oughta get me some sugar cubes so the horse won't shy." He knew he wouldn't find sugar in a henhouse or hanging on a clothes line, but burglarizing a home was unthinkable. McCloud was a safecracker, not a common thief.

He left that evening. Hiking along the narrow dirt road, he noticed lights flickering on the horizon about half a mile away. When McCloud was opposite the cabin, he glimpsed the smoldering end of a cigarette and heard a rocker creak. Unsure whether he had been seen, he kept walking. The moon rose behind him, illuminating a farmhouse settled in an open field on the south side of the road. A faint glow could be seen from the window. Taking his time, McCloud circled around back where he found three horses enclosed in a corral.

Peering through the pole rails, he stood for some time, watching the horses sniff the air and whicker nervously. Eventually, a big sorrel edged its way to McCloud's hiding place, where he poked his nose through the rails.

The convict tried to pet the snorting muzzle and had his hand bitten for his trouble. When the sorrel let go, he turned and kicked the rails with his hind feet as though he were a mule. A lantern appeared at the rear of the house and a man yelled: "Who's there?"

Before McCloud could escape, a shotgun blast added to his woes.

* * * *

Billy's worried face stared down at her as Andrea watched him through a blur of tears.

"You all right?" he asked, kneeling beside her.

"No. I'm not!"

Blood seeped from a wound on her wrist, and he untied his neckerchief.

"Where is he?"

"Ketchum's dead." Billy's voice cracked as he tried to wrap the cut. "I never killed anybody before, Andy."

"Don't touch me," she said, jerking her arm free.

"But I was just—"

"This wouldn't have happened if you hadn't kidnapped me."

Eyes closed, he swayed on his haunches. "Fine way to thank somebody who saved your life."

Andrea pulled herself into a sitting position. "You sent me down here knowing that monster was still around."

Billy's mouth set in a defensive line.

"He was going to kill me—or something worse."

"Nothing's worse than dying."

She touched her cheek and winced. "I'd rather be dead than scarred like him. How could anyone do that to his own son?"

It was several moments before she dared to glance at Ketchum's hulking form, face down on the creek bank. The knife was clutched in his lifeless hand, a bullet hole exiting the middle of his back. She knew he was dead, but convulsed in fear at the sight of him.

Andrea heard a horse approach and spotted Harve riding up the opposite bank. Unable to face him, she crumpled on the bank, burying her head in her hands.

"What happened?" Harve's voice boomed like a vengeful god.

"He was gonna kill Andy," Billy said, pointing to the knife. "And I shot him."

A colorful stream of expletives fused together as Harve nudged his gelding into the swollen creek.

"I'll take Andy back to the cabin." Billy said, gripping her arm. When she resisted, he whispered, "I'll carry you if I have to, but I'll never lay hands on you again." His face was awash with compassion, but she was still repelled by his touch.

"I can get there, myself," she said, jerking free. The effort cost her fresh pain, draining her of what little strength she had left. A few steps on her own settled the dispute, and she was forced to allow him to help her.

When they reached the path leading to the cabin, he swung her into his arms. Carrying her into the cabin's back room, he gently deposited her on a narrow bunk. He returned moments later with a blanket to replace her wet clothing.

"Lay still," he said, his voice hoarse. "I'll be back as soon as I gather your things."

Withheld tears spilled as Andrea awaited his return. Wrapped in a dusty blanket, she relived the entire ordeal. Her cheeks were damp when Billy returned, asking what he could do for her.

"Help me escape," she said, sobbing. Billy hesitated, then left the cabin without another word.

"Damn you!" she screamed. She knew he was still within earshot, and didn't care he would think her anger was directed at him. The wound on her wrist was still bleeding. Easing herself from the bunk, she made her way into the front room. There, she bathed her wrist, then wrapped it with torn strips from a flour sack towel. Filling a discarded whiskey bottle with warm water from the stove's reservoir, she held it against her abdomen where Ketchum had brutally pinned her with his boot. The wet shirt and overalls were replaced with soiled ones and she returned to bed.

The bottle's healing warmth gradually eased the pain, and Andrea drifted into an uneasy sleep. Later that afternoon she awoke to the sound of voices. Several men stood bedside, looking down at her.

"How're you doin', kid?"

"Fine," she whimpered, turning her face to the wall.

"I brought somethin' to cheer ya up." Walt held a small, roughly carved wooden horse in his outstretched hand.

Andrea accepted the gift, her lower lip quivering.

"Hell, don't puddle up on us," Sundance said, frowning. "A man's got to learn to take his licks."

"Leave him be," Walt scolded. "He's been mauled by a damned almighty bear."

Soon after the others filed from the room, Butch pulled a chair to her bunk and straddled it. "I'm sorry what that bully done, Andy." His expression was sympathetic. "I never trusted them Ketchums. He got what was comin' to him. Nobody has the right to mistreat a young boy."

Andrea nodded agreement, her lips still trembling.

"I'll be leavin' here tomorrow," he said, averting his gaze.

Closing her eyes, she choked back tears. He was abandoning her to the other outlaws.

"The Arabian's yours as long as you stay in the Hole, but I wouldn't take him home with you, Andy. They might string you up for hoss thievin.'" Butch chuckled at his own joke, but she realized how close to the truth it was. She tried to laugh with him, but the pain in her stomach was dragging her down, diminishing any feelings she had for him.

"When the bank job's over, Billy will take you home," he promised. "By then you should be feelin' better." Patting her on the shoulder, he reluctantly rose to leave. If he noticed she resisted his touch, he failed to acknowledge it.

Refusing supper, she slept fitfully most of the night and well into morning. Dull rays of sunlight filtered through the dirty window when Billy came to offer her breakfast. He was obviously not in the mood for talk. When he left, she picked at the steak and potatoes. The gnawing feeling could not be appeased with food. She needed to be home, with Gramma using hugs and cayenne tea to heal her.

The following morning she helped Billy prepare breakfast for the others. She found the men quiet and more somber than usual, as though a deadly plague had settled over them. When she later asked about the outlaws, Billy shrugged. He said they were concerned with the bank robbery. Andrea wanted to believe him, but instinctively knew it wasn't entirely true.

* * * *

He found Walt's note after he unloaded the remedy machine. Tom was in no hurry to start for the Hole, although his friend had hinted at something big. He would allow the gelding a couple of day's rest while he solved the problem of moving the still. He couldn't expect his gelding to drag the contraption all the way to the outlaw canyon. What he needed was another pack horse.

He checked the corral and found that Walt had taken the mounts. Pondering his problem, he decided he could risk rustling from a neighboring ranch or he could catch and break a mustang. The later was too much work, so he decided to steal one.

To hell with Lightnin's sensibilities. If Mormon women can share their husbands, Lightnin' can be civil to another hoss.

* * * *

Each day dragged into the next, with Andrea growing familiar with the camp routine. She quietly completed her various chores and was left to sleep alone in the cabin's back room. The men preferred the barn or the out-of-doors, although the inner circle spent considerable time at George Currie's cabin. Alone in the cabin most of the day, she often thought of her childhood home and a life of refined leisure. While scrubbing the stove's greasy surface, she remembered Gramma's lessons in cooking and cleaning, chores she resisted but was now glad she had learned.

"Your mother was lucky to marry a wealthy man," Gramma told her on more than one occasion. "But that's no reason *not* to learn good homemaking skills."

Andrea balked at the idea of marrying below her father's station, although she had recently considered marrying Johnny Mackintosh, a struggling flockmaster. Now that she knew what men were really like, marriage was out of the question. She would buy her own ranch and build a grand cabin when she was twenty-one and inherited her father's estate. But that was more than three years away.

If the outlaws knew she was an heiress, they would hold her for ransom, although there was no one to pay for her release. Her grandparents could be dead and Uncle Jim Bob had probably died in the line shack. Even if he were alive, there was little hope he would part with the money. Grandpa said his only son still owned his first copper penny.

Swallowing her grief, Andrea decided she would return to Alabama when she managed to escape the Hole. Family friends would take her in. She glanced at her hands. Rough and red, the nails were chipped and cuticles peeling. She could not afford more tears. Her time was better spent plotting her way out of this prison.

* * * *

Tom was still wondering where to hide the remedy machine when the towering red walls appeared. The buckskin he had stolen protested the load, bucking like a rodeo bronc. Not only had he bucked off the still, he had nearly gotten away. Tom suspected the clanging noises were causing the gelding's tantrum. He solved the problem by wrapping the machine in Walt's blankets. Sure enough, Buster settled down and behaved himself. Lightning still ignored his new companion, but their kinship would improve once they shared the same corral.

Tom unloaded the still in a secluded area on the leeward side of a sandy ridge. Anxious to set up the contraption, he knew he should first report in at the cabin. As the newest member of the Wild Bunch, proving his worth was more important than a few gulps of brew. Licking his lips, he recalled his first keg of Hole in the Wall whiskey.

Pounding trail dust from his clothing, he remounted Lightning to lead his pack horse south. He hoped he wasn't too late for supper.

* * * *

Flat Nose George Currie wasn't a brilliant speaker but he managed to dominate every conversation. George had arrived the previous evening from Montana, where he routinely rustled cattle and herded them into the Hole. Andrea noticed that everyone seemed to like George—with the exception of the Sundance Kid—although his pranks were usually at the gang's expense.

"A hoss kicked me when I was younger'n you," George explained when he first caught her staring. In profile his eyes bulged across the void where the bridge of his nose should have been.

Andrea tried not to gawk, but found it hard to look away.

"You can call me Flat Nose like ever'body else." He laughed uproariously when he noticed her surprise.

"I'll call you Mister Currie, as my mother taught me."

Flat Nose tousled her hair. "You're a good kid. What're you doin' here?"

"I was kidnapped," she said, staring him down. "Will you help me escape?"

George laughed his way to the corral. He obviously didn't believe her. *I should have told him, 'I'm Butch Cassidy's son.'* She watched him open the gate. *Maybe then he'd let me go.*

A dark-haired, rumpled cowboy rode past the corral with a buckskin in tow. George greeted him by pulling him from the saddle.

The stranger was taller than George, his mustache dark and bushy. Dropping past the corners of his mouth, the heavy soup strainer lent his face a gloomy look, what she could see of it. Flat Nose led him into the barn, and she heard several whoops of welcome. Within the hour, the bank robbing team congregated at the cabin for supper. They later retired to the back room for a serious game of poker. Sundance was the gang's acknowledged card shark, and the others tipped their elbows lightly when he sat in on a game.

The newcomer sat quietly during the meal, increasing Andrea's curiosity. Flat Nose waited until after supper to introduce her to the lanky horseman, who seemed clumsy out of the saddle.

"Peep here helps run cattle to the reservation," he said. "Them Injuns would love to take his scalp, 'specially that hairy lip."

Tom's mouth dropped open, his eyes bulging like Flat Nose George's. "How'd you know about that?"

"About what?"

Tom glanced at his dusty boots. "Nuthin'," he said. "I thought one of them Injuns was after me."

"One of them squaws, maybe." Laughing, he gripped Tom's arm, maneuvering him into the other room.

"How much money you got, Peep? We're about to have a friendly little poker game."

* * * *

McCloud stole a bay gelding east of Glenrock, a hanging offense if he were caught, although hanging was better than prison. After the horse bite, he figured anyone who regularly rustled horses had to be deranged. The shotgun had fired into the air instead of into his hide, but it was more than enough to scare him off. Walking most of the night, he spotted a sturdy bay dozing inside a wire fence. Opening the nearest gate was all it took to lure him out.

"Nice old feller," he said, careful not to let his hand stray anywhere near his teeth.

The gelding was docile enough and probably glad to be free, but McCloud wasn't taking any chances. Tying his shoe laces together, he looped a strand around the muzzle and used the ends as reins. Riding bareback toward the Big Horn Mountains, he stopped that morning to share a sheepherder's breakfast.

"Don't know why you'd wanna visit the Hole in the Wall," the herder said, looking him over. "'Less you're an outlaw."

"Do I look like an outlaw?" McCloud asked hopefully.

"Scalped farm boy's more like it."

"How's an outlaw look?"

"Like a cowhand."

"How's that?"

"Not like you... Not like me, neither. They shore got it in fer us herders."

McCloud was exasperated. "What do I need?"

"First thing's a saddle."

"I'm headed for the Hole to get mine back." He was proud of his quick response. His brain had cleared since the fever left him, although his eyesight was still a bit fuzzy.

"The hole ain't no healthy place for a farmer. Better to buy a new saddle." The old man combed his full beard with gnarled fingers, his grin revealing missing teeth.

Headed north, McCloud resigned himself to stealing items he needed to dress like an outlaw. His chance came late that afternoon when he spotted an outlying bunkhouse on the KC Ranch. The small building seemed deserted, and he could see no riders on the horizon. Loping in quickly, he tied the bay to a crude hitching rail.

He found six unmade bunks clustered around a potbellied stove, along with an assortment of tack and clothing hanging on nails. He tried on an aging Stetson, which covered his eyebrows and the tops of his prominent ears. The only pair of boots pinched his toes, and the worn leather chaps were long enough to trip him up. He'd have to make do.

An empty .30-30 Winchester was hidden beneath a bunk, but he could find nothing resembling a saddle. He hoped to find one at another stop the following day. Searching further, he found a packet of roll-your-own tobacco papers, but there was nothing to roll inside. Realizing the settling sun might bring the cowpokes back, he mounted up to ride.

* * * *

Andrea fell asleep on a mound of blankets while the men played a noisy game of poker. Dawn was streaking the horizon when the game broke up, and she dragged herself to bed. Billy was snoring beneath her window, and she wondered why he slept there. He obviously had no interest in her, and she didn't want his pity.

Awakened from another nightmare, she fought off her blanket, fearing the dreams would never end. Rubbing her eyes, she grudgingly rose to make breakfast, forgetting the men would sleep until noon after their all-night poker game.

Andrea clenched her jaw as she tossed wood into the old stove. Women were nothing more than slaves. It was ironic the outlaws were unaware of her gender. Lifting a cleaver, she hurled it at the wall. A cast iron skillet followed, landing short of its mark.

"Where're you aiming, Andy?"

She was surprised to find Billy yawning on the threshold.

"Who're you mad at this time?"

"Myself." Andrea stooped to retrieve the cooking utensils.

"Throwing them in the wrong direction, aren't you?" Billy quickly backed from the cabin when she raised the frying pan.

When the outlaws trouped into the cabin, Andrea listened as they discussed their final plans for the bank robbery. Harve Logan's younger brother "Lonie" had joined them from Harlan, Montana. He spent most of his time practicing his sharp shooting skills at the Currie cabin with the other outlaws. She often heard a barrage of gunshots echoing across the valley, sounding much like popping corn.

The bank robbing team arrived at the cabin for supper and another poker game. Loudest among the voices, as always, was Flat Nose George Currie's.

"Find any snakes in your boots?" she heard him ask.

"Three cards," Tom said, ignoring George.

"How about cockleburrs under that old saddle blanket?"

Laughter drowned out Tom's reply.

Flat Nose had a sadistic sense of humor, and Andrea cringed whenever she heard his deep-bellied laugh. She knew someone was the victim of another practical joke. It was usually Tom, who never seemed able to retaliate. She wondered whether he was afraid of his tormentor.

Poor Tom. He was so big and dumb that she wondered how he managed to be accepted into the gang. He *was* good with horses, but seemed to stumble over everything else in his path.

She was visiting Aladdin next morning in the barn when she noticed Flat Nose bending over Tom's saddle.

"What's that you're doing?" she asked, knowing he was up to something.

"Ain't none of your business, tadpole." His expression warned her not to interfere.

While she was preparing the mid-day meal, she noticed men gathered near the corral. One of them was drawing a line in the dirt with his heel, another pacing off what appeared to be several hundred yards.

Flat Nose was pounding Tom's back and laughing, which raised layers of gooseflesh on her arms. Whatever they were planning, Tom would get the worst of it.

Andrea pulled pans from the stove's scalding surface and started for the door; but before she could call to Tom, a gunshot sounded and she witnessed the start of a race. Tom's pinto jumped immediately ahead of George's sorrel, but as the two men neared the finish line, Tom slipped sideways and, along with the saddle, fell from his mount.

Andrea spent the next half hour patching him up. "Are you going to let him get away with this," she asked, swabbing a large scrape on the side of his head.

"Let 'em have their fun," he grumbled, rising to leave. Despite his clumsiness and obvious lack of confidence, Andrea felt a special kinship with Tom. Although he was probably unaware, they were both prisoners of the Hole.

Until she could manage to escape, she decided to take part in the activities going on around her. Watching the Logan brothers break range horses provided both excitement and horror. Perched on the top corral rail, she watched a wild mustang they planned to break that day.

Harve told his younger brother to break the first bronc, so Lonie coiled his rope and sauntered around the corral, ignoring the skittish horse. Suddenly swiveling back in the horse's direction, he frightened him into rearing. Before his legs came down, Lonie caught them in a tight loop and jerked the horse off balance. As soon as the stallion went down, Harve twisted his neck to prevent him from rising. Flailing, the horse found himself hobbled.

She was shocked by what she considered excessive cruelty, and was relieved when the mustang was back on its feet. But with his legs tied, he fell again.

Noticing her distress, Tom said, "He's got to learn who's boss."

"I know, but—"

This time the mustang stood still while a hackamore and blindfold were fitted over his head.

"Smart hoss," Tom said, grinning. "He'll behave himself now. He's already learned his first lesson. Some of 'em go down half a dozen times 'fore they get the hang of it."

The Logan brothers rubbed him down and the bronc eventually quieted. Lonie slid a saddle blanket over his back.

"Hold on," Harve warned. "He's not ready for the saddle."

Andrea watched as Lonie stubbornly set the saddle on the mustang's back and began to tighten the cinch.

"Make sure it's tight," Harve growled, obviously annoyed when the horse snorted and hunched his back.

Lonie jerked the mustang's ear to distract him as he mounted. Just as quickly Harve removed the blindfold and hobbles.

"Watch him stand there a while 'fore he notices the hobbles are off." Before the words were out of Tom's mouth, the mustang bolted, knocking Harve to the ground.

"Well, I'll be. They usually don't do that."

Walt raced across the coral to pull Harve to safety as Lonie rode the bucking horse in circles.

Andrea noticed a cut on Harve's forehead, and jumped down from the fence to offer medical aid. Running along the outer corral, she could still hear the angry equine snorts as Lonie remained on the mustang's back.

Harve was already on his feet when she squeezed through the gate. "Damned kid," he said. "I told him to wait."

Until that moment, she hadn't realized how alike the Logan brothers were, and how very different. Lonie was a younger version of Harve, although their temperaments were carved from soapstone and granite. Lonie was usually even-tempered and unwilling to start a fight, while Harve was quick to anger.

When the excitement was over, Andrea went back to cleaning the cabin. Horse breaking stirred up dust that drifted up from the corral, coating everything with fine brown powder. Her days were spent keeping things clean for herself, if not the men. They didn't seem to care.

When Andrea had recovered from Ketchum's brutal assault, she talked Billy into perforating a five-gallon bucket. She dumped ashes from the wood stove into it and repeatedly poured water through, so that lye would leach into another container. Boiled with beef tallow, the concoction became laundry soap so potent it could strip bark from a cottonwood until it was diluted with water.

Then she made milder bars for bathing by whipping in resin and borax that someone brought back from the town of Buffalo. Despite her sudsy successes, she longed for peppermint oil to improve the scent. She also longed for a porcelain bathtub as well as the privacy to use one. Even Gramma's old cast iron tub seemed a luxury in hindsight. If she ever escaped the Hole, she would never again take conveniences for granted.

* * * *

Jim McCloud couldn't find another bunkhouse to raid, but he managed to find an entrance to the Hole before he was forced to eat prairie dogs. The trail leading in appeared wide enough for a herd of long-horned steers, but he was unable to spot an outlaw guard. Lifting the benign Winchester over his head in what he hoped was a sign of truce, he slowly rode into the valley. Before long he came to a cabin, where he expected to find a guard.

A wiry man, no taller than himself, appeared at the door without a weapon.

Surprised, McCloud said, "I wanna visit the Hole."

"What fer?"

"I'm an outlaw."

"That right?" Amusement spread across the scrawny man's face. "Well, there's plenty of 'em roamin' about. Ride right on in and tell 'em what you want."

"Simple as that?"

"I don't make no trouble for them, and they do likewise."

"What if they think I'm a lawman?"

The homesteader grinned. "Not much chance of that. You don't look like any deputy I ever seen."

McCloud gratefully accepted a meager meal before resuming his bareback ride. Although happy he was wrong about strict security, he worried about lawmen sneaking into the Hole. He followed a trail advised by the settler and arrived at the cabin the following afternoon. Noticing activity at the corral, he nudged Outlaw in their direction.

No one seemed to take notice of him as he dismounted. A massively mustached, lanky cowboy eyed him briefly before turning back to watch the horse breaking.

"Howdy," McCloud said. "Looks like some mighty fine mounts you got here."

The other man looked at him curiously. "Don't 'member seein' you around. Where ya from?"

"Leavenworth." McCloud decided the truth was all he had to offer. "I always wanted to see the Hole in the Wall."

"Maybe you oughta talk to one of them fellers over there." He indicated several men in the corral. "They say who stays and who don't."

"If it's all the same with you, I'll just stand here and watch a while."

"Fine with me."

The tall man chewed his mustache for several moments before offering his hand. "Tom O'Day," he said. "Welcome to the hole."

Surprised and pleased, McCloud pumped his hand with enthusiasm.

"You and me are gonna be friends. Why don't I introduce you as my cousin? What's your name?"

"Jim McCloud. You'd do that for me?"

Tom slapped his back. "The boys don't cotton much to strangers... McCloud, did ya say?"

When he nodded, Tom said, "You could be from my ma's side of the family. They was Scots."

McCloud followed his newfound cousin into the corral where Tom presented him to Harve and George.

"What's your specialty?" Flat Nose asked, grinning wickedly.

"Safecracking." McCloud stood straighter and consciously inflated his narrow chest.

"That right?" They looked him over speculatively. "We'll keep you in mind."

"He's a bronc buster." Tom glanced at McCloud as though questioning whether the strange man could stick to a Mustang's back.

"Well, that's a diff'rent story," Flat Nose said. "Why doncha ya stomp the next one."

"He's tired from his long ride." Tom placed a protective arm around the smaller man's shoulders and turned him toward the barn. "He needs to rest up first."

When they reached the barn, McCloud was visibly shaken. "I don't know anything about breaking horses, Cousin Tom. I wish you hadn't—"

"You wanna stay here, doncha?"

"Yeah."

"You and me is gonna take a ride so's I can teach you the what-fors. Then we'll teach ol' Flat Nose George a lesson, but first you're gonna need a saddle and bridle."

Early next morning the two men rode to a secluded area near Buffalo Creek. While McCloud practiced raking his bay with borrowed spurs, Tom rode off to check on his still. When he returned, McCloud was on the ground, the bay nowhere in sight.

"Outlaw went and threw me," he said. "I never had trouble sitting a horse before."

"We call 'em hosses around here. It wouldn't hurt none if you'd started talkin' like me." Shaking his head, Tom said, "We gotta get you some decent clothes while we're at it. But not before we reel in Flat Nose George."

McCloud dusted himself and waited until Tom retrieved his horse. He was then encouraged to remount his bay. He wasn't happy with bronco busting, but knew if Tom withdrew his support, they'd deport him from the Hole.

* * * *

During the night, Tom slipped from his bedroll to pace the corral, like a ghost retracing old haunts. He knew he had to stop George's harassment to earn the gang's respect. A plan had rattled around in his head from the moment McCloud arrived. He felt sorry for the convict, knowing Flat Nose would humiliate him, but at least George's attention had shifted to the newcomer.

It was nearly time for the trip to Belle Fourche. McCloud was faring better than expected, so Tom would arrange the contest within a day or two. That morning he took the buckskin along on their morning ride.

"You're doin' so good," he told McCloud, "that I figured you should try stickin' Buster."

"How good do I have to be?"

"Ten second ride. But don't worry about it none. The buckskin's no better'n Outlaw."

Tom reassured McCloud by climbing on the buckskin himself. Raking Buster with his spurs, he demonstrated his superb balance as the horse humped his back, leaped, and twisted his body.

"See, he don't buck no better'n the bay."

"Then how come you want George to ride this horse . . . hoss?"

"You'll see."

McCloud swung astride and proceeded to rake Buster's ribs. When he stopped, he said, "Hell, Outlaw's a better bucker."

"Hold still a mite." Reaching into Lightning's saddlebag, he extracted a frying pan and large metal spoon. Standing near the buckskin's head, he banged one object against the other. Buster instantly humped his back and squealed as though he had been stung. McCloud seemed to hang mid-air before landing like a sack of corn on the ground. When he caught his breath, he said, "Won't Flat Nose get suspicious when he sees you with a frying pan?"

Tom hadn't thought of that. Now what would he do? Riding back to the corral, he thought of Andy, knowing the boy was an ally. After the noon meal, he'd have a talk with him.

When they finished eating, Flat Nose George focused on McCloud.

"You pigeon-toed, or are those boots too small?"

"They're a little tight."

"Then why'n hell don't you trade with the kid, here? He's sloggin' around like a mule stuck in quick sand."

Andrea and McCloud smiled at one another and agreed to swap boots.

"Now, what's this I hear about you braggin' you can beat me at bronc ridin'?"

Surprised, McCloud looked to Tom. "Uh ... yeah. I can stay on longer than you."

"How much money are you waggerin'?"

"Two hundred bucks," Tom said, noticing McCloud's distress. "And since my cousin's still a greenhorn, we get to pick the hoss."

"Fair enough." Flat Nose rose from the table laughing. "How 'bout now?"

"Tomorrow will do just fine."

McCloud's Adam's apple bobbed noticeably.

Next morning, Tom whistled his way to the cabin and back again to the barn. McCloud looked uneasy, and Tom did his best to reassure him. "Nuthin' to it, cousin. And 'member, you'll git George's money when he flies off Buster."

George strutted across the corral like a banty rooster. Tom noticed that everyone was present to watch the fun, bringing along their freshly filled coffee mugs. Everybody but Andy. Scanning the surrounding area, Tom wondered where the boy could be. He hoped he wouldn't let him down.

"I choose the buckskin," McCloud said.

Flat Nose roared with laughter. "That damned old pack hoss of Peep's?"

"He's a fine buckin' hoss." Tom looked him squarely in the eyes.

"Bring 'im out here, then."

Tom led the buckskin into the corral and watched McCloud mount him. He then climbed the corral fence to wait for Andy. His plan wouldn't work without the frying pan.

Harve held the stop watch, and Lonie gave the signal when everyone found a perch. The buckskin started off slowly, but gave a credible performance as McCloud stuck to his back for the full ten seconds.

Andy was still nowhere in sight, which made Tom's breakfast sour. Looks like the joke's on me again, he thought as George mounted Buster. Tom caught movement from the corner of his eye. Turning, he noticed Andy climbing the fence empty-handed.

Harve was looking at his watch as Lonie raised his arm. "Let 'er buck!"

George got in one long scrape with his spurs before a clatter arose from the rails. To Tom's surprise, the boys were banging their cups with knives, creating noises like a wedding chivaree. George left the saddle within a second or two, landing on his rump.

We're even. Grinning, Tom jumped down to offer George his hand.

"How did you manage that?" George groaned as he got to his feet. Turning to the boys on the fence he laughed, shaking his fist at them.

Tom found Andy smiling near the corral gate. Giving him the thumbs up, he realized the kid was smarter than he looked. He'd be bossing a gang of his own one day.

Chapter Eleven

Andrea had been a resident of the Hole for more than a month when Tom took her aside. He said he would be leaving the following morning for Belle Fourche.

"I'll be goin' over last minute hoss jinglin' with Billy while you get grub ready for the trip." Expanding his chest like an enormous pouter pigeon, he acted as though he were leading the gang.

Following his instructions, Andrea sacked jerky prepared days earlier by cutting beef into strips against the grain and hanging them on an outdoor rack. An army's supply of sour milk biscuits had been baked, after supplies had been brought in from Buffalo. She also set out other provisions the men would be taking with them.

When they entered the cabin at noon, she noticed a lifting of spirits. Even Harve and Sundance were smiling.

"I can feel the money jinglin' in my pockets," Tom said with a mouthful of biscuits and gravy.

"Better not feel it jingling," Sundance chided him. "If the loot's in silver and gold, we'll need a twenty-mule dray team to haul it away."

"Too bad Butch ain't goin'," Tom said wistfully.

"He pulled off some good ones," Flat Nose said, when he had cleaned steak from his teeth with a hunting knife. "Butch coulda started his own bank if he hadn't paid Matt Warner's defense lawyers for that murder charge."

"What about the Castle Gate job?" Lonie asked. "Butch got away with a fortune on that one."

"He didn't pull the jobs off by himself," Harve reminded him. "It takes teamwork, and Elzy Lay's a master planner."

Tom twisted the ends of his heavy mustache. "See's as how everythin's all set, let's have ourselves a snort or two to celebrate."

"No firewater until after the bank job." Sundance raised slightly in his chair, his palms pressed firmly on the table. "Hungover bandits leave a robbery on the back of an undertaker's mule."

"But we gotta take some whiskey along for snakebite," Tom said.

"Hell, yes," Sundance growled, his eyes narrowing. "But we'll tote it in *my* saddlebag, not yours."

Tom laughed self-consciously as Flat Nose glared at Sundance. "Nobody says what *I* can take."

"The two of you would drink yourselves stupid."

"You're not givin' me orders." Flat Nose slammed his knife into the heavy planked table.

Andrea fled the cabin when they jumped to their feet, gun hands at the ready. Rushing down the path to Buffalo Creek, she stopped on the bank to listen, but the shots she expected were not forthcoming. Breathing easier, she was relieved that no one had been killed, although she wondered if a shootout would hasten her escape.

Buffalo Creek's bank was peaceful although painful memories came flooding back. She had spent as little time as possible at the Creek since the assault, and was still uneasy about going there. Memories of Ketchum reinforced her resolve to protect her identity. She had been using a discarded coffee can as a chamber pot, and taken sponge baths in the cabin when no one was around. As an added precaution, she flattened her small breasts with strips of toweling. When her time came that month, she went downstream nightly to wash the bloody cloths.

Skittish as a young colt, she kept track of everyone's whereabouts. Fortunately, the men wore spurs. Although they scarred the cabin floor, they served as snake's rattles, warning of their approach.

When she returned, the cabin stood empty. Dishes were still in place, wiped clean with the biscuits she baked. The rough planked table didn't appear to have moved, although the benches had been pushed aside. She wondered how the men settled their argument.

She knew the Logans would side with Flat Nose George. Tom had probably crawled under the table to avoid the confrontation. She wasn't sure what Billy would have done, had he been there. He had grown more distant as time approached for the bank robbers to leave. Engrossed in their own activities, the outlaws had little time for her, as long as she caused them no trouble. She was aware of Butch's order to "leave Andy be," and felt secure under his absent protection, but she was beginning to feel invisible.

* * * *

Billy slung his line in the creek and slumped against a sandstone boulder. The sun's warmth made him sleepy, and he reckoned that the fish were dozing as well. Slouching, he blocked the sun with his hat. Winding the line around his index finger, he yawned and settled for a nap, but a spiteful fly had other plans. He had tried various fishing holes all morning where he'd previously caught enormous trout, but they produced not a nibble. Squinting at the sun, he realized he had missed the noon meal and searched his pocket for a piece of jerky.

Balancing himself on an elbow, he watched his line float downstream toward a clump of bushes on the opposite bank. He lifted the pole and tugged, realizing the hook had embedded itself in the undergrowth. Groaning, he stood and repeatedly yanked the line. When he couldn't dislodge it, he dropped the pole and hiked around the bend. It was then he recognized the area where he had killed Scar Ketchum.

Billy shivered in the afternoon heat. Memories flashed before him of the scene he encountered weeks earlier. Moments after he had sent Andy to the creek for a bath, he had started to worry, an uneasiness that gnawed at him as though a premonition. Knowing she would be furious if he saw her naked, he hiked along the sandy bank looking just ahead of his toes.

He found the canvas sack of utensils and clothing strewn along the bank, and picked up his pace until he heard someone wailing, raising the hair on his neck. Running, tripping over rocks, he rounded the bend and discovered them on the opposite bank.

Closing his eyes, he tried to dislodge the image, but it continued to run through his mind.

"Stop!" he yelled at Ketchum, but the big man ignored him. "I'll shoot," he warned, drawing his gun before splashing into the creek.

Ketchum's rage was imprinted on Billy's brain. He had tried to swallow his fear as the big man picked himself up, the knife poised for attack. Quivering in thigh deep water, Billy had tightened his grip on the trigger and heard the resulting roar.

He turned and headed back upstream. When he found his pole, he gave it a savage yank. The line pulled loose and whipped back, minus the hook. Hastily rewinding line around the gnarled branch, he started back toward the cabin, fishing in his pocket for another hook.

* * * *

Andrea stepped into the dooryard to look around, but could detect no movement. The corral was empty as was the surrounding area, and so quiet she could hear the flies buzzing and cottonwood leaves rustling. A hawk cried overhead as he wheeled about the valley looking for rodents.

A chilling mist of loneliness settled over her. Deciding to leave the dishes, she ran down the path to visit the Arabian. He was always glad to see her. Aladdin whickered when he noticed her approach. Anticipating a ride, he strained at his tether, tossing his head excitedly.

"Poor fellah," she said, stroking his neck. "It's no fun here alone in the barn."

Not wanting to disappoint him, she saddled the gelding and led him to the corral. The area was still deserted, instilling a sense of freedom.

Mounting Aladdin, exhilaration swept over her.

"No one's here to stop us," she whispered, stroking him. "It's time for us to leave."

Butch wasn't around to keep his promise, and no one knew when he'd return, if ever. There was always the chance the gang had been captured, or killed. It was now or never. Touching her heels to his ribs, she gave Aladdin his head as they climbed the slope beyond the cabin. Glancing about, she urged him in a southeasterly direction, heading toward the narrow break in the red walls. The sun's heat reminded her of the canteen and provisions she should have taken, but it was too late to turn back. Scanning the valley ahead, she noticed a horse and rider standing on a soft swell, watching. Aladdin's haunches pounded over the grassy terrain. Nothing could stop them.

* * * *

Tom sleepily sat his pinto, contemplating his golden mash. He hated the aging process, but knew good whiskey was well worth the wait. Meanwhile, he would make do with the store-bought spirits he had purchased before leaving Lander. He considered the whiskey he was quaffing damned good, although his own brew would outdo any he could buy. If Sundance knew, he'd smash the still and watch the fermenting whiskey soak into the dry earth. What a waste, he thought, shaking his head in disgust.

Following the outburst in the cabin, when the Sundance Kid had been outgunned by the Logans and Flat Nose George, Tom felt the need to fortify himself. He wished that Walt had returned from Bridger Creek to share the bottle with him. Taking another swig, he watched a flock of gulls glide overhead, wondering why the birds had flown so far inland. Butch told him how sea gulls had miraculously saved Utah crops from an invasion of crickets, and Tom wanted to know why a Mormon boy had turned outlaw.

"Circumstances," Butch replied. "I took the blame when some

neighbors broke the law."

Don't seem right, Tom thought hazily. *But a lot of things just don't seem right no more.* He wondered if the others had missed him when they raced for George's cabin to exercise the horses. He had turned off instead for a gulp of hidden brew. Taking another swig, he noticed the Arabian hell bent in the direction of the narrow V-shaped entrance. The kid was on his back, urging the gelding on.

"That ain't no way to treat an Arab," Tom told Lightning.

Dropping the empty bottle, he nudged the pinto's ribs. He swayed a bit in the saddle, but the urgency of his mission seemed to clear his head. Lightning was the best mount a man could ride. The pinto instinctively knew what was expected of him. He was big—over sixteen hands—with the best hocks in the Hole. As Lightning angled off to intercept the Arabian, Tom marveled at the horse's flat croup and high-set tail. The Arab was capable of greater speed than any bronc he had broken to ride. Aladdin might outrun his pinto for a short distance, but Lightning could overtake him. He wasn't worried. There was nowhere for the kid to go.

Grinning wide beneath his bushy, dark mustache, he was thoroughly enjoying the horse race. But from the look on the kid's face, he was anything but pleased. What did he think he was doing, running the Arab into the ground? Butch's soft spot for kids was well known. It would be his undoing one day.

The break in the red walls loomed ahead, and Andy seemed determined to run into them. Tom's brain cleared long enough to realize the kid was trying to escape. So that was it. Didn't he know a posse might be out there, waiting to nab the first horsethief who wandered out?

It was time to put an end to the race. Tom urged the last ounce of speed the pinto possessed to intercept the Arabian. As he leaned to grab the reins, the kid kicked at his hand, jerking his leather out of reach. He'd had enough. Clumsily drawing his gun, he aimed at Andy, ordering him to pull up.

"You wouldn't shoot me, would you?" the kid asked when they had both reined in. "I was just giving Aladdin a workout." Looking directly into Tom's bloodshot eyes, he turned his head to avoid the stench of second-hand whiskey.

"That ain't no way to exercise a hoss that's been stabled," Tom scolded. "He mighta broke a leg, and then I'd have to shoot him. And you, too."

The kid gasped, letting his head drop to his chest.

"I'm sorry, I didn't realize."

"That's the trouble with kids, nowadays. You don't stop to think."

"But Aladdin needs exercise—"

"You was tryin' to get away. You didn't know the hole's blocked off with a boulder, did ya?"

Andy shielded his eyes to stare at the sandstone walls several hundred yards away. The narrow passage between them had disappeared. He glanced back at Tom, who wondered why the kid hadn't taken the longer northeast route, if he was bent on escape.

"You won't tell the others I rode him out here, will you?"

"I sure as hell will."

"Then I'll have to tell them you were drinking."

"I oughta tan your hide."

"I thought we were friends."

Softening, Tom said, "Just 'cause you helped me best George don't mean I'd let the wolves getcha. How far do you think you would get without a gun or bedroll?"

When the kid bit his lip, Tom said, "Get yourself back to the barn and rub the Arabian down. And from now on, you don't ride 'less somebody's with you. I'm gonna tell Billy just that."

"Yes, sir. Don't worry, I won't ride him out here again."

They rode quietly back to the barn. As they approached the corral, Billy was struggling up the slope with a stringer full of trout. A wide grin revealed his even teeth.

"Those for supper?" Tom's special brand of whiskey always left him hungry.

"Flat Nose asked me to catch some," Billy said, holding them proudly. "Says they're good brain food."

Tom smacked his lips "Ain't them nice."

Billy looked to Andy. "Wanna help clean 'em?"

"I've got to rub Aladdin down."

"I'll help," Tom offered. "The sooner they're cleaned, the quicker they'll be fryin'."

Andy shot Tom a questioning look before starting for the barn. Before Tom could deliver his horse care sermon, the drumming sound of hoofbeats distracted him. Billy dropped his fish and crouched with gun hand ready. Staggering along the pinto, Tom clumsily jerked his Winchester free of its scabbard, while Andy stood rooted at Aladdin's head. An agonizing moment passed before they recognized the group of horsemen bunched in formation. Appearing briefly on the rise, they raced down the slope to the barn. Dust rose in a blinding cloud when they reined in short of their spectators.

Squinting through the grit, Tom's curse was lost amid the confusion.

"Where the helluv you been, O'Day?" Sundance yelled from his Appaloosa.

"Took a little detour," Tom replied, momentarily cowed by the smaller man's rage. "And a good thing, too. This here kid was runnin' the hooves off the Arab. Mighta broke a leg if'n I hadn't stopped 'em." He caught himself before he spilled the rest. No sense getting the kid in any more trouble than he already was.

"That's your last excuse." The Sundance Kid's face tightened with anger. "Get on your hoss and come with us."

Tom managed to scabbard his rifle. Weaving his way to the stirrup, his foot missed on the first few attempts. He was relieved that the others had already reined their mounts back toward the rise.

Sure wish Butch was bossin' this job, Tom reflected hazily as he looped a leg over the cantle. Butch understood a man's need for a drink when his nerves were frayed, although he seemed to need fewer than most. The bank job now loomed like an overloaded wagon, with Sundance bullwhacking it. As mean-tempered as Harve was, he, at least, understood a man's right to wash the trail dust from his throat.

Tom nudged the pinto into a trot when he noticed the others waiting. Grumbling to himself, he forced a grin when Harve motioned him to ride alongside.

"You can slip off quicker'n a hen house fox," Harve complained. "You managed to miss target practice and most of the planning. I'm thinking those big ears of yours would make good tobacco pouches."

Tom shook his head to dislodge the cobwebs floating before his eyes. "Don't blame you a bit," he agreed. "I've been spendin' too much time with Billy, trainin' him to jingle the herd."

"And nippin' the sauce while you're at it."

"Them kids git on my nerves." There was no sense denying his drinking. He'd taken a couple of swigs too many and nearly lost control.

"I meant what I said about staying sober until after the bank job," Sundance warned. "Only a fool would ride into Belle Fourche drunk or hungover."

Tom pondered his sobriety as they rode to George's cabin. Tonight, after the others turned in, he would drink the rest of his stash when he rode to check on the still. He should bury the remedy machine before he left. If the kids found it, they could drink themselves sick. Worse yet, they'd probably tell Sundance when the gang returned from Belle Fourche. Reining in at George's cabin, they hunkered down outside, where Harve drew a map of Belle Fourche in the dirt.

"We'll camp on the other side of town in the woods," he said, staring at Tom. "Belle Fourche was rebuilt last year after a fire destroyed most of the buildings. I rode through one night and everything seems to be stacked in the same place."

Harve carved an "X" in the crude map with his knife. "Here's where the Butte County Bank is located. One of us'll ride into town the day before and put his ear to the ground. That'll be you, Peep."

Sundance's frost blue eyes bore into Tom's bright marbled ones. "You're the least known of any of us. Not one reward poster out on you that I can find."

Tom gave him a lopsided grin, relieved he was back in the gang's good graces, although ashamed of his own lack of notoriety. "I'm good at nosin' things out. You can count on me, boys."

"The town sits by itself, a hard day's ride from the Wyoming border, which makes it easier to escape the law. There's over a thousand residents," Sundance said. "With the crowd of out-of-towners arriving for the celebration, the locals won't take notice of a few new faces."

"Sounds good to me," Tom said. "Don't worry, boys. I won't letcha down."

For all his good intentions, Tom was unable to hit one target during firing practice. The others seemed tolerant enough of his sloppy marksmanship. Most outlaws shot wild during robberies, careful not to kill unless it was necessary. Murderers were hunted down until posses dropped from exhaustion, but robberies were considered another hazard of frontier living.

Tom wondered if he could shoot someone at close range if his life depended on it. He hoped he would never find out.

When it was too dark to hit whiskey bottle targets, the men mounted to ride to the cabin for one last home cooked meal. Their spurs rattled like castanets, drowning out the creaking sounds of five worn saddles. As night settled in, they were greeted by the aroma of fried potatoes and trout.

Tom was famished. The whiskey had produced a dull headache, and he craved a nip or two to accompany his meal, although he promised the boys he would remain sober until after the bank robbery.

During the meal, Tom noticed Andy smiling and in unusually good spirits. He ignored the kid whenever possible. Andy's previous hang-dog look got to a man. It made him feel as low as a cockroach and thirsty for a good swig of brew.

Billy even looked more his old self. He might still be a mite down at the mouth, but he looked better. Tom couldn't blame him either. Killing Ketchum must have left a powder burn in his gut.

Tom was feeling better as well. A full belly and a little nightcap after hours would fix him up just fine. Although he'd been uneasy about his first bank job, he was delighted with his new spy role. Although he'd had little schooling and could not remember deciphering anything longer than a wanted poster, he knew spies often determined the outcome of battles. That in itself was cause for celebration.

Supper over, they loaded provisions into saddlebags. Most supplies were left for early morning and a short-legged pack horse. Before Tom could remind Sundance about the snakebite medicine, he saw him shove a pint of Old Crow into his saddlebag. Tom shook his head in disgust. A pint of whiskey wouldn't cure the bite of a newborn rattler.

So much for good intentions. Tom warily made his way from the barn after an hour of listening to heavy breathing and an abrasive snort or two. It was too risky sneaking Lightning out of the barn and, in desperation, he decided to hoof it over the hill to his nearest cache. Walking was a horseman's curse. Legs were made for stretching and wrapping around a good mount's ribs.

He lowered himself to the ground outside the barn to pull on his boots, then stood listening to his companions sleeping. The night was dark, but he knew the Hole as well as his own hands. Glancing down at the outline of his long, out-spread fingers, he knew it wouldn't be easy, but his gnawing thirst was enough to make him crawl over railroad spikes to quench it.

A short distance from the barn, Tom stumbled into a depression. Sharp pain slashed at his ankle and along with the pain, a buzzing sound invaded his head like a hive of mountain yellow jackets. Groaning, he lowered himself to the ground. While massaging his leg, it occurred to him there was whiskey much closer than the still. A pint was stashed in the Sundance Kid's saddlebag.

After several moments of indecision, he decided it was too risky. Harve would relish slicing off Tom's ears, or something more vital, to punish him for his transgression. The decision was made easier when he remembered the cabin liquor shelf. There had to be some of Butch's Old Crow. It wasn't O'Day's special brew, but it would quiet his desperate craving, well worth the pain and effort it would cost him to hobble over there.

The moon's slim crescent had sliced overhead when he limped to the cabin. He heard Billy's snore before noticing his slumbering form near the cabin's back room. Strange how he chose to sleep there. Andy didn't need protection. In fact, from the way the kid had taken over, it was Tom and the others who needed to keep their distance from him.

Wincing in pain, he advanced as quietly as possible through the entryway. The door was left open to let in the night breeze. Edging along the wall, he felt his way into the front room to grope along the wall for the shelf.

Eagerly moving his callused hand over the splintered board, he groaned. The shelf was empty. He frantically searched the lower shelf, where he fingered a smooth surface that was cool to the touch. So thirsty he could have drank the still dry, he took a long pull from the bottle. The instant liquid scorched his tongue, he knew it wasn't whiskey. Gagging, his mouth on fire, he spat the foul concoction to the floor.

Andy heard him and yelled, "Who's there? " The voice was joined moments later by Billy's. A lucifer was struck and he recognized the youngest outlaw.

"What're you doing here?" the kid said, his tone suspicious.

"Thirsty," Tom croaked. "What's in that bottle?"

Andy stooped to retrieve the bottle from the floor. "Kerosene! You didn't swallow, did you?"

"A little." He gripped his throat. "Am I gonna die?"

Billy rushed to retrieve milk that had been stored in the creek. Dick Hale brought it in that evening in a discarded wine bottle, requesting bread pudding. At the time, Tom surmised a wet cow had been found among the rustled herd.

The kid lit a lantern and the room swam before Tom's eyes. Crossing himself, he wondered if he were in purgatory.

Tom's raw throat was closing in on him, fear blocking air to his lungs. Andy guided him to a bench where he groped dizzily for the table to steady himself.

"Put your head between your knees," Andy ordered. "You're not going to die."

The words were reassuring, but what did a kid know about such things? Tom's head raged with real and imagined flames, his stomach joining in as cold sweat trickled over his eyelids.

Billy rushed back with the milk bottle. "Better get him outside, just in case."

Together they helped Tom to his feet and guided him into the yard. Tilting the bottle to his lips, he gagged. He hadn't touched the stuff since childhood. The moment milk hit his stomach, it curdled and erupted through his nose.

"Drink some more," Andy urged. "A sip at a time. Hold it in your mouth to stop the burning."

Tom sagged into a sitting position against the outer wall. Damned kid knew what he was talking about, he did, but Tom would never admit it. His old man would have taken a razor strap to Tom if he'd ever told a grownup what to do. Despite his exasperation, he had a growing admiration for Andy. The kid had smarts and more than a smidgen of pity, unlike Harve or the Sundance Kid, who could cheerfully whittle the ears from a dying man.

Harve's face floated before Tom's eyes. Wiping sweat from his forehead with the back of a trembling hand, he glanced up at the vague figures standing over him.

"You won't tell the boys, will ya?"

"Why shouldn't we?" Billy's voice was heavy with sarcasm.

"If'n you do, they won't let me ride with 'em on the bank job."

"Then I'll go instead, like I should."

"Don't, Billy," Andy pled quietly.

"Why not?"

"You're not a bank robber, and I have a bad feeling about the holdup."

Although Tom's head buzzed with swarming bees, he was aware of a power struggle between the two kids. Forgoing his ready quip that one was trying to redeem the other, he waited to hear who would win. When nothing more was said, he carefully arranged his words.

"I'm a lot older'n you, Billy. And it's my first bank job. I waited a long time for Butch to let me ride along." His words died off into a heavy sigh.

Billy ground his boot heel into the hard earth. "If you don't keep your nose out of the bottle, you'll die with it there." The words were harsh but sympathetic, if one was inclined to interpret them that way.

Tom did. "I'm so sick I won't never touch the stuff again." There was resolve in his voice as he held his stomach with one hand, his head in the other.

"Better get some sleep," Andy urged, helping him to his feet. "It's nearly time to leave."

When Tom reminded them of his injured ankle, they helped him hobble to the barn. With a whispered goodbye, he slumped in the hay for a few hours' sleep. The pain in his ankle and sickness in his gut kept him awake until the first rays of light streaked the horizon.

Someone roughly shook him awake. "Get up, or I'll tie you to your damn hoss and drag you." It was Harve.

Tom groaned and tried to rise, but was so weak his legs refused to move. He was then jerked upright. When Lonie asked him what was wrong, Tom said he had fallen when he went outside to relieve himself. He cringed when the Sundance searched his saddlebags.

"You better not have guzzled the whiskey."

Tom sighed, thankful he hadn't taken the Old Crow.

"If you're too sick, Billy will go instead."

"Hell no, I'm fine. Just give me some grub to quiet my belly."

While the others saddled up, Tom sat gingerly eating biscuits, inwardly cursing the kid for his milk cure. The biscuits refused to stay down, and it took all the strength he could muster to saddle and mount his pinto. Hands shaking, he closed his eyes, swaying so badly that he nearly left his perch. This would be the longest ride of his life.

* * * *

A days' ride from the Hole, Tom thought he was going to die, and was afraid that he wouldn't. Without a drink to numb the pain and warm his innards, he complained of finding no rattlers the entire trip to warrant a sip of whiskey. His alcohol withdrawal had gone through tremors and a variety of ailments, but by the time they reached the South Dakota border, the lanky outlaw was sitting straighter in the saddle, his body nearly free of its miseries.

The six of them had ridden the roughest and loneliest of trails, often forging their own to avoid being seen. Taking their time and allowing the horses plenty of rest, they had seen no one since crossing the KC Ranch.

Tom marveled at thick stands of pine trees interspersed with riotous colored earth and vegetation when they neared the South Dakota border. Black Hills' beauty touched him in a way that made him acutely aware of his mortality, but his thoughts soon focused on his mission and the most effective means of spying on the town of Belle Fourche.

Lonie left them to herd the first batch of relay horses to the Hash Knife Ranch near Ekalala, Montana, where a friend worked as foreman. He would stay with the second string at the pointed buttes until the boys arrived after the bank job.

Circling to the north, they by-passed the town, making camp in the hills some six miles to the east. Once camp was struck, they sat smoking and drinking bituminous coffee, going over final plans for the holdup. Harve didn't need to ask whether Tom was up to his job, for he made a conscious effort to spring from his horse despite the pain in his ankle. He even managed to whistle while unsaddling Lightning.

Next morning Flat Nose baked pones over the campfire in a small Dutch oven, while Walt fried thick slices of bacon. After breakfast, Harve, scratching his thick chin whiskers, gave Tom final instructions.

"Ride in casual-like with your ears open. Listen to local gossip, especially about the bank, and find out whether there's extra deputies on duty. Report back here tonight so we'll know the best time to strike."

* * * *

The main street was crowded with celebrants on the last of the three-day Civil War reunion. Tom rode slowly into town, weaving among matronly women, their neatly-dressed children, and family men newly-hatted in straw. None seemed to be sporting weapons of any kind.

He looked for the saloon Flat Nose said was near the bank. He figured it for the best place to listen in on local gossip. Bruce Sebastian's caught his eye, and he quickly led Lightning to a watering trough before tying him up out front. After loosening the cinch, he wasted little time pushing the bat-winged doors inward.

Tom stood inside the door until his eyes adjusted to the dim light. Making his way to the far end of the bar, he ordered a shot of whiskey, which he downed in a gulp. While the raw sensation warmed his innards, he groaned with pleasure and ordered another. Only then did he lean on an elbow to survey the other occupants.

When the bartender brought him his second shot, Tom asked good-naturedly, "Must be a few drunks in jail from all this celebratin'."

"Good thing it's not winter," the gargantuan barkeep said. "A one-legged drunk tried to burn his way out of jail day before yesterday. The steel cage is all that's left." He took Tom's money and moved on down the bar.

"Imagine that." Tom made a mental note to have a look-see.

Deciding Sebastian's few customers were unfriendly, he sauntered out into the street. His next stop was the Hotel Belle Fourche where he bumped into a trio of mean-faced Civil War veterans as they exited the bar. Tom apologized for his clumsiness, but a big, overall-clad man decided to press his advantage.

"Which side are *you* on?" An enormous hand grasped Tom by the scruff of his neck.

Judging from his accent, Tom chose the south. "My daddy got his hoss shot out from under him at the battle of Antietam," he drawled. Someone had told him that, but his memory was getting fuzzy.

"Good man." The Dixie mountain joined his companions to bully his way across the street.

Tom took the first available stool in the hotel bar. This spy business could be dangerous to one's health, he thought before ordering a third shot of whiskey. There were few people present, and Tom grew bored and left.

He decided to reconnoiter the pink-stoned Butte County Bank building. Staggering along the boardwalk, he entered Giles Hardware Store directly across the street. His feet already tired from walking, he tripped over the threshold and stumbled into a display rack. Pots and assorted cooking utensils clattered to the floor. When he righted himself, Tom looked into the frowning face of the owner, who had been waiting on a customer.

Tom apologized and hastily replaced the cookware. They were still frowning when he left. He then remembered that Harve had warned him not to draw attention to himself.

Light-headed, he retreated to Sebastian's, which he found more inhabited. Seating himself with his back against the wall, he decided he'd better take this spy business seriously. When the fourth shot slid smoothly down his throat, Sundance's voice echoed in his inner ear: "Get drunk and you'll look like a leach can, shot full of holes."

Tom decided to leisurely sip his whiskey.

The only men willing to talk were Civil War veterans, who knew next to nothing about the town. None of them knew a hoot about horse training, and the morning dragged on into early afternoon.

Tom wasn't really hungry, but decided to take advantage of Sebastian's free lunch. He needed to dull the effects of his liquor. Shooing flies, he chose a dill pickle and handful of soggy, boiled eggs. When he finished eating, he walked into the afternoon sun, glanced up and down the dusty street, and returned to his chair against the wall.

The clock over the bar said 2:15.

He was sipping jigger number five when a well-dressed, graying man leaned over the bar. Tom managed to get up and slump next to him.

"Howdy," he drawled. "Which side are you on?"

"I'm damned well tired of hearing about the Civil War."

Obviously a Belle Fourche businessman, he didn't seem interested in recruiting new customers.

"Banker?" Tom asked hopefully.

"No."

"Storekeeper?"

"No."

This was going to be a real tooth-puller. Tom sighed and thrust out his hand. "Tom Barns, rancher from Thermopolis," he said, stumbling over his lines.

Glancing at him from the corner of his eye, the stranger smoothed his curled, waxed mustache. He seemed undecided whether to accept Tom's company, but finally consented to shake his hand.

"George Hair," he said. "I was the Bee editor before the big fire destroyed the newspaper office. I now promote the Gaety Theater. Our first production is scheduled for February."

"That so?"

"A big strapping fellow like yourself would certainly be useful backstage."

Disappointed that Hair hadn't offered him an acting role, Tom said, "I'm here to buy some hosses. Thought I'd take in the celebration."

"Well, it's a real snorter. First the jail burns down, then the picnic grounds get flooded. Next thing you know the bank will be robbed."

Tom caught his breath, his mouth dropping open.

"Guess I'm just a pessimist," Hair said when he noticed Tom's surprise. He quickly downed the rest of his drink, turned, and left the bar.

Sighing, Tom returned to his chair and slid it against the wall. This spy business wasn't his jigger of brew.

Moments later, the bat wings opened, and a shapely red-haired woman entered the saloon. Glancing about, her gaze settled on Tom. Slowly, she moved in his direction. It was early for a saloon girl to be up and about, but he was ready for company. She was built like a racing filly, her long legs visible through her ankle-length gown.

"Hello, handsome," her husky voice said.

"Sit down and keep me company." His words were slurred but she seemed not to notice. "You a Civil War veteran?" he asked, because he could think of nothing else to say.

"Silly," she said, laughing.

"Been in Belle Fourche long?"

"Too long." She watched him through her long, dark lashes.

"Know anything about the bank?"

"As far as I know, it's full of money."

Tom wasted no time offering her a drink. Soon her charcoal-lined eyes and rouged lips were inviting him up to her room. Tom wasn't opposed to the idea.

The clock said 2:45, or was it 3:45? The face was blurred. He'd have to tell the bartender to clean it. Well, no matter. There was still plenty of time to spy on the bank, and it was a short ride back to camp. Besides, this young filly was obviously a resident of Belle Fourche.

Chapter Twelve

Andrea slept late and awoke exhausted from the ordeal with Tom. Little had been said while they returned to the cabin, but she was well aware of Billy's resentment. Rubbing sleep from her eyes, she stood on the cabin threshold and surveyed the area of the corral and barn. No one seemed to be moving about.

Changing into freshly washed overalls, she splashed her face with water from a chipped porcelain bowl. Finger-combing her hair, she padded barefoot into the kitchen where a cracked shaving mirror hung from a rusty nail. Twisting its angle, she gazed into her own large blue eyes and grimaced at her image. The face staring back was unfamiliar, not one she had seen in weeks, or cared to see again.

Her skin had tanned the color of Butch's chestnut mare. Her nose was peeling, and her hair stood out at uneven angles like an anemic sunflower. Cringing, she reached for shears to trim the strands to make them even. She then smeared soft lard on her face and hands to relieve the dryness.

Andrea didn't hear him until he stamped his boots on the threshold. Turning, she caught an amused glint in his eyes.

"What are you made up for?" Billy asked, grinning. "A greased pig contest?"

Glancing down at her lard-coated hands, she laughed. "A pig am I?" Impulsively seizing a wooden spoon, Andrea tapped him on the forearm. "This is to teach you some manners."

"A good spanking's what you need," he said, snatching the spoon.

Billy chased her from the cabin. He caught her a few feet from the door when a bare foot full of cockleburs stopped her. Swinging her into his arms, he carried her into the cabin and collapsed on a nearby bench. Wrestling Andrea across his lap, he paddled her with the spoon. She squealed with laughter and pretended rage, kicking and squirming until he set her on her feet.

"Looks like I caught the greased pig," he said, his solemn eyes riveted to hers.

Andrea stepped back, suddenly anxious from his abrupt change in mood. "We're acting like pickaninnies, aren't we?"

"Pick a—?"

"Children!"

"First it's my manners. Now I'm a child."

Flustered, she changed the subject. "My foot," she said, hopping on the uninjured one. Sitting, she crossed one leg over the other, pointing to stickers protruding from her heel.

"That'll teach you to run outside without your boots." Standing, he started for the door.

"But Billy…"

"I'll be down at the corral working the hosses."

Wiping lard from her face and hands, she pulled on boots to follow him. No one was in sight, and she wondered where the other men had gone.

When he finally acknowledged her, he said the others had ridden north to Buffalo for some overdue hurrahing. The two of them were alone in the southern end of the valley.

Angling off toward the barn, he left her to her loneliness.

"My birthday's next week," she shouted, hoping to prolong his company.

Billy stopped and turned back slowly, surprise registering on his face. "So's mine."

"How old will you be?"

"Eighteen!" He stretched to his full height, several inches above her. "And you?"

"I'm twelve, remember."

"C'mon, Andy, how old are you?"

"A lady never tells her age?"

"Why not?"

"It's an unwritten law. I'll only admit to being thirteen next Thursday."

"The day after mine?"

"I guess that makes us related, somehow."

"How do you figure?"

"A gypsy once told my mother that people born on the same day are like twins. Their souls, I mean. She said they're so alike that they know what the other is thinking."

Frowning, he asked, "You don't know what I've been thinking, do you?"

"No, but I usually know what you're going to do before you do it."

"Hogworsh," he said, looking scornful. "It doesn't matter when you're hatched. And I know what you're gonna do. Curry the horses, carry water to the cabin..."

"I'm going," she said sullenly, following a flat-handed swat to her backside.

"I'm boss here now, and I want things done right."

Billy was taking his responsibilities too seriously. During the days that followed, he spoke only when necessary, appearing only briefly at mealtime. Their conversations were limited to duties he expected her to perform.

"Why won't you let me go?" she pleaded during the first few days they were alone. "I'll find my own way home." She had seen that same annoyed expression when Tom had done something stupid. Words were unnecessary.

"Can't we ride somewhere after the chores are done, or just sit here and talk?"

"Too much work to do," he would say. "We have to get everything ready."

"For what?"

Before she could probe further, he left for the barn, leaving her frustrated and angry.

* * * *

Dick Hale took McCloud under his wing when Tom left the Hole for Belle Fourche. Although Hale's stuttering bothered him, McCloud welcomed a new mentor. When Hale suggested they ride to Buffalo for new clothes and recreation, McCloud was more than agreeable. His first stop in town was to completely outfit himself with the money he won from George Currie. Before he could buy a new saddle, Hale suggested that they visit Beulah.

"B-best scarlet lady in town."

Tom had already told him about Buffalo's pleasure palaces, and from the gleam in Hale's eyes, he knew he was impatient.

"You been to see her?"

"E-ever chance I git."

"Think she would take us both?"

"B-Beulah could h-handle a cattle crew."

McCloud dragged his feet. "Why don't I meet you there later," he said, deciding to return to the general store. "I just remembered something else to buy."

The urge had left him, and he thought of the boy at the cabin slogging around in boots McCloud had stolen from the KC bunkhouse. He felt he owed Andy for his help in unseating George. Without his winnings, he would have had to borrow money from Tom.

More than half his winnings had been spent when he noticed an open safe behind the counter. The clerk was making change for his latest purchase, so McCloud quickly inventoried the contents. A muscle twitched in his left cheek. Breaking into the store would be simple enough, but he'd have to find a drill. Maybe he should pull a daylight robbery while the safe was open.

"Here's your change." The clerk smiled at him as though he were somebody.

McCloud decided not to rob him. Too easy. The real challenge was cracking the safe.

Hale was grinning sleepily when he met him back at Beulah's place. Taking his whisker-stubbled companion by the arm, McCloud led him into the street.

"Ain't you gonna...?"

"No, I got better things to do. The safe at the general store's full of money."

Hale's droopy eyelids abruptly snapped open. "You ain't t-thinkin' of r-robbin' the place?"

"Why not?"

"The b-boys don't never b-bother folks around here. Too d-damn close to the Hole."

"How far do I have to go?"

"D-Douglas is the closest, I'd s-say."

"Got some good safes there?"

"Well, t-there's the hotel and the p-post office."

"Guess I better wait 'til I can grow more hair. Then I'll get me an alias. How does James Dale sound?"

"Nobody e-else's got the n-name that I know of."

"In the meantime, you can call me 'Driftwood' Jim."

* * * *

Lonely and frustrated, Andrea occupied her time searching for wild herbs along the creek. Avoiding the prickly sow thistle plant, she dug dandelions and dropped roots and leaves into a flour sack. The leaves could be chewed to ease indigestion and roots boiled to make a pungent, healing tea. She remembered her grandmother telling her that dandelions also healed wounds.

She found a small, broad-leafed plant that resembled rhubarb, with pale violet flowers. Recognizing it as burdock, she was careful not to stick herself with the brown bristly burrs. She collected leaves, roots, and seeds to cure skin ailments and sluggishness, although she doubted anyone needed them.

On the eve of Billy's birthday, she baked him a cake from sweetened biscuit dough. Pouring batter into a dented lard can, Andrea was disappointed when the cake baked lopsided and sagged in the middle.

With sugar and the last of the milk, she made frosting, piling it high in some areas to hide the cake's deformities. Then, shaving down a well-used candle to smaller proportions, she stuck it in the middle of the cake and wrote Billy's name on the surface with small bits of jerky. Hiding her masterpiece under a bucket on the table, she left it for him to find the following morning.

When she awakened, the cake was still untouched. Standing in the doorway, she could hear metal clanging against metal, the sounds coming from the barn. She hurriedly dressed and scooped up the cake. Trudging down slope, she carried it into the barn, where she found him hammering a metal rod.

"Happy Birthday!"

He continued hammering.

She repeated her greeting several times before he noticed her.

"What's this?" Frowning, he ran his dirty finger through the frosting. Tasting it, he grimaced and went back to work.

Furious, she set the cake down and fled back to the cabin. Fighting tears, she thought how ungrateful Billy was, and how uncaring. Didn't he realize how unhappy he was making her? Didn't he have any feelings for her at all? He was just like the rest of the outlaws. All they cared about were themselves. Billy was headed for ruination and wasn't smart enough to realize that he was riding down the wrong trail.

If he wasn't going to help her escape, she would have to go alone. Lobo wolves be damned. Aladdin could outrun any four-legged beast. Pushing aside her fears of over-night camping, she decided to leave that day.

Gathering up provisions, she dropped them into a flour sack with her few articles of clothing. She was planning her getaway when Billy appeared with the cake.

"What're you doing?"

Swinging the sack behind her back, she said, "I thought you'd like a picnic lunch to celebrate your birthday." Andrea held her breath as cold points of perspiration dotted her forehead.

"Must be something to that gypsy stuff," he said. "I was gonna ask if you'd like to take a ride up north a ways."

Andrea looked into his hopeful eyes and smiled, surprised by his abrupt mood swing. She followed him to the barn where they saddled the horses and rode up the slope past the cabin. A light breeze stroked them from the northwest as they rode, bathed in early morning sun. Muted grasses waved in their direction, already yellowing from lack of moisture.

"I thought you'd like to see the outlaw cave," Billy said. "The James brothers and Civil War deserters hid out there back in the sixties and seventies."

They stopped to let the horses drink from the middle fork of Powder River. A sheer rock face, along the trail to their right, housed a row of swallow nests carved several feet above ground. Chokecherry bushes and buffalo grass grew in thick clumps, the eastern red wall looming behind them, blocking out everything but luminous clouds banked in a brilliant sky.

The orange, hard-packed earth soon gave way to powdery sand, and they dismounted to lead the horses to cliffs overlooking the outlaw cave. The climb upslope ended abruptly with a tilt down to the cliffs and an awesome view of the Powder River, which split the towering walls more than a hundred feet below.

Billy pointed to a dark hole partially hidden by undergrowth a quarter of the way up the steep granite wall.

"Where did they leave the horses?"

"They probably turned them loose up here somewhere in the brush to graze, or they hid them in the cave. I hear there are stalls in the cave."

Seating herself on the edge of the cliff, Andrea peered into the canyon. "Have you been in the cave?"

"No," he said, "and it's time to get back."

Several times during their ride, she ached to broach the subject of leaving. She decided to wait until her own birthday when he might be more receptive. In the meantime, she would see that his day was as pleasant as possible.

The sun was slanting toward the western wall when they rode down the trail to the cabin. Andrea was disappointed when she noticed several horses in the corral. Some of the gang had already returned from Buffalo.

Dick Hale greeted them as they led their horses into the barn. "I h-heard in Buffalo that Bob Divine and some of the c-cowboys from the CY Ranch and the P-Pugsley spread was g-gonna ride up here to round up rustled cattle." Hale's brown eyes bulged, his muscular arms flapping like a plucky rooster.

"Are we gonna try to stop 'em?" Billy seemed as excited as Hale obviously was.

"G-Guess not. The b-boys say they can't sell b-beef to the r-railroads no more cause of the n-new brand inspection laws."

Both men sighed, their bodies sagging.

"B-Butch said there ain't enough m-money in stock stealin' no more. Said bank and t-train robbin' was the real cash."

"Yeah," Billy muttered, unsaddling the roan. Andrea followed suit. After the horses were rubbed down and fed, they headed for the cabin where Billy helped her prepare supper. Jim McCloud soon joined them.

"Well, if it ain't cousin Jim all decked out in new duds." Billy pumped the slender man's hand.

"You can call me Driftwood Jim from now on," he said.

Andrea turned from the stove to stare into McCloud's dark eyes, remembering the first time she had seen him at the corral. His spiked hair was beginning to curl, but still fell short of his large protruding ears. The sparse mustache reached beyond the corners of his lips, and a receding hairline made him appear close to thirty, although she doubted he was much older than Billy. McCloud would have been handsome, she decided, if not for his bloodhound expression. She had never seen him smile.

"Glad you got back from Buffalo in time for supper," Billy said, offering the two men a seat at the table. "We're having spuds and trout from the crick."

Conversation dwelled on whether reports were true that Bob Devine, the CY Ranch foreman, was planning a raid from neighboring Natrona County to retrieve stolen cattle. Billy's "What'll we do?" was promptly settled by McCloud's proclamation of "Nuthin'. Let 'em have 'em. They're not much good to us, nohow, other than a few beef to jerk before we move on to a different territory." He sounded like Tom O'Day's parrot.

Andrea was surprised by his physical transformation and was even more amazed by his confidence. The bumbling farm boy could pass for a seasoned outlaw if one didn't probe too deeply.

She was silent during the prolonged meal, listening to tales of rustlers' butchering techniques, and the selling of stolen cattle to the Union Pacific and B & O Railroad crews as they laid track across the Montana prairie. Hale told them how the bundled hides from butchered cattle had been tied with bailing wire, weighted with rocks and dumped into Buffalo Creek. The hides would drift downstream to be found by ranchers outside the Hole during the spring thaw.

"Tom says Flat Nose George is the best he ever seen with the runnin' iron." McCloud casually wiped his mouth on a new shirt sleeve. "Him and some of the boys could change the CY brand to the TOY or OXO. But the best they ever done was changin' the Old Mallet brand to a dollar sign. It was easy 'til the railroads started asking for brand papers."

Winking at Andrea, Billy said, "I heard they sometimes cut out patches of hide and sewed on new brands with needle and thread."

"S-sew, we d-did," Hale said, chortling.

Scraps of food had adhered themselves to the plates by the time Andrea rose to clean them. Reluctantly, she gathered them up as the conversation continued. Billy's apparent enthusiasm for outlaw ways troubled her. Learning he was her own age had made her even more determined to save him, although she knew she should plan an escape on her own. There was no reason for Billy to think of himself as a wanted man. He had confessed during the ride back from the outlaw cave that he was never directly involved in a robbery. It wasn't too late for him to reform. Why was he so thick-headed?

Next morning she was up before the sun, humming as she buttoned on the new shirt Hale brought back from Buffalo. He was surprised and pleased to learn the shirt and overalls were birthday presents. The nicest surprise was a new pair of boots from McCloud.

She was frying steak and potatoes when Hale sauntered in for breakfast.

"C-can ya read, Andy?" Hale sat at the table, rubbing his stubbled chin and offering a battered newspaper.

Nodding, she wiped hands on her new overalls.

"Take a l-look at this."

Glancing at a copy of the *Wyoming Derrick,* she noticed an open letter to CY Ranch Foreman Bob Devine, allegedly written by a Hole in the

Wall gang member. Someone had circled the letter in pencil. Reading aloud, she laughed at the phrasing and lack of punctuation:

You had better keep your damned outfit out if you want to keep them. Don't stick that damned old grey head of yours in this country again if you don't want it shot off we are the twelve appointed a purpose to get you if you don't stay out of here.

The Revenge Gang

"Who wrote this?"

"I ain't s-sayin' but I'll be watchin'."

Craning her neck, Andrea peered through the window. "Where's Billy?"

"L-last time I s-saw him, he was ridin' north."

"How long ago?"

"A c-couple hours."

Billy knew it was her day, yet he had chosen to ride off alone. Storming out of the cabin, she narrowly missed colliding with McCloud.

"Breakfast's on the stove," she grumbled, heading for the creek.

Sitting on the bank, her head at rest on her arms and knees, she had nearly dozed off when she heard pebbles crunching behind her. Andrea scrambled to her feet, poised for flight. When she saw that it was Billy, she relaxed into a slump, a hand resting on her hip.

"Happy birthday."

Billy grinned sheepishly. Both hands behind him, he made her guess which held her gift. Then, extending his hand, he refused to open his fist. Frustrated to the point of kicking him, she closed her eyes and held out her flattened palm. Something small and hard dropped into it. A beautifully carved gold ring greeted her when she opened her eyes. She was momentarily stunned by his gift.

"Where did you get this?"

"Never mind where. Do you like it?"

"Oh, yes, it's beautiful."

"See if it fits."

Pulling the band over her ring finger, she was disappointed by its size. By process of elimination, she found that it fit her index finger and left it there, moving it about in the sun to admire its design.

"C'mon," he said. "We're going for another ride."

After hurriedly packing biscuits and jerky, they ran down the path to the barn to saddle Aladdin. The Arabian whickered when he saw them approach, so excited they found him difficult to saddle. A slight breeze ruffled her hair, carrying with it the scent of drying grasses. What a wonderful birthday, she thought, admiring her ring. *I should have known he wouldn't forget.*

There was no need to hurry as they set out to the north, enjoying the warmth of the morning sun. Billy didn't say where they were going, but it didn't matter. They spotted a white-tailed deer on a ridge, his huge rack of antlers outlined against the sky. Billy raised his rifle to take aim but she leaned to restrain him.

"Please don't. He's too handsome to kill."

Sighing, he returned the rifle to its scabbard.

Riding leisurely, he pointed out areas of interest, while Andrea enjoyed the valley's array of colors. Just before noon, they reached a tree-lined rise where they dismounted to rest the horses and eat the food from their saddlebags. Before they finished, dust rose from the valley floor a few minutes ride beyond them.

Billy went rigid, shading his eyes as he stared at riders emerging from the cloud of dust. He quickly flattened himself on the ground.

"Must be Bob Devine," he whispered. "Get down so they won't see you."

Glancing furtively behind him, he seemed satisfied the horses were hobbled well below the brow of the hill, out of sight of the approaching riders. He recognized several local settlers riding slowly toward a larger group of cowhands. Passing on the trail, one of the homesteaders turned in the saddle with his handgun drawn. A wisp of smoke arose at the same instant they heard the shot. The report was followed by a barrage of gunfire echoing across the valley as men scurried for cover.

An eerie haze of dust spiraled upward and around the resultant battlefield. Sounds of gunfire ricocheted off canyon walls as though a giant string of firecrackers had been unleashed in a volcanic crater. When the firing at last subsided, they saw several men on foot, their horses dead or wounded. One of the local ranchers was prone, his head against a tree. Several men stood over him. Harsh words drifted up to them, but they were unable to catch their meanings.

"What shall we do?" she whispered.

Billy shook his head but didn't answer. Glancing again at the horses, he finally decided. "Let's get out of here."

They wasted no time riding back to the cabin. The Arabian took the lead, running ahead of the roan until she reined him in, allowing Billy to come alongside.

"We gotta warn the boys," he said. "Devine's men could ride down on the cabin any time."

* * * *

All the doubts he'd had about a lawless career had taken flight in his stomach. There were too many cowpokes and too few of the boys left to put up much of a fight. Glancing at Andy, he noticed her somber expression and wondered how he was going to protect her. Cursing Ketchum for insisting she come along, he realized the best he could do was to let her escape. Women were liabilities in an outlaw's life.

He remembered Matt Warner's pretty young wife, who had been left alone for months while he was off on some far-flung robbery. Dying of cancer, she'd given birth to a sickly son while Matt was imprisoned for murder. He also thought of Elzy Lay's wife Maude, who was seeking a divorce because he refused to settle down.

Although he often dreamed of Andy, he never considered dragging her along on the outlaw trail. He'd see that she got home as soon as the boys returned from Belle Fourche. He had repeatedly told her of his intent, but she continued to press him. Sidestepping the issue seemed his only defense until after the bank robbery. Butch said she could leave then, not before.

His resentment faded. There would be other jobs, and he wouldn't be passed over again if he carried out his duties to the letter. Butch had been hesitant to let him ride along, saying his honest streak was more than a yard wide. That, alone, made Billy more resolved to fit into Butch's mold. He'd never known a more generous, dedicated man. Real outlaws were bankers, cattlemen, and land speculators who pushed defenseless homesteaders off their land. When he thought of the unfair freight fees charged small ranchers by the railroads, he clenched his fists in anger.

Chapter Thirteen

Tom's head harbored a miniature battlefield. A cannon booming from his right temple was answered by rifle volleys from behind his red-veined eye. He raised his head from the pillow as a hob-nailed army marched across his skull.

Groaning, he thrashed about until he untangled himself from the sheets. He was alone in the feather bed. A faint scent of jasmine clung to the sheets, reminding him of the saloon girl. He'd already forgotten her name, his memory a victim of brown bottle fatigue.

Tom groped in the darkness for his trousers, finding them draped across a chair. He found a lucifer in his pocket and searched for an oil lamp. Then, rummaging in his jacket pockets, he withdrew a knife and several coins. His roll of bills from the sale of stolen horses had disappeared.

How would he buy whiskey for the boys to celebrate the bank robbery? Holding his throbbing head, he slipped his toes into an elaborately tooled boot, but there wasn't enough room for his heel. Lifting the boot to eye level, he blinked to clear his vision. Examining the dark leather shaft's design, he decided the boot was his. The boys often razzed Tom about the size of his feet. Horsemen were proud of their well-fitting boots which made their feet seem smaller. Only "Peep" O'Day and sod busters, they said, had underpinnings like mallard ducks.

Tugging the mule ears, he found his right boot slid on easily. When the left one again refused to take his foot, he threw it at the wall. Someone was playing tricks on him. Then, as drum sticks beat a thudding roll in his inner brain, he thought to look inside. Leaning forward to retrieve the boot, dizziness spoiled his balance and he found himself on the floor. Moaning, he rubbed his battle-weary head. As for the spy business, his career had come to an end. Tom knew he was in trouble with the gang. They would most likely use him for target practice when he returned to camp.

He retrieved the boot and turned it upside down, disappointed when nothing fell out. Reaching inside, he found a solid wad of paper stuffed into the toe. Pulling the roll free, he discovered his missing money. He counted nearly four hundred dollars. It didn't matter how the money got there, his luck had changed. Sighing with relief, Tom got to his feet, tugged on his shirt and wrestled with the buttons. When his gun belt was buckled in place, he reached for the doorknob, but the glass ball refused to turn. Wiping hands on his trousers, he tried again. The door creaked open and he peered into the darkened hallway.

Listening, he heard nothing. He took a tentative step, feeling his way to the stairs. Descending as quietly as his trembling legs would allow, he dropped several steps before sitting to clear his head. When he reached the last stair, he noticed an unfamiliar bartender swabbing the mahogany counter. Dim lantern light gleamed from the bar's surface as well as the barkeep's head. A lone customer was slumped over a mug of beer.

"We're closing," the bartender said when he noticed the bedraggled outlaw.

"I need a shot before I leave."

The slight, cross-eyed man swept the room with his good eye. "I guess it'll be all right if you make it quick."

Tom tossed down the whiskey and flipped the bartender an extra coin to show his appreciation. Once outside, he drew in deep night air, marveling at how quickly his headache disappeared. Glancing down the street, he saw a few celebrants howling their last hurrahs.

Lightning stood at a hitching rail across the street, head down in a dignified doze.

"Poor old feller," he said, stroking the gelding's forelock. Tom led the pinto to the nearest watering trough, where he allowed him to drink more than he knew he should. Tightening the cinch, he mounted and rode the dimly lighted street, catching the lingering scent of fried oysters. As he came abreast of the bank, its large plate glass window glared back at him, like a hometown boxing champ challenging an opponent.

"We're gonna knock you over come mornin'," he said beneath his breath. "I'll be rich with sacks of money and whiskey fillin' my saddlebags. Ain't that so, Lightnin'?" He patted the gelding's neck.

Tom dozed several times on the trail back to camp. He awoke to find the gelding nibbling bunch grass. To forestall another nap, he whistled a melodious Irish tune, one he'd learned as a boy. Pondering his family's reactions to his bank robbing role, he decided his pa would be proud of him. His ma, however, would beat him senseless with her rolling pin.

The bank job would earn him his own wanted posters. He imagined them plastered all over the country, his picture tacked to every tree. Everyone would know his name. Raising his chin, he posed for the photographer in his mind's eye. Handsome fellow that he was, he was sure women would be quick to steal the posters to moon over him. A warm, happy glow spread throughout his body.

"Not much further, old feller," he said, when he smelled the embers of a dying campfire. Glancing skyward, he saw the moon skimming treetop level, ready to sink below the horizon. Slowing the pinto to a walk, he whistled a night bird call, then waited for the signal to echo back. Harve Logan was sitting watch at the smoldering campfire, a Winchester draped across his knees.

"Where the helluv you been?" he growled, getting to his feet. "I was about to ride into town looking for you."

"I had a hard time findin' out about the bank," Tom wheezed.

"You been drinking?"

"Just a nip for the ride back. I was talkin' to a hotel bartender. I had to order somethin' so he wouldn't get suspicious."

"What did you find out?"

"The jail burned down and they're takin' the drunks over to Deadwood on the train."

Harve's facial expression was hidden in predawn darkness, but Tom knew he was mad. Positioning the pinto so that Lightning shielded him from Logan's rifle, he worked to loosen a cinch.

By now the others were stirring in their bedrolls. The Sundance Kid sat up and rolled a smoke. "Should have known better than to send a damn drunk into town."

Hurriedly rubbing down Lightning, Tom eased himself to the ground with his head against the saddle. Daylight came all too soon, bringing with it the welcome smells of coffee and frying bacon. Scanning camp with one eye, he noticed everyone moving about. All he wanted was sleep, but he managed to drag himself to the fire. The Sundance Kid ignored him, and Walt shot him a warning look to keep his mouth shut.

Tom quietly filled his tin plate and settled against a boulder. Sundance and Harve seemed over their anger when they gathered to discuss the robbery. Sundance drew a map of Belle Fourche with a sharpened stick and each man went over the job he had been assigned.

Tom's head spun like a child's top. A hammer repeatedly struck his cranium, sending blinding arcs of light across his field of vision.

Staggering to his feet, he felt Harve's narrowed eyes appraising him.

"One drink to satisfy the bartender, eh?"

"Didn't get much sleep last night. Damn rock under my ribs."

Sundance avoided him until it was time to break camp. As they lined up preparing for the trip into town, he gave each man instructions.

When it was Tom's turn, he said, "If you see anything out of the ordinary—extra lawmen, rifles on rooftops or sticking out of windows—ride out of town to warn us before we get there. And keep your damned nose out of the bottle!"

"You can count on me, boys." Tom managed a grin, although the ring of a hammer still reverberated through his skull.

When they were in sight of Belle Fourche, the others halted to wait as Tom rode into town alone. Surveying the street, he saw few people moving about. Although it was only half past nine, the heat beneath his black, wide-brimmed hat was broiling his scalp, forming tiny beads of sweat along his hairline. The more he mopped his face, the thirstier he became.

His mustache twitched nervously as he slowed Lightning to a walk down the middle of the dusty street. Swiveling his head, he glanced at each window and roof of the false-fronted buildings. Inhaling deeply, he caught the various smells of the general store, livery stable, and laundry. Towering over the town like an ever-vigilant sentry was the flour mill's grain elevator.

His attention was suddenly trapped by an open second-story window. A glimmer of light reflected from the sill. Catching his breath, he imagined a rifle trained on his chest. Tom fell over Lightning's neck, then kicked the pinto into a lope as two men rode abreast from a side street, directly into his path.

Tom reined Lightning to the railing along the boardwalk, narrowly avoiding a pileup. Shaken and swearing, he turned to stare into the eyes of a rough-looking farmer who yelled, "Watch where you're riding, you clumsy lout!"

Nudging the gelding away from the rail, he looked back to the window up the street where a young woman leaned over the sill. She was laughing at him, her silver bracelet glittering in the morning sun.

His first stop was Sebastian's Saloon, where he downed a quick shot and purchased a quart of whiskey. An extra half-pint was stuffed in his pocket for medicinal purposes. Resisting the urge for a second drink, he mounted Lightning to ride over to Giles Hardware Store across the street from the bank. Mr. Giles was waiting on a customer and took no more than fleeting notice of him.

Tom browsed for several moments, carefully keeping an eye on the bank through the large front window. The roaring in his head was getting louder, and he knew there was only one cure. Stepping casually through the front door of the hardware store, he looked both ways, noticing nothing more than a few early shoppers. It was a short ride back to Sebastian's. There he downed another shot of Old Crow and bought an extra quart of whiskey, which he stashed in his other saddlebag. The gaunt bartender of the previous afternoon looked at him curiously when he bought the second bottle.

"Still celebrating, I see."

Tom mumbled and left.

Pulse racing, he glanced about. No one appeared to be wearing guns. Squinting, he saw no rifles in windows or hanging from rooftops. He rode slowly back to the hardware store where he pretended to study the merchandise while keeping an eye on the bank. The proprietor moved to the area where Tom stood, asking if he could be of help.

"Just lookin' around," was Tom's reply, a bit gruffer than he intended. He was aware that Giles' interest in him was now more than fleeting.

The store's clock was about to strike ten when, according to plan, Sundance would ride leisurely into town, followed moments later by Harve Logan and Flat Nose George Currie. They would pass by Walt Punteney, who should be leaning against an upright wooden support in front of the Wide Awake Store.

Tom watched a minister enter the bank, followed shortly by three other men. From their clothing he assumed they were local businessmen. Chewing the ends of his heavy mustache, he moved closer to the window, craning his neck as he surveyed the street. Agonizing moments passed before the Sundance Kid's horse moved slowly along the dusty street, followed by Harve and Flat Nose.

Tom stepped onto the boardwalk as his partners tied up behind the *Belle Fourche Times* office. Hurriedly untying Lightning from the hitching rail, he led him across the street to ground-rein next to Harve's big bay. From there he watched the others stroll in through the bank's side door. Stationing himself out front, he scanned the street, gradually edging closer to the door. No one was near the bank, so he disregarded orders and quietly joined the customers patiently standing in line. He wasn't going to miss a thing.

Sundance had already drawn his gun and yelled: "Throw up your hands," when Harve made his move. "All the money under the counter," he said as he shoved a canvas bag at the burly cashier.

The customers immediately raised their hands when Flat Nose leveled his gun. "Make your deposits here," he said, whipping open his canvas bag with a free hand.

Only the merchant Tom met in the saloon complied. The others balked and were in danger of being pistol-whipped when the short, heavily-jowled bank clerk grabbed a pistol from beneath the counter. Pointing it at Harve, he pulled the trigger.

Tom watched in horror as the mechanism failed to fire. Harve cursed the cashier as he wrestled the gun away from him. Although fuzzy-brained, Tom knew Harve was mad enough to kill, but a shot would alert the town. Before they could convince the cashier to cooperate, the side door opened and Giles from hardware store stuck his head inside.

Flat Nose turned from the customers to demand that Giles raise his hands. The man ran instead for his store, yelling, "They're robbing the bank!"

Flat Nose chased him and fired into the hardware store's plate glass window. He missed Giles, but the shot prematurely signaled Walt, who began firing into the air from down the street as though a left-over Civil War celebrant.

"Get the hell out a here," Harve yelled as he rushed through the side door.

Tom still stood in line with the customers, slow to comprehend what had taken place. As his comrades rushed past, he saw the cashier rush to the back of the bank. The customers, their hands still in the air, glanced at one another as Tom belatedly backed out the door, his gun still holstered. Once outside, he fired in both directions, breaking a window at Arthur Gay's store, sending glass shards raining on the customers.

His companions mounted and swung away from the rail as Tom's ground-reined pinto, spooked by the gunfire, followed the escaping outlaws.

"Lightnin'," he yelled, but gunshots drowned out both his voice and whistle. He could not believe his trusted mount had deserted him. Glancing about, he was surprised that no one had tried to arrest him, although the town marshal arrived in time to fire at the fleeing outlaws.

"Don't shoot, they have my hoss," Tom yelled.

Firing stopped. Moments later a rifle report echoed from the flour mill grain elevator.

Glancing up, he noticed a man leaning over the rail, readying for another shot. A horse staggered and fell in the street. Rolling free, the rider shook his fist at the rifleman.

"Damn you, Frank! I was chasing the outlaws."

Raising a hand to shade his gritty eyes, Tom squinted at the rest of the gang who had stopped at a watering trough to look back for him. When Lightning limped up to them with a bullet in his leg, the gang raced off over Sundance Hill.

From the corner of his eye, Tom watched the hefty bank cashier run from the bank. Pointing another pistol, he took aim and fired in the direction the outlaws had fled, although they were already out of sight. Tom glanced about for another horse and spotted a large white mule tied to a hitching rail. Townspeople, who had erupted from doorways, laughed when the tall, unkempt cowpoke climbed on the animal's back. Kicking his ribs repeatedly, he yelled, "I'll git them bank robbers."

The mule refused to move until Tom loudly slandered his ancestors. He then lumbered off in the wrong direction. Tom had already resigned himself to walking when an angry tenor voice yelled: "Get off my mule!" Dismounting, Tom looked around for another mount. He spied a pleasant-looking fellow standing nearby and approached him by asking, "Where can I buy a hoss?"

The man merely shrugged.

Surprised no one had recognized him from the bank robbery, Tom decided to lose himself in the crowd, but first, he would have to make himself inconspicuous by getting rid of his gun. Only the marshal had been wearing one until the shooting started, and Tom marveled at how quickly townspeople armed themselves when the first shot was fired. Lengthening his stride, he headed for a vacant lot between the saloon and newspaper office where a public outhouse stood. Once inside, he hastily unbuckled his cartridge belt.

Selecting one of two holes, he dropped in the belt, holster, and nickel-plated revolver. When the door banged behind him, he decided to stop at Sebastian's for a last quick drink. He had gone only a few steps when a deep voice ordered him to raise his hands.

"You've got the wrong man," Tom said quietly, obediently raising his arms. A shorter man stood before him, his gun pointed at Tom's chest. A blood-stained canvas apron hung from his waist.

A butcher! Tom shook his head in disbelief. Captured by a meat grinder. He would never live this down. Still protesting his innocence, he was staring over the heads of a rapidly growing crowd when he felt someone pat him down. A squint-eyed, wizened little man, no taller than Tom's breast bone, pulled the forgotten whiskey from his pocket. Another man, thicker in the chest but equally short in stature, gleefully lifted Tom's wad of bills, along with several rifle cartridges.

"I-I came for the reunion celebration," Tom drawled. "My old man was a Civil War veteran. He had his hoss shot out from under him—"

"Shut your mouth and stand still," the butcher said.

Tom saw a familiar face in the crowd. The dark-haired man he had asked about a horse was staring at him. Squinting, as though trying to get a better look, he said, "Yeah, I've seen that jasper before. A few minutes ago he was wearing a six-gun."

The butcher handed the man his pistol, grunting with satisfaction. He then asked several bystanders to assist him in turning over the outhouse. Tom cringed and closed his eyes, the buzzing noise growing louder. Repelled, he turned to watch as four men pushed heavily on one side, tipping over the wooden shed. With a rake from Gile's Hardware, they fished out Tom's gun belt.

Lowering his eyes, he groaned.

"You're goin' to jail." the butcher said, a sneer distorting his craggy face, "If you're lucky, the citizens of Belle Fourche won't string you up before the circuit judge gets here."

"Go ahead and hang me, boys," Tom said with his last ounce of bravado. "You'll never see a gamer man die."

Chapter Fourteen

Dick Hale was working a bay in the corral when they thundered down the slope. Before his roan halted short of the pole fence, Billy was shouting.

"C-calm down," the wiry outlaw said.

Drawing a ragged breath, he told Hale about the gun battle.

"There ain't m-much we c-can do." Hale raised his hands in resignation. "If the rest of the g-gang hadn't rode off with B-Butch…"

Billy dismounted. "The cowpunchers are liable to head this way," he said. "I figured you and me and McCloud could hold 'em off from those rocks up the canyon."

"We c-could prob'ly do that," Hale said, nodding. "I'll f-fetch Driftwood Jim."

When Hale left, Billy took Andrea aside. "Hide along the creek," he said. "The cowpokes might make it through to the cabin. If we don't come back, tell Bob Devine you were kidnapped."

His gaze shifted to the toes of his boots. "I know you can ride out of here, Andy. But they might shoot you, thinking you're one of the gang."

His troubled face frightened her. She hated being left behind and briefly considered following him. Gripping her shoulders, he looked at her with concern in his eyes. "How would I explain to Butch if one of them shot you?"

"So that's it. You only care about Butch."

"That's not so." His hands fell to his sides. "I'm just trying to protect you, Andy."

"By leaving me here alone?"

"I thought you wanted to leave."

"Not without you."

"I can't go yet."

Before she could protest, Hale and McCloud arrived leading their horses.

"Stay out of sight until we're back," Billy said in parting.

Anxiously biting her lip, she watched them disappear over the rise, aware of another emotion rippling to the surface. Smiling, she realized that he cared.

Andrea removed her boots and waded across the creek to climb as high in the cottonwood as the slender limbs would bear her weight. Moving branches aside, she could see nothing beyond the cabin or the barn.

The air was restless and laden with dry, heavy scents of summer. Listening, the only sounds to reach her were those of chattering birds and barking prairie dogs. Conversations were muffled by the gurglings of Buffalo Creek. As she watched, a gray squirrel dashed into a hole in the trunk, where roots lay exposed near the water. She waited for him to reappear, but decided he was napping.

A warm wind rustled leaves as it rippled across the creek, making her drowsy. Climbing down to a large fork in the tree, she leaned back, allowing the sun's heat to bake anxiety from her brain. Eyes closed, she drifted into a daydream so pleasant that she hugged herself. Faint popping sounds roused her momentarily, but she settled back in the fork as the afternoon sun banked in a gentle arc and slid toward the western red wall. As she dozed, a snug log cabin appeared in the foothills, shimmering in the bright sun. Green velvet grasses rippled in the breeze where a small band of horses grazed. Several children romped in the dooryard, laughing children with golden hair and hazel eyes. The image dissolved with the sound of hoof beats.

Andrea scrambled into higher branches and craned her neck to peer toward the rise. Cautiously parting leaves, she saw horses milling about, none of them familiar. Climbing down several branches, she crouched, holding her breath as she clutched a limb for support.

A gruff voice sullied the stillness. "Look in the barn," he barked, "while we go through the cabin."

Andrea tensed, afraid to move. Maybe she should climb down and ask for Bob Devine, the CY ranch foreman. He would see that she got home. But thoughts of Billy stopped her. As she perched, undecided, she heard the Arabian's shrill whinny. *They're stealing Aladdin.*

Andrea uncoiled and had begun to climb down when she glimpsed someone leading her horse from the barn—a huge man with dark shaggy hair. She froze, her bare feet dangling from the fork. The cowpoke so resembled Scar Ketchum that she was terrified to move. Behind him a smaller, disheveled man was leading the big bay stallion. Two others led the chestnut gelding and Uncle Jim Bob's quarter horse.

"There's a couple more in the corral," she heard the lead man yell.

Drawing up her feet, she sat immobile, unable to decide. She couldn't save the horses, nor could she prevent the men from ransacking the cabin. Her only option was to turn herself in to the strangers who frightened her. Trembling, her eyes squeezed tight, she quickly reopened them when Ketchum's image returned, along with the painful prick of his knife. Gripping the limb hard enough to numb her hands, Andrea stifled a sob. She couldn't let them see her. If she told them she was not what she seemed, they would probe to make sure. Then the terrible thing she'd feared all along would happen, perhaps many times over. Pressing her forehead against the trunk, she made herself as small as possible.

Before long she heard them ride away, shouting and whooping, as though an Indian war party. She lingered, afraid they might return, but the longer she waited, the more she worried about Billy. Had he been killed or taken prisoner?

She waited long after they were gone to slip from the tree and wade across the creek. Stopping briefly on the opposite bank, she listened, hearing ordinary sounds. Andrea hesitantly climbed the slope to the cabin, but was afraid to go inside. Peering through the open door, she saw the overturned table and broken utensils littering the floor. She skirted the outer wall and stood on the threshold to the back room, where she noticed several spent matches smoldering on her bunk. Struggling, she dragged the mattress out of doors and ran to the water barrel. She found a tin can that she repeatedly filled with water to douse the fire. Then, sitting cross-legged on the ground, she wept.

The warm breeze accelerated to the point of moaning, forming small whirlwinds and whipping cottonwoods until they trembled. When she recognized it was the *banshee* wind, she looked about expectantly for the Irish fairy woman crouched beneath the cabin window. *Bean sidhe* was warning her of another loved one's death.

"Billy," she cried. The cowhands had killed him, or he had done the killing and run away. Cradling her head, she berated herself for being stupid. She should have ridden Aladdin from the Hole when she had the chance, or told the strangers she was a kidnapped young boy instead of remaining in the tree like a frightened squirrel.

Billy should have stayed, she thought resentfully. Fresh tears spilled, drying instantly in the gusting wind. Glancing skyward, she remembered hawks flying over the valley, and wished for wings to escape on the wind.

At twilight Andrea forced herself to return to the cabin. Groping, she found a lantern with a broken chimney. In the dim light, she glimpsed the stove pipe that had been wrenched from the ceiling, and the old wood stove that was turned on its side. Running her hand along a shelf near the stove, she unearthed the shaved candle used to decorate Billy's cake. Remembering it was her own eighteenth birthday, she felt her throat constrict.

The corner shelf held an overlooked match which she struck to light the candle. The room appeared even more devastated bathed in candlelight. The cattlemen had destroyed her home. Andrea had never considered the cabin home until now, but realized how much she cared for the men who peopled the Hole in the Wall canyon—at least some of them.

Righting one of the benches, she wedged the candle into a small knothole. She then tried clearing debris. While gathering broken glass, she pricked the palm of her hand. Before she could remove the sliver, she heard the sound of horses descending the slope. Hurrying into the other room, she slipped from the side door and ran toward the creek.

"Andy!" The voice was McCloud's.

Heart thumping, she returned to the cabin in time to glimpse his surprise. McCloud hesitantly backed through the doorway. Jutting on either side of his body were a familiar pair of legs, the booted feet dangling.

"Billy's hurt," he said.

She noticed Hale supporting the rest of Billy's body.

"Looks like them cowpokes wrecked this place," McCloud said frowning. "Clear a spot on the floor, will you, Andy, and lay a blanket down."

She did as she was told. Locating the horsehair broom Hale brought back from Buffalo in his rifle scabbard, she hastily swept the area clean.

"They took all the blankets," she said tearfully.

Hale told her to untie the bedroll from his saddle. When they laid Billy down, she could see that he was wounded. His shirt was soaked with blood, and he was apparently unconscious.

"Who shot him?"

"He tried to keep them yahoos from coming this way." McCloud wearily removed his hat. "I told him there was too many of 'em, but he was afraid you'd get hurt. He crawled up on a ridge to get a better look. That's when he took a bullet in the shoulder."

"But how...?"

"We hid him in the rocks and tried to stop the bleeding. They musta been in a hurry to get to the cabin 'cause they didn't take on the rest of us."

"Billy needs a doctor," she said, biting her lip until it bled.

"He said to bring him here. Said you could fix him up. We had to wait 'til that bunch of cowpokes left."

"I've never treated a bullet wound."

"Billy said you could. 'Sides, you're the only doc we got. By the time we kidnapped one from Buffalo, Billy would prob'ly bleed to death."

Andrea shuddered. She hadn't considered that possibility.

"We'll help. Just tell us what you need."

Andrea frantically looked about. "I need to boil some dandelion roots, but the cowhands wrecked the stove."

"I'll b-build a campfire." Hale started for the door.

"Help me get him out of his shirt," she said. The bloody garment was already unbuttoned and pulled from his trousers. McCloud finished cutting the shirt away from Billy's shoulder. His body was sweltering. She had to find a way to lower his fever.

"Bullet went clean through, so there's a hole on both sides." McCloud carefully positioned Billy so the larger exit wound was visible.

"We need more light." Leaning close, she cringed at his loss of blood.

"There's a lantern in the barn. I'll get it while you make him some medicine."

A handkerchief covered the chest wound. It was saturated and dripping. She had to stop the bleeding. "Billy, if you can hear me, I'll do whatever I can to heal your wound. Please don't die," she said, unable to hold back her tears.

Andrea clenched her fists. *Get hold of yourself. Think! Remember the verse from Ezekiel to stop the flow of blood.* She had witnessed her grandmother's gift of healing, knowing that it worked for those who believed. She had to try. While she prayed, the words came back:

And when I passed by thee, and saw thee polluted in thine own blood, I said unto thee when thou wast in thy blood, Live. Yea, I said unto thee when thou wast in thy blood, live.

She repeated the verse several times before Hale appeared in the doorway, pretending to ignore her tears. "N-need anythin' else, Andy?"

"Some clean towels."

"I'll s-see what I c-can find."

Andrea found her bag of herbs in a corner where the raiders had flung it aside. After blood clots had been cleaned from Billy's wound and dandelion roots boiled long enough to suit her, she dipped a piece of toweling into the potent dandelion tea.

McCloud retrieved both pieces of toweling from the water with his knife. When they cooled sufficiently to serve as compresses, Andrea placed them over the wounds. She then set the dandelion tea aside and boiled a pot of water for the dried burdock. She recalled her grandmother's instructions: "One level palm full of dried herbs to each pint of water. Boil half an hour, then simmer another thirty minutes."

While the burdock boiled, she wore a path between the campfire and her patient. Billy had not regained consciousness, and Hale positioned himself to prevent further injury when he revived. When the burdock decoction had boiled half an hour, Andrea could wait no longer. Preparing an herbal paste, she spread the mixture on pieces of boiled towels. When they cooled, she applied them to the wounds. For the remainder of the night, she sat beside him on the floor, her hand resting on his arm. She alternately prayed and dozed.

Sometime between midnight and dawn, she dreamed of her grandparents. Their faces were in shadows, and she strained to bring them into focus. Gramma frowned while delivering a lecture Andrea was unable to hear. Before her image faded, Buford Wilson glared at her from his sick bed. She tried to explain to him why she had not escaped, but he refused to listen.

"Grandpa!" she cried, waking herself from the dream.

The lantern still lighted Billy's face. He appeared to be sleeping peacefully, but she was seized with fear she would wake to find him dead. Placing two fingers on his throat, she found his pulse steady but weak. She placed her palm on his forehead, uncertain whether his temperature had fallen. It was still much warmer than her own.

At daybreak, Hale and McCloud returned to check on her patient. Both faces were puffy and drawn from a restless night. When she told them his condition had not changed, Hale said, "I'm gonna m-make sure all t-them raiders left the hole. And if you n-need anythin', I'll g-git it from one of the homesteaders."

Andrea shook her head to clear the fuzziness. "More towels," she said. "And onions and honey. I need garlic to cure him of infection."

Hale and McCloud exchanged quizzical glances as though her list was a bit peculiar.

"Please hurry," she said, rubbing her eyes. "Onion and honey broth will keep him quiet when he comes around."

Yawning, she recalled Jake Edwards and regretted not treating him with garlic. She consoled herself with the thought that nothing she could have done would have saved him.

"You better sleep while you can," McCloud said, when Hale left the cabin. "I stuffed some hay in that mattress they tried to burn. Why don't you rest while I keep an eye on Billy."

Nodding gratefully, she insisted her patient needed the mattress more.

McCloud dragged it in, and she helped lift Billy onto it. She covered him with both men's blankets.

"Don't see how it makes a difference when he's knocked out," McCloud said. "But if it makes the doc feel better..."

"It does," she said, smiling. She was tempted to kiss his stubbled cheek in gratitude, but remembered boys didn't do that sort of thing. Instead, she extended her hand. "Thank you, Mister McCloud."

"Don't be so damned formal. Call me Driftwood Jim."

"Yes, sir ... Driftwood."

"That's better, now get some sleep. We don't need no grouchy kids around here. Grumpy, gall durned doctors are even worse."

Andrea obediently curled around Billy and slept. When she awoke the sun was overhead. McCloud was seated on one of the benches, smoking.

"He's shivering," the convict said. "Reckon he's gonna be all right?"

Touching Billy's jugular vein she said, "His pulse is much stronger."

McCloud's face mirrored his relief. For a moment, she thought he was actually going to smile.

"Anything else I can do?"

"Gather some sagebrush leaves. Gramma says sage tea will cure the chills."

"Always wondered what the durn stuff was good for."

After McCloud rode off to find Hale, she carried a handful of sagebrush to the campfire. As soon as water boiled, she poured it over the small gray leaves and allowed them to steep. Later, while crooning and stroking Billy's hair, she noticed his eyelids flicker open.

"Andy?" He tried but was too weak to lift his head.

"How do you feel?"

"Like I was dragged through a knot hole."

"Take this." She supported his head so he could drink from the cup. He gagged but managed to keep it down.

"Sagebrush tea," she said when he glared at her. "I'll sweeten it with honey when Hale gets back."

Andrea was filling him in on what had happened since the shooting, when she heard the sound of horses approaching. She panicked, afraid the raiders had returned. Rushing to the door she looked up slope toward the rise. To her relief, she recognized the riders.

Hale dismounted and rushed in, trailed by McCloud, seemingly out of breath. His words were unintelligible.

"They killed Al Smith," McCloud shouted over Hale's stuttering.

"Who killed him?" Billy's voice was weak.

"Devine or some brand inspector named Joe LeFors. Nobody knows for sure, but word's out that LeFors shot him in the back. He wouldn't let nobody give Smith a drink of water while he was layin' there dyin'."

"Smith's a rancher. Why'd they kill *him*?"

"Said he was on the rustle."

Billy groaned.

"Devine's hoss was killed. Him and his son Lee and some of the cowpokes was wounded." McCloud rubbed his forehead. "And that's not all. When Hale was over to Bob Taylor's Ranch this morning, he heard that Cousin Tom got himself arrested in Belle Fourche."

Andrea's hands flew to her face. "Oh, no. Poor Tom. What about the others?"

"Seems they got away. But there's posses out everywhere looking for 'em."

A muscle twitched in McCloud's left check. "The worst thing that's happened is the governors are deputizing everybody to shoot us all on sight. It's turning into a regular war. Most of the boys from Montana and Wyoming are getting up a meeting. They'll be heading south to Brown's Hole—a whole army of 'em."

Billy glanced at Andrea. Shrugging, she hoped the gunshot would had have convinced him to quit the gang, but he seemed bent on rectifying the situation, somehow.

"We'd better get the hell out a here," McCloud concluded. "Ride south to Brown's Hole or Robbers Roost as soon as you're able. It's not safe here no more."

"What about Butch and Sundance and Harve?"

"Hell, Billy, them boys don't w-worry about us none," Hale said, squatting beside the mattress. "If we're g-gone when t-they git here—*if* they ever git here—they'll k-know where we went." Hale indicated a small knothole in the back wall, little more than an inch from the ceiling. "'Sides, we can leave 'em a n-note up yonder."

"Let's sleep on it." Billy's voice was fading. "There's time to decide tomorrow."

"You're r-right. I'm tired, too. S-so's my thinker."

Later, when Hale and McCloud had gone to the barn, Andrea changed Billy's poultices before brewing him a calming broth of onion and honey. McCloud's news had upset him, and he needed to relax. They had already been forced to restrain him.

"I'll tie you down if you don't lie still," she threatened. "You won't be able to ride for several weeks."

"I can't just lay here while the Hole's overrun," he said. "They'll finish me off if they find me."

"They're not coming back," she said, crossing her fingers. "Hale and McCloud are taking turns standing guard up the trail. If they see anything, we'll move you down along the creek."

"I can't stand being helpless, and I hate for you to see me like this."

She smiled and patted his face. "I don't mind. It gives me a chance to practice medicine. My patient is doing just fine."

"I don't feel fine."

"You will. Now behave yourself or I'll pour more garlic into you … without the honey."

By the middle of the third day Billy's fever was down, but she continued his medication. Hale brought food back from one of the neighboring ranches, and Andrea heated chicken stock swimming with onion and garlic. Although Billy had been quiet and uncommunicative before the shooting, he now talked incessantly. He seemed itching for an argument, and Andrea grew weary of his demands.

"Do you still want to be an outlaw?" she asked, her patience worn thin.

When he didn't answer, she said, "I've been thinking about us robbing banks and mail trains." Her voice trailed off as she gathered courage. "We could be king and queen of the outlaws."

"You don't mean that." His hazel eyes bored into hers. "I thought you wanted to go home to your grandparents."

"We're both adults now," she said, sitting beside him. "We can do whatever we please."

"You're not the sort of woman to rob a bank." Shaking his head, he said, "You're doing this for me, aren't you? You think that's what *I* want?"

Nodding, she whispered, "I promised myself I'd stay if you lived."

Eyes closed, he attempted a laugh. "I've been thinking about a horse ranch in the foothills."

"And?"

He said nothing more for several moments, then, "The boys are depending on me to take care of things while they're gone."

"Hale and McCloud can manage."

"They're depending on *me*. I gave my word."

"What if they're arrested and never come back? How long will you wait for them, Billy?"

Chapter Fifteen

Rumblings of a good-sized crowd penetrated the small window, increasing in volume with each heartbeat. Crazed insects ravaged Tom's brain. Sweat drenched his dusty clothing and his stomach ached with emptiness. If only he had a drink.

He'd spent the night in a scorched steel cage, the remains of the burned city jail surrounding him. A crowd of townspeople had grown steadily, openly taunting him with hangmen's ropes and a variety of weapons. When the marshal realized they were becoming dangerous, Tom was transferred to his office.

The door swung wide, admitting a short, swarthy deputy wearing a worried frown. Helping Tom from his chair, he led him down the hall.

"The crowd's getting nasty," he said, adjusting his gun belt. "We'll take you to Deadwood on the train before those yahoos work themselves into a lynching."

"But I'm innocent."

"Don't matter none. You're gonna get your bucket kicked if we don't get you out a here." They rounded a corner and walked into an anteroom where several men stood, deep in conversation.

"The freight train for Deadwood will be along in twenty minutes," a balding man said, glancing up. "We'd better get him over there with as many men as we can deputize."

Nodding, the slightly-built lawman checked Tom's handcuffs and nudged him into a chair. "Sounds like a good idea."

"I'm hungry," the prisoner whined, staring gloomily at the polished floor.

"You'll have to wait 'til Deadwood," the deputy said as he prepared to leave the room. "If that crowd gets a hold of you, you won't never need another meal."

Tom listened while the men discussed the safest route to the train. Compressing his neck, he cringed at the thought of an angry mob stringing him up on the nearest pole, as Rawlins citizens had done with

"Big Nose" George Parrott. Tom knew the local doctor had ordered a pair of shoes made from Parrott's hide. He imagined a saddle could be made from his own.

Within minutes the deputy returned with reinforcements. Pulling Tom to his feet, he said, "We're gonna walk you to the depot. If you hear me yell 'Run,' you better move them legs as fast as they'll go."

Tom glanced down at the grim-faced deputy and swayed on his feet. Noise from the street sounded like a dog fight. He could hear the words: "Lynch him!" echoing like a chant. He balked when the others started forward, digging in his heels as the men behind him began to shove.

"If we don't get you on the next train, they're reliable to rush the building. The townspeople are fighting mad about the bank robbery."

Tom lowered his gaze to the boot heels ahead of him. The door opened and the crowd confronted him like vicious dogs. Stepping up their pace, the small knot of deputies propelled him, head and shoulders above the rest, down the street to the depot.

"Hang him!" someone yelled nearby. A rock sailed past Tom's head, narrowly missing his nose.

The deputy in charge yelled, "Run," his grip like a vice on Tom's arm. Hands still cuffed behind him, Tom quickened his pace, stumbling and nearly falling into those ahead. As they approached the depot, he saw the waiting train with steam billowing over the freight cars; the smell of burning cinders aggravating his senses in the mid-day sun.

Standing beside the train was a stout, older man, his eyes shadowed under his cap. Motioning them toward an empty box car, he stepped aside as deputies helped Tom aboard. Just as quickly the trainman signaled the engineer. Rocks, thrown by the angry crowd, bounced off the train as it jerked forward, its whistle shrieking.

They led Tom to the end of the car and seated him with his back against the wall.

"I know it ain't no fun with your hands cuffed behind you," the deputy said, "but we can't take a chance you'll make a break."

The twenty-two mile trip to Deadwood was miserably long. Trees sailing past the open door and the swaying motion of the freight car riled his empty stomach, which threatened to erupt at any moment.

"Ninety-seven dollars was all they got," one of the deputies said, laughing. "That was Sam Arnold's deposit from the Wide Awake Store."

"I heard it was only fifty. Clumsy damned bunch of bank robbers, if you ask me. It was probably a first attempt."

"Yeah. Good thing nobody got shot."

"You're forgetting Joe Miller's horse. Frank Bennett shot him from the grain elevator, thinking he was one of the outlaws." Deputies roared as Tom slid further onto his spine, attempting to distance himself from the discussion.

Few people waited on the platform when the train pulled into Deadwood, much to Tom's relief. As they boarded a wagon for the trip to jail, deputies bragged it was the most inescapable lock-up in the country.

Tom's small cell made him feel like a caged animal. Rising from the steel floor and running horizontally from reinforced corner posts, were bars as thick as his thumbs, forming three-inch steel squares. It would take a month of Mondays to saw through one of them.

He remained in his cell, lying on his back most of the day, tracing unfamiliar trails in the ceiling. Throat dry, his head felt squeezed to half its size. When he sat, his hands and legs twitched like a nervous filly.

Days passed quietly, except for an occasional drunk who insisted on tormenting his cell mates with off-key singing, or a belligerent sot who complained at the top of his lungs. Tom had been arraigned on the charge of bank robbery, and was awaiting trial. That night when the deputy shoved a supper tray into his cell, he said, "I hear they shot the horses out from under your friends."

"That was one of the townspeople," Tom said, scoffing at the report.

"It happened later. Posse members have the saddles."

Tom erupted from his self-imposed stupor, sitting alert for the first time since his capture. "Where'd you hear that?"

"Sheriff Fuller organized a posse and chased them down." A smirk altered his weasel features. "Seems the bank cashier and some of the town's leading citizens took off after them."

Tom was suddenly apprehensive. "Did they catch 'em?"

"Not yet, but you can bet your boots they will. The sheriff notified neighboring states, including Montana. So posses are out looking for them."

Tom sank into his narrow bunk. He dismissed the deputy by rolling onto his side, thinking: *We shoulda cut the telegraph wires.*

* * * *

His wound was healing without infection, and she knew his bouts of grouchiness were a positive sign. Used to his attempts at drawing her into arguments, she took some pleasure in baiting him, as long as his temper held.

"How long are you planning to stay?" she asked a week after the shooting.

"As long as I'm needed."

"If you take me home, my grandparents will help you file a homestead of your own."

"I hate to say this, Andy, but your grandpa was pretty sick when we left. And Ketchum likely broke your grandma's neck."

Andrea knew he was right. She had come to the same conclusion on her own. "Then I have no one," she said, her throat constricting.

"You must have other relatives."

"Uncle Jim Bob's probably dead, too, and my father's family lives in France."

He sighed. "I can't keep fending for you, Andy."

"I thought you cared about me." Tears filled her eyes.

"I-I do, but..."

"Is it because I'm ugly?" She pulled at her cropped, unruly hair.

"Hardly. I'm afraid somebody will find out and claim you for his woman."

"Is it because of Ketchum?"

"No." He handed her his kerchief. "That wasn't your fault."

"What then?"

"I'm a wanted man."

"You're not." Smiling at him through her tears, she said, "You've never stolen anything."

"Guilt by association, Andy. I'm a member of the gang."

"You can change your name and shave your head like Driftwood Jim," she said grimacing.

"I'd always be afraid strangers were coming on my land to arrest me."

"But how would they know?"

"Soon as I'm able, I'll find a way to take you home."

Andrea sat while he dozed, staring at chinked log walls, wondering how she could get through to him. Her heart swelled when she considered his loyalty, but his stubbornness formed a hard knot in her throat. At last so weary she was nodding off, she blew out the lantern and covered herself with the quilts Hale bought from local ranchers. Billy's frown swam before her eyes as she sank into a troubled sleep.

* * * *

Rough, unkempt men were turning up in the Hole in increasing numbers, alone and in small groups. Their common objective was to flee the four-state governors' pact to exterminate outlaws. Some discussed leaving the states for Alaska or South America. Others were in favor of forming a lawless army to rid the country of cattle barons and crooked politicians.

Andrea awoke one morning with a foul-smelling man standing over here.

When she gasped, he said, "What's a purty little thing like you doing here?"

Cowering, she tried pulling the blanket over her head, but he jerked it from her reach. Knees pulled tight to her chest, she wrapped her arms around her overalled calves, cringing when a filthy hand touched her head.

"How come you ruint your hair?" He pulled her thick cropped mane as though measuring its length.

A wide shadow fell across her pallet as someone entered the room.

"Leroy! What are you doing to that kid?"

"This ain't no kid."

Andrea yelled in the deepest voice she could muster. "Get your hands off me, you lousy varmint!"

Surprised, the man drew back, allowing her to roll from the quilts. Scrambling past the wide, scruffy man standing near the door, she ran screaming down the path to Buffalo Creek. Collapsing on the bank, she trembled uncontrollably. Hale found her soon after hiding in the cottonwood.

"W-We run them hombres off, Andy. S-sorry they scairt you so b-bad."

"What were they doing here?"

"Lookin' fer a p-place to stay."

"Don't they know this is Wild Bunch headquarters?"

"Yeah, b-but most of 'em wanta join up. I told 'em me and McCloud are j-just caretakers. We ain't even official g-gang members."

Andrea hurried back to find Billy. While climbing the slope, she thanked God she had an ear for outlaw vernacular and the sense to sleep in her overalls. Fading into the background when strangers arrived, she wore a discarded felt hat to hide her hair, and rouged her face with soot to disguise her features.

Since mending the cabin's furniture and righting the old wood stove, Hale and McCloud spent their time playing cards and spinning well-told tales. As days passed, rustlers and horse thieves continued to filter through the valley. Hale identified several as highwaymen. She knew Billy disapproved of them, insisting killing was wrong, although robbing banks and trains was just getting even with the corporate thieves.

Billy was convinced Butch Cassidy was a Western Robin Hood, and made him sound philanthropic. During one of his more talkative moments, he told her of the rancher's widow Butch had saved from dispossession.

"Butch gave her five hundred dollars to pay off the mortgage. Then he held up the scoundrel banker after he left the ranch."

Andrea had heard the same story told of the James gang, but didn't contradict him. Butch was his idol, and Billy was convinced the outlaw was well-intentioned. He did admit, however, that the others made him doubt the dubious call of lawlessness.

A week after he had been shot, Billy was able to walk a few steps to a chair.

The night he had enough strength to dine with them at the table, Hale and McCloud announced they were planning to attend a shooting match at a sheep ranch east of the Hole. They would spend their prize winnings in Buffalo, while gathering the latest news.

"Them sheepherders got a lotta nerve challenging us to a shooting match," McCloud said, pulling the makings for a roll-your-own from his leather vest pocket. "Everybody knows they can't hit a barn at five paces."

"I heard they've been practicing," Billy said. "Can't blame 'em after all the raids the boys have pulled on 'em. And don't forget the cattlemen."

"I guess you're right," McCloud said, thoughtfully. "I'd probably do some sharp shooting, myself, if I was being picked on."

"What's the grand prize?" Andrea asked while clearing the table.

"Just money we're all putting up. Depends on how many's shooting." She wished them luck.

"Too bad you can't come along," McCloud said to Billy as the men were preparing to leave. "Andy says you ain't been out of the Hole since you got here. Sure you don't mind us leaving for a few days?"

Billy shifted his weight on the bench, grimacing with shoulder pain. "Why don't you bring back some supplies from Buffalo," he said. "Andy will write a list."

As soon as they left he seemed to withdraw, as though brooding. Next morning when she brought his breakfast, she decided she had waited long enough.

"When are we leaving, Billy?"

He continued to chew his food.

"Why won't you answer me?"

He stared at her a long moment before answering. "I haven't decided. I need more time."

"You have another week. By then you can travel. If you're still undecided, I'll walk away from here alone."

A small laugh escaped his lips. "You can't do that."

"I'll find my way to a ranch where someone will help me."

"But Andy..."

"My name is Andrea. Or have you forgotten?"

"Of course not, *Andrea*." He banged his cup on the table to emphasize her name. "What you seem to forget is that *I'm* in charge here now. You won't leave until I say so."

Rising slowly from the table, he shuffled to the door. Taking a few tentative steps into the yard, he stopped to gaze intently to the north.

"There's a cloud of dust coming from the direction of the herd," he yelled. "I'm not leaving you alone this time."

Rushing to the door, she eyed him with disbelief. "I thought you were too weak to ride."

"I'll manage."

She saddled Pepper and led him to the cabin. When she tried to help Billy mount the roan, he brushed her hand aside and swung into the saddle on his own. Once seated behind the cantle, she saw that he had strapped on his gun.

"Do you think you'll need that?" she asked, patting the holster.

Without a word, Billy nudged the gelding forward, but winced when the gelding gained his stride. Following the same route they had taken on their previous ride, they dismounted below the brow of a hill. Andrea climbed the rise where they had witnessed the gun battle. Misty clouds of dust swirled skyward as cowhands whistled and prodded the remaining cattle from the Hole. She counted nearly thirty men, including a man whose badge reflected the morning sun. Hurriedly retracing her steps, she told Billy what she had seen. When she mentioned the badge, he decided.

"Let's go."

"You mean we're leaving?"

"I'm not shooting it out with another bunch of cowpokes," he said over his shoulder. "We'll load supplies and leave the Hole."

Her heart sank when they started down the slope to the cabin. A familiar horse was in the corral and Flat Nose George greeted them with a scowl.

"Where is ever'body?"

"They made dust for Buffalo," Billy said, slowly dismounting. "Some cowpunchers are running off the herd." He nodded to the north.

"Let the settlers fight 'em. We got more important matters."

"Such as?"

"Bank job in Red Lodge, Montana. The boys are there now gettin' ready. We'll meet 'em in Lost Cabin in a few days. Then we'll all leave for Brown's Hole."

"But I've got to take Andy home."

"Load all the gear on as many hosses as you can herd," George said, as though Billy hadn't spoken. "Be ready to leave when the boys come through here after the bank robbery."

After they told him of Bob Devine's raid, and that no horses remained, Flat Nose described the Belle Fourche bank robbery. A posse's lucky shot had brought down the Sundance Kid's prized Appaloosa. The outlaw managed to escape when he climbed on double with Harve. The next day, Harve's horse was shot as he jumped a barbed wire fence.

When asked of Butch's whereabouts, Flat Nose told of Butch's recent trip into Dixon and Baggs, small neighboring towns on the southern Wyoming border.

"I hear the boys shot up Baggs real good. Then they rode over to Dixon to fill it fulla lead. Some party." George's eyes gleamed as he described the action.

"You gonna bust Tom out a jail?" Billy asked.

"Peep can rot in Deadwood, for all I care. I dunno how he lived this long without gettin' his neck stretched."

"He almost did. We heard the townspeople in Belle Fourche tried to string him up."

"Poor Tom," Andrea said, almost inaudibly.

"Poor Tom nuthin'. I don't wanna hear his name again."

George Currie rode away early next morning. He warned them again in parting that the gang would be riding through following the Red Lodge bank robbery. "Have ever'thing ready," he said.

"Let's leave now," she urged as soon as Flat Nose topped the rise.

"Can't." Billy clenched his jaw.

"Why not?"

"They're depending on us." He ended the discussion by shuffling into the cabin and lying down.

For the rest of the week Billy remained adamant in his refusal to leave the Hole. His strength was returning, but he grumpily favored his left arm.

Hale and McCloud returned from Buffalo on Tuesday, with a sack of potatoes and other supplies. The shooting match, she soon learned, was a sore subject.

Among the flour sacks of food, Andrea discovered a small bag of horehound candy.

"Weren't my idea," McCloud said, shaking his blood-hound face. "Billy told me to get some. I reckon he figures you got a sweet tooth."

Billy denied ordering candy while at the same time offering her a piece. His generosity extended no further. Retreating behind his wall of silence, he said no more than necessary.

Andrea was weary of his attitude, as well as her slave treatment in the presence of the others. When Hale and McCloud left for Lost Cabin, she insisted, "I mean it, Billy. I'm leaving—with or without you."

"You'll wait 'til they pull off the bank job. They won't stay long. They'll be heading south for Brown's Hole."

"And if they want you to go along?"

"I won't."

A few days later, Hale and McCloud returned with four sorry-looking geldings.

"L-lost some on the w-way," Hale said in greeting.

"If they looked like these, it doesn't matter much." Billy shook his head in disgust.

"We ain't g-gonna race 'em, B-Bill. J-Just gonna use 'em fer pack hosses."

When the horses had been loaded with gear missed by the cowhands, Hale and McCloud led them back to Lost Cabin. A swayback mustang was left for Andy to ride.

Billy stubbornly waited for the bank robbers' return. Hiding behind his mask of silence, he lingered until the morning Lonie Logan rode in.

* * * *

Tom O'Day didn't bother to track time as his trial date drew near. He was dozing in his cell when a commotion in the bullpen woke him. Lifting his head from the mattress, he looked into the glittering gray-blue eyes of

Harry Alonzo Longabaugh. Stopping briefly at Tom's cell, Sundance shot him a look he knew meant to keep his mouth shut. Behind him loomed Walt Punteney and Harve Logan, whose wrist was noticeably bandaged. All were handcuffed and scowling.

"Howdy, stranger," Sundance said as he was pushed forward. "The name's Roberts. This here's my brother Frank." He nodded in Harve's direction. "I met this other fellah along the trail."

Tom nodded as each man passed, his heart sinking into his knees. When the deputies left, he pressed against the bars, whispering: "Where's Flat Nose George?"

"He wasn't around when the posse caught up in Montana." Sundance groaned, flexing his bowed legs.

At least one of them was still at large. Tom breathed easier, knowing it was only a matter of time 'til they found a means of escape. Butch's friends would see to that. Glancing at the steel-barred windows, he shook his head, wondering how it could be done.

Tom's daily routine changed little; the others deliberately avoided him. Days were spent mainly in his cell, lying on his back, dreaming of a green-acred horse ranch. His jail mates walked restlessly about the bullpen, smoking constantly and speaking in muffled tones Tom was unable to hear.

Harve agitated him most. Climbing the bars one-handed, he never seemed to rest, making Tom nervous with his constant movement.

For three weeks Tom endured his outcast status, wondering why the others blamed him for the botched bank robbery. Had he not done as he was told? he thought miserably. Was it his fault old man Giles stuck his nose in the bank during the holdup? Had he not risked his skin spending all day in Belle Fourche and half the night spying on the town?

Tom's quarantine lifted the night the weasel-faced deputy slipped a note into Harve's cell on his supper tray. Later, when lights were out, he heard the news. "Five saddle hosses will be waiting for us in Spearfish Canyon the night of Halloween," Harve whispered.

"You're jokin'."

"If I was joking, I woulda said some witches were waiting to boil you in oil, you lummox."

"Where's this Spearfish Canyon?" Tom was relieved that someone was talking to him, although in anger and total darkness.

"Some miles from here near the B & M Railroad Station."

Tom crossed himself, thinking the eve of All Saints Day was a fine time for a jailbreak. He hadn't set foot in church since his old man died, but his family's religion was indelibly stamped on his soul.

The prisoners seldom spoke among themselves during the following week so as not to alert the jailer. Each man studied at his leisure the thirty-foot square bullpen, outer corridor, and rectangular steel box which housed the combination lock. The lever automatically locked the cells, so there was little contact between inmates and their keepers. Prisoners were allowed to mingle in the bullpen during the day, but were locked in their cells at night.

For the rest of the week Tom wondered how anyone could break them out of jail without staging an armed assault.

* * * *

Voices were drifting up from the corral when she awoke that morning. She knew immediately it was Lonie Logan although his back was turned as she glanced from the doorway. Standing in the middle of the corral, he was gesturing with both hands as he spoke to Billy. Hurriedly combing her hair, Andrea dashed her face with water before trotting down the path to the corral.

She arrived in time to hear Lonie say, "Take five saddled horses to Spearfish Canyon. Buy some from the Lazy H Ranch if you have to, but make sure they're good long distance runners."

"Andy and I are the only ones here," Billy explained. "Everybody left to meet up with Butch."

"The law's watching our old ranch in Montana, so I can't get hosses from Jim Thornhill. He's the friend who took over when Harve shot Landusky in self defense."

"We can take 'em," Billy said. "Andy's good with hosses, and the two of us can handle 'em. Nobody would suspect two young cowpokes taking stock to the sale in Spearfish, especially if we've got papers."

Lonie chuckled. "You're a good man, Billy. I wish you'd gone to Belle Fourche, instead of Peep."

Andrea cleared her throat. "Nice to see you again, Mister Logan. Where are the others?"

"They're in the Deadwood jail. Harve stopped a bullet in his wrist." Hanging his head, he stared at the ground.

"But weren't you along?"

"Harve had me take the first batch of relay hosses to the Hash Knife Ranch. A friend let me leave 'em in the hoss trap. I went back to Harlan after the second pick up."

Turning to Andrea, he said, "Billy tells me you wanna be an outlaw."

"Yes, sir," she said, glaring at Billy.

"Think you can help herd some saddle hosses to Spearfish?"

She nodded, forcing a smile.

"Then it's settled."

* * * *

Winds were blowing progressively stronger and colder, scooping dirt particles from distant ridges. Earlier, when Billy had been well enough to leave unattended, Andrea had searched through an old trunk in the barn and found a discarded wool jacket. She mended it and shortened the well-worn sleeves. With summer fading from the Big Horns, she wore the jacket constantly. She was wearing it when she followed Billy from the barn early the morning after Lonie's departure, astride the sway-backed mustang she had named Chester.

"What kind of name is that for a hoss?" Billy asked, grimacing. After a quick inspection, he laughed. "I guess you're right. Most of his weight is hanging in his chest, like Flat Nose George."

He told her a rancher beyond the eastern entrance to the valley would sell them horses and hopefully the saddles they needed. Carefully recounting the four hundred dollars Lonie had given him, he folded the money and stuffed it into his trouser pocket.

Billy set a steady pace after they left the cabin. They traveled northeastward over homesteaded lands with their own small herds of cattle. Setting up camp early that evening in a sheltered draw, they left before daybreak the following morning. By the time the sun rose, the foothills had been left behind. The rolling grassland stretched to the horizon in monotonous tones of fawn and pale ocher.

Billy recalled making a trip over this same route with Harve Logan two summers earlier. Harve told him of the Johnson County War and pointed out the trail ridden by fifty-two cattlemen and Texas mercenaries in 1892. The invading cattlemen's mission had been to kill seventy Buffalo city officials and suspected cattle rustlers.

"They wound up killing two settlers they thought were rustlers," Harve said. "One of them, Nate Champion, died with twenty-eight bullet holes in him. The cattlemen holed up at the TA Ranch between here and Buffalo, where the townspeople were fixing to blow 'em up with the cattlemen's own dynamite. But soldiers from the fort rescued the cattlemen, and they got off scott free." Harve acted as though the incident had happened yesterday, instead of several years earlier.

Billy pondered the miscarriage of justice, comparing it unfavorably with the harmless raids of the Wild Bunch. He didn't understand why wealthy cattlemen had gotten away with murder, or why President Benjamin Harrison had called out federal troops to protect them. He was convinced money would always buy freedom, no matter how heinous the crime.

He was still mulling over the injustices of the world when they arrived at the Lazy H Ranch. The scent of dried grasses mingled with the pungent odor of manure drifting on the chilly morning wind. October snow was on its way.

"Awfully quiet for a horse ranch," Andrea said as she rode alongside.

"Maybe they're taking a *siesta*."

Billy worried no one was around to sell them horses. The ranch house squatted in a wilted meadow, apparently abandoned with the exception of several unkempt horses grazing in an adjoining pasture. He took the lead as they walked their geldings into the yard and tied them to a rail post. When no one appeared, he knocked. A few moments passed before the door opened little more than a crack, and a woman's voice demanded to know their business.

"We're here to buy some saddlers from Mister Hardy, ma'am."

"Well, he ain't here. He's gone off with the posse looking for outlaws." Her small, dark eyes narrowed suspiciously.

Billy glanced sidelong at Andrea, surprised to find her edging toward the yard. The door opened wide enough for him to glimpse the woman's drawn features, framed with graying hair.

"Can you sell us some hosses, ma'am?"

"Whatcha need 'em for, son?"

"Some outlaws stole ours a few days back."

The door opened wider and the woman invited them in. A rifle was carelessly slung over one thin arm as she questioned them about the theft. Andrea resisted the urge to roll her eyes when Billy explained. He said they'd been camped at Tongue River, where outlaws rustled their saddle horses.

"Our pa sent us down here to buy some more," he said, "and we heard your ranch was the best place to get 'em."

She herded them from the back door into the corral. When shown several shaggy broomtails swatting flies along the fence. Billy shook his head.

"No, ma'am. We need good saddlers, like the ones that were stolen."

"All right, then, follow me."

Refocusing their eyes in the dim light, they followed the gaunt woman into the recesses of the barn. Standing in rough-hewn stalls in the back, with light filtering through cracks in the wall behind them, were horses Billy recognized from blooded lines. Checking them over, he commented on the hocks and withers of some, the fetlocks and cannons of others. When finished, he chose five horses: a bay, dun, grulla, pinto, and a gray, all of them over fifteen hands.

"We need saddles and bridles," he said, closing the deal.

"That'll be four-twenty-five."

"We only got four hundred. These are good hosses, but we didn't come here to be robbed."

"I'm not gonna dicker," the woman said evenly. "Ain't ya got nuthin' to trade?"

Billy pulled the linings from his pants pockets and let them hang. "That's all I got."

Andy glanced down at the gold ring he'd given her and slowly twisted it from her index finger. Biting her lip, she offered it hesitantly.

Stepping into the forenoon sunlight, the woman revolved the ring in her fingers, then popped the band between her teeth. Billy noticed a glint of amusement in her dark eyes when she said, "Reckon it's worth twenty dollars."

He looked to Andy, shaking his head.

"It's all right, Billy. We need the horses *and* the saddles. We have nothing else to trade."

"What about the hoss Andy's riding?"

"I wouldn't give you five bucks for that old nag," she said, laughing. "This ring will do just fine."

After the woman had laboriously filled out bills of sale, Andy saddled the gray and led the pinto and Chester. Strung out behind Pepper were three others on a specially rigged lariat.

The sun was already arcing toward the southern spur of the Big Horn Mountains when they rode away from the ranch, cutting their own trail over rolling grassland toward the South Dakota border.

Chapter Sixteen

They camped that night in a wooded area near a partially frozen stream. Too tired to heat a tin of corned beef, they chewed jerky and washed it down with water from the stream. Billy banked the fire and they wrapped themselves in heavy quilts to lie within its warmth.

Yawning, she said, "We're leaving for my grandparent's ranch after the horses are delivered, aren't we?" She heard his sudden snore from the opposite side of the fire.

"Billy, I know you're awake."

The raspy sound increased in volume.

You've developed evasion to a fine art, she thought as she snuggled inside her quilt. Sighing, she allowed her mind to drift back over the past five months, from her kidnapping to the loss of Aladdin and her beautifully carved gold ring. Convincing Billy to leave the gang had become an obsession.

Why was he so stubborn? His professed feelings for her were nothing more than meaningless words. Cupping hands over her lower face, she blew warm breath to thaw her nose and chin. Despite Billy's presence, she felt dismally alone. Although she had not refined her feelings for him, he had become the most important person in her life. Convincing him to quit the gang was for his own sake as well as hers.

Billy groaned, and she watched him shift position on the cold, hard ground. He wasn't sleeping any more than she was.

"We need to talk," she said.

He snorted before launching into a full blown snore.

Pulling herself upright, she waddled to his side of the fire, enveloped in the heavy quilt. Lowering herself to the ground, she tapped him on the head.

"You're a coward, Billy Blackburn. I thought you were brave. Someone I might spend the rest of my life with."

He rolled onto his back to stare up at her. "You would?"

"Would what?"

"Spend the rest of your life—?"

"I was wrong."

"You know I'm no coward." Billy bolted upright, the quilt crumpling around him.

"You've been lying to me all along."

Studying his tented knees, he was silent for several moments. "I-I'm not right for you, Andy," he said at last. "You're from a good family and you're smart ... and beautiful."

His pathetic expression reminded her of a chastised young boy, but she resisted the urge to hug him.

"I'm not Daddy's little princess any more. Mother said if I remained chaste, a good man like my father would marry me. Now no one will believe..." Her voice broke as she stared into the darkness.

Groaning, he reached to gently pull her close. When she shivered, he hugged her to his chest. "You're a hard case of stubbornness, Andrea Bordeaux. We'd better get some sleep."

The sun was up before they awoke. Billy was stirring in his quilt, his arms around her in an ardent embrace. Unable to move, she panicked, thrashing to free herself.

Sighing, he released her. "You don't trust anyone, do you?" Jerking free of the quilt, he hastily picked up his saddle.

"You kidnap me and expect me to trust you?"

"I killed a man to save your life, Andy. And you must have forgotten about the wolf."

"That makes me your slave for life?"

"No! I'm taking you home as soon as we report back to the Hole."

"There's no one left at Hole in the Wall."

"The boys'll be back as soon as they break out a jail."

"They might not let us leave."

"I gave my word," he said, moving to his gelding. "I keep my promises. To you *and* the boys." Refusing further discussion, he set the saddle on Pepper's back.

Andrea helped him break camp, ignoring the jerky he offered when they were ready to leave. Food was the last thing she wanted. Resisting the urge to hurl a pebble at him, she mounted the gray muttering, "Stubborn jack of apes!"

They rode in silence the remainder of the day, Andrea growing more morose as time dragged on. Famished, she heated two tins of corned beef that evening. After they ate, she cleaned the utensils, and burrowed into her quilt without a word. If words didn't get through to him, maybe silence would.

The following afternoon they sited a huge tapering monolith, resembling a petrified tree stump jutting from its base.

"Must be Devil's Tower," Billy shouted over his shoulder, breaking the silence. "I heard Flat Nose George talking about it. He said there's an Indian legend about a giant bear making all those scratch marks on the sides while trying to rescue his mate."

Andrea focused on the tower, ignoring him. Imagining herself stranded there, calling for help, she wondered whether he would try to rescue her. She maintained her silence that evening when they struck camp, noticing with satisfaction that he was chafing under the solitude.

"Ignoring me won't do you any good," he said as they made camp. She gave him a withering look and moved away from the fire. It wasn't long before icy wind nudged her back. Finished cleaning the utensils, she pulled the quilt around her and bedded down for the night. Hearing him rummage through a saddlebag, she peered from the rim of her quilt as he withdrew a small metal object. Pounding it hard against his palm, he launched a harmonic serenade. The music was so mournful that Andrea choked with emotion. She tried shutting it out by covering her ears, but the plaintive notes seemed to penetrate her soul, creating an inner cloud of thunder and raindrops. Sleep eluded her that night long after she heard his honest snore.

Next morning, as they preparied to leave, a stranger rode into camp astride a handsome buckskin. Shabbily dressed, the bewhiskered, florid-faced man tipped his hat, inquiring whether the horses were for sale.

"We're delivering them to a ranch near Spearfish," Andrea said quickly, crossing fingers behind her back.

"Which ranch?" Small, close-set eyes squinted at her from beneath his dingy, low-crowned hat.

"I forgot the name but we have a map," she said, staring him down.

"Let's have a look."

Billy placed a protective arm around her shoulder. "Don't want to bother you none," he said. "We can find it."

"Got papers on them hosses, son?"

"Sure do, if you wanna see 'em." Billy hurried over to Pepper and lifted the papers from his saddlebag.

Holding them within inches of his eyes, the man nodded. "Looks to be in order. Can't be too careful with so many hoss thieves about."

"Yes, sir. Guess we'd better leave." Billy retrieved the papers and nudged Andrea ahead of him. They wasted no time mounting their horses and leaving camp. The stranger quietly sat his buckskin and watched as they started off in the direction of the South Dakota border. Turning in the saddle to check the trailing horses, Andrea glanced back at the motionless rider. While they climbed toward the border, she felt an uneasiness, but pushed it aside to marvel at the Black Hills' autumn beauty. She was tempted to call to Billy, to tell him how wonderful it would be to build a cabin there, but remembered she wasn't speaking to him. She noted with satisfaction that her silence was causing his shoulders to slump. Billy withdrew a map from his pocket to study the drawing. Halting, he raised in the stirrups, shading his eyes to peer up the trail.

"I think it's this way," he shouted, pointing.

The uneasiness returned when she swiveled to look beyond old Chester. Nudging the gray forward, she decided on a temporary truce. Riding alongside Billy, she said, "That man was up to something."

"I know he was. We'd better get off the trail."

Billy rode downslope to the stream, leading the horses into the center of icy water. Andrea followed, turning often to survey their back trail. The gray was shivering in hock-deep water, tossing his head and emitting a cloud of warm breath in the chilling morning air. She leaned forward to whisper in his ear, "Good boy, it's not much further."

Patting him reassuringly on either side of his quivering neck, she wondered how the others were doing. Ahead of her, Billy's string appeared docile and resigned to their discomfort. Her own string seemed as cold as the gray, but the pinto was rebelling, tossing his head and whickering. Talking to him, coaxing him, she was able to quiet the gelding. It was then she noticed a thin veil of dust rising from behind a forested hill they had ridden past.

"Billy," she cried. "Look!"

His worried expression told her she was right. They were being followed. Billy picked up the pace, going ashore on a rocky flat where the trail would be lost, at least temporarily. Glancing back at her, he grinned as though he were enjoying a steeple chase. Nagging pains shot from the base of her skull into her shoulder blades, from frequent twists in the saddle. Andrea had seen nothing to indicate they were being pursued since wading ashore, and found it exhilarating to out-smart whoever was following them. She understood why Billy and the others enjoyed a good chase, but was tiring of it rapidly.

He stopped beside a stream late that afternoon and dismounted. Tying the reins to a gnarled limb, he climbed into an oak to survey the area. Reining in beside Pepper, she gazed up at him questioningly.

"Can't see a thing," he said breathlessly. He then dropped to the ground. "Looks like a good place to camp."

Andrea shrugged. She was relieved to see him in good humor, but was wary of his intentions. She went about unsaddling the gray in silence.

"You're not playing deaf and dumb again, are you, Andy?"

The corners of her mouth drooped as she lifted her shoulders and brows.

"Fine." He carried his saddle to a nearby rock. Glaring at her, he said, "I'll bed down here, and you can sleep over there." He indicated the oak tree.

Dousing the cooking fire before darkness crowded in, Andrea drew the heavy quilt about her. The night was colder than the previous one, and there was little sleep in camp that night. Both of them were puffy-eyed and grumpy the next morning as they prepared to break camp.

Neither spoke as they saddled-up and rode out. Studying the map, Billy turned south, climbing a steep slope through thick stands of snow-skiffed pines. The wind thrust a frozen dagger, slashing at exposed skin. Drawing her collar as high as it would reach, she lifted her shoulders to protect her stinging ears. The gloves Billy had given her dwarfed her hands, but she was grateful to have them.

Eyes heavy from lack of sleep, she had dozed off when a cracking sound caused her chin to recoil from her chest. Blinking, she realized Billy had halted and raised his hands.

"Don't move!" A stocky, filthy man was perched on a boulder, his rifle trained on Billy. "Thought you lost us, didn'ja?" Cackling like one of Gramma's hens, the gunman swung his rifle in her direction.

"Dismount!"

"We're taking these hosses to the sale," Billy said.

"We'll save you the trouble."

"You're making a mistake." Billy slid from the roan, his arms aloft and grimacing with shoulder pain. "These hosses belong to Butch Cassidy."

"And I'm the sheriff of Spearfish." The horse thief's homely face twisted itself into a leer.

His attention shifted to Andrea. When she dismounted, Billy edged between them. "This is my brother, Andy. We're taking the hosses to the Wild Bunch."

"You think I'm stupid?" The stranger had a brutal laugh. "Them boys don't hire no kids."

"We're gang members," Andrea shouted, her hands above her head.

Before the conversation could develop further, they were distracted by the flanking motion of three additional horsemen.

Laughing uproariously, a newcomer yelled, "I see you corralled 'em, Barney. Mighty fine pieces of hoss flesh." Short, dark, greasy-haired and dirty, they resembled the man called Barney, who appeared to be the eldest.

"These here kids are bigger liars than you are, Shotgun," Barney said chortling. "They say they're takin' them hosses to the Wild Bunch."

"Hell, I'm Butch Cassidy and I aim to take delivery right here." Shotgun vigorously scratched his groin.

There would be no reasoning with these animals. From their smell, they had worn the same clothing since the spring thaw.

"You boys must be related," Billy said.

"We're the Edwards Brothers," Shotgun boasted, lifting his sagging chest. "The best gall durned hoss thieves in the Black Hills."

"Edwards?" The muscles in Billy's face relaxed. "Jake Edwards is a close friend of ours."

"Never heard of no Jake Edwards." Barney lowered his rifle. "You got any more stories to tell 'fore we shoot the both of ya?"

Shaking off Billy's arm, she shouted, "We're telling you the truth. Don't you know what the gang will do if you harm us?"

"I reckon they won't know once you're buried." Shotgun snickered.

"The Wild Bunch is planning to rob the Spearfish bank tomorrow," Billy said. "There will be more posse men combing this hills than you've ever seen." He turned slowly as he spoke, looking each man in the eyes.

"These hosses are legally registered to Butch Cassidy," he added. "If you don't believe me, take a gander at the papers in my saddlebags."

Barney shook his head. "They don't register no hosses to outlaws... Do they?"

"They do in Utah." Billy pressed on, his tone confidential. "That's where these beauties came from. Andy and I are Butch Cassidy's grooms. Andy rides his race hosses. He's a jockey."

Andrea nodded agreement, praying the horse thieves were as dumb as they looked.

"I'll be damned." Barney looked to his brothers for their reactions.

"If you'll allow me, I'll show you the papers." Billy edged slowly toward Pepper. "You'll be pinning targets on your chests if you take 'em," he said. "Everybody knows who owns these hosses, and they'll be sure to tell the gang you stole 'em." The speech left him breathless.

Shotgun jammed his gun in Billy's ribs. "Git them papers," he said. "We'll see who's storytellin'."

Andrea tensed as Billy carefully pulled the strap on his saddlebag, the rifle barrel still pressed in his side. Slowly lifting the papers with a thumb and index finger, he showed them to the Edwards brothers, who had lined up before him as he held the documents in both hands. With Billy's back to her, she glanced from one grimy face to another for some sign of disbelief.

"Whadda ya think?" Shotgun looked to Barney for a decision.

"Looks mighty official to me."

"We ain't got no quarrel with the Wild Bunch." The smallest horse thief had a pained expression.

"You're right about that, Stubby. Maybe we oughter let these young fellers be on their way." Barney spat a stream of tobacco juice, which dampened Billy's jeans.

"I reckon ol' Butch wouldn't mind if we took a few coins for our troubles," Shotgun ventured, a look of childish innocence on his heavily stubbled face.

"And you'd be welcome to 'em *if* we had some," Billy said with mock sympathy. "But a couple of bandits took our money back a ways. They'll be dead men when the Wild Bunch hears about it."

"And so they should." Barney wagged his head vigorously. "You boys better hurry along so you won't be late." Shouldering his rifle, he waved his brothers into a huddle, out of earshot.

"Let's go," Billy hissed. "Don't let on you're afraid."

Heart threatening to hammer from her chest, Andrea mounted the gray and followed Billy slowly up the trail. When he rode abreast of the Edwards brothers, he raised his hand in a farewell salute.

"We'll put in a good word for you with Butch," he said smiling.

The trail curved down a thickly forested hill, and Billy increased the pace until Andrea found it reckless. Afraid to look back, she rode low over the gray's neck, dodging limbs, her eyes trained on the grulla's tail ahead of her. Heart still pounding, her lungs expanded until she thought they would shatter.

Dark lowering clouds threatened to erupt into a snow shower. Andrea could smell the moisture as it stung her nostrils. When the pines thinned, she braved a look back up the trail, surprised to find only the pinto trailing behind. Chester, her sway-backed mustang, was missing.

Billy finally halted and motioned her alongside. "You all right?"

"Yes, but I thought..."

"They'd kill us?"

She nodded.

"Me, too, Andy. But when you yelled the gang would get 'em, I remembered something Butch once said: 'When you're cornered, come out swinging.'"

"I don't understand."

"Remember that jasper on the buckskin?"

"Yes."

"When he looked at the papers, he held them close to his eyes, but they were upside down."

"He couldn't read?"

"Yeah. So I gambled that the Edwards brothers couldn't read either."

"But how could you be sure?"

"They would have had to stand on their heads to decipher the bills of sale."

Andrea flushed with pride. "I'm sorry I called you a coward."

Reaching to touch her arm, he said, "I've been acting like one."

They were still sitting their horses, smiling into each other's eyes, when the first snow began to fall. Andrea looked skyward as tiny flakes of ice landed on her upturned face.

"Chester's gone," she said.

"I know. They cut him loose when we started down the first slope. We're lucky that's all they took."

"But our food's in Chester's saddlebags."

"Can't be helped," he said, turning his gelding up the trail. "Let's find the railroad station. We're almost there."

Nearly an hour passed before Billy halted and pointed to his right. "There's the depot," he yelled, a grin stretching his handsome face.

"Are you sure?" Her chattering teeth chopped her words.

Nodding, he started down the embankment onto the rutted road, riding cautiously as snowflakes swirled about his shoulders. The riderless horses picked their way down the slope behind him.

A small wooden building appeared deserted when he rode past. Scanning the area, he withdrew the map from his pocket. Billy stopped several hundred yards along the B & M Railroad tracks and waited for

Andrea to reach him. Glancing along the iron rails, she shielded her eyes to prevent the snow from blinding her. Large flakes had begun falling heavily since their descent onto the road.

"We can't leave the horses without feed," she said. "They might freeze to death before Tom and the others get here."

"Maybe the station's unlocked."

Squeezing Pepper's ribs with his knees, he turned the animal caravan back in the direction they had come. Before they reached the small clapboard depot, they noticed large white letters painted across the slanting roof. There was no doubt this was Maurice Station. Billy swung down from the roan and stomped his numbed feet at the door. Rattling the knob, he turned back frowning.

"Wouldn't you know," he said, disgustedly.

"We've got to find a place to get warm." Sliding from the gray, Andrea brushed snow from the small window and peered inside.

"There's a stove and some wood piled against the back wall. I don't see another door, but that window might be unlocked."

He hurried around back, returning a moment later, grinning. A skeleton key dangled from his gloved hand. "Found it on the back sill," he said, inserting it into the lock. The door creaked open, and they stepped inside, a musty odor greeting them.

"Start a fire," he said, "while I rub down the hosses and hobble 'em under the trees."

Checking the flue, she swept aside accumulated ashes with a gloved hand, and scrupulously laid kindling in the bottom of the stove. When it lighted, warmth penetrated her clothing and thawed her numbed skin, the heat increasing her exhaustion. Yawning, she forced herself to the back window to check on Billy's progress.

The wind had picked up, hurling thick horizontal streaks of snow past the window. Gasping, she rushed to the door. Once outside, she lowered her head and barreled around to the back of the building, where she could scarcely make out Billy's form. The horses were bunched together for warmth, their tails to the wind as he worked to loosen a cinch. By the time he pulled the saddle free, the snow had stopped falling.

"Shortest blizzard I ever saw."

"Let's hope so," he said, still rubbing down the gray.

"The wind will get rid of the snow if it doesn't start up again."

Looking skyward, she knew chances were slim that snow would not resume. Finished with the horses, they staked them a hundred yards behind the station where they could graze, in an area sheltered by towering pines. They then ran a foot race back to the station. Billy arrived first and held the door for her. The room was warm, and they wasted little time gathering around the stove. While she thawed her hands, he wrapped his arms around her, pulling her close. Nestling her head on his uninjured shoulder, she welcomed his embrace.

"Isn't this better than ignoring me," he whispered.

Nodding, she murmured, "Only thing nicer would be going home."

"I've been thinking on that."

She pulled back to gaze into his hazel eyes.

"We'll go as soon as we're rested from the trip back to the Hole."

Wrenching free of his embrace, she rushed to the door. "I'm not going back to the Hole. I'm going home to my grandparents."

"You'd get lost, Andy. Too much open country out there," he said, reaching for her. "I have to leave the gang on good terms, or I'll be spending the rest of my life looking over my shoulder."

As much as she wanted to sweep that possibility aside, she knew it was true. He would have to negotiate his withdrawal from the gang. Folding her arms across her chest, she studied the planked floor.

"All right, Billy."

Twilight was fading as they huddled wrapped in their quilts beside the stove. Exhausted from the day's ordeal and lack of rest, they slept while the wind shrieked outside the drafty station. Worried about the horses, she slid quietly from her quilt at dawn to stare through the back window, relieved that snow had not resumed. Snuggling again close to Billy, she slept.

Winds died with morning's first light. Peering through tired eyes at the young outlaw, Andrea promised herself to follow him wherever his inner trail led. She hoped it would lead back to the ranch, but if it didn't, she resigned herself to whatever fate he chose for them. Sighing, she knew it was a promise impossible to keep.

Billy got to his feet, stretching. "Feels like the fire could use some more wood. And I'd better check on the hosses."

Andrea dozed while he was gone. When she awakened, he was stoking the fire. They were chewing jerky from his jacket pocket, huddled over the stove, when he announced they would start back that morning for the Hole.

"But the horses…"

"I found the place we're supposed to leave 'em. I gave 'em enough slack to graze and get to water. They'll be fine 'til the boys get here tonight."

He had scarcely gathered her into his arms when they were startled by the station door opening.

"What the sam hill's going on in here?" a base voice boomed. Andrea gazed into the transparent eyes of a paunchy, graying man who appeared to have been trampled by a steer. Pulling at his rumpled uniform, he peered at them suspiciously.

"How'd you kids get in here?" His voice was harsh and authoritarian.

"We found the key on the sill," Billy explained. "It was snowing and—"

"I oughta have you arrested," he barked, pointing a beefy finger at them.

"We were robbed by the Edwards brothers." Andrea indicated the direction they had come.

"Those low lives? What did they take?"

"My horse, Chester."

"Well, that's still no reason—"

"We'll be on our way," Billy said firmly. "Sorry if we caused you any trouble."

Quickly gathering their gear, they rushed past the station master and onto the icy road.

Wind had picked up, carrying with it fine grains of snow. Carrying her quilt, she slipped and nearly fell. When they reached the horses, he packed their remaining supplies into Pepper's saddlebags. Their food supply was meager, only a few pieces of jerky Billy had discovered in his pocket.

"Why aren't we taking the gray?" she asked, huddling between horses. "I thought there were only four men in jail. How far is Deadwood?" she asked before he could answer.

"I'm not sure. Must be quite a ways on foot."

"Why aren't we leaving the horses close to town?"

"I'm just following orders, Andy. I do what I'm told."

"Isn't it time to think for yourself?" Andrea bit down hard on her lip, wishing she'd kept that bit of insight to herself.

Billy stiffened, drawing himself to his full height. "Get on the hoss, woman, and close your mouth before the wind freezes your tongue."

Chapter Seventeen

Walt lounged in his jail cell most of the day. During the evening meal, he quietly told Tom that the cage door between the bullpen and outer corridor would be left unlocked.

The others still avoided Tom, including the black man William Moore, who shared their cell block. Moore had been charged with murder, and was even surlier than the Sundance Kid. Tom was wary of the heavily muscled Moore and kept his distance.

The clock above the office door said eight-fifteen. The supper trays had been cleared away, and Harve was pacing the bullpen in short strides, an eye on the time. Each man had closed his cell so that it appeared locked, and was leaning against the bullpen bars.

Nervously chewing his mustache, Tom heard the hinges creak as the office door swung into the cell block, signaling the prisoners to gather near the corridor. The jailer, John Mansfield, rubbed his receding hairline before announcing: "Time to get back in your cells, boys."

"The lock box must be broken," Harve said off-handedly. "The cell doors won't open." He swung the bullpen door into the outer corridor to demonstrate that the locking system was awry.

Tom held his breath, afraid the bluff wouldn't work. The weasel-faced deputy had been bribed to leave the door unlocked, and Harve was sure the jailer would investigate without calling the sheriff for protection. He glanced at his fellow inmates as they prepared to dash into the corridor when the unarmed jailer entered the cell block. Sundance positioned himself along the bars near the cage door and waited until Mansfield entered the corridor. When the jailer's diminutive wife followed with a key dangling from a large ring, Sundance slid his foot into the opening, preventing her from locking the door behind her husband. Wrenching the door open, he slapped the screaming woman and pushed her into a cell.

Moore first struck Mansfield, knocking him against the bars. Walt and Harve then took turns punching him until he was down. Moore kicked him repeatedly in the ribs as Tom watched, flinching with each blow.

"Drag him in the cell with his old lady," Harve said. "Let's get out a here."

When the cell door was locked, they rushed through the office and into the open courtyard, where Moore jumped the fence on his own.

Tom hiked down Carney Street with Walt until they reached the creek, following it to the railroad yard. Tom was winded before they reached the summit of McGovern Hill, where he stopped to mop his brow. When he reached Walt, he noticed distant lights fluttering along the ground like lightning bugs. He knew men with lanterns were searching for something or someone.

Hurriedly changing course toward Blacktail Gulch, they dared not run and draw attention to themselves. The boys were waiting for them on False Bottom Road.

"Helluva night for a jailbreak," Harve said. "Clouds over the moon and it feels like snow."

Lights flickered from Whit's Half-Way Ranch on the old Carbonate Road when they cut through the underbrush. Before sunup they crawled under bushes well off the road and slept, huddled together for warmth. The wind was chilling, the ground even colder. Tom volunteered for the first watch, but fell asleep soon after the others.

Twilight had descended on the Black Hills when they started out again, staying off the road until it was dark. Blisters had already formed on his heels, and Tom lagged well behind his companions. As he sat to pull off his boots, he heard hoof beats growing louder from the vicinity of the road. Well ahead, he noticed his companions dart out to surround a horse and rider.

"Grab him," he heard Harve yell.

The rider used his whip. Rearing, the horse scattered men like match sticks. Before loping off down the road, he dragged an outlaw with him. Tom could hear them cursing as he limped toward them.

"Where the hell were you?" Harve snarled as he dusted off his clothes. "We could have held him down with another man."

"What good is one hoss?" Tom asked defensively.

"Two of us coulda rode him to Spearfish canyon and brought back the hosses."

Tom hung his head.

"We better get out a here before that farmer meets up with a posse." Walt started off into the brush.

"Let's separate," Sundance said. "We'll meet you two in Spearfish Canyon."

An hour later Tom slumped to the ground, calling out to Walt, "I gotta rest. My feet hurt."

His friend turned back, grumbling. "All right, but only for a minute."

Once seated Tom felt around him, gathering twigs and small pieces of dry brush. Reaching into his pocket, he retrieved a lucifer and struck it on a rock.

Walt's eyes widened with alarm "What the hell?"

"I killed a sage hen with a rock before dark." Tom extracted a small bird from his belt. "Thought we'd have ourselves a little supper."

"What if somebody sees the fire?"

"Stack some rocks around it while I skin the bird."

"If my belly wasn't touchin' my backbone, I'd say you're crazy, Peep."

Tom hurriedly stripped the bird of its feathers, then skewered the hen with a branch and carefully rotated it over the flames. As he was taking meat from the stick, a horse whickered from the direction of the road. Dropping the bird, Tom nearly stumbled into the fire in his haste to follow Walt, who had already vanished into the brush. They ran until Tom could go no further. Crawling under a clump of bushes, they lay down to rest. Walt was snoring before Tom could make himself comfortable. The ground was unbearably cold, the breeze heavy with the feel of snow. Tom's sleep was troubled and filled with cold, blistered feet.

A gunshot shattered their dreams, devastating the sill dawn air. Peering around the bush, they noticed a young man standing nearby holding a bloody rabbit. Heavy frost covered the ground, which Tom mistook for snow. Glancing at Walt's sleep-creased face, he saw him motion in the opposite direction. Crawling after him, he heard the sound of voices in the distance.

During the morning they labored through thickets in the hills south of Spearfish. Weary beyond anything he had previously endured, Tom kept dropping back, holding his growling stomach. Annoyed, Walt waited for him, making furtive signs for him to hurry. Early that afternoon they spotted a rutabaga growing in a field alongside the road. Against his better judgment, Tom scrambled to pick it. When he had scarcely eaten his share, he heard hoof beats and spotted men riding in his direction.

Sighing heavily, Tom stood and raised his hands. "I've had enough boys. Don't shoot!"

"Damn you, Peep," Walt snarled, indecision working his face. Tom wasn't sure whether his partner was about to run, risking a bullet in his back, or saving his energy for an assault on Tom's midsection. He was relieved when Walt hesitated a moment too long and sat down hard on the edge of the road, swearing.

They were handcuffed and pushed into a two-seated buggy, their ankles shackled with heavy chains linked to the custodial bracelets for the trip back to Deadwood.

* * * *

Wind velocity increased as they rode toward Sundance, Wyoming. Billy smiled to himself, remembering that Harry Longabaugh had earned his moniker from the small town near the South Dakota border. The Sundance Kid served his first jail term for stealing a horse, gun, and saddle from the nearby Triple V Ranch.

Squinting at the sky, he said, "Sure hope this storm blows over." He tried to keep his tone light, although dark, lowering clouds had him worried.

Andy's weight had increased against his back, her grip gone limp on his waist. When she didn't respond, he knew she had fallen asleep. He liked having her close but her dependence was causing him concern. The thought of taking her home bothered him even more. He had felt sorry for the skinny little scamp with chopped hair and a face that resembled a lopsided watermelon. When the swelling and bruises faded, her personality took on a more confident air, and he worried others would notice her beauty. Several had called her 'purty boy' and made coarse remarks behind her back, which only fortified Billy's resolve to protect her. He admired Andrea's courage, despite her recent naggings. Taking her home had been his plan all along, when the time was right. Why couldn't she understand his responsibilities to Butch and the gang? They were his only family.

Her weight seemed to be shifting to one side. Reining Pepper, he reached to grasp her arms.

"Andy," he said, gently shaking her. "Should we stop here and rest?"

She moaned, gradually increasing pressure on his waist. Yawning, she said, "No, let's go back to the Hole before it snows again."

"Hold tight then. Pepper will have to sprout wings." Nudging the roan with his heels, Billy settled lower in the saddle, resigning himself to a faster pace.

Light snowflakes were spiraling from a charcoal sky when they rode southeast of Sundance. Wind had shifted from north to west, buffeting them from the right as they hunched over the roan. Snow swirling in hypnotic circles made him dizzy until he closed his eyes.

Although Andy had buried herself in the quilt, he sensed her shivering. His stomach ached with hunger, and he debated whether to save the few remaining pieces of jerky for their evening meal. They had no money and nothing left to trade. Perhaps a friendly rancher would invite them in for supper, if they could find one.

After an incalculable length of time, the wind slackened and snow fell as though it were weighted, targeted for the ground instead of his eyes. A thick white mantle covered the rolling hills. Sitting erect, shielding his face with a gloved hand, he squinted to determine direction. They seemed stalled in a quickening white curtain. Berating himself for not riding into Sundance, he turned to look back at the gelding's tracks, which were rapidly disappearing.

"What's wrong?" she asked sleepily.

"Nuthin'." He kicked Pepper gently with his heels. If the snow didn't let up soon, they could become lost. Billy didn't want to consider the consequences.

Light was growing dimmer. He followed a muted glow, knowing the sun set south of west during early November. If they could stay this course, they should arrive at the eastern entrance to the Hole in the Wall canyon within four or five days. But before darkness settled in, they would have to find shelter.

Pepper was tiring under the double load, his breath labored. Billy slowed the roan to a walk, searching for any kind of haven from the storm. There seemed nothing out there but endless waves of lustrous white hills.

Andy was quiet. He knew she was no longer dozing, and her silence bothered him.

"You all right?" he asked, turning his head to one side.

"Yes, Billy, but where are we?" Her tone was more intense.

"We're somewhere southeast of Sundance. We'll stop as soon as we find a place to stay."

"And if we don't?"

"We will," he said, forcing a laugh. "There are sheep camps out on the grasslands. It's just a matter of time 'til we find one." He hoped his voice belied his lack of conviction. No need worrying Andy. He was troubled enough for them both.

Her shuddering was more pronounced, and he gripped one of her gloved hands with his free one. If they lived through this frozen nightmare, he promised himself he'd never let go, but he knew chances were slim they would survive the night. Flakes were heavier now and falling like a barrage of frozen bullets. When he reached to pull the quilt over his head, the ache in his shoulder increased to a steady throb.

Visibility was limited to Pepper's ears, which twitched constantly to prevent them from freezing. The snow-choked air was closing in on Billy, forcing his breath in short gasps. Sweat trickled down his chest although the temperature had dropped low enough to freeze his brows in a permanent scowl.

He was unaware of the building until they were upon it. The steep-roofed wooden structure suddenly appeared out of the whiteness, as if by magic. Dismounting, Billy trudged around the edifice until he found a small covered entrance, admitting him on its south side. When no one answered his knock, he opened the door cautiously and peered inside. Striking a lucifer, he noticed a plaque which said he was standing in the vestibule of the Inyan Kara Methodist Church, Wyoming's first country house of worship. The plague also said it had been built six years earlier.

"Andy," he called as he burst from the church. "We're saved."

Slogging through ankle deep powder, he led Pepper to the entrance and tied him to a post.

"Nobody's here but we can sleep in the pews."

She nodded silently.

Helping her slide from the roan, he carried her inside. She appeared so tired that Billy worried she might be sick. Spreading her quilt over a front row bench, he shook out his coat and placed it under her head. Then, bending to kiss her forehead, he told her to get some sleep.

A small stove stood in the corner of the room, but Billy could find no wood to fuel it. The parishioners must bring wood for tithings, he thought, as he tightly closed the outer door.

When he had tended to the roan, he wrapped himself in his quilt and tried to get comfortable on the bench next to Andy's, but it was a cold, restless night. As the first rays of light filtered through the rectangular panes, he rose, deciding it was time to leave. Stepping from the vestibule, he saw that it was still snowing although the fall appeared to have tapered off.

"Time to go, Andy," he said, pulling her to her feet. "We'll pray for another church with softer benches."

Pepper seemed rested and anxious to be on his way. Having foraged for grass, he kept up a steady pace, crossing over several small frozen streams before snowflakes took on immense proportions. Billy stuck out his tongue to catch the flakes, but spat them out when he experienced their metallic after taste.

He was dozing when the gelding lost his balance. They were descending a slope when the roan stumbled and landed on his knees. Losing his grip on the reins, Billy tumbled over the gelding's head. There was no air in his lungs to amplify his cry of pain when Andy fell across his back, still wrapped in her quilt.

Billy's thoughts were of dying. Searing pain filled his chest, and he was unable to breathe. Andrea attempted to roll him onto his back.

"Billy?" she shrieked, staring into his eyes.

Grimacing, he managed to nod his head, but the effort shot waves of pain the length of his spine.

When she pulled away, he croaked, "Pepper." He heard the gelding's whicker and knew that he was down.

Unbuttoning his coat, she pulled his shirt aside to check his shoulder wound. Satisfied that it wasn't bleeding, she moved to the roan to comfort him, but Pepper seemed inconsolable. Tossing his head, he repeatedly tried to regain his footing but fell back to his knees.

Billy feared Andrea would lapse into hysterics. He was relieved when she reached for the gelding's bridle and tried to help him rise.

"Get up, boy," she pleaded, but the roan kept sinking in the snow. She stroked his forelock and neck until he quieted. By the time Pepper resigned himself to lying on his side, Billy was able to pull himself into a sitting position. Pain was lessening and breathing becoming easier. Groaning, he struggled to his feet and carefully shook out each leg.

"Doesn't feel like anything's broken," he said, gasping.

Relief flooded Andy's face as she continued to stroke the roan. "I think we're in a small stream bed. Pepper must have slipped on the ice."

Billy nodded his agreement, his breath still in short supply. As he knelt to touch the roan's legs, he noted soft swelling in the extensor tendons that crossed in front of the knees. The roan's cannons appeared uninjured when he gently ran his fingers over the tendons. Untying the kerchief from his neck, he dried Pepper's legs and probed for a rupturing of the bursae sack. If the synavial fluid, or joint oil, had leaked out, his legs could be permanently stiff. Billy was relieved no oil had been released.

Pepper nickered softly and blew through his nostrils.

"Is he all right? Can he stand?" she asked.

"I think so, but he needs to get his footing." As he spoke, Billy reached for his quilt, which had been flung aside when he fell. Smoothing the cover carefully under the roan's legs, he pulled on the bridle, urging Pepper to stand. The horse made several attempts before gaining a foothold.

"Let's walk him a ways to see if he's all right." Billy shook his quilt and draped it over his shoulders.

Trudging off into the thick white veil, they walked carefully until ice no longer hid beneath the snow. Pepper stepped hesitantly, but didn't appear to be limping. Gripping one of the stirrups, Andy dragged along, head down, clutching the quilt around her. Each step was painful as Billy tramped forward gripping the headstall, watching the gelding's progress. When they crossed a large drift, snow crept in over his boots. Before long he could no longer feel his toes. His body screamed to recline but he had to keep going. The alternative was much worse than frostbitten feet. When they climbed another low hill, he was satisfied Pepper's injuries were confined to skinned knees. They then mounted to ride blindly through the storm.

* * * *

Fine grains of sand-like snow had been falling for nearly an hour when the outlaws spotted several horses grazing in a roadside pasture. Twilight was graying the Black Hills, and they decided to wait for darkness.

"Sure wish we had field glasses," Harve said, squinting.

"Hard to tell what shape they're in."

"Purdy big for saddle hosses."

Half an hour later they found that Harve was right. The farmer's draft horses were lumbering and slow as well as uncomfortable riding bareback.

"It'll be New Year's before we get back to the Hole," Sundance complained.

"They'll have to do 'til we find something faster."

The two men rode within sight of a wooden bridge where moonlight betrayed a party of horsemen stationed near the approach.

"Whoa," Sundance whispered.

"Looks like a posse."

"What'll we do?"

"We can't outrun 'em on these old plugs, so you better follow my lead."

Riding single file, the outlaws advanced on the bridge, where Harve broke into a Scottish drinking song.

"Halt!" someone yelled.

"You boys got somethin' to drink?" Harve hiccupped loudly.

"A couple of damned drunken farmhands."

"Where you headed?" another voice asked.

"Home, I reckon," Harve said, slurring his words. "If you ain't get no hooch, we'll find somebody who does."

"They might be some of the prisoners," a young rider said.

"Escapin' on a couple of draft hosses?" The laugh was chorused by several others.

"Seen any strangers on foot lately?" another man asked.

"We been drinkin' at Paddy's place since day 'fore yesterdee," Harve drawled.

"Then you better get your asses home. There's a storm brewing. We don't wanna find you stiffs in a snow bank, come morning."

Harve nudged his horse into a walk, crossing the bridge without further incident. He resisted the urge to kick his mount's ribs, knowing a three-legged dog could outrun him.

"Oh, there's somethin' in the bott'le for the mor-nin'." Harve sang at full lung capacity in his best Scottish brogue.

"Shut up, you damn fool," a posse man yelled. "Them jailbirds can hear ya twenty miles off."

Chapter Eighteen

Darkness brought with it a sense of suffocation. Snow was falling so heavily that Andrea felt she could no longer breathe. Hunched over the roan, they had traveled until daylight dimmed in what they hoped was a straight line. Unable to continue, she begged him to stop.

"Pepper's done in, anyway," Billy said. "We'll have to bed down in the snow."

He chose a flat area on the leeward side of a rolling hill. Between them they hobbled Pepper and covered him with a quilt. Then, wrapping themselves in the remaining quilt, they clung to one another, shivering.

The snow continued, quietly layering insulation against the rapidly dropping temperatures. Snuggling for warmth, neither spoke for several moments.

"It'll get colder before morning."

When she didn't respond, he hugged her until she gasped. His closeness spawned strange, uneasy feelings. Nuzzling his throat, she momentarily forgot the storm. He shifted uneasily, sleep eluding them both.

Billy then surprised her by whispering, "I couldn't let you go."

"What do you mean?"

"I was afraid you'd get lost, or killed by an animal—"

"Oh. I thought you would miss me."

"That, too."

"This may be our last night together, and you've never even said you love me."

"I do, Andy."

"Why is it so hard to say?"

"I guess I thought you wouldn't believe me."

"Just say it."

He brought his mouth down on hers with an urgency that frightened her. Current surged the length of her body, his passion overwhelming her. Breathless, she struggled feebly, an alarm sounding somewhere in her brain, but she was too aroused to resist when his body covered hers, hands caressing her face, lips moving to her eyelids, throat and ears, warming them with his breath. She was floundering and no longer cared. The storm didn't matter. Billy's love would keep her alive.

The kisses stopped. He whispered, "God, I love you."

She was embarrassed when tears rimmed her eyes.

"Don't cry. You know I'd never hurt you."

"You already have."

Before she could explain, a sharp cry of pain sliced through the silent storm. Billy groaned and pushed his head from the quilt, his desire gone limp. The scream came again, louder this time, although they could tell it was from a distance.

"Mountain lion?" she asked, trembling.

"It sounds human." Easing himself from the quilt, Billy stood listening, one hand reassuring his nervous gelding.

"Somebody needs help. We'd better get over there."

Billy helped her into the saddle. Leading the gelding, he stopped several times to listen as heavy snow continued to fall. When she heard the voice again, she was sure it was a woman, but what could cause such agony?

"Over there," he said, pointing.

She noticed faint light. Seating himself behind the saddle, Billy reached around her for the reins. Within minutes he dismounted near a sheepwagon and helped her from the saddle.

"You better knock," he whispered. "They'll be more likely to open the door if they know a woman's out here."

Climbing the wooden steps, she hesitated before rapping on the Dutch door. She heard a gasp and clatter of metal, and nearly fell from the steps in her haste to retreat. Billy moved up, blocking her path, his gun hand at the ready.

The door's upper half opened outward, and a man no taller than herself appeared wide-eyed with surprise.

"We heard screams and wondered if we could help." She extended a snow-encrusted glove.

"*Madre de dios!*" a tenor voice said. "*Mi mujer es dar a luz.*"

"You need help? Uh—*Necesita ayuda? Soy mujer.* I'm a woman." She allowed the quilt to slide from her head.

"*Si, muchas gracias.*" The sheepherder stared at them incredulously before motioning them both inside.

"Where'd you learn Mexican?" Billy asked as he followed her up the crude wooden steps.

"My mother's housekeeper was from Madrid, but I've forgotten most of what she taught me."

Another cry startled them as they stepped inside. Lying on a rumpled bed at the end of the wagon, a small, dark-haired young woman gripped the wooden frame. Perspiration glistened on her forehead, her black hair tousled in damp, tangled strands.

"Aiiiiiieeeeeeee," she cried, taking no notice of them.

Memory of a neighbor's childbirth stabbed at Andrea's conscience. She had accompanied her grandmother to the birthing, but had done little more than hold the woman's hand. Gramma had delivered a stillborn child, the mother suffering excruciating pain.

Andrea shivered with fright.

"*Donde esta el aqua caliente?*" she said haltingly, glancing about for boiling water. Andrea remembered Gramma heating a kettle of water to sterilize the umbilical scissors.

"*Aqui, aqui,*" the man said, pointing to a pot of water simmering on the small wood stove in the corner near the door.

Heat collecting near the arched canvas ceiling made Andrea dizzy, and she shed her quilt before sitting on the bed. Looking down at the woman, she smiled, patting her hand reassuringly.

"*Ayudame!*" the woman cried, grasping her wrist.

"I *will* help you." Andrea nodded but wondered what she could possibly do. She noticed tears glistening in the sheepherder's dark eyes, his full mustache drooping sadly about the corners of his trembling lips.

Billy stood awkwardly inside the door, fidgeting. Modesty told her that men should wait outside, but the storm belied that notion. Indicating the small table and two bench seats, she said, "*Sientese, por favor.* Sit down, Billy, before you collapse."

Turning to the sheepherder, she asked, "*Tiene damas?*"

"*Si.*" He pulled a battered checkerboard from the cupboard. Seating himself at the small table facing the bed, he scattered a handful of checkers across the board, beckoning Billy to join him.

Andrea removed her gloves and washed her hands. She then wet a towel in the small basin to dab the woman's brow.

"*Como se llama?*" she asked between contractions.

"Rosita," the woman replied, smiling faintly, her large, dark eyes frightened.

"Andrea," she said in return, pointing to her chest.

"*Su pelo?*" Rosita touched her own hair.

Andrea laughed nervously as she smoothed her cropped locks. "*Tijeras de ovejas,*" she said, pantomiming the cutting action of sheep shears.

Rosita's laughter was cut short by another squeezing pain. Gripping Andrea's hand so hard that it hurt, she cried, "*Jorge, me moriendo!*"

Tears running down his checks, the young sheepherder rushed forward to gather Rosita into his arms. "*No, no, mi corazon. Lo siento. Lo siento.*"

Billy turned in his seat to face Andrea, an uncomfortable questioning look on his face.

"Rosita thinks she's dying," she said, "and Jorge's feeling guilty."

Billy flushed, lowering his eyes. "I'm gonna see about Pepper."

"I wish you would stay."

"I'll be back," he said, pushing the door open. "Call if you need me."

A chilling draft invaded the sheepwagon, reminding Andrea of the storm. Before she could worry about Billy wandering about in the snow, Rosita cried "*Bebe!*" Her face reddened as she bore down.

Jorge's huge brown eyes widened like a frightened puppy.

"*Esta bueno,* it's all right," Andrea said to comfort him. Lifting the blankets, she draped them around Rosita's upturned knees.

"*Tiene impermeable?* Or some canvas," she added in English, unable to remember its Spanish equivalent.

Jorge rushed to the cupboard, returning with a folded yellow slicker. Smiling her thanks, Andrea slipped the raincoat under Rosita's hips, covering it with a blanket.

The young sheepherder knelt beside the bed, holding Rosita's hand in both his thin, trembling ones. Sitting midway on the wooden frame, Andrea applied light pressure to the woman's knees, pressing them apart to allow passage of the baby.

"*Empuje!*" She remembered Gramma demanding that her neighbor push during the final stages of labor. She had thought it harsh and unnecessary at the time, but used that same tone with Rosita The woman needed no instructions. The baby's head was already emerging from the birth canal.

"*Empuje!*" she demanded once more, gently easing the infant's mucous-slicked head toward her. Rosita strained and bore down, gritting her teeth. Turning the tiny body so that each shoulder slipped free, Andrea was able to pull the baby into a cold, new world.

The baby didn't cry, which frightened her even more. Jorge motioned frantically for her to hold the baby by its feet. Cringing, she slapped its red little bottom and was relieved to hear the child's lusty wail.

Quickly inspecting him, she announced, *"Es un nino! Que guapo!"*

Dark haired, red-skinned and wrinkled, he was held for his parents to behold. Telling them their son was handsome was a small lie, not worthy of crossed fingers to nullify it. The baby resembled his father and would be handsome one day, but she thought he now looked like a puckered little monkey.

Jorge's grin was so wide that Andrea could have counted his teeth. Rushing to the wood stove, he dipped sheep shears into boiling water, swirled them around and brought them back. Wiping them carefully with a flour sack towel, she hesitated. Where did one cut the umbilical cord? She wished she had watched her grandmother more closely. He pointed to a spot several inches from the baby's naval, and she nodded gratefully.

The sheepherder helped his wife expel the afterbirth while Andrea cleaned the baby and wrapped him in a blanket. When the baby was safely in his mother's arms, Andrea pulled on her jacket and wearily walked into the storm. She found Billy leaning against the sheepwagon, stroking Pepper's mane. The snow's intensity had decreased to light swirls.

"It's a boy," she said quietly.

"I know."

"Why didn't you come in to congratulate—"

"Because," he said, looking away.

"What's wrong?"

"I could have done that to you."

"Oh, Billy. Come inside," she said. "Let's have a look at the baby."

He reluctantly followed her into the wagon.

Jorge's teeth shone like piano ivory when Billy offered his hand, mumbling congratulations.

Andrea slipped past them and knelt beside Rosita and the child. *"Se llama el nino lo mismo que el padre?"* she asked slowly.

Rosita smiled. "Si, Jorge Ernesto Guillermo Sanchez."

"She named him for his father," Andrea translated. "And one of the names is yours—*Guillermo'*— William."

A corner of his lip lifted in a smile.

She sensed his embarrassment and was not surprised when he again retreated out of doors. After tying a quilt securely to Pepper's back, Billy returned to sleep the remaining hours of the night with Andrea on the sheep wagon floor.

Next morning, Jorge prepared them breakfast of sausage, biscuits, and grease-drenched potatoes. He was still wearing his toothy grin when he thanked Andrea profusely. Before they left, with one of Pepper's saddlebags stocked with sausage and biscuits, Andrea sat for several moments observing the sleeping child. Peacefulness had settled in, replacing the pain and fear of the previous night. She sighed, wishing Billy were as kind and devoted as Jorge seemed to be.

Glancing up, she caught his attention and motioned him to the bed. Frowning, he allowed her to pull him near.

"Aren't they beautiful?" she whispered.

"Yes," he admitted, "they are."

Gruffness crept into his voice. "Let's get going. If we're lucky, we might make the KC Ranch by tomorrow night."

Jorge pointed them in the right direction and they waved until the sheep wagon faded into the mist. Half a foot of snow had accumulated and by dawn, the storm showed no sign of letting up.

"I've been thinking about last night," Billy said, squinting at the sky. "What would Jorge have done if we hadn't come along?"

"Sheepherders help deliver lambs."

"But he was so…"

"Nervous?"

"That's the word."

"He couldn't bear Rosita's pain, but he knew how to deliver the baby." She was relieved the birthing had gone well and that her prayers had been answered. The baby had probably saved their lives.

They stopped briefly for a noon meal on the sheltered side of a rolling hill. Snowfall had decreased, and they were able to use cairns as landmarks. Jorge had told her the rocks were piled on the open prairie to prevent sheepherders from becoming lost. As long as daylight persisted, they had some hope of finding shelter. If they didn't find shelter by nightfall, Andrea planned to do some serious praying.

* * * *

Tom swung one leg over the other and stretched his arms beneath his head. Back in his old cell, he cheerfully settled his body into grooves he had previously worn in the mattress. Walt occupied the adjoining cell and was still glaring at him. Despite his nasty look, Tom knew his friend was grateful for a full belly and warm place to sleep. Jail wasn't so bad. The food was regular and fair-to-middling.

He questioned the new night deputy when the supper trays arrived.

"Heard anything about the boys?"

"Still loose, I reckon. Sheriff posted rewards of $625 for each of 'em."

Tom hoped they had reached the waiting horses. If not, they were worn down and half-starved by now.

"Bye-the-bye, boys," the stoop-shouldered deputy said on his way out. "Sheriff found five saddle horses hobbled in Spearfish Canyon. Damned near froze to death. Nice horses, at that."

Tom cursed, hitting the side of his bunk.

"Shut up, Peep," his partner said. "If you'd rode with Red Cloud, General Custer woulda won the battle."

* * * *

Snow fell in slanting sheets, pushed by an accelerating wind. They should have stayed with the sheep wagon, Billy berated himself, but a crying baby would have driven most men into the storm.

"Are we going in the right direction?" Andy sounded only curious.

He wasn't sure of anything. Gripping the reins in his teeth, he pulled his hat lower, the quilt closer, as he settled into the saddle. Until the wind picked up, Pepper seemed relatively unaffected by below freezing temperatures, or his fall on the ice. Billy worried the roan might develop some sickness of the lungs. He leaned forward, listening for coughing or wheezing that could signal trouble. Pepper's breathing sounded normal. The gelding was, however, growing skittish. Small ears laid back, he was looking about as he moved through the snow as though wary of what lay ahead. Billy tensed, scanning the monotonous landscape, squinting through streaks of snow.

"What's wrong?" Andrea's voice was sharp.

"Nothing."

"We're not lost, are we?"

"Of course not." Lost was the least of Billy's worries. There was something out there causing the gelding's apprehension. It could be anything. Coyotes. A posse. He doubted the latter. Most people had better sense than to travel in a Wyoming snowstorm. Billy cursed himself again for his stupidity. They had been lucky to stumble upon the sheep wagon. Tonight, that luck might not hold.

He thought he heard a howling noise but dismissed it as the wind. Pepper was not convinced. Nervously tossing his head, the gelding whickered a warning, sidestepping when the snarling form of a wolf appeared in the mist, effectively blocking their path.

"Easy boy." Gently stroking the roan's neck, he swiveled his head slowly to whisper to Andy, "Sit still and don't let on you're afraid. There's a wolf up ahead."

She groaned and leaned around him to look. Some ten feet ahead, a gaunt, gray wolf stood guard over an enormous fallen ewe. They had obviously interrupted a long-awaited meal. Red-eyed and growling viciously, the wolf stood motionless, as though waiting for them to make the first move.

Pepper shied to the left, high-stepping as though his feet were on fire. It was all Billy could do to keep him from bolting. He reasoned that he couldn't shoot the wolf without spooking the roan. Pepper was on the verge of rearing and unseating them both when Billy decided the wolf was more interested in a meal than he was in attacking them. Sweat beaded his forehead and rolled down his face. Slowly massaging Pepper's neck, he eased him to the left, away from the dead ewe. He wished he could see the gelding's eyes as the wolf was watching them. He was afraid Pepper was telegraphing the fear they all felt. Thank God they were downwind from the wolf.

"Good boy," he said softy, applying light, even pressure to Pepper's flanks. As he spoke, the wolf moved forward to resume ripping flesh from the ewe.

Billy waited several moments before crouching slowly, pressing his elbows into Andy's arms, which encircled his waist. When she clung tightly to him, he kicked the roan into a fast start, reining him at an angle away from the wolf.

Neither of them looked back. Holding his breath, Billy prayed Andy was able to hang on. Pepper wasn't the fastest sprinter on the high plains, but he was well-trained and possessed great stamina. If any horse could outrun the wolf, it was his roan. He doubted they were being followed. The wolf only seemed interested in an immediate meal, one unable to fight back. His gelding ran a long while before Billy reined him in. Turning to check their back trail, he was satisfied they were out of danger.

He now feared they were off course. Dismounting, he swiveled, trying to get his bearings. Which way was West? Andy was no help. When he lifted her from behind the cantle, she wanted to be held. He resisted holding her for more than a moment, knowing he had to keep his wits.

The roan was wearing down. "We'd better walk for awhile," he said, "and give him a rest."

Gripping the headstall, Billy led Pepper toward the failing light. Andy walked behind, gripping a stirrup and following in the tracks Billy had made through half a foot of snow. They had to find shelter. The hills were steeper now with deep gorges running east and west. Rock piles towering over their heads were barriers to reckon with. Perhaps they could find a cave in the rocks where they could camp. They couldn't go on forever.

The temperature continued to drop. Billy knew it sometimes dipped to minus forty degrees, although it was early November, not the middle of January. He didn't think it was below zero, but couldn't be sure. No one could survive in temperatures that cold for long, especially riding double on a worn out horse.

Patting Pepper affectionately, he willed himself to reach their destination. Turning to check on Andy, he noticed Pepper nearly dragging her. Halting, he insisted she ride, reasoning that ninety pounds was much less than their combined weight. She appeared to be in worse shape than Pepper. None of them had gotten much sleep the previous night. He was beginning to wonder if even he had the stamina to continue. The constant ache in his shoulder was nearly unbearable.

Twilight was approaching when clouds began to break up, with patches of blue in the western sky. He turned to glance at Andy and share a weary smile. When darkness descended, the snow stopped falling, but they had not yet sighted shelter on the horizon. Boots crunching through a thick mantle of snow, Billy's spirits heightened when the moon sprayed its first rays of light across the frozen terrain. As it rose, the moon's reflected light illuminated the snow's surface, as though dawn had broken behind them.

Turning again to gaze at Andy, he noticed her eyes were closed, her gloved hands gripped tightly over the saddle horn, as though she were praying. Glancing skyward where stars glimmered overhead, he noticed one so large and brilliant that he wondered how he had missed it. Billy changed course slightly to the north, heading toward the star.

The barren dunes were endless as the moon reached its apex and began its descent. Afraid to stop and rest, he feared his body would refuse to continue; their bones found the following spring picked clean by wolves.

Chapter Nineteen

A light snow was falling and clouds hid the moon. Exhausted, they found a large cutbank on the leeward side of a bluff, where they stopped to rest. Billy looped Pepper's reins over a small chimneyed rock, and kicked snow from beneath the overhang. Huddled in their quilts, they slept a few hours until dawn.

When Andrea awoke, she discovered that snow had stopped falling. Shaking a thin, insulating layer from her quilt, she exclaimed, "Thank you for answering my prayers."

Billy groaned and sat up. "I do my best, Andy."

"Not you, silly. Let's make breakfast and be on our way." Glancing skyward, she saw large patches of blue sky among the scattered clouds.

While they were thawing Jorge's sausage and biscuits over a small sagebrush campfire, Billy admitted he had never liked sheep.

"Why, because the gang won't stoop to steal them?"

"I'm my own man," he said heatedly.

"If you hadn't kidnapped me, I'd be herding sheep of my own."

"I know," he said, reaching for her.

Andrea pushed him away. "You won't even consider herding a small flock?"

"No!"

"Then we have nothing more to talk about."

"Your way or none at all!"

The gelding's frightened whicker startled them both. Crouching beneath the overhang, they noticed someone standing near the gelding, with a grip on his headstall.

Coarse laughter caused them both to freeze. "Need some help?" a base voice asked. "Sounds like a couple of wildcats caught in a trap."

The stout man wore grimy buckskins and tall rawhide boots. A saddle was slung over one shoulder. Andrea knew fur traders were extinct, so he must have crawled out of someone's history book.

"Amos Cross," he said, extending his hand.

"William and Andrew Blackburn," Billy said, standing to grasp with his own.

The stranger scrutinized Andrea, his black hair hanging loose in long greasy strands past his shoulders. "Ya don't say. I coulda swore…"

"He always gets teased about his looks," Billy said. "We were thinking of shaving his head and having him grow a beard."

"Too young for that." Cross leaned for a closer look.

"What're you doing on foot?"

"My hoss stepped in a hole back a ways. Had to shoot 'im." Shifting his attention to Pepper, he said, "How much for this big feller?"

"He's not for sale. We're breaking camp and heading for the KC Ranch."

"Just came from that direction. Purty rough country. Easier to walk than ride."

Andrea sensed Billy's alarm and hurriedly gathered their gear. "They'll be looking for us if we're not back soon," she said, edging toward Pepper.

"Our old man's the KC cattle foreman," Billy told him.

"Yeah? What's his name?"

When Billy hesitated, Andrea's throat constricted.

"Abe Blackburn. Everybody knows that. Him and the boys are probably out looking for us now. We were expected yesterday."

Cross's grin resembled a sneer. "What're you two doing out here in the Badlands?"

"We took some hosses to the sale in Spearfish. We didn't count on a blizzard blowing in."

"That right?"

She found Cross staring at her whenever she glanced up. Edging toward Pepper's opposite saddlebag, she decided to stow their cooking utensils.

Pepper snorted and tossed his head when Billy placed the saddle on his back. Andrea hurriedly loaded the saddlebags and moved to one side, keeping both men in sight. She was prepared to climb the bank if there was trouble. While Billy tightened Pepper's cinch, Cross again grasped the headstall. The gelding sidestepped and whickered.

"Nice hoss you got here, son."

"He's mean-spirited and doesn't like strangers."

"Oh, he likes me all right. Don'tcha big fella?"

Cross abruptly swung his tattered saddle, hitting Billy in the ribs and knocking him to the ground. Quickly lifting Pepper's reins, he slid his foot into the stirrup. When Andrea screamed, the roan spun toward her, throwing Cross off-balance. Bolting toward the arroyo, Pepper dragged the stranger with him, his heel still caught in the stirrup. Billy's shrill whistle failed to stop the gelding. Continuing up the rocky gorge, Cross flailed and bounced his way to the top.

"Pepper," she cried as he disappeared over the rim.

Billy was on his feet and running. She watched him climb the draw and vanish. Following, she dug in her heels and scrambled over the embankment, but there was no one on the horizon. Heart pounding, she glimpsed a path in the snow. Following, she saw that it led to a huge mound of rocks with a thick snowy mantle. She heard a troubled voice before she rounded the nearest boulder.

Andrea found Billy kneeling beside Amos Cross, Pepper ground-reined nearby. When he noticed her approach, he warned, "Stay back. You don't need to see this." Turning his head, he retched.

Circling so that she could see, she gasped when Cross's crumpled body was visible.

"He's dead." Billy wiped his mouth with his sleeve.

Another dead man. Stunned, she sank to her knees in the snow. "No," she wailed. Jake's jaundiced face swam before her eyes.

"We've got to bury him so the wolves don't get him."

"How?" she said, sobbing. "The ground's frozen."

"With rocks."

She noticed him going through Cross's pockets. "What are you doing? Robbing him?"

Billy's head jerked up and he glared at her. "He was gonna steal Pepper."

"Two wrongs never make a right."

"We need money to get you home, Andy."

"Once an outlaw, always an outlaw," she said angrily. She refused to help him bury Cross. Mounting Pepper, she watched him carry rocks heavy enough to damage his spine. When he finished, he said, "You wanna say some words over him?"

"I already have. And while I was at it, I prayed for your soul."

Billy appeared crestfallen. "Survival," he said lamely.

They had ridden for nearly an hour when they crossed a wide, deeply rutted trail. "This must be the bloody Bozeman," he said, dismounting. "Trail heads north to the Virginia City goldfields. If we take it, we'll wind up in Montana."

"Then we should be going that way," she said, pointing, knowing full well Billy was the trail blazer.

"We'll change course to a more westerly direction," he said. "The Bozeman runs north by west." Checking Pepper's feet, he was relieved to find them free of trash. Examining the roan carefully, he decided he had better walk. For the next hour, he led his horse over hills growing steeper, the gullies deeper.

Before they reached the rim of a steep rise, they found an arroyo blocking their path. Pepper was wearing down, and Andy would have to walk. He searched the horizon for Pumpkin Buttes, but the sun's glare on snow blinded him. Squinting, he followed the movement of a herd of antelope, failing to notice the depression ahead of him. Sliding on snow-covered sand, his feet went out from under him, and he nearly fell into the gully. He heard Andy's cry of alarm and felt her hands beneath his arms, helping him to his feet. They then surveyed the terrain that lay ahead. Deep arroyos spread in every direction as far as they could see.

Badlands! He didn't remember traveling this way before. Maybe the Buttes were south instead of north. Forming spectacles with his hands, Billy strained his eyes to determine what lay on the horizon. To his left was a low range of mountains heavily wooded with pine. Where were they?

"We're lost, aren't we, Billy?"

No sense lying to her. "Yeah, I guess we are."

Andy shook her head but said nothing.

"We need to find three buttes," he said. "Do you see them?"

She shook her head. "Can't the sun give you directions?"

Billy looked at his shadow and calculated their course. It was impossible to travel through the arroyos in a straight line. They needed a distant landmark to guide them. There was nothing but a thick blue haze to the West.

"If we angle to the northwest, we should see the Big Horn Mountains before the sun goes down." Crossing her fingers, she said, "By then we should be out of the badlands."

He grudgingly admired Andy's smarts. She always seemed to have a ready answer, like she thought he couldn't figure things out for himself. Stopping to gaze to the south, he decided to keep the low range of mountains on his left. Eventually, they should reach the southern spur of the Big Horn Mountains.

"This way," he said, leading Pepper into a wide draw. Behind him, Andy slipped and fell although she was gripping Pepper's stirrup.

"Keep going," she said, regaining her footing. "This is more fun than sledding."

Surprised, Billy marched with renewed vigor. Andy was a fine companion, he thought, despite her nagging. Too bad they had not met sooner, before he became an outlaw.

After many hours of skirting deepening arroyos, the sun was setting slightly to the south, but they had not spotted the buttes or the Big Horn Mountains. Shading their eyes, they continued to evade one arroyo after another, unable to determine how many still lay ahead. Soon they would be forced to camp for the night. When Billy suggested another cutbank, Andy seemed receptive until a wolf howled nearby.

"Keep going," she said. "There's got to be someone living out here somewhere."

"Nobody in his right mind would live in a place like this."

A few moments later, Andrea cried, "Look." A thin trail of smoke was outlined against the tree-covered foothills to the south.

Undecided, he stopped. It would take them until dark to reach the smoke. Was it a line shack or someone camped on the edge of the arroyos? Billy's mind raced back to their earlier encounter with Amos Cross. He couldn't risk another horse thief. He realized they were spotlighted by the setting sun, as well as blinded by it. Whoever was out there had seen them by now. A good tracker could easily find them once the moon rose high enough to reflect light from the snow.

Holding his hand to screen the sun, he looked back to where he had seen the smoke trail. There was no sign of it now, and he moved forward to get a better look. Billy heard Andy's warning too late. The earth crumbled beneath his feet and he fell forward, losing his grip on Peppers headstall. The sun disappeared and darkness enveloped him until sparks briefly shot before his eyes.

* * * *

"I heard the Wild Bunch was camped near Wamsutter."

"Yeah, but word got around so quick that guards were posted at all the banks along the Union Pacific, clear on into Evanston."

A wind-tanned rancher spat tobacco juice at a cuspidor and adjusted his boot on the rail.

"My brother-in-law was hired as a special guard down at the Sweetwater Coal Company payroll office," the rotund bartender said, wiping Red

Desert dust from the counter.

"They musta been shaking in their boots wondering when Butch would come riding in."

"When they spotted all them extra guards, the gang pulled up stakes and headed south."

"Is that a fact?"

"Gotta give Cassidy credit, though."

"How's that?"

"He knew there was too many guns laying in wait."

"Yeah, some saddle tramps recognized the gang when they rode into Wamsutter."

The small, southern Wyoming railroad town, halfway between Rawlins and Point of Rocks, temporarily harbored the Texas members of the Wild Bunch, Will Carver and Ben Kilpatrick. Average and quietly unassuming, Carver was a half foot shorter than dark-haired, ladies' man Kilpatrick, who was nicknamed the "Tall Texan."

Although Butch and Elzy Lay considered the area "ripe picking's," they weren't foolish enough to attempt robberies under full alert. While Elzy led the gang south into Colorado, Butch rode north for Lander and his confidant Mary Boyd Rhodes, a half-blood Shoshone. She lived as his common-law wife until Butch was imprisoned for horse theft.

Butch rode north of Lander to the Jakey's Fork Ranch. Margaret Simpson had been a second mother to him while he worked for the family prior to his arrest. The Simpsons greeted him warmly, avoiding any mention of his prison sentence until after supper when Butch brought up the subject, himself.

"Lowest point of my life," he said, "but the warden and guards treated me well."

"It was a sad time for us," Margaret Simpson said, patting Butch's hand.

Her husband glanced down at his work boots, unable to meet Butch's eyes. "It was especially hard because another Simpson prosecuted the case."

"Will was just doin' his job..."

"With a third grade education," John said, shaking his head, "they let him pass the bar exam in open court before three judges. Lucky he married a school teacher who taught him Latin and proper English, or he'd still be clerking in a grocery store."

Margaret Simpson said, "We'll never forget the long ride you made through the storm to bring back medicine when the children were sick."

"You folks was always good to me, like my own family."

Before he left, he asked Margaret to write a note to his friend, asking her to meet him at the usual place. She wrote dutifully, and he wondered whether she suspected his true relationship with Mary.

When he arrived in Lander the following day, he stopped to visit Gene Amoretti, the local banker.

One of Amoretti's clerks delivered the note to Mary while the two men discussed old times. Amoretti had been a struggling young rancher neighboring the Simpson spread where he and Butch became friends.

At the appointed time, Butch kept his rendezvous in the foothills of Shoshone Forest. Checking her back trail, he made sure she hadn't been followed. The slender, dark-eyed young woman clung to him as he stroked her raven hair. Berating himself for continuing their relationship, he knew he had caused her more than her share of pain. He was also aware that she worshiped him.

"How's Olie?" he asked good-naturedly, although he still resented the ranch hand she had married while Butch was in prison.

"He's well. You know he'd kill us both."

Shrugging, he asked, "And little Mary?"

"She's growing like a young colt. She's six summers now." Mary hid her face in his chest, unable to stop the tears.

Lifting her chin to gaze into her eyes, he said, "If I'd known..."

"She's doing well on the reservation. You know I couldn't keep her."

"If I hadn't been railroaded into prison, we'd be married with our own place and lotsa kids by now. You know I love kids."

"I know they love you. Lander people say George Cassidy is one of the finest men they ever knew."

Lowering his face to hers, he kissed her gently, then led her to a blanket spread upon the ground. Taking his time, he savored each touch as he slowly unbuttoned her dress, caressing her olive skin. Hanging from her neck was a gold chain and cross, duplicating the one she'd given him for safe passage. There was no need to tell her how much he loved her. She knew, but he told her repeatedly. They were both aware the stolen moments had to end, but they prolonged their euphoria as long as possible.

"I should have waited for you," she said, snuggling close as he lay spent and drowsy.

"Folks can be cruel. I know how you must have suffered."

"I didn't know you'd come back."

"The Cattlemen's Association blackballed me, and Otto Franc swore out another phony hoss stealin' warrant. I had to leave Wyoming, but not before I ran off fifty of his best hosses."

"You stole them?"

"No, I scattered 'em from hell to Houston."

Brushing stray hair from her forehead, he said, "I been thinkin' on applyin' for amnesty. Then I could work for the railroad honest as a guard."

"But how?"

"An old lawyer friend of mine by the name of Doug Preston in Rock Springs."

"But the governors are swearing out warrants on all the outlaws."

"I know. I also been thinkin' of goin' to South America. I could send for you…"

"I don't know, George. I think I am…" She flushed and patted her slightly rounded stomach.

The day was nearly exhausted when he rose, helping her to her feet.

"Where will you go now?"

"New Mexico. I'll be workin' at the WS Ranch near Alma. If you decide to send a message, I'll be usin' the name Jim Lowe."

Lifting her into the saddle, he led the mare down a narrow path toward Lander.

* * * *

Andrea had been squinting at the ground, avoiding the setting sun when Billy fell into the arroyo. When she realized what had happened, she fell to her knees on the rim and repeatedly called his name. Shading her eyes, she found that the gorge was deeper than most they had encountered. When her eyes adjusted to the shadows, she spotted him on his back, his head against a rock.

Billy can't be dead, she told herself as she retrieved his lariat. Tying it securely to Pepper's saddle horn, she led him to within a foot of the gorge. She then ground-reined him and lowered herself with the rope. Crumbling soil made her slip and bang her knuckles against the embankment. Crying out in pain, she heard Pepper whicker, and felt the lariat jerk in her hands.

"Pepper," she called, attempting to calm him before she made her final descent. She envisioned him rearing and pulling her out of the arroyo, dragging her as he'd done Amos Cross. Her heart pummeled her chest so hard that she found it hard to breath.

"Billy," she called when she finally caught her breath. "I'm coming down to help you."

Billy didn't answer. *Please God. Don't let him die.*

The roan stopped moving, and she slowly lowered herself to the bottom of the arroyo. When she looked up, it seemed a hundred feet to the rim, although she knew the rope was only fifty feet long. Twilight was already fading into darkness. When she looked down, she could not detect her own feet. Two hesitant steps later, she tripped over Billy.

Groping, she felt his head and something wet and sticky in his hair. Clumsily untying the kerchief from his neck, she held it against what she perceived was his wound. Placing two fingers on his juggler vein, she was relieved to feel his pulse. Thank God he was still alive, but how was she going to get him out of there. Peering skyward, she could only discern faint light overhead and a vague sprinkling of stars.

She talked to Billy for some time, but he never even groaned. The snow beneath them was melting from body heat, and they both were getting wet. It was then she heard Pepper's frightened whicker.

The rope! She panicked when she heard it sliding up the embankment. Leaving Billy, she groped along the arroyo walls, unable to locate the lariat.

"Pepper," she cried in anguish. "Please don't leave us down here."

Andrea heard a voice and thought she was hallucinating. A moment later someone called, "Are you all right down there?"

An angel's voice. It had to be. She had died, without knowing it, and gone to heaven. She stumbled back to Billy, praying that more than his body remained.

"Hello," the voice called again.

"Help," Andrea cried. "Please get us out of here."

A light shone from above and a face peered over the edge.

"We'll lower the rope," a woman said. "Tie it around your waist and we'll pull you out."

"The horse?"

"We've got him." The end of the rope landed on her head.

"Billy's hurt."

"We'll get him next. Are you ready?"

The angels tugged gently, and Andrea fought her way to the rim. Kneeling on the edge, she noticed two small figures clad in baggy trousers. Long dusters and large slouch hats made them appear even smaller. One of them held the lantern and Pepper's headstall. The other offered her a hand, a small callused one, but warm to the touch.

"Are you all right, dear?"

"Yes, but…"

"We're the Barlow twins," the soft voice said. "I'm Elvira and this is my sister Elizabeth." The woman holding Pepper and the lantern dipped her head in greeting.

"I-I'm Andy Blackburn," she said.

"Andy? That's a strange name for a young lady."

"I'm not a lady," she protested. "I'm a 13-year-old boy."

"Nonsense," Elvira said. "Let's see about getting your young man out of there." Without further comment, she tied the rope around her own waist, and with her twin's help, lowered herself into the gully. Elizabeth's lantern followed her sister down the hole, and she held it above her head, as Andrea steadied Pepper. Afraid of crumbling dirt and snow on the rim, Andrea stood back and prayed. Within minutes she heard Billy groan.

"He's all right," the tiny woman called. "Just give him a moment to gather his wits."

The moon was beginning to peep over the horizon when Billy crawled from the arroyo. Andrea backed the roan slowly from the rim until Billy was on his hands and knees. Gingerly holding his head, he asked what had happened.

"We'll talk about it back at the cabin," Elvira said, insisting he mount his roan.

When they hesitated, Elizabeth said, "We know the arroyos so well we could navigate them in our sleep."

"We've even given them names," her sister said, laughing softly. "The one you fell into is Juan Bad Horse. You picked one of the deepest arroyos." Her voice trailed off as she started forward.

"Juan Bad Horse?"

"He's a renegade Indian who leaves the Crow reservation to ambush travelers," Elvira said. "Bad Horse robs and kills people like yourselves who come this way."

"But how did you know that we—?"

"We scan the area every night before dark with field glasses. We have for years."

"You mean you live here?"

"Born here," she said. "We'll talk about it later." Leading Pepper, the old woman made her way on foot around each arroyo, without breaking stride. Andrea followed on a dark mare, ready to warn the others if he seemed to be slipping from the saddle.

Within a quarter hour they reached a large log cabin engulfed in scrubby pines. Andrea noticed a wooden platform perched high along the side of the structure, assuming it to be the sisters' lookout post. Dusting themselves before they went inside, Andrea was surprised by the neat, well-furnished interior.

The furniture, although crudely constructed, was cushioned with brightly-flowered material that Andrea was unable to identify. Sinking into the cushions, she felt as though she had, indeed, arrived in heaven.

"Let's take a look at your head." Elvira led Billy to the dining table. While her sister held the lantern, she carefully inspected his wound.

Pushing his head forward, she said, "You're not dizzy, are you?"

Resisting, he said no.

"Superficial wound," she declared. "You just took a nap to rest your weary bones."

Billy closed his eyes and rested his forehead in his hands. He yelped and glared at them both when tincture of iodine was applied to his scalp.

Elizabeth brought in snow wrapped in a towel to hold against his head. She told him to relax, and stroked his head. Billy glanced at Andrea as though he were under attack. She smiled at him, telling him how fortunate he was to have someone fussing over him, but he seemed so uncomfortable that she insisted on holding the ice pack herself.

"Time for supper," Elizabeth announced as both sisters busied themselves at the stove. Andrea was afraid Billy would refuse to eat mutton stew, and was pleasantly surprised when he emptied his bowl a second time.

Seated at the table, Andrea took a closer look at their benefactors. They were older than she imagined. Late sixties, she guessed. Their faces were deeply tanned and wrinkled from the elements. They were both slim and youthful in their movements, however, and her head was filled with questions.

When Elvira finished her stew, she set her spoon aside, saying, "I know you're curious about us living here alone."

"Alone?" Billy said. "Where are the men?"

"We never married," Elizabeth said. "Our father killed a man in self defense and hid in the badlands for years, living off wild game. How he convinced our mother to move out here is still a mystery."

Elvira smiled at her twin, saying, "Before they died, our parents accumulated a herd of cattle."

He grinned, interrupting her with, "Longhorns, Angus, white-faced Herefords? You still got 'em?"

"No, we tired of pulling them out of arroyos, so we traded them for a flock of sheep. We graze them in the mountain meadows."

"Sheep?" Billy grimaced but said nothing more.

"Why did you never marry?" Andrea asked, quickly changing the subject.

"Not many men would brave the arroyos to come courting," Elvira said wistfully. "And those who did are not the kind to settle down."

"We've run some of them off," her sister said, smiling. "Juan Bad Horse was one of them."

"Bad Horse? That renegade you mentioned?"

"Yes, you need to keep a watch for him when you leave. Hopefully he's back on the reservation."

Andrea watched the Barlow twins following dinner, wondering about the survivor when one of the sisters died. They seemed content with their lives on the edge of the badlands. She hoped they would live forever. They didn't need men to complicate their lives, she concluded, glancing at Billy. Stubborn, reckless, undisciplined males. In less than three years her father's estate would be hers. She could then live wherever she pleased. She might even find a man like her father to share her life. Shaking her head, she reasoned that was too much to hope for. No, like the Barlow sisters, she would make a life of her own.

"You must be tired," Elvira said as she rose to help her sister spread pallets on the floor. "We're sorry we don't have better sleeping accommodations, but we have so few visitors."

They both thanked the twins and bedded down for the night. Next morning they were served lamb chops and potatoes for breakfast, and Billy ate his fill. While they were preparing to leave, Andrea noticed an entire wall in the sitting area filled with books. No wonder they're so well-spoken, she mused. There probably wasn't a school within a hundred miles.

Elizabeth handed them an oil cloth-wrapped bundle Andrea knew was their lunch. Thanking them profusely, she waved until the cabin was out of sight.

"They're wonderful, aren't they?"

"Who? The spinster sheepherders?"

"Call them anything you like. They're angels all the same. If not for them, we could have died in the arroyo."

"Hogworsh," he said. "We'd have climbed out this morning."

"What about Pepper? He might have fallen in a gully and broken a leg."

"Then we'd have walked out of here."

"Like Amos Cross?" Andrea glared at his back, making a mental note to thank him and forget him when they reached her grandparent's ranch. Why in heaven's name had she not asked the Barlow sisters to hide her until Billy was out of sight? She hung her head, berating herself.

They rode in silence, skirting the endless arroyos. Billy was holding his head and groaning when she was abruptly jerked from the roan. Before she could scream, a hand covered her mouth and she was dragged into the nearest gully. Pushed face down into the snow, Andrea was crushed with her assailant's weight while her hands were tied behind her. Unable to breathe, she forced her head to one side. Spitting snow she tried to yell, but her neck was wrenched to the point of snapping.

"Make noise," he warned, "you die."

Chapter Twenty

They left the winded draft horses standing near a fence that separated a grain field from rolling pasture. Grazing a quarter mile from the narrow dirt road were several sleek Appaloosas with sparse tails swishing flies from their mottled rumps.

"Nice looking mounts," Sundance said, leaning on the top rail. "Too bad they're not rigged for riding."

"Guess we'll have to bareback it a while longer."

The sun had not yet shown itself on the horizon, but they knew the owner would be leaving his farmhouse soon.

"Time to corral 'em. All we need is to get caught on foot in open pasture." Harve climbed the fence and dropped to the other side. "The one on the left is mine!"

"Victory's to the swift."

His challenge sent Harve scrambling with a head start. The ground was slick with intermittent snow, and he slipped and fell to his hands and knees, allowing the taller man to overtake him. Digging in his heels, the Sundance Kid bowlegged his way across the field, slowing his pace to a crawl when he neared the horses.

The nearest Appaloosas turned their heads to eye him inquisitively, and he knew they might take flight at any moment. Extending his hand as though holding an offering, Sundance quietly stood waiting. The gelding on the left finally gave in to curiosity.

"Good boy," he said, reaching to stroke its muzzle. Gripping him abruptly in a neck lock, he told Harve, "Get your arse up there."

Harve mounted and offered his hand to another gelding which seemed unusually skittish. The others soon lost interest and were grazing away from the road. Nudging his mount in their direction, Harve intended to herd the horses back toward his partner, but noticed a wagon moving toward them from an adjoining field. Racing back toward the Sundance Kid, he yelled, "Get mounted."

His companion lunged for a sturdy mare but she veered off, following a wall-eyed gelding. Harve's Appaloosa stopped short, blocking the path of a barrel-chested gelding. He deftly herded him back in his partner's direction. With the grace of a matador, Sundance grabbed a handful of mane and swung onto the horse's back as he rushed past.

"Somebody's coming," Harve warned. "Can't tell if he's armed."

Sundance leaned to unlatch a gate, and they were off down the road before the wagon reached the pasture.

Both men felt vulnerable, lacking weapons and riding gear. If a posse caught up with them now, raised arms would be their only defense, and that wouldn't guarantee their survival. Late that afternoon they rounded a bend where a large barn had been erected on a rock-studded plot.

"Worst place I ever saw," Sundance had remarked earlier when they stopped to relieve themselves. "How can farmers grow anything in this stony ground?"

"Probably hauled in top soil." Harve pointed to a distant grain field.

"I'm afraid I'd starve to death."

"That'll happen soon enough if we don't find some grub."

The barn was deserted but for a few pieces of tack hanging from freshly constructed walls. A worn hackamore was a welcome sight, along with a fifty-foot lariat and several soiled horse blankets.

"No good without saddles," Harve said.

"But they just might keep us from freezing tonight."

Later, tying the horses on a short lead rope to allow them room to graze, the outlaws bedded down in a copse of trees.

Sundance agreed to the first watch. Before Harve closed his eyes, he said, "Good thing we spotted that posse before we got to Spearfish Canyon. I've had enough jail time to last me a while."

"But we'll have to double back for the relay hosses at Hash Knife."

"Too far, and we're liable to run into another posse."

"Pure waste of horse flesh and saddles."

"Can't be helped."

Sundance settled himself against a tree. "I have to admit it was a stroke of genius when you bluffed your way through that bunch at the bridge."

"You can thank Peep for saving our necks. I did what he would have done."

"That fool would have invited the entire posse home with him."

They started out next morning before daybreak, stiff, hungry, and cold. The Appaloosas' naturally streaked hooves were heavily encrusted with mud, but they seemed in better spirits than their riders. At midday they were traversing a narrow draw when two horsemen appeared on the nearest ridge, signaling them to halt.

"They don't look like lawmen to me." Harve readied his gelding for possible retreat.

"Could be part of a posse."

"No rifle scabbards that I can see."

"Most posses don't require rifles."

"Yeah, some of 'em ride along just for the hell of it."

The strangers picked their way down a snowy ridge, the squat man in the lead still holding his hand for them to wait.

"A coupla saddle bums," Harve said. "We might as well hear what they have to say."

Within minutes they arrived, flush-faced and excited. "There's a posse waitin' in ambush down a ways," the stout one said. "If it's you they're waitin' fer, you'd best foller us."

Sundance nodded when Harve warily glanced over at him. What did they have to lose, besides a couple of winded Appaloosas?

"Know where we can find fresh mounts," Sundance asked when they stopped to rest several miles north.

"Sure." The tall, dark, lanky one spoke for the first time. "Buck Majors' place is a coupla mile from here. Reckon he can afford to lose a few more hosses." His partner agreed.

The Major's Ranch lay nestled in a rock-rimmed canyon, cut by a narrow stream. Plentiful grass fed a large horse herd, but snow was covering the grazing land at an ever increasing rate.

"How do we grab hosses and get back up the canyon without being seen?" Sundance's empty stomach was making him surlier than usual.

"Don't worry 'bout that none. We'll git 'em fer ya," the chunky, pitted-face bum said. "Good practice for the two of us, eh, Jed?"

Grinning, Jed replied, "Yeah, Hossfly."

"While you're at it, rustle up a couple of saddles and some grub."

Reaching into his saddlebag, Hossfly retrieved several twists of jerky. "Feast on these 'til we git back."

"What's in it for you?" Harve asked, suspicious.

"Figured you wouldn't mind us ridin' along to the Hole. Maybe joinin' the gang."

"You know who we are?"

"Whole country's out lookin' fer ya."

They waited until dusk to lead their horses single file down a narrow trail onto the canyon floor that was choked with varying levels of snow. When they were out of sight, Harve said, "I don't trust 'em."

"Hell, you don't even trust me."

"They could turn us in for the reward money."

"Yeah, they know we're not the Roberts brothers."

Harve pulled off a boot to vigorously scratch his instep. "We can either wait to see if they're on the level, or waylay 'em on their way back."

"How do we know they'll be alone."

"We don't, but we can be where they don't expect us."

Tethering the horses some distance from the canyon rim, they followed the tracks downslope for several hundred yards, taking up positions separately behind boulders. Snow had fallen steadily all afternoon, but they appeared to be on the dwindling edge of the storm.

Nearly two hours passed until laughter floated up the trail, waking the Sundance Kid from a light doze. Crouching, he and Harve waited until the two thugs were opposite them, leading the horses.

"Majors put up quite a fight, didn't he?"

"Not as much as his old lady."

"How much money did we git?"

"Dunno. Didn't take time to count. Reckon it'll last fer a while."

A ray of moonlight sliced through the scattering clouds. As Jed and Hossfly passed, the fugitives noticed two saddled horses and two bare backs they were leading up the trail. Harve signaled his partner to mount one of the saddled grullas. Once astride, they cut the ropes and quietly rode upslope until they reached the summit. Then, before the two men could step into leather, the outlaws rode past, nearly trampling them.

Hossfly swore as they scrambled to mount.

"Reckon they're testin' us."

"They best not push us too far, or we'll leave 'em like we done the Majors."

"We shoulda buried 'em, Hossfly."

"What fer?"

"We coulda used the ranch for a hideout."

"We're gonna join the Wild Bunch. We don't need no damn hoss ranch."

"When the posse finds the bodies, they'll be after us."

"No they won't. They'll think them two jailbirds done it."

"If the short one's Harve Logan, he'll kill us 'fore we git to the Hole."

"In case you haven't noticed, Jed, them two don't have no weapons. And I'm not about to give 'em mine."

* * * *

Sundance had hoped to outdistance the yahoos, but when the moon reappeared they'd come within pistol range. Without guns they had little chance of overpowering them, so they were stuck with the bums for a while. Hossfly had been adamant in his desire to accompany them to the Hole.

There was always the chance they could out-maneuver them. If that proved unlikely, once back on home turf there were ways to get rid of the thugs, if they weren't first intercepted by a posse. He wasn't looking forward to an all-night ride, but traveling during the day was tantamount to suicide. They were in open country now. They had to reach the cover of the Big Horn Mountains by daybreak.

Remembering Ketchum and his gaunt sidekick Jake, Harve's ready anger surfaced. He wasn't going to lead these new drifters into the Hole, although the Wild Bunch had all but abandoned the hideout. Turning, he signaled Sundance.

"We're gonna hafta to jump 'em," he said, when he rode alongside. "I'll take Hossfly. The stringbean's yours."

Slowing the horses to a lope, they waited for the others to catch up, but their pursuers seemed to be pacing themselves accordingly.

Sundance's lips set in a grim line. "Looks like they don't trust you either."

If they doubled back, the saddle bums would be alerted, Harve told himself, remembering the Smith and Wesson strapped to Hossfly's hip. He knew he was in no position to knock him from his horse, and that the only place to overpower him was on the ground. But Hossfly outweighed him by at least forty pounds.

"Pull up," he yelled to Sundance. Reining in, Harve dismounted and stopped to lift the grulla's hind leg. Sundance swung down and crouched beside him.

"Be ready to hit 'em and grab their guns."

Hossfly and Jed approached cautiously, halting some five yards behind.

"What you boys stoppin' fer?" he yelled. "It's a ways yet to the Hole."

"Damn worthless hoss you stole is lame. Get down and have a look."

"I'll take your word fer it."

"Got a lucifer so I can see what's wrong?"

Hossfly grumbled as he walked his paint closer. When he was within five feet he leaned to toss a small packet at Sundance.

The matches hit him in the chest and dropped to the ground. "You stuck to that hoss?" Sundance stooped to feel around him in the dark. When he found them, he struck a match on his boot heel and knelt to illuminate the horse's hoof, shielding it with his body from Hossfly's view.

"I never seen anything like this." Harve held the grulla's trembling leg with both hands as the animal tried to kick free.

"Neither have I," Sundance said. "How did that happen?" He lit another match as the two men huddled together, holding the leg at an angle. He snuffed the light when he noticed Jed dismount.

"Either of you boys know anything about horse shoeing," he asked. "The Wild Bunch could use a good farrier."

"Fraid not," Hossfly said. "That's why we brung some extry mounts. Pull the saddle off the grulla and slap it on the gray." He tugged at a lead rope and the gray trotted forward.

Harve nodded wearily and began to loosen the cinch. They were both too tired for a fight, but if these bums insisted on following, they were doing so at their own risk. They would shake them at their first opportunity.

* * * *

W. O. Temple refused to enter the cell until Tom was seated on his bunk. Walt figured the attorney felt dwarfed by Tom's six-feet-three-inch frame.

"Good news, boys!" Temple said, when the cell door closed behind him. "I got you a change of venue."

"A change of clothes is what we need."

Ignoring Walt's remark, the lawyer said, "The trial will be held next March. The court interviewed thirty Belle Fourche residents, and all but three of them said they're prejudiced in favor of conviction."

Both prisoners groaned.

"I s'pose they all got relatives and friends in Deadwood that feel the same way." Walt sat heavily on his own bunk, feeling dejected.

"Not necessarily. Mister O'Day has become quite a celebrity around these parts. The afternoon crowd at Carter's Resort thinks he should run for public office. They enlisted the services of Mister Shockley, the *Times* editor, to serve as his campaign manager."

"Is that right?" Tom immediately perked up.

"Indeed, and I understand that a number of unmarried ladies have asked the sheriff for permission to visit you."

Tom patted his hair and proceeded to brush the front of his shirt. "Well, tell 'em I'm ready for company."

Clearing his throat, the lawyer said, "I'm afraid the sheriff has denied permission. He says it would create a public nuisance."

Both prisoners swore.

"But I have some further good news."

"What's that?"

"I got myself appointed court reporter for the *Deadwood Independent*."

They looked at one another through the bars and shrugged.

"That means I'll be writing accounts of the court proceedings for publication."

They gazed at him expectantly.

"Gentlemen, you may not be aware of the extent that newspapers influence public opinion."

"You mean you can convince the jury to turn us loose?"

"Well…" Temple turned to survey the cell corridor. In a quiet voice he said, "The jurors aren't supposed to read newspapers during the course of the trail, but I'm sure some of them will."

"And if they don't?"

Expanding his chest, he said, "At least residents will know what a fine job I'm doing for the defense."

When Temple left, Tom said, "That feller's pretty damn stuck on his self."

"I reckon he earned it."

"Since I'm so popular, maybe I oughta be my own lawyer. That'd save Butch a pile a money and he'd be so grateful."

"Forget it, Peep."

* * * *

They camped at dawn on the northern Wyoming border, south of the Crow Reservation. Exhausted from his long ride, the Sundance Kid wanted nothing more than a few hours' sleep, but he was forced to keep an eye on his benefactors.

Hossfly and Jed obviously were in a similar mood because he was refused guard duty. He and Harve were told to roll up in their borrowed blankets and sleep in a sandy gorge.

"Jed'll watch fer awhile," Hossfly said, dragging his saddle to the rise.

"Then I'll relieve 'im."

Sundance watched as Hossfly arranged his saddle so he wouldn't be taken by surprise. Head against leather, he grinned at them from the sandstone ledge above. Sundance thought he resembled a demented Cheshire cat.

"Better get some shut-eye," Hossfly said. "Don't worry none about Jed. He knows what'll happen if he closes his eyes."

Sundance had no doubt he'd kill him.

Cutting lower branches from a thick scrub pine, Jed leaned against the trunk, watching his two captives as well as the terrain. He seemed unperturbed by his partner's threat. The thickly-forested hillside hid them from a posse and there could be several in the area. The Hole in the Wall Trail was well known in these parts. Even Crow braves could be looking for Wild Bunch members. Although Sundance had not seen a wanted poster, he knew the rewards were high.

When Hossfly drifted off, Harve whispered, "Think we can take 'em?"

"Forget it. They'll drop us before we're halfway up the gorge."

"Yeah," Harve grumbled, turning on his side. "Wake me if the stringbean dozes."

Eyes narrowed to slits, Sundance kept his own watch. By the time the sun had peeked through scattered clouds, he had half a dozen plans, if an opportunity arose. When the guard changed, he nudged his companion awake. "It's your turn," he whispered, knowing Harve would have plans of his own. But when his partner woke him later, he was told to mount up and ride. Harve's eyes were dark-rimmed and sunken, evidence of his lack of sleep.

Snow was falling heavily in the mountains, and the draws were becoming dangerous. Any loud noise could set off an avalanche. Sundance thought for a long while about setting off a snow slide to his advantage, but how would he warn Harve? Turning his head, he noticed the others following at a safe distance; Hossfly watching Harve, the stringbean with his eyes trained on him. So that was the way things were stacked. What would happen if he were to attack Hossfly? Would that confuse the issue long enough to gain an advantage?

The four men halted when a horse neighed nearby. Sundance heard buzzing behind him and noticed the two thugs in a huddle. Without waiting for their decision, he nudged his horse into a thick stand of lodge pole pine. Harve followed.

"Any ideas?" Harve whispered.

"Avalanche."

"You crazy?"

"Haven't figured it out yet, but I will."

"Who do you s'pose is up ahead?"

"If I knew I wouldn't be sitting here."

Hossfly rode up to them saying, "Jed's scoutin' ahead. Better keep quiet 'til he gits back."

The fugitives glanced at one another, knowing now was their chance. Two against one, but Hossfly must have read their thoughts. Backing his horse down the slope, his hand remained on his holster. "You fellers still thinkin' of testin' me?"

Sundance and Harve shook their heads and shrugged.

Jed was back within minutes. "Whoever was up there's gone," he said. "The trail leads on down the northern slope towards the reservation."

"Somebody out huntin'," Hossfly said. "Nuthin to worry about."

Maybe not, Sundance told himself, but he'd keep a lookout from then on. These two thugs were the least of his worries. A posse could be waiting in ambush farther up the trail. As heavy as the snow was falling, their tracks would disappear before they reached the rise.

* * * *

Hard-packed snow stabbed her cheek like a dull knife blade. Gasping for breath, Andrea feared her life was over. After agonizing moments, the weight lifted from her back and she was jerked to her feet. The bitter-tasting hand again gripped her mouth as she was pushed forward, deeper into the arroyo.

Although she had not seen his face, she knew it was the renegade, Juan Bad Horse. The Barlow sisters had warned them about him, but she and Billy had become complacent in their travels. If only Billy were here, she would never leave him or think ill of him again.

"Who you with?" her abductor whispered harshly, pushing her against the arroyo wall.

Taking his hand briefly from her mouth, he allowed her to answer. "My brother." Before she could scream, the man banged her head against the embankment.

Dazed, she bit her lip, determined not to cry. Looking at him for the first time, she thought she had descended into hell. The wild eyes and matted hair accompanied a wide flat nose and badly scarred face.

His thick lips were cruel, his front teeth missing. Scar Ketchum was handsome in comparison. Was this a man or the devil?

Pulling at her uneven hair, he grinned crookedly. When he lifted a knife from the scabbard on his belt, she closed her eyes and prayed aloud: "Our father who art in heaven, hallowed be thy name, thy kingdom come, they will be done, on earth as it is in—"

"Where father?"

She opened one eye slightly and stopped praying. "Dead."

"His woman?"

"Dead, too."

He nodded. "Yellow hair."

She wasn't sure whether he was asking a question or making an observation. "Yes, mother had yellow hair."

"How woman die?"

"Train wreck."

He grunted. "Iron horse."

A tear escaped from the corner of an eye. Her hands were tied behind her back and she tried to brush it away with her shoulder.

The devil looked at her curiously. Pulling her into a sitting position, he jerked her head back to look in her face.

"How many moons?"

"Moons?" Her mind raced back to something she'd read in her father's library. Moons? Years? Age?

"Thirteen," she said, remembering to lower her voice.

"Small," he said, shaking his frightful head. "Too small kill," he added, almost as an afterthought.

Holding her breath, she waited for what he had in store for her.

"Keep," he decided at last.

Andrea closed her eyes, sighing inwardly. She would say no more than necessary. She prayed he was unaware of her gender.

Roughly hauling her to her feet, he dragged her further down the arroyo where his spotted pony was tethered. Pushing her down again, he commanded, "Stay." He then disappeared from sight.

If she were able to stand, she would not get far before he caught her. Making him angry would only jeopardize her life.

Where was Billy? Had he been killed? "Dear God…"she began. A fine skiff of snow sprinkled over her, making Andrea instantly alert. Someone was on the rim above her.

Was it Bad Horse or Billy? She craned her neck but was unable to see anything but the overcast sky. A horse whinnied nearby, but it didn't sound like Pepper. She held her breath when more snow fell into the arroyo. Andrea thought she heard a hissing sound, but snakes were hibernating this time of year. Glancing fearfully about, she was afraid one had been awakened early.

"Who's there?" she called.

"Shush," someone said, the voice vaguely familiar.

Was Billy trying to rescue her?

Andrea closed her eyes and concentrated on listening. When a gun went off nearby, she cried, "Billy!"

Eons passed before she heard someone coming down the arroyo. The Indian wore moccasins, but this was someone in boots. She was surprised when a small figure wearing a floppy hat appeared in the bend of the gorge.

"Are you all right, dear?" she asked.

"Elizabeth?"

"She's catching up with Billy."

"Bad Horse?"

"I'm afraid I had to kill him, dear."

Andrea exhaled slowly. "Why did you follow us?"

"My sister and I were afraid something like this would happen. We took a shortcut and watched you through field glasses from a distance."

"You truly are an angel, Elvira."

"A pretty young girl like you has no business out here in the badlands," she said, untying her wrists. "Do you trust me enough to tell me why?"

Andrea hugged the woman and cried. When she had dried her eyes, she told her the entire story, from her kidnapping to Bad Horse dragging her from the horse's back.

"We'll take you home with us," Elvira said. "If that young man doesn't have the sense God gave him, he'll have to suffer the consequences."

"No, you don't understand. Billy's not a real outlaw. He never committed a crime. He just needs someone to make him see the light."

"Do you think you're up to the job?"

"Yes, I do. He's starting to come around."

"I've known men like him, dear. They never settle down. They're like wheat on the wind. Wherever they happen to light is where they stay, until another gust blows them somewhere else."

"Billy's not a drifter, Elvira."

"As long as you're sure."

They heard a voice calling.

"My sister's back. Are you ready to go."

They climbed the arroyo to find Elizabeth sitting her bay and leading Pepper. There was no sign of Billy.

"Where is he?" Andrea cried.

"Back a ways. I'm afraid your young man is hurt worse than we thought."

Andrea mounted Pepper and waited for Elvira to retrieve her chestnut mare. They followed Elizabeth, skirting arroyos until they found Billy lying on his back near the rim of a shallow gully.

Dismounting, Andrea hurried to see what she could do. She found him conscious but in pain.

"My head feels like a river's running through it," he said. "I can't seem to keep my balance."

"Concussion," Elizabeth said.

"Might be."

"It's not a good idea to move him. We'll set up a tent in that gully's flat area."

"But how...?" Andrea glanced anxiously at the twins.

Elvira peered down at her shadow. "It's about noon. I'll ride to the cabin and rustle up some poles and blankets. Elizabeth will return to help you as soon as we bury Bad Horse."

"How can we ever thank you?"

"You helped us get rid of a murdering renegade. That's thanks a-plenty."

Both women unsaddled Pepper and built a shelter before they left. When Andrea covered Billy with their quilts, his eyes fluttered open. Noticing her scrapes and bruises, he tried to sit. She gently pushed him down.

"Fell off Pepper, too?" he asked.

"No, I'll tell you about it later."

"Now," he insisted.

Andrea hesitated. "The sisters saved me from Bad Horse."

When he moved his head in confusion, she told him what had happened. Billy groaned and closed his eyes. She knew he was berating himself for not protecting her.

"You must have been unconscious in the saddle when it happened," Andrea said, attempting to salve his pride. "I remember you were slumped forward when Bad Horse grabbed me. I thought you were dozing off."

"I'm sorry I got you into this."

"It wasn't your fault. Harve Logan could have stopped Ketchum from kidnapping me, but he didn't."

"Don't worry about me. I want you to stay with the spinsters until I'm well enough to ride."

"Angels," she corrected him.

"Yes, that's twice they saved our lives."

Andrea smiled. Billy *was* worth saving. Glancing off to the West, she noticed storm clouds on the horizon.

More snow? She didn't think they could survive another storm, but how would she get him to shelter? It was a long ride back to the Barlow cabin.

Chapter Twenty-One

When Elizabeth returned from burying Bad Horse, she helped Andrea move Billy to a more sheltered area. Elevating him several inches above ground on one of the quilts, they managed to lift him into the shallow gully.

"Feels like more snow tonight," the older woman said. "I don't like leaving you here alone."

"You can adopt us." Andrea nodded to the far end of the gully. "We're both orphans."

Elizabeth smiled and patted her face. "You'd get tired of this place before long. Not much to do other than herding sheep." Taking Andrea's arm, she walked her down the slope, out of Billy's earshot.

"How long?" Andrea asked.

"I'm not sure he'll stay down, dear. He's a stubborn young man."

"That I know."

"Keep him quiet tonight. I doubt he'll lie still after tomorrow morning."

Andrea looked back at Billy, knowing he would insist on leaving.

"I noticed he has a gun. Keep it handy tonight in case of animals. I haven't seen a wolf lately, but you never know."

Andrea nodded, remembering.

Elizabeth stooped to retrieve sagebrush that had blown into the gully. "You'll need a good supply to stay safe and warm tonight."

By the time Eliza returned with tent poles, food, and blankets, they had a good-sized pile of fuel for the fire. Billy slept until well after the twins left. When he woke, he insisted that he was feeling better.

"We've got to leave tomorrow for the Hole, Andy."

Gritting her teeth, she said, "There must be posses everywhere looking for the gang. What if they've been captured?"

"I'll be there just in case."

Stoking the fire, she lay awake until the moon was bright overhead. Was Elvira right that Billy was a drifter? She raised her head to gaze at him in the moonlight. He looked so young and gentle. Once the remaining outlaws had retreated to Brown's Hole, she would have him all to herself, with no outside interference. She drifted off to the soft patter of wet snow falling on the small tent.

Andrea awoke shivering. The fire had gone out. Lifting the corner of a horse blanket, she pulled more sagebrush from the pile. Snow had buried the campfire, and a fresh fire would soon go out as well. How would she keep Billy warm and the wolves at bay?

Sliding Billy's gun into her overalls pocket, she started a new fire, shielding it with the horse blanket. As long as she crouched there, the fire was sheltered. If she fell asleep, she knew it would die out. The wind picked up, blowing snow into the gully. She feared the tent would blow away, although the twins had anchored the poles well. Listening, she thought she heard a growl, but dismissed it as the wind.

No *bean sidhe* tonight, she prayed. When she opened her eyes she thought she saw an Irish fairy woman dancing at the end of the gully. Her long white hair was flowing in the wind, and she seemed to be getting closer. Andrea squeezed her eyes, then looked again. It was still there. She must be dreaming. She had dozed off and allowed the snow to snuff the fire.

A quick glance told her the campfire needed more fuel, but she couldn't take her eyes from the fairy. Dancing closer and growing larger, it was coming in her direction.

"No," she screamed, and it stopped, but she could hear Pepper's frightened whicker behind her.

Billy raised his head in the tent and asked, "What's wrong?" Groaning he laid back on the quilt.

"A bad dream," she said, but the fairy was moving again, taking the shape of an animal. The fire was no longer there to protect them, and there wasn't time to start another.

Sliding the gun from her pocket, she stood and took careful aim. When the animal was within several yards, it leaped toward her. Firing the gun she collapsed, striking her head on the ground. The animal was on her chest, smothering her with its weight. Shrieking, she tried to roll free.

Billy yelled, so close that it hurt her ears. Gasping for breath, she was aware of something sharp against her throat. The animal was lifted from her chest as warm blood oozed over her skin.

"Andy?" His voice broke as he crushed her to him.

"I'm all right," she said when she was able to catch her breath. "Is it dead?"

"You must have shot 'im through the heart."

Scooping snow from the gully floor, she washed the blood from her throat, and then took a closer look at the wolf. The animal appeared lifeless, but Billy took no chances. Taking careful aim, he shot it through the head. Pepper reared, threatening to dislodge his tether. Quieting him took some time. When they crawled back into the tent, they were both shivering. Pulling her close, he held her while she cried.

Next morning a light snow was falling, but the wind had gentled to a breeze. She knew they couldn't stay, but dreaded renewing their trip.

"Are you sure you can travel?" she asked, worried he would fall from the saddle, or die of a brain hemorrhage.

The Barlow twins' borrowed gear was left where it could be easily retrieved. When it was time to leave, he carefully mounted Pepper, with one hand holding his throbbing head.

Andrea refused to take her arms from his waist. If he slid to one side, she would do her best to keep him in the saddle. If he fell, she would fall with him. After a while they stopped in a sheltered draw to rest and place another snow pack on Billy's head.

"I'm all right," he insisted. "You don't have to keep fussing over me."

"Someone has to look after you."

"You know how that makes me feel?"

"Time to go," she said, wishing she had held her tongue.

They rode the rest of the day, still skirting arroyos although there were less of them now. When night came, they both dismounted and walked, thankful that snow provided enough light to continue. Resigned to spending another night in a gully, they noticed the outline of a tall wooden structure in the distance. Exhausted and numb from the cold, they continued until they reached what appeared to be a huge tipi frame. Billy dropped Pepper's reins next to the rough planking. Thick wooden crosspieces climbed the tapered tower.

"What is this?" she asked, afraid she was hallucinating.

"A derrick." Billy crawled inside the triangular frame. "This must be the Shannon field. I heard about an oil strike east of Jackass Springs and north of Teapot Rock."

"You mean—?"

"It's an oil well derrick."

"But where is this place?"

"We're south of the KC Ranch." He smiled. "Too far to make it tonight. We're probably five or six hours ride from the entrance to the Hole."

He noticed the shadowy outlines of additional derricks, standing like awkward giants pointing to the stars. A log cabin stood on the outer rim of the field and he led Pepper in that direction. Were anyone home, they would be sleeping at this hour. Even before he knocked, he knew the cabin was open. Wyoming residents rarely locked their doors. If they were away, travelers were welcome to stay and eat whatever food was available. It was simply a matter of survival.

Still, he was wary when he eased the door inward. The cabin's interior yawned black and silent, as forbidding as any cave. The planked door squeaked a warning as tiny feet skittered across a wood surface. When the door closed, the only light was reflected snow filtered through a dirty window. Lingering odors of oil and sweat would have seemed more repulsive had they not been so tired.

"Anybody here?"

When no one answered, Billy reached into his pockets and found them empty. Swearing beneath his breath, he inched cautiously into the room with arms extended, searching for an oil lamp. Creeping behind him, Andrea gripped his belt.

"I found a lantern. Might be a lucifer on the table." He swore softly. "I've got a splinter in my thumb."

"Find a match?"

"No, let's have a look in the saddlebags?"

When they left the cabin, they discovered Pepper missing. Drawing his gun, Billy scanned the area around them. Snowdrifts curved knee deep like sand dunes along the front and sides of the cabin. The only tracks visible, other than their own, were those of a large-footed cat. A trampled area where the gelding had been ground-reined indicated he had fled in the direction they had come.

Billy pursed his lips and whistled, a long, piercing sound that made her tremble. She called to Pepper in a pleading voice. Why would he run? Had a mountain lion spooked him?

"Wait inside while I track him." Gripping her arm, he pulled her toward the cabin.

"No, Billy. You should be lying down."

"I've got to find him."

"Then I'll go with you."

"It's dangerous out there, and we're both exhausted."

"Let's wait until daybreak. I'm sure he'll come back on his own."

Sighing, he pushed his way into the cabin. Several moments passed before he found matches on the hearth. Lighted, the lantern exposed a few pieces of dusty, makeshift furniture. Six narrow bunks were stacked along three walls, dried clods of mud and refuse strewn on the floor. Only oilfield roughnecks had lived there.

An ample supply of wood lay beside the hearth. He lighted kindling and while he built the fire, Andrea slapped a stained, shuck filled mattress. Rising dust made her sneeze.

"Latch the door and get some sleep while I look for Pepper." Billy's palm raised to prevent an argument. "I'll be back soon if I don't find him."

"But Billy—"

Lightly kissing her lips, he pulled his hat lower and opened the door. A tepid wind was blowing a fine spray of snow in the direction the gelding had taken. Latching the door behind him, she moved to the misted window to watch him disappear among the oil derricks.

As she rubbed the pane for a better view, she saw the first flare of dawn igniting the horizon. Worried the wind would whip up a ground blizzard, she stood at the window waiting for his return, until a weary chill forced her back to the fire. Shuffling to one of the bunks, she removed her boots and brushed snow from her overalls. Wrapped in the quilt, she drifted into an uneasy sleep.

A banging noise awakened her. Bleary-eyed, she glanced about, noticing the logs had burned to embers.

"Billy?"

"Open up." He sounded out of breath.

Unlatched, the door swung wide, allowing wind to spatter her with snow. He hastily pushed it closed behind him.

"Pepper?"

I couldn't find him," he said. "I nearly got myself lost. Ground blizzards are worse than snowstorms. If it wasn't for the derricks, I'd never have found my way back."

He tossed another log on the grate and briskly rubbed his hands, waiting for wood to ignite. Shivering, his reddened face filled with regret, he said, "I really got us into trouble, didn't I?"

"The storm's not your fault."

"I shoulda hobbled Pepper."

Andrea sighed, her hands rising in a helpless gesture. "We were both so tired..."

"That's no reason to get careless."

She blanched at his self loathing. "What can we do if he doesn't come back?"

"Walk to the KC. Maybe we can borrow a horse to get to the Hole. But we'll have to wait 'til the wind stops blowing snow around."

"We could starve by then."

"Not if I can snare a rabbit." Billy stooped to gather rawhide and sticks from the floor.

Andrea laughed, imagining him stalking a jackrabbit in the middle of a ground blizzard. Before she could apologize, he slammed out the door.

She prayed she wouldn't find him later in the snow.

* * * *

"How're we gonna pay big-time lawyers like Temple and McLaughlin?" Tom asked, after Temple left his cell.

"He said not to worry. It's all arranged."

"By who?"

Walt said, "Butch takes care of his own. You can bet your cookie duster that's where the money came from."

"I'm surprised Temple's still on the case. The sheriff said the townspeople was gonna string him up, instead of us, when we broke jail."

"He oughta been strung up for lettin' the judge get away with settin' bail at fifteen thousand dollars," Tom said. "That's twice the reward offered for Butch after the Castle Gate robbery."

Leaning close to the bars, Walt whispered, "I got me an alibi."

"How'd ya do that?"

"Temple says a coupla Thermopolis boys'll testify I was havin' supper with 'em the night before the bank robbery, a fast three-day ride from here."

"What about me?"

"You was captured in Belle Fourche the day of the robbery. You couldn't have been in Thermop."

"That means I'll hang for robbin' the bank when I didn't get no money."

"Quit your caterwaulin', Peep. Temple's gonna get you out a here."

"How's he gonna do that?"

"If Butch sent enough money, witnesses can be bought to say you was dancin' with some rancher's daughter at the time of the holdup. How do I know what a lawyer's gonna do?"

"You mean lawyers hire folks to lie?"

"Money'll buy anything. You oughta know that."

"What about your alibi in Thermop?"

"Friends of Butch's. They'll likely do it for free."

"It pays to be in the Wild Bunch, don't it?" Tom's dropping mustache curled itself above a wide grin.

"I wouldn't count on that, Peep."

"What're ya sayin'?"

"While you was lollygaggin' in your cell, I was listenin' to what the boys had to say after the bank job."

"Yeah?"

"You've been throwed out a the gang."

"What for?"

"They think you're a bungler and a drunk."

"I have a few snorts now and then."

"Ain't nuthin' you can do about it, Peep."

"Butch'll take me back."

"He's long gone with the rest of the gang."

"Then you and me can start our own gang."

"Not me, pardner. I'm goin' straight."

* * * *

Andrea awoke when he returned. Removing his boots, he reclined on the bunk next to hers. Twilight was settling when she woke again, still so tired she resisted rising until she heard his mattress rustle. The room was cold and nearly dark, a banshee wind screaming to get inside.

Billy left to check the snare, returning with a plump rabbit. When it was skinned, he skewered and rotated it over the flames. Settled by the fire after supper, she noticed a peculiar glint in his eyes.

"Why are you looking at me that way?"

"Just noticing how beautiful you are." His hand reached tentatively to stroke her cheek.

"You really think so?"

"You don't know how many nights I've laid awake thinking..." he lowered his gaze to the hearth, "about having our own hoss ranch in the foothills."

"How would we buy horses?"

"Well," he said, gathering enthusiasm. "One bank job ought to do it."

Instantly angry, she slammed her plate against the hearth and sprang to her feet. "I should have known," she cried. "You're entirely hopeless!"

"How else can I stock the ranch? Steal the hosses?"

"You've never considered honest work, have you?"

"Do you know how long it would take on cowpoke's wages? I'd be an old man past thirty."

"But at least you'd earn the money honestly."

"Where would you live, Andy? Cowhands stay in bunkhouses or on the open range."

"We could homestead a place nearby."

"That kind of life ages a woman fast."

"But you never thought to discuss it with me, did you?"

"I can't ask you to live that way. Alone most of the time."

"But you'd risk your life robbing a bank, maybe getting killed?"

"That wouldn't happen. I'll ride with Butch."

A tear glistened on her cheek. "Why do men become outlaws, Billy?"

He shrugged.

"Because it's exciting?"

"That's part of it, but more important is getting even with all those corporate thieves, like the bankers, railroaders, and land grabbers."

"That's Butch talking."

"It's true."

"The only way to defeat corporate thieves is to go into politics."

"Politicians are as corrupt as bankers, maybe worse," he said, getting to his feet.

"What is it you really want?"

He stared at her a long moment. "Having somebody believe in me, no matter what."

"I was willing to do that."

Placing both hands on her shoulders, he pulled her gently to him. "I'm gonna get us a grubstake the best way I know how."

Resisting his embrace, her voice grew shrill. "How? By robbing a bank?" Stooping to grasp a piece of kindling, she pointed it at him menacingly.

"Aw, Andy, I was only kidding."

"No, you weren't. You meant it."

"I love you," he said, reaching for her.

Backing away, she tossed the stick into the flames. "I give up on you, Billy. I don't care how many banks you rob, or how many horses you steal. If we ever get out of here, I'm going home ... alone!"

Moving to his bunk, he sat down hard on the edge, holding his head in his hands.

Andrea sat by the fire until she heard him snore. Twisting her fingers, she decided that reforming him was impossible. She wasn't sure whether he had been serious about the horse ranch *and* the bank robbery, or whether he had been testing her. Either way, she could no longer trust him.

I've been a fool. Billy never intended to quit the gang.

The wind had gentled by the following morning, the sky nearly clear. Sunlight illuminated small, scudding clouds when they peered through the doorway.

Andrea shuddered, wondering what had become of Pepper.

"We'd better get going," he said, running a hand through his hair. "Good thing the Chinook blew most of the snow away."

Grimacing, they drank melted snow from tin cups she found in the cupboard. Securely closing the cabin door, they headed north toward the KC Ranch. Threading a path among the wooden derricks, Billy lapsed into silence for the next hour.

Andrea squinted west toward the Big Horn Mountains. Climbing ground swells, they shaded their eyes against the glare of drifted snow. Still no sign of Pepper. Billy noticed an animal watching them from a distant ridge, but agreed it was an antelope.

"Pepper couldn't have gone far," he said to reassure her. "He was worn down. It's not like him to run off like that."

"You don't suppose he went south, toward Casper?"

His answer was a long screeching whistle, which pained her ears. Pushing the quilt hard against the sides of her head, she anticipated another blast. Instead, he clapped his hands against his thighs, sadness etching his young face.

"Walk faster," he said. "It's a long way." Rolling hills were covered with short, wheat-colored grass and small, scattered clumps of sagebrush, its tiny gray leaves flecked with gold. They waded through a number of curved snowdrifts, rather than skirt them, as the land began a long gradual upward slope.

"Let's rest a minute," she said, easing herself to the ground.

"Don't get comfortable," he warned. "We have a long way to go."

"How's your head?"

"Never felt better."

She knew he was lying but said nothing more.

Sitting with their backs together for support, Andrea was ready to doze when something caught her eye. Leaning forward for a better look, she thought she saw a large, reddish-barked tree that had been felled by the wind. Its color stood out against the splotchy pale yellow and white landscape. Trees were rare on the rolling, short-turfed grasslands, and she had never seen one of that hue. She gasped when she realized the object wasn't a tree. Tears rimmed her eyes when Billy reacted to her sudden intake of breath.

As soon as she pointed, he must have known. Leaving her seated on the ground, he climbed the slope for several hundred yards. When he knelt beside the roan, she covered her face and cried, great racking sobs that erupted from deep within. Poor Pepper. At some level she had known he was dead when he hadn't returned that morning.

She took her time getting there, knowing that Billy was grieving. Standing anxiously behind him, she waited while he emptied one of the saddlebags. Reaching around his waist, she hugged him, and he quietly accepted her sympathy. Moments later he handed her the biscuits and sausage, still wrapped and partially frozen. Although hungry, she put them aside, knowing the lump in her throat would prevent her from swallowing.

Kneeling briefly to run a hand across Pepper's withers, she found the coarse red and white hairs stiff to the touch. The gelding's legs were drawn close to his stomach, his muzzle partially submerged in snow. His body was rigid and cold, but she was unable to identify any wounds that may have caused his death.

* * * *

When Billy had filled his own pockets with the contents of the saddlebags, he offered her a few cartridges, handkerchiefs, and odds and ends to carry in her overalls. He attempted to retrieve his rifle from the scabbard, wedged beneath the roan, but gave up trying.

"Pepper froze to death or died of exhaustion," Billy said, swiping at moisture on his cheek. His mind focused in the past, he took Andrea's hand and started north. He said nothing more until they stopped again to rest. "Let's eat," he croaked, reaching for the flour sack she had slung over her shoulder.

The biscuits were thawing but hard, the sausage slick with congealed grease, but he ate with relish. Andy seemed to be nibbling, and he urged her to eat her fill. Her eyelids were swollen and red but she had not cried since leaving the roan.

"I'm not very hungry," she said. "How much farther?"

He squinted at the brilliant cloud-banked sky. The sun was as high as he thought it would rise, and they needed to move on.

"I don't think we're halfway there," he said. "We're gonna have to make better time. Eat," he insisted, and watched her force down a biscuit.

Billy crouched to fill the tin cups with snow. Helping Andy to her feet, he slid an arm around her shoulder and guided her to the north. He didn't want to think about Pepper. Butch had given him the roan when he first arrived in Brown's Hole. The gelding had been his best friend and confidant when the others rode to rustle cattle, leaving him alone in the backwoods cabin on the ridge. They spent days traveling the hog backs, looking down on ice-choked streams and thickly forested mountainsides, rarely encountering another soul. They had been lonely days, but time that filled him with an awe of nature's vastness and beauty. He resolved then never to leave the West, nor to part company with his roan.

His throat burned when he tried to swallow a ripening lump, his eyes stinging with distress. He couldn't let Andy see him cry. He had to be strong and get them both to safety. Letting go of her hand, he turned to gaze to the east, quickly swiping at his eyes and blowing his nose. He was grateful when she faced west, pretending not to notice.

"I thought we'd see a sheepwagon or ranch house by now," he said, when the terrain sloped downward into a ravine.

Andy was falling behind and there were dark patches beneath her eyes. If she fainted, he knew he couldn't carry her as far as the ranch, no matter how little she weighed. She was too stubborn to accept his help, but he would never leave her. They would camp wherever she fell, and he would look after her. Squinting at the bright sky, he noticed the sun already sinking toward the mountains. There was probably less than four hours of sunlight left, and he had no idea how far they had traveled. His feet hurt, and he couldn't wait to remove his boots.

The air was warmer and they no longer needed the soiled quilts. Carrying them was a burden, but they could not be sure where nightfall would find them. Sunlight was fading beyond the Big Horns when they saw a newly constructed building setting alone on the opposite bank of Buffalo Creek.

"What is it?" she asked, stopping to rest. "A new ranch house?"

"Danged if I know. Let's have a look."

Limping along the bank, they saw several weathered logs lying together, straddling the partially frozen creek. Billy helped her get her footing and followed as she placed one boot carefully on each log, balancing her weight between the two. Scrambling up the opposite bank, they circled the rough wooden rectangular structure. POWDER RIVER COMMERCIAL COMPANY was painted over the door. Billy tried the latch and was surprised to find it locked.

"I heard some talk about starting a town here on the KC Ranch. This must be it."

"With no streets or houses?"

They heard a drumming sound and watched a horse and rider approach, trailed by a pack mule. The rider raised his hand in greeting. A huge man drooped beneath his large brimmed hat, overflowing an ample saddle. His long brown hair curled beneath the dusty Stetson, framing vaguely familiar features.

"I'm lookin' for the Lost Cabin Mine," the stranger drawled. "I cain't find it, so I figured I'd look for my brother Homer. Last I heard, he was at the Hole in the Wall."

"A lot of prospectors have come through here looking for the mine. Nobody found it as far as I know." Billy remembered the boys discussing the mine. A group of Swedish miners from the Black Hills had discovered placer gold there in 1865, a dozen or so miles north of where they now stood. Five miners had been killed by Indians, but two had ridden away with more than seven thousand dollars' worth of gold.

"I came all the way from Texas," the stranger drawled. "Can you direct me to the Hole."

"Better than that," Billy said. "We'll take you there, if you'll let us ride."

The big man eyed them curiously. "What're you two doin' out here on foot?" He stretched his flabby neck as though looking for their mounts.

"We were caught in the blizzard and lost our hoss," Billy explained, sizing up the muddy black gelding, which stood a good seventeen hands.

Billy was uneasy. He knew he'd never met the man, but there was something troublingly familiar about him. The big man was a stranger, he reasoned, pushing aside his gnawing concern and attributing it to weariness.

The big man chuckled, looking back at his mule in the dwindling light. "Elmer lost most of his load, so I reckon one of you kids can ride him a ways."

The mule was barrel-chested and sturdy, carrying a bed roll and half a canvas sack of supplies. There wasn't a pick or other mining tool to be seen.

"We're a team, "Billy insisted." We stay together."

Andy stepped back to appraise the black gelding. "If your horse can carry you, your mule can carry both of us."

"Smart-mouthed little bugger, ain't ya?"

"No, sir," she said contritely. "But you need us as much as we need you."

"Git on the damned mule, then. Let's git movin'."

Head pounding, Billy pulled himself astride the mule. Arranging his quilt across Elmer's haunches, he helped Andy mount the mule behind him. The animal was stubborn and dirty, refusing to move when the stranger tugged at his reins.

"There's too much weight on his back," the big man said. "One of you young'uns has to git off."

Billy kicked the mule hard in the ribs while twisting one of his ears. The mule bucked and leaped forward, nearly unseating them. When they were even with the mule's owner, he tossed Billy the reins. Laughing and slapping his huge thigh, he said, "Ain't never seed ol' Elmer move that fast. Guess he can handle the load."

Elmer took the lead after they forded the creek, heading west into the valley. Darkness was moments away when Billy found the trail leading south. The Hole in the Wall cabin was still a good many hours away. Giving the mule his head, Billy hoped that Elmer would stay on the trail in the dark. The stranger didn't say how long he had been in the saddle, and Billy worried the mule would give out before they reached the outlaw cabin.

Bare cottonwood branches scraped them as the moon rose full and brilliant above the Big Horn Mountains. Snow lay deep in the draws and progress was slow. Elmer trudged on, his pace varying little with the terrain. When they reached the Red Fork of Buffalo Creek, the mule refused to move.

The stranger rode alongside, chuckling to himself. "Elmer's had enough. He won't budge another inch 'til mornin'."

Billy slid from the mule and helped Andy dismount. "Guess we'll be spending the night here, then." He spread his quilt at the base of a huge cottonwood.

"How fur is the hole?"

"A few hours' yet."

The big man took his time dismounting, and Billy thought he heard the big horse groan. When the stranger ducked beneath the black's neck, he formed a huge pyramid, his dirty trousers straining over his pear-shaped body. He obviously enjoyed the reaction he caused by towering over smaller men, for a wicked grin spread across his face.

"The name's Bart Ketchum," he said, extending a mammoth hand. "I'm a cousin to Black Jack, the famous outlaw."

He cringed when Ketchum squeezed his hand. "B-Billy Blackburn," he said, flinching in pain.

"And the little feller?"

"My brother, Andy." Billy spoke quickly, fearing Ketchum would break her hand. "He doesn't talk much. He's kinda sickly, and I'm taking him home."

"What's he doin' out here?"

"Our family's homesteading in the Hole."

Ketchum seemed satisfied for he abruptly yanked his bedroll from Elmer's back. When he had kicked a spot clear of rocks and snow, he spread his blankets and set about hobbling the black.

Andrea arranged her quilt next to Billy's, and they huddled on the ground beneath the cottonwood. Leaning his head against the bark, he watched the big man unsaddle the gelding named for his outlaw cousin.

"When you kids gonna build a fire?" Ketchum was tying the mule's reins to a low hanging branch.

"I didn't think we needed one." Billy slowly unwrapped his quilt.

"It's colder'n hell," Ketchum complained, then laughed at his own antithesis. When the fire was banked and Ketchum snoring in his bedroll, Billy allowed his muscles to unwind. Moving closer to Andy, he whispered, "Scar Ketchum's brother!"

"I know," she whispered back. "What are we going to do?"

Chapter Twenty-Two

Light snow was falling when Sundance glanced back at his captors. If the trail had not been narrow, he would have signaled Harve of his intentions. Jumping the saddle bums was foremost on his mind. He suspected that Harve's thoughts were riding the same trail.

His hat shielded his eyes from the snow, but the brim narrowed his range of vision. The trail was steep and dangerous, and it took all his wits to keep his stolen gray from slipping over the edge. It would soon be dark, and he didn't relish making camp with Hossfly and Jed.

Tonight, they would have to overpower them and relieve them of their weapons. They wouldn't get near other Wild Bunch members if he could help it. Even if they did, there wasn't a beggar's chance in Hades that Butch would allow two trigger-happy thugs in the gang, especially now that outlaws were in danger of extinction. They would be lucky to leave the country without bullet holes in their backs.

Harve pulled up short ahead of him, causing his gray to balk. "Something's up the trail," he said.

"You sure?"

"My hoss's acting up."

Could be anything from a posse to a mountain lion.

Sundance dismounted and held his hand for silence. Climbing an embankment, he cut a path through the trees. Angling away from the trail, he heard Hossfly's graveled voice complaining behind him. Let Harve handle him, he thought, as he circled back toward the trail.

When he reached the summit, he peered from behind a massive pine. Snow fell silently and lay so deep that he sank in over his knees. Pulling his sheepskin collar higher, he hunched his shoulders and waited, breathing shallowly. They weren't far from Little Goose Canyon where Butch and Elzy had worked as wranglers after the Castle Gate payroll robbery. The rancher was Butch's friend, but he wasn't sure he was receptive to other gang members.

He couldn't risk leading Hossfly and Jed to the ranch. From bits of conversation he overheard following their horse stealing raid, he was sure they'd killed the horse ranch owner and his wife. Not only killed them, but tortured them as well.

"See anythin'," Hossfly said behind him.

"Not even a bob cat."

"Let's get goin' then," he said, moving out of range.

"Nobody's left at the Hole," Sundance said, attempting to discourage him. "Butch and the others rode out weeks ago."

"Don't matter none. We'll just ride along to keep you company. Sees as how we went to all the trouble of gettin' you hosses, Butch oughter be plumb grateful to let us join the gang."

"I guess you don't know about the four-state governor's pact?"

"Packed governors?"

"You don't read newspapers, do you?"

"Never had no need—"

"Outlaws are being hunted down and exterminated."

Hossfly spat a stream of tobacco juice, staining the freshly-fallen snow.

"We're leaving the country as soon as we arrange for passports."

"Pass ports?"

"Papers to travel out of the country." Sundance bit his lip; he'd said too much. If Hossfly decided his captives were useless, he might try to kill them.

"We'll see what Butch has to say."

He considered throwing snow in Hossfly's homely face. Instead, he led the way back to the horses, following in his previous tracks. When they arrived at the site, they found that their companions had left without them. From the corner of his eye, he noticed Hossfly's hand on his gun. If Harve had jumped the stringbean, Hossfly would take his revenge on him.

"They must have seen something up the trail," Sundance said, squinting through the snow for some sign of a struggle. He saw nothing to indicate Harve had taken the upper hand.

"Why'd they take our hosses?"

"We'd better find out."

Struggling upslope, Sundance glanced about, expecting an ambush. Stopping to listen, he felt vulnerable on foot without a weapon, and Hossfly at his back. When the grade finally leveled off, he saw other tracks mingled with Harve's and Jed's. A posse had intercepted them while he and Hossfly were slogging through the snow.

The saddle bum swore when he reached the rise.

"Keep your voice down," Sundance said. "Our saddled hosses told them we're in the vicinity."

"I'll blow every damn one of them to smithereens," Hossfly threatened, still keeping his distance.

"One gun against an entire army?" Sundance shook his head in disgust.

"You got a better plan?"

"The longer we stand here, the further they'll get away."

The square-head glared at him. "I'm right behind you."

Sundance left the trail. Noticing a large formation of boulders through a clearing in the trees, he headed in that direction. Maybe he could spot the posse in the distance. While he was at it, he'd catch Hossfly off guard and relieve him of his gun. When he reached the rocks, he glanced back at the saddle bum, who was wheezing like a winded bronc. Sundance could outrun him in the trees, but he might need his gun to rescue Harve, *if* he needed rescuing.

Gripping a handhold in the snow was no small feat, and he lost more ground than he covered. Finally reaching the top, he peered into the distance, but could see no farther than a copse of trees some fifty yards away. Darkness was crowding in. Unless it stopped snowing and the posse built a campfire, finding them would be next to impossible.

Climbing down, he made a mental map of the terrain. He would keep moving until he outdistanced Hossfly. Then, if he didn't find the posse, he'd double back and catch him by surprise.

"Keep it quiet from now on. Sound carries in the mountains. We don't want the posse knowing where we are."

Hossfly sneered at him, but kept his peace.

It would be dark within minutes. The moon wouldn't be up for at least two hours, so there was plenty of time to lose the burly thug. Sundance slogged through the snow in a straight a line so Hossfly wouldn't get suspicious. Moments later he heard branches move and caught movement from the corner of his eye. Ducking behind an enormous pine, he stopped to look back. A gunshot took him by surprise, but shock was quickly replaced with anger when Hossfly exclaimed, "Biggest damn buck I ever seen."

"You idiot! Now every lawman within fifty miles knows we're here." Sundance angled out of sight, moving as fast as the snow would allow. When he had placed enough trees and distance between them, he slowed to a walk. Glancing back he saw that there was still enough light to follow his trail. A blind centipede could follow in total darkness. Speed was his only weapon until he found a limb he could use as a club.

He had walked for the better part of an hour when he caught the scent of smoke. Licking his finger, he tested the wind. It seemed to be coming from the northwest, so he changed course in that direction. Although knee-deep snow slowed him down, he was grateful for the added light that kept him from stumbling into the undergrowth. He wondered what kind of progress Hossfly was making behind him.

Deliberately circling a huge pine, he jumped onto a pile of rocks and leaped off into the opposite direction. That should slow him down for a while.

At one point in his descent down a steep slope, he imagined he heard voices. Stopping to listen, he decided it was only the wind whistling through the evergreens. He caught another whiff of smoke, stronger this time, and with it the scent of frying beef. His stomach growled and he realized for the first time that his feet hurt.

The pines had thinned, and he glimpsed a spark of light in the distance. Snowfall was lighter, the flakes reduced in size like grains of sand. His visibility increased along with it, despite the darkness. Avoiding the open meadow, he stayed within the trees, moving slowly, keeping the campfire in sight. Within minutes he was able to detect several men moving about, setting up camp. Harve and Jed were nowhere in sight. Exhausted, he found himself a flat rock on which to sit while he watched the men at the fire. It wouldn't be long before Hossfly caught up with him.

If his calculations were right, the moon wouldn't be up for another hour. He had to act soon. Reluctantly rising from his hard perch, he edged his way along the tree line, scanning the men seated in a circle around the campfire. Several were in various stages of food preparation, and he estimated there were seven of them.

When he was on the northern edge of the trees, he spotted Harve seated in profile. The stringbean was sitting next to him, partially hidden. Their hands didn't appear to be tied, and he thought he heard his partner laugh.

What's going on?

If it was a posse, they were the most lenient bunch he'd ever seen. He stood watching them for some time before remembering Hossfly. The damn fool would start shooting and ask questions afterward. Sundance roughed up his hat and tugged it low over his brow. Pulling out his shirt tail, he shouted a greeting and sauntered into camp.

"Got a handout for a hungry cowpuncher?" he said, warily watching the men seated with Harve.

"Where's your hoss?" one of them asked.

"Guess I had a little too much to drink last night and forgot to tie him up. He ran off on me."

Harve laughed along with Jed. "Looks like another horse stomper down on his luck. If it hadn't been for these good posse members, we woulda bedded down hungry."

"Mighty neighborly." Sundance squeezed in between Harve and Jed.

"You might as well throw in with us," Harve said. "We're headed on over to Little Goose Ranch to get us winter jobs."

"That right?" Sundance gave Harve a hard look. "I'd be grateful if you'd loan me a mount."

"We brought a partial string. If you've a mind to ride along, you can ask for a wrangler's job."

"I'm plumb grateful," Sundance said, crushing his partner's hand to warn him.

Harve flinched. "These fellers thought Jed and me were Wild Bunch."

Sundance forced a laugh. "You mean you and this feller next to me? Ain't that a hoot?"

"I told these gentlemen that we got lost trying to find the Little Goose Ranch."

"How far off were we?" Harve turned his head to ask someone across the fire.

"Didn't miss it by much," a wizened man said. "We'll show you the way in the morning."

"Much obliged," Harve said, "but we should be getting there tonight. They might give the jobs to some other cowpokes."

"You're welcome to spend the night with us. We got plenty of grub."

Sundance winked at Harve. Nodding, he rose from his seat before the fire, saying, "I think this waddie's right. We should be on our way."

"Not before supper," a posse man said.

"The cook at the Little Goose Ranch'll have some leftover beans. We don't want you boys running low."

Quickly saddling their horses, they were preparing to leave when they heard a shot. Sundance groaned as he wheeled his mount away from camp.

"Hossfly," Jed said, attempting to block their escape. "We gotta wait for him."

"Damn fool's gonna get us killed." Harve rode close enough to Jed's dun to knock him from the saddle. The two men kicked their horses into a fast start. Behind them a battery of shots were fired. Riding low, they raced behind a stand of trees, unsure where the posse was aiming.

"They know now we're not just cowpokes," Sundance said, when they rode up a second rise and stopped for a backward glance. They could still see the fire through the trees, although no one was in pursuit.

"Maybe they'll think Jed and Hossfly are us," Harve said.

"Nobody would mistake those two for Wild Bunch members."

"You're right about that."

"At least we lost them. Let's ride a ways, then get a few hours' sleep. Feels like a draft hoss rolled over me."

They rode until the moon was high before they bedded down in a shallow cave. Harve's snores were loud enough to be heard back at camp, and Sundance was bleary-eyed next morning when a nudge in the ribs woke him. Dawn was streaking the horizon and someone was staring down at him. Blinking his eyes in the faint dawn light, he saw that it was the homely face of Hossfly Slater.

"Thought you'd lost us, did'nja?"

Sundance groaned and reached to shake Harve. "Look who's here, pardner," he said. "Our good friends and benefactors."

Harve woke with murder in his eyes. "Nobody wakes me until the sun's up and lives to tell about it," he growled.

Sundance thought he saw Hossfly flinch. So he *was* afraid of Harve. "Where've you been?" he said. "We got tired of waiting for you?"

"We had some business with the posse." Hossfly snickered.

Harve grimaced when he glanced up at him. Whatever these two had done, the Wild Bunch would be blamed for it.

"Glad you could join us for breakfast," Sundance said. "If we had some grub."

"We've got plenty of grub. Did a little shoppin', you might say."

Jed glanced at Hossfly and giggled.

"I'm not hungry," Sundance said. "Let's get back to the Hole."

Harve looked over and nodded. "By the way," he said, "Why do you two wanna join the gang?"

Hossfly looked at Harve as if he'd lost his mind. "Don't everybody?"

"Outlawing's not what it used to be," Sundance said. "You can't earn a decent living anymore."

The yahoos exchanged a look and laughed. "We done right well for ourselves."

"When you're in a gang, you have to split the proceeds. The more members, the less you earn."

"There's more'n one way to thin a gang," the square head replied. "I got all kinds of ideas to talk to Butch about."

I'll bet you do, Sundance thought grimly. *But you won't get near Butch Cassidy.*

Hossfly must have recognized the anger in Sundance's face because he wasted no time mounting up. He watched as they took their time saddling and tightening cinches.

When they were ready to leave, Harve said, "You keep those guns holstered from now on, or I'll personally see them emptied in your gut."

* * * *

For the next hour Billy considered his alternatives, dismissing a plan to sneak away on foot. His legs ached and his feet cramped when he removed his boots. He could feel Andy moving restlessly beside him, rubbing the calves of her legs. They would likely be miserably sore by morning.

Ketchum's snoring was even-paced. Billy doubted the big man was faking. Still, he was hesitant to move from his spot under the cottonwood, afraid he would wake him. There was only one solution, steal the big black gelding. He wondered about taking the mule, knowing Elmer was unpredictable.

When he whispered his plan to Andy, she quietly eased herself from the quilt, draped it across her shoulders, and made her way to the gelding. While she stroked Black Jack's ears and neck, Billy pulled boots over his burning feet and crawled forward to unhobble the horse.

Ketchum snorted and turned over in his bedroll, facing them. The saddle and bridle were under the big man's head, so they would have to ride bareback, if Black Jack didn't give them away before they could mount him. The hobble untied, Billy gently looped the rope around the black's neck and handed the end to Andy. She continued to pet the horse and nuzzle him. When he glanced again at Ketchum, he was still on his side, the ancient Henry rifle cradled in both arms. As an afterthought, Billy freed Elmer from the cottonwood limb, hoping he would follow along on his own. Their escape would be easier if Ketchum was left without a mount.

Andy hurried to retrieve her boots. Billy led the gelding along the bank until Ketchum was out of earshot. Black Jack sidestepped nervously when Billy helped her onto his back. His only protest was an indignant snort. Before they plunged into the icy water, he slid a knife between his teeth and removed the belt from his waist. Slicing an incision in the middle of the leather, he slipped it over the gelding's head to form a headstall.

The black obediently followed him into the creek, the cold water shocking Billy fully awake. When they reached the opposite bank, he heard the mule braying from the other side. Bart Ketchum couldn't be far behind. Scrambling astride the black, he reached around Andy for the makeshift reins and kicked wet heels against the gelding's ribs. They had gone but a few yards when the big Henry roared behind them, the bullet splitting a limb near Billy's head.

Crouching over the gelding, they raced off behind a clump of cottonwoods, maintaining cover until they were out of rifle range. Then, circling back to the south, they kept a steady pace until the red walls loomed tall in the moonlight.

Dismounting, they led the gelding up the trail to the entrance, glancing back to determine whether they had been followed. When they reached the slope to the cabin, they noticed several unfamiliar horses in the corral. The cabin was dark, and Billy dismounted with a hand on his holster.

He crouched to one side of the heavily planked door and slowly pulled the latch, easing the door open with the toe of his boot. When the hinges squeaked, a baritone voice demanded that he throw down his gun.

Recognizing the voice, he yelled, "Don't shoot! It's Billy!"

A lantern sputtered to life, illuminating the tired faces of Harve and Sundance. Harve appeared to be unusually happy to see him and his Colt revolver.

"I'm gonna borrow your gun, Billy. I'll see that you get it back."

Surprised, he noticed they were unarmed. "Sure, Harve, might as well take the gunbelt while you're at it."

Sundance was his usual cantankerous self. "Where the helluv you been?"

Billy told them briefly of their trip to Spearfish. While recounting their return trip, he remembered Andy was still astride the black. He was reluctant to rile the ill-tempered outlaws, who interrupted him to tell about the aborted Red Lodge Bank robbery.

"We borrowed hosses along the way," Sundance said when Harve stopped for air.

"If it hadn't been for a couple of Montana saddle bums, we'd be back in jail by now, or pushing up sunflowers in some sodbuster's field."

The door opened and Andy marched in the cabin with her hands in the air. Behind her two homely, rough-looking men followed her through the doorway, their guns aimed at her back.

"Now hold on." Billy jumped to his feet.

"Put your guns down," Harve said. "That's Andy, our cabin boy."

"Hell, he squealed like a damned girl when we jerked him off his hoss." The shorter, square-headed man's greasy hair fell across his pitted face.

"Looks like one too," his lanky companion agreed.

"I'm no girl," she said, turning to kick the shorter man in the shins. Before he could recover, she scurried to the back wall, behind Harve and Sundance.

"Leave him be," Harve warned. "We don't hold with mistreating kids."

"What's he doin' here?" the injured man said.

Billy's fists clenched at his sides. "We might ask you the same thing."

Harve stepped between them, his hands held in a peaceful gesture. Had Billy not been angry, he would have appreciated Harve's rare display of diplomacy.

"This's Hossfly Slater and his partner, Jed Waller. They saved us from an ambush in Montana."

Billy nodded but refused to offer his hand. He noted with satisfaction that Hossfly was still holding his shin. From Harve's expression, he didn't seem pleased to have the strangers along. Sundance must have invited them.

When Billy told them of stealing Bart Ketchum's gelding, they laughed—including Hossfly, whose natural expression seemed to be a sneer.

"Better hope his cousin don't hear what you done," Hossfly said. "I hear ol' Black Jack can be right mean."

"He's crazy as a loon," Sundance muttered.

Harve was obviously angry. "When Ketchum hears you killed his brother, he'll be tracking you 'til his mule drops out from under him. We planned to leave at sunup, anyway. It might as well be now."

"Where are you going?" Andy asked from the back wall.

"Brown's Hole for awhile, then down to a ranch in New Mexico," Harve said. "We have jobs there as cowpunchers whenever we need 'em. A good place to lay low."

Billy had been aware of Andy's imploring look long before she spoke. He hoped ignoring her would keep her quiet, and was surprised when she left her haven along the wall.

"I'm not going," Andrea said, confronting Harve. "Mister Cassidy said Billy could take me home."

"The hell you are," Sundance said heatedly. "You're not riding off to tell where we've gone."

Billy was quick to defend her. "Butch said—"

"There's no time for that."

"Then I'll have to quit the gang and take Andy home." The words were out before he realized he'd said them.

Sundance's face settled into an angry scowl. "Do you know how many men would give their eye teeth to ride with us? You ungrateful little whelp!"

"Let's go," Harve demanded, gathering up a few belongings. "Andy, load this stuff in the saddlebags."

Glaring at Billy, she immediately set to work

"We've only got one hoss," Billy protested, "and he's worn down."

Sundance groaned. "Too bad we rode down our entire string by the time we got here, or there would have been some extra hosses."

"It's best that we don't all ride together," Harve said impatiently. "Get some sleep and leave with Hossfly and Jed at daybreak." He glanced at Sundance, who nodded his approval.

"We'll leave you a couple of fresh hosses at Walt's place when we get to Bridger Creek," Sundance said.

His hand resting on Billy's gun, Harve warned the newcomers: "See that the kids are well taken care of." He started for the door, then turned back to glare at Hossfly, his eyes narrowed to slits. "If anything happens to 'em, there won't be a place left to hide, not from me."

From their downcast expressions, Billy realized the strangers were afraid of Harve, but he was uneasy at the prospect of riding with them. His fears soon proved well founded. Not long after the two men left, Hossfly turned his gun on Billy and ordered them both to the barn.

"Git yore tails out a here."

"But Harve said to take care of us." Andy protested.

"That's just what we're doin'. Makin' sure you don't git yourselves in no trouble."

When they reached the barn, they were ordered into the hay loft, while their guardians spread their bedrolls on the ground beneath them. Hossfly hammered the ladder loose to leave his charges stranded. Exhausted, they slept until dawn when they were awakened by the ladder bumping against the loft.

"Git down here. We're leavin'." A bristled, ugly face showed itself above the loft floor. Hossfly's small, dark eyes drilled into theirs.

"I said move!"

Before they could rouse themselves from the hay, a shot rang out, causing splinters to rain down on them. Rank laughter echoed throughout the barn as Hossfly descended the ladder.

Andy's eyes were frightened when Billy helped her to her feet. "Hold your fire," he shouted over the edge of the loft.

The saddle tramp glared at him while waving his .45.

"We're coming." Angrier than he had ever been, Billy climbed down. He glanced up to see that Andy was following. He considered jumping Hossfly and pistol whipping him, but was afraid Andy would be shot during the struggle. He stepped from the ladder instead, squaring himself before the tramp and blocking him from her descent. Hossfly's laughter continued as his gun waved them toward the corral.

"The black's done in," he said, his harsh voice grating. "We'll have to ride double to Bridger Crick. Unless the two of you would rather walk."

When they reached the corral, their wrists were tied in front with rawhide. Hossfly lifted Andy and her quilt behind his bedroll, and warned her to behave. Seated behind Jed, Billy's glance slid in her direction. Head down, her shoulders were hunched as she half-heartedly gripped the saddle strings.

Some outlaw he was. They were treating him like a wayward child. He wasn't able to protect himself *or* Andy. He worried she was thinking the same way.

Knowing he could push Jed from his horse and chance an escape, he also knew Andy would be left to receive the full brunt of Hossfly's anger. If he jerked Jed's gun free of its holster and shot him, would there be enough time to hit Hossfly without endangering Andy? He couldn't risk it.

When they reached the entrance to the canyon, Jed scanned the boulder-littered valley to determine whether Ketchum had tracked them in the dark. Emerging from the passageway, they saw nothing moving between them and the horizon. The sun's first light was at their backs as they rode away from the red walls, a healthy Chinook thawing snow from dormant grasses.

During late morning they stopped for a quick meal below a ridge covered with snow-dusted pine. When they started out again, they kept to the ridges where snow had been swept clean by the wind. It was well after dark when they arrived at Walt Punteney's cabin on Bridger Creek. The place had been abandoned since Walt was arrested and jailed with Tom in Deadwood.

A note awaited them from Sundance. Hossfly handed the note to Billy, claiming his eyes were too tired to read. The note said they had purchased two good brood mares, a paint and dun, from old Pop Corey. The horses were stabled in the barn, along with a couple of ten dollar saddles. It also said Pop's son Pete had returned from Lander, where he learned from the sheriff that Tom and Walt had been recaptured. Their trial date had been set for the following spring, but the sheriff doubted there was enough evidence to convict them.

"Brood mares," Hossfly said. "Think you can handle ridin' a couple of bloated nags?" He laughed when he untied Andy's wrists so that she could prepare a meal of bacon and beans.

"Wait'll folks hear the Wild Bunch is nuthin' but a bunch of snotty-nosed kids."

"When Harve finds out how you've treated us—"

"Who says he's gonna?"

During supper, Billy noticed Andy wasn't eating. She appeared sick, and she glared at Hossfly as he noisily gobbled his food. He feared she would say something to infuriate their captors.

She did. "Were you raised in a pig sty?"

The words stopped Hossfly mid-chew. One arm abruptly swept dishes from the table. While the others gaped at him, the saddle bum jerked his long-barreled revolver free of its holster.

"That's uncalled for," Billy yelled, jumping to his feet.

Hossfly took careless aim at a large hurricane lamp and squeezed off a shot. Thunder reverberated off the log walls, the concussion severely punishing their eardrums. Laughing, Jed joined in the after dinner entertainment by shooting up the furniture. An acrid cloud of gunpowder hung in the room, causing them all to cough.

* * * *

Andrea was awake long after they climbed into the loft and the ladder had been taken down. Shuddering, she relived an earlier moment when Billy whispered he didn't know how they were going to escape. Hossfly again shot into the rafters, yelling, "Shut your mouths. No talkin'."

She marveled at Billy's calm. He had simply turned on his side and gone to sleep. Shifting uncomfortably in the hay, she was unable to sleep. Her body ached and her head swarmed with escape plans. Burrowing into her quilt didn't help. Her guardians' coldness seemed to have chilled her from within.

Chapter Twenty-Three

Billy's arm was draped across her waist when she awoke at dawn. Gently pushed away, he sat up yawning and brushed the hay from his hair. He seemed relieved when the ladder bumped against the loft, signaling them to climb down.

"The paint's yours," Hossfly said gruffly, handing Andrea a piece of jerky. "Git 'er ready."

Billy was offered a long-legged dun. When they had finished saddling the mares, their wrists were again tied with rawhide.

Motioning them to follow, Hossfly warned, "Jed's ridin' drag with his hog leg handy. So don't try nuthin' stupid."

Riding single file behind Hossfly, Andrea imagined herself a captured criminal, with Brown's Hole looming as a formidable prison. The hideout lacked the Hole in the Wall's towering sandstone walls, but its remoteness insured her inmate status. She knew Brown's Hole was by now crowded with outlaws of every persuasion, all fleeing the four-state governor's pact to exterminate them. She couldn't hide her gender much longer. Shuddering, she wondered if Butch would still protect her, knowing she had misled him.

Despite their captors, she was relieved to be astride the paint. Riding behind Hossfly had been a loathsome experience. From the smell of him, he had earned his nickname honestly. Jed was equally scruffy, but his height and thin build reminded her of Jake, whom she remembered fondly. Jed didn't seem to harbor the meanness that seeped from Hossfly's pores, although he too enjoyed gunplay. Andrea imagined herself a running target in the middle of the barren Red Desert. She wouldn't do anything to anger either man.

Billy seemed preoccupied. He had avoided eye contact with her since leaving Bridger Creek. She was sure he had decided against quitting the gang. She didn't blame him. Harve Logan and the Sundance Kid had forced that decision. She was surprised when he stood up to them back at the cabin, although he now seemed cowed by these two tramps. If they didn't escape soon, she knew Hossfly and Jed would kill them.

They spotted a sheep camp early that afternoon. Hossfly pointed out the lone wagon and Jed agreed it was a good place to stop for their next meal. "How 'bout some mutton stew?" Hossfly asked, turning in the saddle, his sullen mood improved.

She watched Billy shrug. It didn't matter what they wanted. The ugly one had decided.

The sheepwagon's canvas top resembled a snow drift in the distance. If snow had fallen here on the prairie, the wind had blown it away. As they rode nearer she could hear bleating ewes. A canvas tent was pitched on the leeward side of the wagon, among thick clumps of sage. Wind was blowing briskly out of the southwest, carrying grit in swirling gusts, whipping pale strands of hair into Andrea's eyes. Before they reached the camp, a slim herder stooped to leave the tent. When he noticed them, he raised a hand in greeting. Jed and Hossfly returned his wave.

"We won't have much trouble with that youngun'," Hossfly said. Jed laughed in agreement.

Andrea caught her breath when the herder pushed his large tan hat back from his forehead, the sun revealing a handsome face. She recognized Johnny Mackintosh, her former suitor from her grandparents' neighboring ranch. It seemed a lifetime since she had considered marrying him.

Wrists still tied, she pulled the dirty quilt awkwardly over her head and lowered her eyes when they came to a halt near the wagon. Positioning the paint so that she was partially hidden behind Jed's wide-rumped grulla, she prayed Johnny wouldn't recognize her. He would try to rescue her, and was not adept with a gun.

"Got some stew for a buncha hungry trav'lers?" Hossfly asked, dismounting.

"I was just about to make some," she heard Johnny say. "You're welcome to sit a spell while I peel some spuds."

"The boy here can help." Jed twisted in the saddle to locate Andrea.

Shaking her head, she turned away until Hossfly tugged at her foot, insisting she dismount. "Take that damned quilt off your head," he demanded. "You look like an albino Injun."

Reaching to slice through the leather thong between her wrists, he did the same with Billy. Once her feet touched the ground she hunched her body, walking between horses. Leaning to scoop a handful of crumbling earth trampled by their horses, Andrea rubbed the dirt into her face. When she reached the wagon, she sat cross-legged, her back to the tent, all but hidden within the folds of her quilt. She knew she was defenseless without a weapon, but even if she had a gun, she didn't know whether she could kill someone.

The *bean sidhe* wind seemed to be gaining strength, moaning as it unmercifully teased the tent. Andrea wondered why the tent hadn't been blown across the prairie. Shuddering as she scooted closer to the sheepwagon, she wondered whose death the wind warned of next. Probably her own.

She glimpsed a heavy wooden walking stick leaning against the steps. Quickly reaching to grasp the tip, she dragged it under her quilt, noting with relief that the others were preoccupied with tethering the horses. Johnny emerged from the tent with a sack of potatoes under his arm. Lowering her head when he appeared, she shaded her forehead to hide her face. Glancing up through slightly spread fingers, she watched him hesitate. He set the sack down next to the sheepwagon steps and turned back slowly in her direction. Hunkering down in front of her, he sat back on his heels to stare, shielding his eyes against the gritty wind.

"Andrea?" Johnny's voice was sharp with surprise. "My God, are these the outlaws who kidnapped you?" The harried movements of the wind seemed suspended as Johnny's words echoed through the camp.

Andrea shook her head. Lifting a finger to her lips to silence him, she glanced toward the horses, where Hossfly and Jed had been a moment earlier. She saw them straighten like ramrods. Before she could warn Johnny, Hossfly was standing over them, a curious leer spreading upward from his thick protruding lips.

"Andrea?" Hossfly repeated, jerking her to her feet. "I knowed you wasn't no damned boy." Dust swirling angrily along the ground swept into her eyes. Frightened, she steadied herself with the cane, still hidden beneath the quilt. Her free hand clutched the quilt around her.

"So that's why you wanna leave," he shouted at Billy over the roaring of the wind. "Found yourself a little woman."

Hossfly laughed as he dragged his captive toward the tent. "We'll have ourselves a little fun," he yelled to Jed. "Ain't had us a woman since the Majors ranch."

Blinking grit from her eyes, she pressed the cane into the hard, cracked earth and attempted to dig in her heels. The tramp's callused fingers crushed her arm as the wind blinded her. She was powerless to stop him.

Johnny emerged from the tent with a rifle. Facing into the wind, he squinted as he fumbled with the barrel. Before he could aim the gun at Hossfly, the outlaw released Andrea long enough to draw his own weapon. Her cry of warning came too late. Andrea watched in horror as he aimed at Johnny and pulled the trigger, a gust of wind spoiling his balance. The resultant roar triggered an instant wave of anger as she watched Johnny stagger and fall. Shrugging off the quilt, Andrea grasped the cane in both hands. Mustering strength, she swung it at the back of Hossfly's head, and swung again until he crumpled.

She froze when Jed swung his gun from Billy to level it at her. Screaming, she dropped the cane to hide her face.

When the gun fired, she only felt the wind. Slowly spreading her fingers, she saw Billy wrestling the pistol from Jed's grip. A dust devil engulfed them. When the gun fell, Billy pounded him repeatedly with his fists.

"Johnny!"

Sprawled on his back, a pool of blood spread outward from the hole in his upper chest. Tears blurred her vision as she caressed his face. Fleeting memories of his callused hands stroking her waist-length hair caused her throat to constrict. Glancing up at Billy's stricken face, she realized that Johnny's gentleness was what she missed most in him, yet the hurt in the young outlaw's eyes stabbed at her heart. She was jolted by the fact that she loved them both.

Johnny's pulse was faint but he seemed to be breathing. Carefully unbuttoning his shirt, she noticed the wound high on the right side of his chest. She prayed the bullet had missed his lung. The bleeding had to be stopped and quickly. Turning, she saw Billy tying Hossfly's hands behind his back. Wiping tears, she asked him to carry Johnny into the sheepwagon. When they had lifted him onto his bed, she hastily searched the wagon and found clean towels and a canister of sugar. Sprinkling the wound generously, she repeated Gramma's special prayer to stop the bleeding.

"He needs a doctor," she said as she bandaged him with strips of toweling.

Johnny mumbled, "I love you, Andrea," before losing consciousness.

Billy's betrayed expression prompted her to grip his arm. "Please listen," she said. "There's something I have to tell you." When she finished, Billy hurried down the wagon steps without a word. Following, she pleaded with him to drive the sheepwagon into Wolton to find a doctor.

"Do you love him?" he asked.

"Does it matter?"

"I guess not."

He hitched Johnny's horse to the wagon, then tied Jed's senseless body behind his saddle. Hossfly, meanwhile, was yelling obscenities while lying on his stomach in the dirt. Billy silenced him with a greasy rag. Bound securely, he was tied to the back of the wagon. He could either walk or be dragged to the town of Wolton.

Billy drove while she led the horses, heading east, the dust storm raging around them. They traveled along the southern Big Horn foothills, arriving in Wolton at dusk. After carrying Johnny into Doctor Bryant's office, Billy said, "The sheriff'll probably lock me up too." His expression said he didn't really care.

"Don't worry," Andrea said, attempting to reassure him. "Everything will be fine."

When he left to herd their former guardians down the street to jail, she returned to the doctor's office to see about Johnny. The doctor allowed her a brief visit, and she leaned to kiss his brow.

"I love you, too, Johnny," she whispered, but she doubted he could hear. Searching for his pulse, she was relieved to find him still alive. When she stepped back onto the boardwalk, Billy was leaving the sheriff's office down the street. Hurrying her pace, she reached him as he untied his dun from the hitching rail.

"What happened?" she asked, alarmed by his angry expression.

"The sheriff's out a town," he said through clenched teeth. "And the deputy's dumber than a dead mule. He locked 'em up but Hossfly'll talk his way out before the sheriff gets back."

"Not if I have anything to say about it."

Storming into the jail, she planted herself before the short, red-haired, young deputy.

"Is there a reward offered for the men who kidnapped me?"

Surprised, he pulled his boots from the desk and stood to acknowledge her. "You're Andy Bordeaux?"

"I am, and if there's a reward, this man earned it. Billy rescued me from those scoundrels." She turned to grip his arm.

"Those are the men who kidnapped you?" The deputy turned to stare at the cell. "But I thought—"

"I don't know what else you would call it. They tied us up and dragged us here from the Hole in the Wall. If Mister Blackburn hadn't taken their guns away, I wouldn't be standing here now." She wouldn't implicate Billy and the others for her kidnapping, but Horsefly and Jed deserved imprisonment.

Billy started to protest.

"Don't deny it," she said, glaring at him.

Turning to the deputy, she insisted, "Come with us. They shot my friend, Johnny."

During the walk back to the doctor's office, the deputy said a thousand dollar reward had been posted for her return. He wasn't sure of the details.

Andrea's knees nearly buckled. Who could have posted the reward? Certainly not Uncle Jim Bob. Her grandparents must have survived, but where did they get the money? Grandpa's savings had been nearly depleted when he bought the flock of sheep. She had to get back to the cabin.

If the young lawman doubted Andrea's story, the evidence lay in Doctor Bryant's office. Johnny was still drifting in and out of consciousness, although the physician assured them he would recover. Andrea lifted Johnny's limp hand to her lips. Kissing his tanned skin, she held his palm against her check, promising to return as soon as possible. Doctor Bryant smiled, telling her he would relay the message. She then asked a disheartened Billy to accompany her to the ranch. Refusing the reward, he tightened saddle cinches and helped her mount her mare.

The following day they rode east in silence. When they reached the Powder River, the silver moon was full, the stars brighter than she had ever seen them. Crossing the river, they headed south toward Pine Mountain and her grandparent's sheep ranch. The lunar glow was directly overhead when they first glimpsed the cabin settled placidly in the foothills near the creek's middle fork. Andrea's heart hammered when she found the cabin dark and apparently deserted. Billy must have sensed her fear for he swung down and hurried to the door.

Once inside he struck a lucifer and searched inside the cabin. Light flickered through the small window, and she held her breath until he reappeared.

"Andy," he called. "Come quick."

Trembling, she gripped the pommel and lowered herself to the ground. When she hesitated, he hurried over to place an arm around her shoulder. Then, quickly tying the horses to a post, he led her into the cabin and lit an oil lamp. To her surprise, the room was just as she had left it. The big brass bed still stood along the east wall, her own bunk neatly made across the room. Dusty mahogany furniture was arranged in between.

"Where are they?"

"Your grandparents left you this."

Sinking into the nearest chair, she held the carefully penned letter close to the oil lamp. Dated the previous Sunday, it read:

Our dearest Andrea,

We are moving back to Casper today. I am sorry we could not wait any longer. Grandpa's health has not been good and he needs to be near a doctor. We sold our sheep to Johnny Mackintosh and offered a reward for your return. Bob Devine's cowhands could not find you in the Hole in the Wall but the Pinkertons we hired have talked to people who saw you with a young man on horseback. We pray that he brings you home soon.

Your Uncle Jim Bob fought off an army of outlaws to rescue you but they got the best of him. I am afraid he has not been up to tracking them since. We are moving to Jim Bob's house and leaving the cabin and furniture to you and Johnny as a wedding present. We pray every day for your safe return.

All our love,

Gramma and Grandpa

"Why are you crying, Andy?"

"Because I'm so happy they're still alive."

"I'm glad I was able to bring you home." His eyes said he was lying.

"I couldn't have made it without you."

"I'm not so sure of that," Billy said, managing a tight smile. "You swing a mean cane, Andrea Bordeaux. I hope Johnny knows what he's getting."

"What he's losing, don't you mean? Johnny's sheep will be scattered from the Rattlesnake Mountains to the Colorado border if we don't ride to the Mackintosh Ranch tomorrow to tell them about the shooting."

"I'll ride along that far." He unwound, getting slowly to his feet.

"You're not staying?"

Glancing at his hands, he said, "I'm sure you can find someone to help with the ranch 'til Johnny gets better."

"But I thought—"

"I'm no sheepherder, Andy."

"What are you planning to do?"

"I thought I'd find a job at a hoss ranch."

"You mean that?"

"I'm not cut out to be an outlaw." When he looked into her eyes, they were smiling.

"If you're serious about reforming, I know of a ranch in the foothills. The horse herd is small and the pay's not much, but I predict a substantial raise when we're both twenty-one."

Laughing at his puzzlement, she stood to embrace him. "We've got the start of a darned good horse herd standing in the yard. Let's move our brood mares into the corral."

Epilogue

Andrea Bordeaux became Mrs. William Blackburn the following Sunday in Casper's First Methodist Episcopal Church, her grandparents, uncle, and townspeople in attendance. The Blackburn horse raising venture was successful and the couple was further blessed with two handsome, hazel-eyed sons and a daughter who closely resembled her mother.

Johnny Mackintosh survived to become a wealthy flockmaster in the Spring Creek area, where cattlemen killed thousands of sheep and murdered three herders in 1909, prompting sheep growers, the Mackintosh clan among them, to hire range detectives to keep peace on the Wyoming plains. After one of the cattlemen died, leaving a suicide note implicating the others, the culprits were imprisoned.

Actual Wild Bunch members suffered similar fates. During the spring of 1898, Tom "Peep" O'Day, who was never allowed to ride again with the Wild Bunch, and Walt "Wat the Watcher" Punteney were found *not* guilty of the Belle Fourche bank robbery. Punteney returned to the Bridger Creek area where he lived a quiet life.

Tom O'Day was arrested by Casper Sheriff Frank Webb in 1903, and charged with herding twenty-three stolen horses. He was sentenced to six years in the Wyoming Penitentiary. When released, he returned to his former haunts in Lost Cabin, where he married, homesteaded in the Shoshoni, Wyoming, area, and was last seen in the former outlaw hideout as late as 1926. He died in South Dakota in 1927 following a runaway wagon accident.

Margaret Simpson became postmaster of Jackson, Wyoming, the town she named in honor of mountain man David Jackson. She was also the mother of Wyoming Governor Millard Simpson and the grandmother of U.S. Senator Alan Simpson and his brother Peter.

Suspected rustlers Bob Taylor and Al Smith, who were involved in the shooting incident between local ranchers and Bob Devine's cowboys, may not have actually rustled cattle, but it was common practice during that era to "borrow" enough of an absent owner's herd to start a cattle ranch of one's own.

Author Brown Waller says in *Last of the Great Western Train Robbers* that Butch had a wife and two small children in the Salt Lake area, and that he was negotiating amnesty with Utah's Governor Heber Wells, which never came to pass. It was also rumored that Butch Cassidy's Shoshone lover gave birth to a daughter.

Robert Leroy Parker (George "Butch" Cassidy) and his cohorts: Harry Alonzo Longabaugh (the Sundance Kid), Harvey Logan (Kid Curry), and Butch's close friend William "Elzy Lay" Ellsworth (William "Mac" McGinnis) laid low for over a year, probably working as cowboys. Then, on June 2, 1899, Harve Logan led a raid on the Wilcox train in southern Wyoming. Accompanying Logan were his brother Lonie, their cousin Robert E. Lee (alias Bob Curry), Will Roberts (John Dalton), and Flat Nose George Currie.

The bandits blackened their faces, tied long bandannas over their noses, and flagged down the train at half past two in the morning. Dynamiting the mail car, they got away with what the Union Pacific estimated at $3,400, although more than ten times that amount has been reported over the years.

Harve Logan is blamed for the shooting death of Douglas, Wyoming, Sheriff Joe Hazen near infamous Tea Pot Rock, following the robbery.

Butch Cassidy and the Sundance Kid have been credited with the Wilcox job, as well as the Tipton (Wyoming) train robbery, but noted historians agree that Cassidy wasn't actually involved. He and Elzy Lay may have planned the robberies, but both were probably holed up at the WS Ranch near Alma, New Mexico, or Brown's Hole while the robberies took place. Lay did participate in the Rio Grande train robbery in New Mexico a month after Wilcox, and was sentenced to life imprisonment for the crime the following year.

Lay had been wounded twice by a pursuing posse; and one of his two accomplices, Sam Ketchum, brother of "Black Jack" Ketchum, died of lead poisoning. Lay's good conduct earned him an early release from prison.

Lonie Logan and Bob Lee escaped to Harlan, Montana, following the Wilcox robbery, where Logan operated the Curry Brothers Saloon. His cousin Bob worked as a part-time bartender and gambler. They soon fled Harlan after passing some of the stolen bank notes, leaving behind Lonie's common-law wife Elfie Landusky, step-daughter of Pike

Landusky, who had been killed by Harve Logan in a saloon shootout.

Learning that the Pinkerton detectives were after them, they rushed to Cripple Creek, Colorado, where Lee plied his trades. Lonie immediately left for his aunt's home in Dodson, Missouri. Elizabeth Lee was apparently unaware of her nephews' criminal activities, or that of her son Bob's.

Pinkertons traced Lonie Logan to Dodson, and on February 28, 1900, he was shot to death escaping his former childhood home. Bob Lee was arrested the same day in Cripple Creek, and sentenced to ten years in the Wyoming Penitentiary, with three years suspended for good behavior.

Harve Logan is credited with killing more men than the dozen or so he actually shot, one of them a New Mexico stock detective during April of 1900, while Logan worked at the WS Ranch near Alma.

Flat Nose George Currie was killed by lawmen that same year near Thompson, Utah, where he had gone back to his former trade of cattle rustling.

The Wild Bunch struck again in another daring Wyoming night robbery, August 29, 1900. Harve Logan, Ben Kilpatrick, and two companions that historians cannot agree upon, robbed a Union Pacific train near Tipton. The loot taken from the dynamited mail car has been reported as high as $55,000, although the railroad claimed it lost less than $55 in spendable cash.

The following month, Cassidy, Carver, Longabaugh, and Logan robbed a bank in Winnamucca, Nevada, hauling away an estimated $30,000.

Later that fall, Longabaugh, Logan, Carver, and Kilpatrick met at Fannie Porter's bordello in San Antonio, where Logan's girlfriend Annie Rogers, and Carver's friend Lillie Davis worked. Etta Place, the Sundance Kid's companion, was also present.

By the end of the year, Cassidy joined the four men in Fort Worth, where their infamous picture was taken and subsequently labeled "The Train Robbers' Syndicate." Cassidy reportedly sent a copy of the photo to the Winnamucca bank with his note of appreciation for their money.

Early the following year, the Sundance Kid and Etta Place sailed from New York for South America as Mr. and Mrs. Harry Place, while Butch returned to the West.

Harve Logan and Ben Kilpatrick were then involved in a killing on the Kilpatrick Ranch near Eden, Texas. Carver was with them in Sonora, Texas, soon after, and died of six bullet wounds fired by lawmen in a bakery. He had been reportedly shot while raising his hands. Ben

Kilpatrick's brother George survived with five bullet wounds and was taken into custody. When they heard the shooting, Harve Logan and Ben Kilpatrick rode out of town.

During July 1901, the duo held up a Great Northern train near Malta, Montana, with "Deaf Charley" Hanks and another gang member, whom author Dale Schoenberger says may have been Laura Bullion, Carver's former girlfriend. The bandits got away with $40,000 in unsigned bank notes.

Harve Logan and a companion then rode back to the Landusky, Montana, area to kill the neighbor who had gunned down Logan's one-armed brother Johnny five years earlier, on land adjacent to the brothers' former ranch. The neighbor reportedly died of a stomach wound the following day.

Harve Logan and Annie Rogers traveled the country extensively, as did Ben Kilpatrick with Laura Bullion. Rogers was arrested later that year in a Nashville bank when she tried to exchange some of the stolen bank notes from the Great Northern train robbery. Logan fled town when he learned of her arrest.

"Deaf Charley" Hanks stayed on in Nashville, and narrowly eluded arrest while passing one of the bank notes in a local store. Hit over the head with a policeman's club, he managed to escape, but was killed by lawmen the following spring in a Texas bordello.

At approximately the same time, Ben Kilpatrick and Laura Bullion were arrested in St. Louis, and imprisoned for passing altered bank notes. Two months later in mid-December, Harve Logan was arrested alone near Knoxville, Tennessee, with more than $2,000 worth of the notes in his possession. Logan went to trial in September 1902, charged with more than twenty federal counts of forging and counterfeiting bank notes. A local celebrity while in the Knoxville jail, he was visited by many women, including at least one who proposed marriage. He was also visited by the governor of Tennessee, who allegedly shook Logan's hand.

During that time, Logan signed a statement which exonerated his girlfriend Annie Rogers, and she was subsequently released from custody.

In November 1902, Logan was found guilty on ten of twenty-three counts, and sentenced to twenty years in prison, plus $5,000 in fines. Allowed to remain in the Knoxville jail until his appeals had run their course, he escaped a year and a half later astride the Knoxville sheriff's horse. The lawman was later implicated.

Harve Logan is credited with robbing a Cody, Wyoming, bank in November of that year. Some say he then joined Cassidy and Longabaugh in Argentina, where he was killed by a wild mule. There are many reports of his demise, including the taking of his own life following a June 7, 1904, train robbery near Parachute, Colorado. He and two unidentified companions were said to have gotten away with an insignificant amount of money, and Logan was seriously wounded the following day by a local posse member. He reportedly shot himself in the right temple to avoid imprisonment, because his Knoxville jail stay had seriously impaired his health.

Harry Longabaugh and Etta Place returned to New York from South America during the spring of 1902, seeking medical treatment for the Sundance Kid. Meanwhile, Butch Cassidy filed on land in a remote area of Argentina, under the name Santiago Ryan. The Sundance Kid and Etta Place returned to Argentina in August, moving into a ranch house with Cassidy, where they lived a somewhat peaceful life until January of 1905.

Cassidy and Longabaugh may have grown bored with Argentine ranching or run short of money, for they returned to a life of crime. A good horsewoman, Etta Place accompanied them during their first few robberies. They held up a bank on Argentina's southern coast in 1905, completing two more holdups that year, one of them in neighboring Chile. The following year another Argentine bank robbery was followed by a railroad payroll in Bolivia, and a mining payroll in Peru.

During late 1906, Etta Place went home with what was rumored to have been a pregnancy. Longabaugh accompanied her to a Denver hospital, then promptly left town. Nothing more is known of Etta Place, although some say she gave birth to a daughter and married in the Denver area.

The following year, Butch and Sundance were hired by the Concordia Tin Mines in Bolivia, where they worked sporadically for several years as payroll guards, making frequent robbing forays elsewhere in the country.

Historian James D. Horan claimed the infamous pair was killed during November of 1908 by Bolivian soldiers following the Aramayo-Francke payroll robbery. Dale Schoenberger said it was Bolivian police who killed them in a remote village several days after the robbery.

Other biographers, including Butch Cassidy's sister, Lula Parker Bentenson, swore that Butch did not die in South America, but returned to this country to live a respectable life until his death. Larry Pointer, in his book, *In Search of Butch Cassidy,* pinpoints the cancer death of William T. Phillips (Cassidy's reported alias) in Spokane, Washington in 1937, and quotes from Phillips' unpublished autobiography.

Edward Kirby claims in *The Rise and Fall of the Sundance Kid* that Harry Alonzo Longabaugh returned from South America to live out his life as Hiram Bebee, a mean-tempered recluse who died in prison for murder. He reportedly disclosed his true identity, although few believed him.

The remaining member of the Wild Bunch, Ben "The Tall Texan" Kilpatrick, was released from prison in mid-1911, vowing to go straight, but was killed attempting a train robbery in his home state the following year.

Jim McCloud and "Stuttering" Dick Hale, although not members of the Wild Bunch, *were* members of the Hole in the Wall gang. McCloud was a friend of Tom O'Day, and spent the majority of his life in various prison cells. As James Dale he cracked the A.B. Daniels Saloon safe in Douglas, Wyoming, during late summer of 1898, for which he served three and a half years in the Wyoming penitentiary. The year after his release in 1902, he robbed the Buffalo, Wyoming, post office, and was suspected of cracking the town's Occidental Hotel safe.

Not long after his release, McCloud reportedly shot a flockmaster in the Thermopolis area, then rode into town a few months later to rob the post office, later holding up the Buffalo-Sheridan stage. Following one of his arrests, he escaped jail in Cheyenne with the infamous Tom Horn in 1903. They were recaptured within the hour, and Horn was hanged shortly thereafter.

McCloud returned to Leavenworth and a succession of prison sentences. He died there during his mid-sixties, following sentencing for violating the Marijuana Tax Act and selling liquor to Oklahoma Indians, according to Doug Englebretson's book, *Empty Saddles, Forgotten Names.*

"Stuttering" Dick Hale was called "a superb horseman, crack shot with both rifle and pistol, and an expert in handling the lariat," according to A. J. Mokler in his *History of Natrona County* (Casper, Wyoming). Classed as one of the Hole in the Wall gang, a blanket label for hundreds of lawbreakers who drifted in and out of the valley, Hale is said to have been a partner of Otto "Gentleman Horse Thief" Chenoweth, a well-educated artist from Massachusetts, who allegedly fell in with some congenial central Wyoming horse thieves.

Hale had been charged with horse and cattle rustling and train robbery, with rewards totaling $3,000 for his arrest when he was wounded by a posse's bullet in Johnson County, Wyoming, in 1901. Captured, he soon escaped and was tracked through Colorado to Thompson, Utah, where George Currie had been killed the previous year. Hale was never recaptured or heard from again.

About the Author

J ean Henry Mead began her writing career in 1968 as a news reporter/ photographer in California, and staff writer and correspondent for the statewide newspaper, the Casper Star-Tribune. She later served as editor of *In Wyoming Magazine* and *Misty Mountain Press*. While freelancing for the *Denver Post's Empire Magazine*, other articles were also published domestically as well as abroad. She published seven nonfiction books as well as two novels and edited and ghostwrote a number of others. While serving as national publicity director for Western Writers of America, she established the Western Writers Hall of Fame, and wrote *Maverick Writers*, a book of interviews with famous authors, including Pulitzer Winner A. B. Guthrie, Jr.; Louis L'Amour; and Elmore Leonard. Her blog articles may be read at http://westernhistoricalhappenings.blogspot.com/ and at Murderous Musings at http://www.murderousmusings.blogspot.com/ as well as her website: JeanHenryMead.com

Afterword
by Jack Herrmann

Deep inside the heart of every intelligent and sensitive reader is a persistent desire to write.

In these individuals, experience, observations and thoughts (gained through the process of living) keep tweaking a wish to make a cultural contribution by means of the written word. All writers have this need. Some writers answer that need successfully. Other writers don't. Unfulfilled writers lack two crucial advantages they must have to gain mastery of the craft: confidence in their own ability, and the necessary training to hone their skills. It is a shame. Every unfulfilled writer continues to merely dream. Every reader loses.

I don't know how many times I've heard, "I've got a story to tell, if I could just write like this." If it is there, inside, it can be brought outside. So, if this is a description of you, what can you do about it? All that needs to be done is to learn that writers write and good writers write better.

As far as skill is concerned, know this: most writers cannot be placed in any sort of genius category.

They all do have this in common, though: 10 percent talent and 90 percent desire. They all can have fun developing their abilities. They all need to know where to find the help.

Where do you go to find that help? Formal scholastic training is costly and time-consuming. Correspondence lessons are similarly expensive and generally do not give benefit of peer group aid, or allow for sudden inspiration, or fun in learning. Face-to face writer's groups have necessary time-scheduling requirements, which can be difficult to maintain within the busy demands of life .

Perhaps you have enjoyed this book. If you have, you should know that this author had similar problems, but found a way to solve them.

Have a look at a web-based site described by Writer's Digest Magazine as one of the best online locales for writers: "Writers' Village University" and its affiliate, "F2K." Both sites were created with specific things in mind: simplicity, effective learning through course study, peer feedback and, most important, emphasis on mind-committing rather than wallet-emptying. Take a look at these.

F2K: A FREE series of six one-week courses designed for beginning writers. Intermediate and advanced writers take this full course as a refresher, or to socialize with and encourage beginning writers. Then, too, F2K is a great way to start writing again and to break writer's block. It is offered six times a year. Check it out by going to:

http://www.wrtersvillage.com

WVU: Writers' Village University is a living, breathing community of support and training curricula, totaling 200+ courses, seminars, study programs and workshops. Each is designed to help bring an aspect of your writing up to higher levels, be it fiction or nonfiction, poetry or literature.

Course scheduling is set so classes can fit into your personal time-slots. To insure this convenience, they are repeated several times each year. You can take what you need, when you need it. No examinations. No cranky teachers, and no impossible assignment demands. Just intelligent guidance and friendly, invaluable student feedback. The cost is, by far, the best value for writers anywhere. Here's where to find more information:

http://www.writersvillage.com

T-Zero - the Writers' Ezine: This is another free service (and also a paying market) offered by WVU bringing you details on:

*Editing
*Writing tips
*Exercises
*Fiction, non-fiction and poetry (Paying Market)
*Hints and practical encouragement

T-Zero has become a premium monthly Webzine designed to keep writers well informed. You can subscribe to it, and check out the current issue and the archives, at:

http://thewritersezine.com

Seize the moment. Become the writer you want to be. Have fun, learn much and. . .

Astonishing luck,

Jack

Order Form for ePress Books

ALL BOOKS may be ordered online from our website at
http://www.epress-online.com.
All ePress books are available as eBooks - price each - $5.99
Some are also available in print, trade paperback
$14.99 plus shipping and handling.

FICTION

Mystery/Suspense
Absent the Soul - BJ Bourg
A Cobweb on the Soul - Nadene R. Carter
Cadaver - John P. Matsis
Knight Errant: Death and Life at the Faire - Teel James Glenn
Pathogen - John P. Matsis
Switcheroo - Herbert Holeman
Under a Raging Moon - Frank Zafiro - *eBook only*

Fantasy
A Faerie Ring - Michael Honeth
Death at Dragonthroat - Teel James Glenn
Eagle of the Kingdom - Joanne Hall
Hierath - Joanne Hall
In Exile - Joanne Hall
Nola and the Goblin Mountain - aj dryna
Return to UKOO - Don Hurst
Sister Warrior - Teel James Glenn
Stolen Tome - J. Brian Jones
Tales of a Warrior Priest - Teel James Glenn
The Boy and the Warrior - Julia Macdonell
The Daemonhold Curse - Teel James Glenn
Windwalker - Donna Sundblad

Genre Specific Romance
Dancing on the Edge - S.L. Connors

American Historical Fiction
A Lesser Form of Patriotism - G.G. Stokes, Jr.
Benning's War - Jeffrey Keenan
Echoes of Silence - Nadene R. Carter
Escape, A Wyoming Historical Novel - Jean Henry Mead
Gold - Steven Bartholomew

Science Fiction
Needle - L.L. Whitaker

Mainstream Fiction, Poetry, and Short Story Collections
Other People's Lives - Betty Kreier Lubinski
Dunbar Station - L.L. Whitaker
Word Castles, a book of Poetry - Tom Spencer

NON-FICTION - Craft of Writing
Pumping Your Muse - Donna Sundblad
Them's Fightin' Words - Teel James Glenn
The Magic & the Mundane - P. June Diehl
The Sense-ible Writer - Nadene R. Carter

Made in the USA
Lexington, KY
04 May 2011